LIPS ON MY HEART

A MERCY RAVENS MC NOVEL BOOK 1

M.J. MARINO

♡ Enjoy,

M.J. Marino

COPYRIGHT

Lips On My Heart - A Mercy Ravens MC Novel 1

By: M.J. Marino

Copyright © 2020 by M.J Marino

Cover Design: Amy Queau of qcoverdesign.com

Editing: Christa Desir

❀ Created with Vellum

DEDICATION

For my husband and our three boys.
Thank you for keeping me on my toes.

THANK YOU

Hello Awesome Reader,

I wanted to personally thank you for purchasing my first self-published novel. It means so much to me that you are reading something of mine, and I appreciate it from the bottom of my heart.

Writing has always been a hobby of mine, but becoming a published author seemed so daunting a task, I shelved the idea for many years. Eventually, I realized the only thing holding me back from making my dream a reality was myself. So I dusted off my computer and sat my butt down until I finally wrote something that I wanted to share with others.

Josephine and Maceo developed in my head overnight and I instantly fell in love with their chemistry. Their story came to me so naturally that my fingers had to race to keep up with my imagination. Within a month, I had written the start of their love journey, and now you get to enjoy it.

The self-publishing route has been a journey in itself, but I'm finally learning the ropes, and will be publishing more about these two lovebirds in the very near future.

My wish for you, dear reader, is that you get lost in the fantasy, place yourself in the characters' shoes, and live a different life if only for a moment.

Enjoy!

M.J. Marino

ABOUT THIS BOOK

Not all the best decisions in life come from making logical choices. Going off the path most chosen sometimes brings you to where you were always meant to be.

Josephine Holland doesn't veer from the path of least resistance. She may appear fragile like a pixie, but Josephine takes control like a dictator with a Napoleon Complex. An awful ex-boyfriend has left her with a sour taste for any future relationships. Josephine wipes the slate clean for a fresh start in Fort Collins, Colorado. With no time for nonsense, Josephine busies herself with her start-up design company and hopes for the best.

Maceo Tabares, a man who oozes trouble, is only interested in no-strings-attached hookups. The former Navy SEAL's life is dangerous, and a target is always on his back. A relationship would only complicate things. Tired of the vagabond lifestyle, he chooses Fort Collins as his headquarters for his crew, with plans of expanding his security company. Maceo longs for stability, but having an *old lady* to share his life with is not in the cards.

So when a chance encounter on a hiking trail has these two conflicting characters running into each other—literally—neither one is interested in anything beyond a stolen moment. What neither of them expected was for a spark to form after that single encounter—a spark that would burn down their defensive walls and throw their clear-cut paths into unfamiliar territory.

Josephine's reaction is to flee while Maceo's is to pursue.

Josephine has no intentions of seeing Maceo again, but fate intervenes. When she meets her new client, Atlas, President of the Mercy Ravens MC, she comes face-to-face with Maceo, and all bets are off.

When a potential stalker puts Josephine in danger, Maceo will stop at nothing to protect the woman who has consumed his life. Several hurdles must be cleared for them to have a fighting chance, but will their love be enough fight off all those that want to to do them harm? Will love conquer all for these two headstrong lovers?

CHAPTER ONE
MACEO

There's nothing quite as refreshing as an early morning run—well, for me at least. Though it's not like I have much of a say in the matter. I'm used to waking up at the crack of dawn.

Living as a Navy SEAL for ten years changes you. It conditions you and organizes every aspect of your life 'till you run like a finely tuned engine. After my retirement from the navy two years ago, I'm still up by five o'clock each and every morning, regardless of what recovery mission I'm currently involved in or how hard I've partied the night before.

God, I've missed the quiet of this place. It's good to be back home.

The peace it gives me as I run along the Cache la Poudre River and Rocky Mountains is almost enough to silence the demons. Almost, but never fully gone. This near-perfect atmosphere is the reason why I've decided to set down roots here in Fort Collins, Colorado with my men and take my security company to the next level.

My workout isn't helped by the fact I've only slept for three hours. This run is killing me, which only pushes me harder. I'm not a runner by any stretch of the imagination. I'm a fighter and a heavy weights kind of guy. But I like the challenge and thrive on it. Plus, I need the cardio in my daily routine. My eyes are burning, my lungs and legs are bitching at me, but I welcome it. It reminds me I'm alive when many of my brothers in service no longer are.

Doesn't help that it's been nearly three months since I've had sex. Back to back missions don't exactly give me enough time to find a sweet little thing I'm willing to be balls deep in. Unlike some of the guys on my crew who will fuck any woman who wants their dick, I'm more selective in my choice of bedmates. I'm not willing to risk my health for a quick fuck—regardless of always keeping my member covered and being tested regularly—it's not worth the risk.

A fuck buddy with no strings attached is not something most women go for, leaving my playing field extremely limited. I could be a bigger dick and promise a woman flowers and a happily-ever-after to get her in bed, but I won't. I give it to her straight and let her decide if she can handle it when I'm gone.

I don't do relationships—I never have, and I sure as fuck don't plan on it in the future. I've seen too many relationships go bad while in the navy. I made a 'no relationship' rule for myself early in life. There are only three ways it ends—cheating, divorce, or death. In my case, it would probably be death, and there's no reason to involve a woman in my messy life. The fact I haven't found a woman who can change my mind only solidifies my view on it.

Happily-ever-after doesn't exist—at least not for most people. Hence, it's a bachelor's life for me, but damn if my cock isn't angry with me for holding it back.

Thinking about getting my dick wet makes it twitch in response, as if begging me to make it happen soon.

Yes, I know you want to get laid. No, I'm not ignoring you. I'm presently waiting for the right playmate to walk into my life.

It's been thirty minutes since I've started on this trail, and I'm ready to head back to the house when I see the shape of someone up ahead running my way. Another early riser. My eyes home in on the gorgeous figure.

It's a petite young woman with light brown hair pulled back into a messy ponytail. Her toned sun-kissed legs are accentuated by the short running shorts. I want to see her backside to confirm if her ass is as firm as my imagination guesses. Her face is thin and oval with an elfin nose and luscious pink lips. The tank top she's wearing is suctioned to her tight body, outlining her perky breasts, which are bouncing hypnotically as she runs.

My once-twitching dick is now semi-hard, and my mouth instantly salivates as I take in the tiny little thing running toward me. *Goddamn, she's a wet dream come true!* It's as if God himself was listening and sending me exactly what I need.

A smirk spreads across my face as our paths converge, but my smile falls when I see the fucking hellhound barreling down on her from behind.

Like flipping a switch, I go into full SEAL mode, charging right toward the pretty pixie who doesn't have a clue as to the danger she's in.

"Hey!" I yell to get her attention. But she doesn't hear me. I get closer, and I see she has fucking earbuds in, putting her more at risk than I originally assessed.

I scream again as I run, waving my arms over my head and hoping the movement will catch her attention.

She spots me this time and stops in her tracks, her eyes going wide.

"Fuck!" I race faster to reach her. I didn't want her to stop. The beast of a dog is sure to attack her if she doesn't move.

Before she has a chance to say a peep, I'm on top of her and flinging her over my shoulder, OTS survival-style, and running in the opposite direction of the huge black dog.

The pixie screams as I race away, the dog barking as it charges us.

"It's okay. I gotcha." But her screaming only continues, probably because she saw Cujo chasing after us.

"Help!" she screams as she squirms and kicks violently under my tight hold over her firm thighs. I really shouldn't be thinking about how good her legs feel under my touch, but I can't help myself.

"HELP!"

"I got you, baby. He won't hurt you."

The dog's barks are getting closer, which, I won't lie, makes me panic slightly. The fucking hound is mammoth. I'm used to dealing with terrorists, killers, mafia—people, not feral animals the size of a damn mountain lion. I need to get us to higher ground immediately.

"Fuck!" I grunt as the dog closes in on my heels.

A boulder comes into view up ahead and it's the only place we can escape to before dog is on us. As soon as I'm close enough, I use the hand not wrapped around her perfect petite body to hoist us both up on the rock.

The dog comes charging at us, jumps, but falls short. Doesn't stop him from trying again, barking and bouncing around the rock like he's on a fucking pogo stick. It's the reason I haven't set down the woman still hanging over my shoulder.

"Someone help meeeee!" She pounds on my ass with her fists. I know she's hitting me with all her might, but I honestly can't feel a thing; my body is conditioned to handle anything thrown at it.

"Shh," I coo, pulling her down my body and holding her close to my heaving chest, keeping her far away from the devil who circles in bounds around the boulder. I pull out her earbuds for her to hear me better. "You're safe, sweetheart."

She shoves against me. "What the hell is wrong with you, you goddamn giant!" she shouts, looking up at me with coastal blue eyes. *Fucking stunning.*

Confused by her anger, I frown but don't let go. She's tiny—her head barely coming to my chest, which makes me imagine how fun it would be to throw her around on a bed. My cock chooses this inopportune moment to twitch in agreement while pressed against her stomach. This makes her go into full-on panic mode, pushing against me to wiggle free.

"Easy," I chide, holding tightly to her lush body. I can't risk her falling into the path of the killer dog.

"Let go of me! You sick twisted motherfucker! You keep your dick in your pants or I'll fucking bite it off, I swear to God."

Bite my penis off? Jeeze.

Clearly, she's freaked out and I need to reassure her, but I can't help a chuckle from escaping me. This pixie has a mouth on her, and damn if it's not the sexiest thing ever.

"Look, calm down. I'm not going to touch you," I say, fighting a smile.

"Stop laughing at me!" she seethes. I laugh again. Her temper is too damn cute, exactly like her.

"Let me go," she growls.

My eyes track the dog circling us like a shark. "Not a chance in hell."

"Seriously, let me go, now!" she demands.

"And watch that thing rip you to shreds?" I point at the dog. "The beast was chasing you, and it would have been on your back if I hadn't swept you up and climbed both our asses here."

My beautiful pixie stops hitting my chest and looks at me with her eyebrows raised nearly to her hairline. "You thought I was in danger?" she asks, like I'm ridiculous.

"It was going to maul you," I say firmly, wrapping my arms tighter around her slender frame to hold her closer. *Fuck, she fits perfectly.*

She shakes her head. Giggles erupt from her before she looks at the dog. "Hades, silent!"

The fucking dog stops barking.

"Hades, sit."

The dog sits back on its haunches, waiting patiently for her to give the next command.

What. The. Fuck.

The woman turns her elfin face back to me with the most beautiful smile, showing perfect pearly teeth.

Well, I'll be damned. I just saved a woman who didn't need saving.

5

"The hellhound is your dog?" I question, still refusing to release her.

"He's not a hellhound. He's a Cane Corso, and he's my baby," she says defensively.

I look from her to the giant dog—whose massive tongue is hanging out, making him look like he's smiling—and back to her again. "If he's your dog, why don't you have him on a leash? And why was he running you down?"

She sighs. "Everywhere I go with him, he needs to be on a damn leash. Some places make me muzzle him because of his breed. But he's a good boy—all bark and no bite. Rolls over on his belly to children, for crying out loud. This is the one place I let him run loose where he goes unnoticed. He was sniffing trees, fell behind, and was trying to catch up to me. Hades only freaked out when he saw you grab me and run."

I roll my eyes. "You named your hellhound after the god of the underworld."

She snorts. "Fitting, don't you think?"

I laugh. This woman is fucking funny. A beauty with a sense of humor.

"Um, now that you know my dog isn't going to kill me, will you please let me go?"

"Yeah, sorry." Reluctantly, I release my hold on her. She felt too damn good near my skin. She takes a deep breath—as if to calm herself—and gives me a shy smile, which I return.

Lithely she slides off the boulder and opens her arms to Hades, who bounds right into her embrace. He knocks her flat on her beautiful ass, licking her all over. Giggles and squeals erupt from her. I can't help the grin spreading across my face. The dog has to weigh more than 150 pounds, beating my pixie by at least fifty, but clearly, he's her baby; he even tries to crawl into her lap.

"Yeah, it's okay, Hades. Mommy's okay, big boy. Thank you for trying to protect me. I love you, too. Who's Mommy's good boy? Yep, it's you, yes it is," she says in a higher-pitched voice.

Chuckling, I slide down the boulder next to her. Hades growls in warning. Apparently, he's not a fan of mine. My smile widens because the big beast is protective of his *mamá*.

"Hades, no! I know he scared us, but this is Mommy's friend, um..." She looks to me.

"Maceo," I answer.

She nods before looking back to Hades. "This is Maceo. He's okay. He thought Mommy was in trouble and was trying to help. He's sorry he scared us. Okay, big guy?"

A snigger slips past my lips and I run a hand through my unruly hair. "It's funny how you talk to him, like he actually understands what you're saying."

Hades growl. "Hades, no growling," she warns before turning her attention back to me. She stands to her full height, which I'm guessing is no more than five-two, making me well over a foot taller than her. "Of course, he does. Every damn word. He's the smartest dog."

Amused, I laugh, but in the corner of my eye I catch Hades, who is baring his teeth at me, making no noise behind his *mamá's* back. The dog is smart, I'll give him that, hiding the threat he's making to avoid being reprimanded. Maybe he does comprehend humans.

"Well, he's definitely protective of you."

"Yeah. I heard enough horror stories about Colorado's wildlife to know I wanted to get the biggest, toughest dog to accompany me on my runs—for both companionship and protection. I adopted him from the Humane Society, but his name was different. They named him something obnoxious: Licorice." She makes a face of disgust and I shake my head. "One look at his sweet golden eyes and I was sold. Brought him home and we've been inseparable since."

No longer seeing me as a threat, Hades snorts and starts investigating a nearby brush pile.

I need to know who this little spitfire is before she goes on her way. I extend my hand to her. "Well, I guess proper introductions are in order. Maceo, but you already know it." I give her my best panty-dropping smile, praying it works on her. From the pretty blush growing on her cheeks, I'm guessing my charm is having the desired effect.

"Josephine," she says in a soft voice as she takes my hand. We shake hands for a moment, and I bring the back of her hand to my lips to place a kiss on her silky skin. I don't know what possessed me with this fucking chivalrous behavior. I've never kissed someone's hand before. But something about her makes me want to put my hands and lips all over her, right here and right now, while still being a gentleman.

"Josephine," I murmur. "Beautiful name for a beautiful woman."

She giggles and I swear to God it sounds like little bells, perfect and musical. She's fucking gorgeous, and it makes my chest ache. I palm the area with my free hand to ease the pain. She rolls her bright blue eyes, but she's clearly flattered based on how her blush spreads from her face to her cleavage. "My, aren't you the charmer."

My grin turns wolfish and my inner asshole takes over. "I'm hoping to charm the pants right off you."

Josephine blinks, shocked. "You're bold." She shakes her head as if to clear it.

Still holding her hand, I pull her closer till I'm bending down to her ear. I'm so fucking close I can smell the citrus scent of her skin mixed with what I know is the scent of her arousal. It's fucking euphoric and nearly primal. "Is it working?"

Her pupils dilate and the corners of her mouth turn up. "Not at all."

She lies. I chuckle at the challenge she's presenting.

Her bright blues narrow at me. "I'm not that easy."

Maybe true with the men in her past, but I can tell by the flush of her skin and the way she's shifting her thighs together, I'm affecting her as much as she's affecting me. I may have a shot at being the exception.

I don't need to get to know a bedmate in order to have sex with her. Honestly, being willing, attractive, and clean is enough. I'm not in it to form a connection; it's just sex. And the women I've hooked up with before are of the same mindset.

But Josephine isn't the typical woman I go after, and if she was, she would already be trying to run a hand up my body. Josephine is... surprising in some odd way I can't discern. She needs to be wooed, and to feel connected to any man she allows in.

These are uncharted waters for me. But looking at the little beauty and how enticing her body is, I'm willing to give it a whirl.

"Of course you're not easy, and I'm sorry if I gave you the wrong impression. Can't blame a guy for trying." I eye her up and down appreciatively, watching her blush deepen. "I think if you gave me the time of day, you'd see we have more in common than not."

She smirks. "Like what?"

I've got her attention, and now I need to sell myself like an infomercial host. "For starters we both enjoy running and staying in shape."

She nods but isn't biting—yet.

"We're both early risers. We enjoy being out in nature and appreciate quiet surroundings. And we can find humor in disastrous first encounters."

Josephine grins. "You're right, we have more in common than I expected. But it's not enough to 'charm the pants off' of me."

Ugh. I've never had to put this much effort into winning a woman over. They typically take one look at my cut body, and are all game. This one's willful and...amazingly, I like it.

"What does a man need to do to win your approval? I mean, I already swept you off your feet, rescued you from the *Hound of the Baskervilles*, and climbed a mountain to bring you to safety. Aren't I enough of a knight in shining armor?" I joke, keeping it light.

Baby, if you take a chance on me, I promise your body won't regret it.

I don't chase women, *ever*. They come to me willingly, and when I'm done with them, I'm done. If this woman isn't interested in what I'm offering, I'll leave her alone and go on my merry way. But damn if this blue-eyed pixie doesn't make me want to beg like a fucking dog for any kind of affection she'd give. Going three months without sex must be messing with my head.

Josephine laughs nervously and I can't help but inch closer, her laughter like a beacon. My semi-hard cock is now nearly erect. Goddamn, I have no control around this pixie, and it both arouses and scares the shit out of me. I'm used to being in control and calling the shots, but Josephine—she's bringing out my carnal needs. I need to seal the deal with this woman, and *now*.

With my cock aching for attention, I contemplate if it would be overstepping to lean down and offer her a kiss. My eyes hold hers, searching for consent, but Josephine takes me by surprise.

"Oh, to hell with it," she says in a husky voice, before pulling my face down to hers where salty sweet lips brush against mine.

Holy fuck! How did I get this damn lucky with this woman?

The featherlight touch of her velvet lips is enough for me to let loose my feral side. My left hand snakes into her hair, while the other wraps around her tiny waist, pulling her against my body. I deepen the kiss, enjoying her silky lips against mine. Gently, I press her back into the boulder, careful to avoid setting off Hades—I definitely don't want him cock blocking me. I lean into her and experience more of her heavenly body.

She moans into my mouth, granting me access to swipe my tongue against hers. Lord, she tastes like mint, heaven, and sin all rolled into one.

Her slim fingers graze up and down the hard-muscled panels of my shirtless abdomen, while my hand roams over her slim hip and down to the curve of her ass. Never have I wanted to smack an ass as much as I want to right now. My hand twitches, but I resist.

We break the kiss and I lean my forehead against hers, both of us panting for air. Her eyes hold mine and her fingers toy with my waistband. If she's looking for approval, she's got it. Hungry for her, I crush my lips to hers. Her small hand molds around my huge, erect cock over my workout shorts. I can't stop the growl of approval from leaving my lungs if my life depended on it.

Shit, this is escalating quickly.

I'm not in control, only following her lead, and I'm sure as shit not going to stop it, knowing her intentions. *No.* I'm going to stoke this fire burning between us and take the reins. If she wants to cop a feel, I'm going to take it to the next level.

My hand moves from her ass to the front waistband of her shorts, and slides underneath the thin material, finding her hot center wet and ready. I bite back the groan working its way out of my chest. My cock thickens at the notion of being covered in her juices.

Her head tilts back, giving me access to her slender throat. I take full advantage, by licking and kissing it. Fuck me—she breaks out in goosebumps—and I nearly come, knowing I'm giving her as much pleasure as she's giving me.

I circle my thumb on her precious nub before slipping two fingers between her slick folds and plunge inside of her. *So fucking tight, maybe I should have started with one finger.* I don't want to hurt her, only bring her pleasure.

"Yes," she moans and angles her hips.

Ah, hell! That little moan is like a shock to my heart.

My fingers curl to hit the secret ball of nerves deep inside of her, wanting to make her pussy vibrate. My other hand untangles from her hair, and I hook her leg and cradle it in my elbow, trussing her up against the rock so my fingers hit her tender spot better. I swear to God she's purring as she rides my hand, chasing her own pleasure.

I focus on her radiant face and watch her come apart from my fingers alone. Her head is tossed back, her eyes closed tight, and her pretty little mouth parted in a perfect O. Fucking gorgeous, but I need to see her aqua eyes when she peaks.

"Look at me, baby," I command gruffly.

She obeys, showing me those bright blues of hers—swimming with the ecstasy I'm giving her. She's the sexiest temptress I've had the pleasure of fucking. She's close; her legs are shaking, and her gasps have turned into moans.

I hear movement behind me and look over my shoulder to see Hades cautiously approaching. He doesn't trust me. He probably hears the soft cries of his *mamá* and has come to investigate.

Shit. "Um, Josephine?"

Josephine looks over my shoulder at her hellhound and holds up her hand, stopping him. "It's okay, big boy. Go lay down."

Reluctantly, Hades goes and flops down under a tree.

My eyes reconnect with Josephine's, and my fingers and thumb work her into a quivering mess.

"Let go," I order, barely able to control my own arousal.

Her eyes roll back into her head, and she cries out as she detonates around my fingers, filling my palm with her wet sweetness. Her pussy clenches hard on my fingers, and my dick starts to weep with jealousy.

My groan can't be contained anymore. "Fuck, baby, you're killing me."

My pixie opens her eyes and all I see is more wanton need than what was there to begin with.

Thank fuck for that.

Needing to taste her spunk, I pull my fingers out of her and raise them to my mouth, where I suck them clean. And it's my turn to roll my eyes into the back of my head with pleasure. She tastes sweet and creamy —it's like fucking ambrosia and it only fuels my already heightened need.

A soft moan escapes her as she watches me feast on the essence lingering on my fingers. She pulls me to her lips and kisses me deeply, her tongue working hard against my tongue barbell.

Fuck me, that's hot! Most women don't like to taste themselves, but clearly my little pixie is all for it. She has quickly become my favorite person in the world.

My head is swimming with lust. I only half register that she's pulling my heavy cock out from the top of my shorts. I was hoping she would return the favor with maybe a hand job or, God willing, a blowjob, but my mind explodes as she pushes down her own shorts to bare her succulent wet pussy to me.

Thank the fucking saints above for sending Josephine to me.

Instinct takes over and I'm grabbing her under her firm ass, hoisting her up to my waist. She wraps her slender legs around me, strong and ready for the ride I'm going to give her. I line up my thick cock to her entrance and swipe it several times across, coating it in her wetness. As wet as she is, we're still going to need extra lubricant. My fingers felt how tight her hot little pussy is. And I don't want to ride her dry with all nine inches of me. Keeping her happy is my number one priority.

Christ. Why does it feel like I'm falling for this woman when I only know her first name? It's a little unsettling, but in the heat of the moment I shove it aside.

Before I drive myself into her, I need to look in her eyes and make sure this is in fact what she wants. I'm all for picking up women and having a good fuck and then saying my goodbyes, but if this is going fast for me, it's probably going even faster for her. I cup her cheek with my free hand and force her to look at me. Her lust-filled eyes meet mine.

"Please," she whispers. "I want you inside of me."

Fuck me. She's begging for my cock. Who am I to deny her?

Ah hell, I'm not covered. Why didn't I realize this as I coated my length with her juices?

I never go raw. I'm clean. I was recently tested and I've been abstinent for months, but I don't know this woman from Adam.

Is she clean? Is she on birth control? Where is she in her ovulation cycle? Does she care if I'm not using protection?

My dick is screaming 'who gives a fuck.'

Torn, I hesitate. She reacts by grabbing my cock to entice me into her warm center.

"I don't have protection," I say regretfully.

"Please, I have no STIs, I swear. Just please fuck me, Maceo," she whimpers.

Oh Christ! "I don't either, but are you sure you're okay with this?" If she's fine fucking in the open without protection, I'm all on board.

She bobs her head anxiously.

Greedily, I slide in to the hilt in one thrust. She gasps, and her sex squeezes my dick. *Jesus*, I nearly come. Her molten hot pussy is a tight sheath around me; she's like a second skin. I wait a moment for her body to adjust to my girth before I start to move—slow at first, and she hisses from the intrusion. It's not until she starts panting that I move my hips faster and *fuck me* if she doesn't meet me thrust for thrust.

I kiss her tenderly, contrasting the force of my hips. She caresses my face with her slender hands and looks deeply into my eyes like she's searching for my soul. It's not long before we're both slick with perspiration from our lovemaking.

Lovemaking? I shake my head. Where the fuck did that come from?

Josephine wraps her arms around my neck and I wrap my arms tighter around her waist, and we're totally enveloped around each other. Definitely not my norm. We're fucking holding each other as I drill into her harder and harder, and I couldn't be more pleased with the fact we're embracing. She's mewling and I'm practically growling.

Fuck, this is too much. Embarrassingly, I know I'm not going to be able to keep this up much longer.

Heaven answers another prayer for me. "M—Maceo, I—I'm coming," she cries. My name on her lips as she climaxes is the sweetest sound. My chest nearly explodes hearing her scream my name. Suddenly, I'm flying over the edge.

"Fuck, fuck, fuck!" I roar, shooting my load deep inside of her. My orgasm goes on and on, her pussy clenching around me from her own release.

My God, that was the best orgasm I've ever experienced. And I've had a lot, making me a damn expert.

14

I look at her lovely face and she's probably having the exact same thought, bringing the biggest fucking grin to my face. I'm pretty proud to be the best she's had, and the only one to give it to her from here on out.

What the actual fuck, Maceo? We've fucked once and I'm already thinking of forever. I've never been with a woman more than once. But fuck if this tiny pixie isn't making me rethink my own rules. One and done isn't going to cut my urge for Josephine. I need more of her and it terrifies me.

Josephine must sense me tense up, because she pulls away and assesses my reaction. Here I am, in the middle of trying to figure out how I can keep this woman with me, and she's realizing what the fuck we did.

Her hand rises to her forehead. "Oh. My. God."

I shoot for humor, making light of the delicate situation we're in, to keep her calm and with me. "Why, thank you. But seriously, call me Maceo."

She groans and starts to pull away, leaving me no choice but to slip out and set her down. *Fuck*—my dick is bitching at me to push back into her and keep her speared on me. My gut twists as I watch her hastily pick up her shorts and tug them back on. Reluctantly, I pull my own back up, and I catch her arm as she turns away.

"Hey," I say gently, stopping her retreat.

She refuses to meet my gaze, shaking her head. "I can't believe I did this. This isn't me. What the hell was I thinking?"

"It's okay. No worries. Fuck, that was amazing." I bring her hand to my heart. "You feel that? My heart is still fucking racing like a freight train."

Blue eyes fly wide and she quickly pulls her hand away from my heaving chest. "Oh, God. This was a bad decision."

"Wrong!" I counter. "It was the greatest decision. And we're going to do it again, and again, and again."

Yep, you're mine and I'm keeping you. Wait... What the hell, Maceo?!

Sex was supposed to clear my mind, not fuck it up. I want to slap myself for thinking shit about forever with this woman, even if she made me come harder than anyone else.

Josephine is fucking shaking now and clenching at her abdomen. "No, we won't be having sex again."

I snort. "You can't fight this chemistry between us, Pixie. It's primal and instinctive. No use trying to go against it and wasting precious time. Come back with me to my place and let me take care of you again."

There's no way I'm letting her go 'till I get my fill of her. I'll reschedule my appointment for this morning to make it happen.

Josephine's face blushes a deep scarlet. Does the blush spread all the way down to the lips of her pussy? I bite my bottom lip, picturing the image.

"Nope. Not happening." She quickly looks down at her watch. "Shit," she says with clear panic. "I don't have time for this. Hades! Come on, boy. We need to hurry home."

Hades hasn't moved from his spot under the shade of the tree off the trail, and he makes no attempt to get up. I don't blame him. Early as it is, it's fucking hot.

Scowling, I fold my arms over my chest. "Where is home exactly?" If she thinks she's going to ditch me after the best lay ever, she's got another thing coming.

I don't want to scare her away by getting all possessive, but a switch has been flipped inside me and I don't think I can stop myself from tracking her down. Finding people is my damn job. I'll find her, woo her little ass 'till the cows come home, and have her in my bed where she fucking belongs before the end of the week. It would just be preferable if I could convince her to give me an actual shot first.

"Yeah, I'm not telling you," she scoffs, calling for her dog again.

"Yeah, well, you may change your mind if you end up pregnant with my baby," I say heatedly. Fuck me if the idea of having a child with this woman doesn't thicken my cock with pride.

"We didn't use a condom, per your request. You may not want

anything to do with me right now, but I take responsibility for my actions and you may actually want me involved if there's a kid. You know what, fuck that, I *want* to be involved, whether there's a baby or not."

Jesus, did I just say that out loud?!

Her eyes bulge at my confession, but then quickly narrow. "I have an IUD; we're good on the baby end, thank you. My last boyfriend didn't want kids and insisted on it."

I glower. "He made you get an internal contraceptive device?"

She looks agitated as she shrugs. "He was adamant."

What the fuck? What kind of man insists on his woman using an invasive contraceptive? Her ex sounds like a real prick. "But you're not with him anymore?"

She sneers with revulsion. "No. And I haven't been with anyone since."

"Aside from me, and that's exactly how it's going to stay," I sing with confidence, happy she seems disgusted with her last boyfriend.

"You can't be fucking serious," she stutters.

"Like a heart attack," I confirm, cocky as always.

She shakes her head again. "We don't know anything about each other. This isn't a realistic expectation."

"We knew enough to give in to each other though we met fifteen fucking minutes earlier," I counter. "And that right there confirms there's something between us."

Bewilderment spreads across her face. "You're irrational!"

"And you're *very* rational, which makes this relationship fucking ideal because we balance each other out."

It looks like she's considering my offer judging by the wild look on her face, and my heart swells with hope. She only needs to see it my way, and we can be together until we've had our fill.

You're a damn liar, Maceo. Considering how she fucked me, I'll never get my fill.

Fuck me. I want this woman for my own. Damn my rules.

"I have to go. I have a business meeting I can't miss." She whistles for Hades, who finally gets up and pads toward us.

My heart starts to jackhammer. This can't be the end. I can't let her walk away. "Don't resist this, Josephine. We have something between us."

"You don't know that," she mumbles with a tremor in her voice.

"I fucking feel it in here," I say as I put my hand on my chest. "And you feel it, too. You're just being stubborn. But I won't let you ignore it. I'll remind you every damn day and night what we have if you let me."

My pixie looks at me gobsmacked before she turns on her heels and dashes away with Hades over the crest of the hill.

For a moment, I'm in shock.

She's fucking running! Oh, hell no.

I've never seen a woman take off—that move has always been reserved for me. Shit, half the time I have to shake them off before I close the damn door.

Snapping to attention, I recall there's a parking lot nearby and I dash up the hill to confirm my suspicions. I arrive in time to see her climb into a white Subaru, and she peels out of the parking lot. Not fast enough to avoid me catching her license plate, though. My lips curl into a smirk. If she wants to challenge me, I accept.

CHAPTER TWO
JOSEPHINE

What the hell is wrong with me? I had sex with a complete stranger in a fucking nature preserve where any Tom, Dick, or Harry could have watched.

Fear of jumping off the deep end after a chance encounter had me running for the hills—literally. I couldn't get out of there fast enough. Good thing Hades was on my heels, or I might have left him behind.

I speed out of the parking lot, but I allow myself one last look in the review mirror. Fuck if my heart doesn't leap into my throat when I see him standing in the lot with his hands on his hips and a smirk on his handsome face. I force myself to accelerate when every fiber in my body is screaming at me to stomp on the breaks.

Shame consumes me as I speed back to my condo, hoping and praying I can get ready fast enough for my morning appointment with my biggest client in over a year.

This was not how I planned my morning when I set out for my daily run. I was up by five and out the door no later than a quarter after with Hades. Running is the only time in my schedule when I unwind and meditate. It brings me the peace I need to tackle the rest of my hectic day. I was minding my own damn business, not bothering a soul in the world, before everything went batshit crazy.

I was running the trail wallowing in a pity party over the past year's events. Over a year ago, I was a content woman working at the firm of my dreams, and on the arm of a man I was in love with. But the fucker broke my heart and didn't give two shits about stealing my dream from me. I try to brush off the bad vibes while I weave my way along the trail.

All of a sudden—BOOM—this walking sex-on-a-stick barreled in to me and threw me over his massive shoulder like a bag of flour.

I laugh through my tears thinking of how I pounded against his chest and kicked at his shins, making his arm constrict around me tighter than a damn boa. He explained himself—his only concern was to save me from Hades. Looking at Hades from an outsider's perspective, I totally got his reasoning.

And fuck me if Maceo wasn't charming the pants right off of me like he wanted. His proximity was enough to make me drunk with need. His soft lips on my knuckles only made me want those lips all over me. The warmth of his arms holding me close sent shivers of pleasure all through my body and deep into my lower belly. His voice hypnotized me, and I gave into his charisma and unspoken sexual requests.

Choking on my tears as I drive, I want to blame my rash decision —having sex with a total stranger—on not having sex for a whole damn year. I haven't felt compelled to be involved with anyone else since I broke up with Jacob.

It had only been Jacob since freshman year in college. If I'm being honest, Jacob didn't bring much to the bedroom. Most of the time, I had to finish myself off in the bathroom after the fact; Jacob was a two-pump chump.

Maceo—my stomach flutters and my thighs squeeze together—Maceo was a sex god who was clearly ready to lay me out. A voice in my head I never listen to—the irrational part that had me leave my life the last time I paid attention to it—was screaming at me to jump his bones.

So what did I do? I took the fucking leap.

Before I knew what I was doing, my hands were running all over his hard body and groping him through his shorts, where I could feel he had a frenum piercing. I never intended for things to get carried away the way they did. I should have stopped it right there, but his hand slid past my soaked panties, and his thick fingers were inside me, circling my clit. My body turned off my mind, and I pushed my hips forward to ride his hand like I was starving for his touch. His commanding voice was all I needed to go over the edge.

Without hesitation, I stripped both of us and begged Maceo to fuck me bareback. *Reasoning be damned.* Not when he impaled me on his long shaft, or kissed me fervently, or in our final moments before we exploded together, I never belong anywhere else but with him.

Our happy encounter ended right there. Reality came crashing down hard while I was still perched on his dick, which I swear never went soft. Shame and dread bubble up inside me. I fucked a man I just met and know nothing about.

As if that isn't bad enough already, the crazed look of possession in his dark eyes scared me more than anything else. But it was those small touches he gave me after I came to my senses which had me second guessing everything. His words about our partnering being inevitable had me painting a picture in my head with him by my side. And fuck me if it didn't feel *right*.

My mind drifts back to the present as another sob escapes my throat and tears prick my eyes. *What the hell am I doing?* Was Maceo right when he said not to fight this? I shake my head to clear the absurd notion.

It's not long before Hades and I are pulling up to the condo. I race with him up the steps, and I immediately go to the kitchen to put dog food in Hades's dish. I grab a glass of water for myself, but I regret it instantly because I can no longer taste Maceo's kiss on my lips.

Enough! These ridiculous thoughts have to go.

On autopilot, I navigate myself around my condo, pulling out my best business clothes and highest stilettos before turning on the shower. I step into the hot blast and scrub any remainder of Maceo from my body. Thank God I splurged on waxing last week because I'm damn near out of time to get ready.

Finished, I dry off quickly and throw my hair in a towel, brushing my teeth for the second time this morning, and beginning my daily moisturizing treatment. After stepping into my undergarments, I slip into my black pencil skirt and sheer white blouse—only slightly provocative, which never hurts in sealing a business deal.

By now my hair is dry enough to blow out and throw up into a French twist. A couple of bobby pins, a dab of perfume on my neck and wrists, and I'm good to go. I step into my heels, grab my purse and computer case with my portfolio, before kissing Hades' big head and running out the door.

Trying to get my head in the game, I focus on what I need to accomplish. *I need to score this deal.* My whole career is riding on landing stable projects, and right now I'm getting pretty desperate. I deserve better—at least that's what I keep telling myself.

To say it's been a struggle would be an understatement—it's been fucking awful. I've taken every single design job I've gotten my hands on, which has limited my creativity and often forced me to work with some shady-ass characters.

Like Lorenzo Bianchi, the mob boss who hired me to build an illegal casino under his family's Italian restaurant. The dude is still sending me flowers in hopes I'll finally break down and take him up on his offer of a date. *Hard pass.* Or the freaky religious group I had never heard of before, who asked me to build a temple into the cliff face of the Rockies. I swear they were a cult. And countless sleazy landlords wanting cheap and shabby work, while asking top-dollar from tenants.

At least I've had enough local clients now to have a decent portfolio, and some contacts for production around Fort Collins. This is not where I saw myself at twenty-seven, but here I am nonetheless.

Today, it's all going to change. I'm meeting with my first multimillion-dollar client on a project which is sure to take months to complete. My first stepping-stone in the direction I want to go: up.

My client, who goes by the name Atlas—that's it, one name, like Cher or Beyoncé—asked to go over my plans at a local diner, where he and his motorcycle pack have breakfast every morning. No problem. I'm more than accommodating to the needs of my prospective clients. Plus, meeting over breakfast seems like a relaxing way to learn more about this new customer's needs.

Pulling into the parking lot, I have to maneuver around a dozen motorcycles. Not unusual, since this diner is known for serving bikers. I've passed this place a million times, and there's always a motorcycle gang gathered here. I park and climb out of my car, reaching to grab my belongings.

A low whistle and a couple catcalls reach my ear as I'm bent over. I stand to my full height, which is helped by the four extra inches I'm sporting, and I straighten my back before glaring at the two MC members behind me.

They snigger but otherwise don't say anything to my face. I turn and head to the diner.

"That one's a hellcat," one of the men says.

I roll my eyes. Maybe taking this project was a mistake. I will not tolerate being sexually objectified, and I have had my fair share of it over the past year. Even though I've grown a thick layer of skin, there's only so much I will take. This biker I'm meeting and the group he's affiliated with may be beyond my comfort zone. I hope this isn't my last straw.

Minimizing the natural sway of my hips to avoid further harassment, I make my way into the crowded diner. Bikers and scantily-clad women pack the restaurant. As I take in the wardrobe choices of the women hanging on the huge men, I realize my sheer blouse will be less appealing than I originally thought.

I pivot to see if I can pinpoint my client. He told me in our last email to 'look for the biggest guy in the room, with the leather cut reading Atlas and President.' His description does nothing to help, because all these men are huge, and I feel a little awkward staring at their chests to read their vests.

It probably doesn't help that my client has no idea who he's looking for either. The fact we've only communicated through email has given nothing away about my identity.

Most of my clients are shocked when they discover I'm a woman. I purposely shorten my name from 'Josephine' to 'Jo' in order to land bigger fish.

In my industry, men are the dominating force, especially when it comes to clean lines and modern architecture. Women are always associated with the softer touches of design. It's annoying as hell.

Midcentury modern has always been my springboard, and it pisses me off I have to trick people. But until I make my mark in this industry, I fear I have no other choice.

I turn in a half circle and freeze when my eyes make contact with the person I'd vowed—only an hour ago—never to see again.

Maceo, looking sexy as sin, dressed in ripped jeans and a skin-tight faded black tee, sits in a big circular corner booth by himself. His inked arms drape over the back like he fucking owns the place. He looks so casual in scuffed combat boots, and his MC leather cut reads *President* followed by...*Atlas*. To add insult to injury, he's looking right at me with a devilish grin and smoldering eyes.

Fuck. My. Life.

This could not be any worse if it were written for a drama TV series.

This Goliath of a man is too damn good-looking for his own good. His huge rippling muscles are barely hidden underneath his T-shirt. His tan skin highlights his long black eyelashes and dark brown eyes —those eyes, nearly black, have the power to reel me in and make me disappear. His shiny raven-black hair is shaved close to the scalp on the sides, but longer and flipped back on top, making me want to run my hands through it—again.

Early morning dark scruff is the only facial hair on his strong, chiseled jawline. His corded neck makes me want to press my lips there and feel his pulse. Legs as thick as my waist, and strong as hell, are stretched out in front of him.

Hot damn! I'm pretty sure I'm staring with my mouth hanging open for the second time today.

The way his eyes scan my body convinces me he's remembering our previous tryst, and his tongue snakes out along his full bottom lip, showing me a hint of his barbell piercing.

With the tightest smile I can muster, I walk toward him 'till I'm standing at the head of his table.

"Atlas," I say as casually as I can, but I can still hear the growl in my voice.

His grin spreads to cocky. "Jo," he purrs. "Or would you prefer Josephine?"

My eyes narrow. I both like and dislike him using my full name. It sounds lovely coming from his lips, but it's *too* intimate. "Jo is fine, thank you."

"I like Josephine better. I'm sure you won't mind, seeing as the customer is always right, yeah, Josephine?" he says wickedly, raising one full, dark brow as if to challenge me.

My fist clenches around my computer case, but I maintain a casual face. At least I hope so. "Of course. Whatever you're comfortable with."

Maceo stands from the booth 'till he's hovering over me, and fuck me if he doesn't smell like our earlier lovemaking.

The asshole never washed me off. My nostrils flare, and I swear he knows exactly what I'm thinking.

"Sorry if I smell *musky*. I ran out of time this morning, too preoccupied. Please have a seat."

Rat bastard! I pucker my lips and raise my eyes to the ceiling to

25

gather my composure before I slide into the booth. He follows beside me and plants himself against me, his leg grazing mine. I scoot over to break the connection, but his body fills in the vacant space.

Keeping distance from him while I sit here is fruitless—he's not going to settle on giving me personal space. I give up and allow his body to brush against mine, hating and loving the connection all at once.

A waitress approaches our table. "What can I get ya?"

Frazzled, I grab the menu and quickly skim it. The gyro omelet with feta cheese and spinach is right up my alley. I order it along with a coffee. Maceo chuckles to himself before looking up at our waitress with a proud-ass smirk. "You know what I like, Bonnie."

"Two gyro omelets and coffees coming right up," she clucks before returning to the kitchen.

I close my eyes and shake my head. Of course, I had to order his favorite off the menu. The smug *sonofabitch* is gloating right now, probably thinking this is one of many things connecting us, adding to the list he rambled on the trail this morning.

Bonnie returns with our coffees before disappearing again. We both reach for the creamers at the same time, grazing each other's fingers, sending little shocks of electricity up my arm. I pull away quickly and Maceo smiles, grabbing a creamer cup. "Want to share? I don't use half of this thing."

I nod. "Yes, actually. That's perfect." No point in being wasteful.

Maceo tops off our coffees and we both stir our mugs. I raise the cup to my lips and blow before taking a long sip, while Maceo watches me over the brim of his own mug.

I clear my throat. "Well, Atlas, I—" I begin, but he cuts me off.

"No, Pixie. To everyone else I'm Atlas, but to you I'm Maceo."

I bite my tongue to keep from arguing. It's bad enough he's using my given name, but it's a whole other ballgame making me use his. It connects us on a deeper level. Why does he insist on my use of his first name? We had sex one time. It's not like we're a couple.

"Maceo." It comes out like a caress around my tongue, reminding me of the last time I used it. He was balls deep inside me, making me scream his name through my climax. My face heats from the memory.

The smug asshole knows exactly what I'm remembering from the way his grin widens. Now I know why he wants me to call him Maceo—it's a reminder of what occurred between us.

He drapes his arm behind my backrest, encasing me without actually touching me. The gesture is far too personal, but I don't pull away. *What the fuck is wrong with me?*

Distraction, I need a distraction. "We've got some time before the food comes out. Would you like to see the blueprints and virtual tour?"

Atlas—I mean, Maceo—had requested my services as an architectural engineer after he viewed my portfolio on my website, stating my edgy designs were exactly what he was looking for. He wanted me to build him a giant housing complex he referred to as a 'clubhouse' for the Mercy Ravens MC crew.

"Please, I can't wait to see what you got," he says in a husky voice. The sexual innuendo is not lost on me.

Oh Lord, help me.

Doing my best to ignore the rush of blood swirling in my lower belly, I open my laptop, plug in my flash drive, and pull up the plans for the MC headquarters. I start with the tour because it's easier to visualize a design when you're walking through the program. Maceo leans in, eagerly watching and listening to my detailed layout.

"I got the impression you wanted more of an apartment atmosphere with a common area, instead of a dormitory. The outside is all clean lines, rock, metal, and cedar. You walk into the grand entrance to a wall of local stone, which directs you around either side to the main living room—or gathering area—which will be filled with several distressed leather couches and light walnut end tables. The stone wall functions as a fireplace on the living room side, and a privacy barrier from the front door looking in."

Maceo nods in approval. "Good."

"To the left of the gathering area is the kitchen, which will have dark flat panel cabinets, stainless steel appliances, brass finishes, and white quartz countertops. We could do concrete counters in a lighter finish, if you would prefer. Next to the kitchen is the open dining area, with one long banquet table and industrial metal chairs. To the right of the gathering area, is what I call the billiards room; two pool tables, a couple dart boards, a poker table, and a full bar with TVs mounted on the walls. Plenty of high tables and stools for entertaining."

Maceo grunts his endorsement, and he sucks off some butter on his thumb from the toast. I flush, my dirty mind recalling when he sucked my juices off his fingers. Witnessing him taste me with desire flooding his eyes was like a shot of pure lust to my core. Remembering this makes me want his pierced tongue on my sex.

Jesus, I'm throbbing. I cross my legs, trying to combat the ache between my thighs.

I clear the lump in my throat. "The back of the first floor will be reserved for a large conference room, with a full tech area for your, um, meetings."

What possible meetings with state-of-the-art equipment a MC gang might have is beyond me, but Maceo demanded it and I always deliver.

"The rest of the main level will be dedicated for offices, yours being the largest, as well as two separate bathrooms.

"The entire first floor will have matted gray walls, plenty of windows for light, but tinted on the outside for extra privacy. Ebony-stained trim and mission-style doors. And the acid-stained concrete floors will hold up all the heavy boots tracking through," I say as I look around at the huge members of the MC, taking in the women hanging on them. "—or high heels."

My hypocritical thought is not lost on me. I have no right to judge these women, especially after what I did this morning. I shake my head in self-disgust.

Maceo raises an eyebrow and leans on his massive inked forearm, giving me nowhere to look but into his intense eyes. "The only heels I care about are the ones on your dainty feet. I don't give a fuck about anyone else's, or who the fuck they're attached to. You know, you're really cute when you get all jealous, like a kitten showing her claws."

"I'm not jealous," I say too quickly, but my heart goes pitter-patter at his confession.

He smirks. "Right. Just like I wasn't jealous hearing my brothers compliment your fine ass when you waltzed in here. Wearing those skyscraper heels, showing off your killer calves, and pushing your perfect tush into their grab zone. Nah, I wasn't jealous at all."

Holy hell, that's hot! Blood rushes to my cheeks and I clear my throat.

"Moving on to the second and third floors. That's where the individual bedrooms are, twenty in all, with en-suite bathrooms and sitting areas, ten per floor. You said you wanted separate spaces, so I assumed it included everything, seeing as you referred to the clubhouse as a home. You said you're all one big family, but still need detox space from each other."

"We do need separation. I'm thirty fucking years old, and I want my own space with something larger than a twin bed to stretch out on. All of us are crammed into a rented three-bedroom ranch we've been using as a club headquarters for the past year. You're looking at sixteen people living under fifteen-hundred square feet.

"We're sick of renting, tired of moving from town to town, and living in motels. I decided to stay put 'till I found us our permanent home, but there are no houses large enough to accommodate our numbers. That's why I purchased the hundred acres to build our MC clubhouse.

"We're a family. Some of us, this is the only family we've ever known. But as much as I love my crew—my brothers—I fucking need my space. I like this layout a lot," he admits.

My heart hurts a little when he confesses how the MC is the only family many of them have. It's incredibly tragic and it makes me curious about Maceo's family life, if he has one outside of this club.

I clear the emotion from my throat. "The bathrooms will have black penny tiles on the floor and large gray subway tiles in the showers. Same cabinets as the kitchen, with similar counters and finishes. Each bedroom will be able to hold a king-size bed, dresser, and two floating nightstands. Recessed lights will be in all the corners, the exception being the bedrooms, which will have an additional ceiling fan light. As far as flooring, I would like to stick to softer surfaces like carpet, but a nice hardwood in a birch or maple finish would be easier to clean, which might be ideal."

"Nice," he compliments. "Definitely hardwoods on the upper floors. I'm all for easier cleaning."

"Noted," I say, adding it to the plans before returning to the tour.

"Now, as a bonus, I've added a lower level with individual storage lockers for each member, and an industrial-size laundry room with multiple washers, dryers, stationary tubs, and folding tables. The pièce de résistance is a full gym with weights, benches, treadmills, punching bags, and a boxing ring. I know you didn't request it, but you mentioned every member was ex-military. I gambled on you all still training and being in top condition."

Maceo slaps his hand on the table, making me practically jump into his arms. "Fuck yeah, that's awesome!"

"Okay, good," I say, a little surprised by his excited reaction. "I added a large outdoor patio with a grill station and pavilion. I wasn't sure if you wanted an open pit for bonfires, or if you wanted an outdoor fireplace. I've made two options for you to view and pick from."

"Outdoor fire pit, hands down, but larger," he says confidently.

I quickly make the changes he requested and have him review the results. "Perfect," he says.

"Well, this pretty much wraps up the house. Is there anything I've forgotten, or is there more you would like to add?" I ask.

He nods. "A shop."

I pull up a new tab and start messing around with the program.

"By shop you mean a place to work with tools, like maybe a pole shed?"

"Yeah. We need a place to work on the bikes, trucks, and SUVs."

"A mechanics garage?"

He smiles broadly, happy I'm catching on to his requests. "Exactly."

"With all the bells and whistles?"

"Quote me and I'll decide from there."

"Give me a moment." I focus on the program and add in a workshop. Luckily, I already designed one of these six months ago, helping me breeze through the process. Bonnie comes through and drops off more food before disappearing again. I work while eating my breakfast.

Before long, I have something which is sure to meet his expectations. "This is a fairly large shop, but considering the number of vehicles you own, I believe this will more than meet your needs."

Maceo leans over to view my proposal and smirks. "Damn. You added a hydraulic lift, too."

"If we go with this plan, I'd like to keep it to the left of the property. It's built into the cliff and obscured from view of the road. I'd like to maintain the aesthetic, making the house the center of attention. We can make a circular drive, having you round the front of the house before heading to the shop, which will still leave plenty of green space in front. I also want the garage black with either a red metal roof or the reverse, seeing as the MC colors on your cuts are black and red."

"I'm good with that. Whichever you decide will look best since you're the designer."

I nod and implement my changes into the program. "Not like I want you to go for broke, but what about adding a couple garages along here to keep your vehicles out of the elements in the same color palette?"

"Protecting the bikes and other vehicles will definitely be a plus."

I add those in while we both eat, and I work.

"What's the damage, Pixie?"

I blow out a breath. This is always the hardest part of working with an individual because of the sticker shock. More often than not, I'm forced back to the drawing board, slicing and dicing my original plans to fit the needs of my client while still keeping their wallets happy.

I turn my computer to show him the expense report with the full total at the very bottom. Maceo reads through it and takes a bite of his omelet before nodding. "Looks good to me. When do we start?"

I blink. There's no way I heard him correctly. I quoted him for damn near five million dollars and he didn't bat an eye. In a designer's world, this is a dream come true. "Maceo, you did see the total, correct?"

He lowers his dark eyes to mine. "Yes, and after all the shit I made you add, it's still under the number I had in the back of my head. Where do I sign?"

Holy fuck. I did it. I landed my first multimillion-dollar project, and I didn't need to fight with my client to design it the way I wanted. I pull up the electronic contract, and he signs away his life on the dotted line.

He winks at me. "Looks like you're stuck with me for the next few months."

I'm giddy to the point I could kiss him. As if my body agrees with my subconscious, I catch myself leaning in. Maceo's coal eyes go wide, and he wraps his arm around me, pulling me flush against him and meeting me halfway to seal the deal with his lips.

God, his kiss is like water in a desert, and I can't stop drinking him in. His tongue skims across mine, and my libido jumps to new heights when his firm calloused hands are painfully perfect on my soft body. The musky scent of sex on his skin doesn't cover up the woodsy scent underneath, and it all acts like kindling to the fire burning low inside of me.

How is it possible I've missed his soft lips against mine when they were on me an hour ago? Once again, he has me moaning, and he's taking full advantage of my open mouth by dancing his tongue with mine.

I'm too caught up in the moment. It's not until the diner erupts in claps and whistles from the other MC members that I recognize my mistake, and I violently pull away from him, pushing myself up and out of the circular booth.

Flustered, I grab my purse and laptop, before I remember I'm a damn professional. "I'll email you the final details and your copy of the contract later today. If my contractor can get on board and have our crew lined up, we will be breaking ground next week. Start to finish should take four months, weather permitting."

I spin on my heels and haul ass out the door. I've got my car door open and I'm throwing my shit into the passenger side when I'm spun around by my waist. Maceo slams my car door, pinning me up against it.

"Nu-uh, Pixie. You can't run away this time," Maceo says, pushing his chest against my small breasts, caging me in.

"I'm sorry. It was a mistake to kiss you back there," I say, breathless.

Maceo runs his nose along the side of my neck, making my nipples go rock-hard and poke through my shirt. "A mistake," he echoes. "We need to make more mistakes if they turn out like this morning."

I gulp. "I don't get involved with clients. I never have and never will. This morning at the preserve, I didn't know who you were. But I agree the kiss in the diner was entirely my fault, and I take full responsibility. I apologize if I misled you, but I will not jeopardize this business deal. Therefore, I cannot be involved with you. Plus, I'm not interested."

Maceo's dark chuckle against my ear is his only response, and he pulls his face back to look in my eyes. My mind goes blank and I lean in. He covers the distance in a nanosecond and presses his lips against mine. More than anything, I want to continue this kiss, but this is wrong. I turn my head as I'm about to give in to him.

"Stop fighting this, Josephine," he growls with a smoldering glare. "And don't give me the 'no client dating' bullshit when you're the one initiating everything with me."

I balk. "I have not!"

"You made the first move on the trail, you kicked it off again when you leaned into me in the diner, and you just did it again here by your car. For someone who says she's not interested, your actions say otherwise," he counters, smug, ripping a hole through my delusion instantly.

Shit. He's right. I am the one who started all of this.

I'm desperate now. I know my will is disintegrating the longer I'm connected to him, and I simply can't allow it. My one and only relationship was a shitshow and my career is at risk. I cannot gamble on a high-risk relationship with a former Navy SEAL biker club president.

"I have another appointment," I lie. He's the only client I have right now.

Maceo's eyes narrow at me suspiciously. He has no way of knowing if I'm lying or not, but the way his eyes are scrutinizing me, I'm not entirely sure he can't tell.

I try a new approach. "Hades has a date with the groomers." Not an appointment with a client, but one for my dog, which is totally true. He's well overdue for a bath and nail trimming.

Maceo gives me a pointed look, like he's calling me out on my bullshit, but he takes a step back from our embrace and opens the car door for me. I slide into the seat, jumping when he leans across me to buckle me in. The gesture is totally sweet, but completely inappropriate for the 'no client relationship' rule.

Before I can object, he breathes me in and presses his lips to my temple—fuck me if it doesn't make me want to pull him into the car and have my way with him.

Stop giving him openings, Josephine!

He steps out and gives me his panty-dropping smile, making my heart do back flips again. "I'm picking you up tonight and we're going out."

"I told you, I don't—" I start.

"Fuck your rules. Fuck *my* rules. The rules are null and void now, don't you think? We're going out, we're going to have a great time, and we're going to see where the night leads us."

"Is it your norm to turn into a commanding asshole?" I snap.

Maceo barks a laugh. "Stop shooting me down, and maybe I won't turn into such an asshole. Come hell or high water, we're going out tonight."

Irritated, I turn away from him. "Why do you even want to bother with me?"

Maceo looks at me, curious, like he's trying to figure out this exact question himself before smiling. "You mean aside from the awesome sex?"

Typical guy. "Maceo—" I try again.

But he puts a thick finger to my lips to hush me. "Give me your business card."

Confused, my brows pinch together, but I reach into my purse anyway and hand him one.

He takes it from my fingers, looks down at it, and meets my gaze with a sinful smile. "See you at six." He closes my door and swaggers back into the diner, my eyes glued on his fine ass.

He doesn't have a clue where I live.

Quickly, I start my car and hope he doesn't turn around before I get out of here.

CHAPTER THREE
MACEO

S trutting like a cock, I know she's watching me walk all the way back toward the restaurant, because I can see her in the reflection of the diner windows. It makes my heart race knowing my little pixie is checking me out.

Back inside, I'm greeted with back slaps and more whistles from my crew. I walk up to the counter to pay Bonnie for our breakfast. As I wait for my change, my mind drifts back to the little pixie.

I knew I would find her and have her back by my side when she drove off this morning, but fuck, I had no clue it would be in the following hour. Imagine my surprise when she twirled around and locked eyes with me. Shock was written all over her face, followed by the wanton desire she desperately tried to conceal. Her eyes traveled all over me before narrowing. She took in my leather cut, homing in on my club name.

Well, tie me up and spank me happy.

My little pixie, Josephine, was Jo Holland. How fucking ironic is it fate was already working to bring us together for the past three weeks?

We'd only been able to speak via email the past few weeks while I worked a job in Colombia, I had no idea the 'Jo' in my head was actually a woman—a smoking-hot woman who fucked me better than my wildest dreams could have imagined.

Punk's voice carrying across the diner brings me back to the present. "Damn, Atlas. Who was the sweet thing?"

Smiling like a damn fool, I decide to fuck with them. "That there —" I point at her white Subaru speeding out of the lot. "—is my future wife, gentlemen. Mind your fucking tongues when you're talking about your *first lady*."

The diner erupts in thunderous laugher and more whoops and whistles. They know I'm joking since I've never been serious about a woman before, but I have to admit, keeping Josephine permanently feels *right*. It scares the fuck out of me.

Gauge is at my side, leaning in, letting me hear him over the ruckus. "When the hell did you find time to fuck our architect? You only met her this morning," he says with envy.

Fuck yeah, I met her this morning, and fuck yeah, I was already buried balls deep inside of her, but fuck him if he thinks I'm going to share any shit. I smile broadly at Gauge before taking the stool next to him. "I don't kiss and tell."

"Since fucking when?" Chase asks on my other side.

I smirk. "Since I saved a pixie from a hellhound and scaled a mountain."

Chase raises a pierced eyebrow. "What the what?"

I shake my head and laugh. No point in trying to explain the story without spilling the beans on all the sweet details. *Fat fucking chance.*

Instead of answering, I pull out my pixie's license plate number from my wallet and hand it to Chase. "I need an address for the owner of this license plate. Tell Steve Shields at the station her name is Josephine Holland. It should help him pull her info faster. I need it no later than five this afternoon."

"Why? What's going on this afternoon?" Chase asks.

"I'm taking the pixie on a date," I answer.

Shocked, Chase and Gauge glance at each other before looking back at me. I know the look. It's the 'what the fuck happened to him' look. It's how we used to look at our SEAL team when one of them fell hopelessly in love. 'Date' is not a word I've used before when talking about hooking up with a woman, and these two shits caught it.

Annoyed, I glower. Do I plan on fucking Josephine tonight? Absolutely. But oddly enough, I want more from her than just getting horizontal. Chase and Gauge can go to hell.

"Um, no problem," Chase says as he takes the license info between his fingers, pulling out his phone and walking outside.

I turn back to Gauge. "I'm not sure if I'm coming back this evening. Only contact me if you absolutely need to," I inform my second-in-command. In other words, he knows to keep a look out and not involve me unless it's life or death.

"Sure thing," he says. "Are you sure getting involved with the designer is a smart move?"

"I don't give a cock-suck if it's smart or not. It's what I want. I'm stuck with this woman for up to four months; I might as well make the most of it." *There, that sounds like me.*

Gauge snorts. "Or by the end of the project you'll have figured out a way to make her your old lady."

How dare he joke about me being committed to anyone!

I'm about to backhand him in the chest when, without warning, my mind flashes images of Josephine—in my arms with her legs wrapped around me, the slender curve of her ballerina neck, and her coastal blue eyes staring deep into mine.

I bite down hard on my tongue to stop myself from moaning.

"Damn, Atlas, are you sure she hasn't got you pussywhipped?" Gauge laughs and cracks an imaginary whip.

Fuming but unable to show he's getting to me, I grunt. Grunting is safe, and he can't read into it. What I really want to say is 'there's no other pussy I would want to be whipped by. She's fucking it and I don't care what any of your sorry asses say about it.' But I can't admit it, especially when I don't understand what the hell I'm feeling. All I know is I want more of Josephine, more than what we had on the trail this morning.

"Shit, man, I never thought I'd see the day when Maceo Tabares would settle down," Gauge continues to poke with a smirk, sipping his coffee.

I suck in my lower lip and bite it, anything to stop myself from showing my cards. This is the last thing I saw for myself.

Gauge eyes me suspiciously and slowly puts down his coffee. "Atlas?"

"Hmm?" I don't look at him.

Gauge leans in. "Are you shitting me?"

Fuck. Am I that obvious?

Gauge's eyes go wide and he quickly looks around the diner to see if anyone is listening to us before forcing me to look at him. "Do you like her, like her?"

Groaning, I rub a hand over my face. "I don't know what the fuck it is, okay. All I know is one time isn't going to do it for me."

Gauge's eyes bulge. "Holy shit!"

I want to tell him he's got it wrong. I want to tell him she's just another notch in the bedpost. I want to tell him I fucked her out of my system, and I'm ready for the next. But I *can't* because it's a lie and I don't lie to my brothers.

Gauge straightens up, stunned. "I feel like there's been a death in the family."

"Will you fucking stop?" I snap.

Gauge leans toward me again. "Bachelor Atlas is dead and committed Atlas is born. I mean, it's not a bad thing."

Is he screwing with me? Of course, this is a bad thing. Most relationships don't work. My job is dangerous, I have enemies who seek vengeance, and I'm gone a lot. What woman would want to stick with me through all that shit?

"You're only saying this because you want a more permanent relationship with Opal," I growl.

Gauge eyes narrow at the mention of Opal. "Watch it, Atlas."

Oh, I so have him. "I can't wait till you finally admit there's more between you two—other than hooking up every damn night."

Gauge's face grows red. *Yep, he's pissed.*

"Think about how awesome it's going to be when I'm hitched and you are too. Our kids will grow up together, and we'll celebrate the holidays like one big happy family," I joke louder.

Gauge's head whips around, making sure no one overheard, especially Opal. "Will you keep your damn voice down?"

I chuckle, but then I'm picturing what I just said in my head. I can see our kids running around outside, catching fireflies in jars while Gauge and I and our wives laugh around a bonfire.

Gauge waves his hand in front of my face. "Are you fucking serious?"

"What?"

"You're actually daydreaming about this shit?"

I shrug. So what if I am? It's a fantasy—it's not like it's actually going to happen. There's a pang in my heart and I rub my chest. *Shit. I really want this to happen.*

Gauge squeezes his eyes shut and runs both his hands through his brown hair. He groans before looking at me. "Ah, this shit's okay for you, but don't be going and putting these ideas in my head."

I look him dead in the eye. "This 'shit' is okay for both of us."

We stare long and hard at each other before looking away.

Gauge's fingers steeple in front of him and press to his face, like he's trying to pray the thoughts away. I'm no better. My leg bounces uncontrollably, and I pinch the bridge of my nose.

I growl in frustration. If I can't talk about what I'm going through with Gauge, who the fuck can I talk to? I decide to let my thoughts out. "Even if I wanted to pursue a relationship with her, she's not on board. Apparently she's living by the same 'one and done' code as me since her last boyfriend."

Gauge sniggers. "Never thought a woman would give you the shaft."

"This one's stubborn," I admit. It's easier to talk about my feelings for Josephine knowing Gauge is in the same position with Opal.

Gauge gives a firm nod. "Good for her. You fucking need someone with a backbone who will challenge you. All those past bitches rolled over and took whatever you gave them. It's why this one has you wrapped around her little finger. She doesn't and won't put up with your shit."

"All true, but it's more. One look at her and I was snagged. It's fucking fate, I tell you," I say, leaning back in the stool and crossing my arms over my barrel chest.

"You don't believe in that shit," he counters.

I turn my deadpan-face to him and raise an eyebrow. Both of Gauge's go up. "You're telling me the sex is so good you're rethinking your fucking relationships theory?" he scoffs.

I shake my head. "You have no fucking clue. Or maybe you do," I say as I see Opal across the diner staring longingly after Gauge.

"Motherfucker," Gauge mumbles into his coffee. "Enough of this brother-bonding shit."

Gauge and I have been best friends since we met at boot camp. Just a couple of eighteen-year-olds, angry at the world, finding themselves and their way by becoming SEALs. We found brotherhood through our shared trials and victories. I trust him with everything including my life, and the feelings are mutual.

When I decided to retire after a decade of service, Gauge followed my lead, and he never batted an eye when I suggested we should cruise the country. Chase left the SEALs after seven years of service to follow us. And Punk served his four years before joining our crew. We have a dozen MC members now, but these guys, my motley crew—Chase, Gauge, and Punk—have been with me long enough to know I'm fucking breaking all my rules for Josephine.

Needing to shake off my nerves, I stand and stretch before slapping a hand on Gauge's shoulder. He nods and stands to follow me out, needing no words to know I want to ride. Punk falls in line and we walk to our bikes where Chase is already waiting.

My phone pings with a text from Chase containing Josephine's address. I smirk and climb on my bike, pulling out her business card.

When I requested her card, it threw her, but she obeyed and handed one to me. One quick glance and I knew it had her cell number, giving me another way to keep in contact with her.

"I didn't even need to reach out to Steve at the station. Her address isn't unlisted," Chase says, climbing on his own hog.

I frown. Well, that isn't safe at all. I'll talk to her about changing her address to unlisted when I see her tonight.

I shoot her a text.

Don't forget about tonight, Pixie. I'm coming for you.

With a nod to my brothers, I start my bike and pull out with Gauge at my right, Chase and Punk behind. We make our way out of the city and let loose. This is our first real ride since coming back from Colombia less than twenty-four hours ago. We all need it. The wind whipping around us and the constant rumble of our engines puts us in a meditative state. We all have our own demons, but in this moment when our tires hit the open highway, we're finally free.

The sixty-mile drive to Denver gives us a little reprieve before we meet with our next client. He's some rich investor named Henry, who's being blackmailed by an ex-lover with pictures of him in some compromising positions. Henry reached out to us through our security company website.

The guy's in a sore spot. To his family and colleagues, he's a mild-mannered straight guy, when in reality he's a closeted gay man into S&M. He was tied up and blindfolded when pictures were taken without his consent.

Lucky for Henry, cyber work is a damn breeze for us. Chase was the intel specialist on our team back in the SEALs, and fuck if he ain't a straight-up hacker now. The guy is scary with what he can find out and get into with only a computer. Chase prefers to keep things as legal as possible, but when we're in a pinch, he has no problem breaking a couple laws for the greater good.

It doesn't seem fair, what Henry is going through. He wasn't hurting anyone by enjoying his sexual needs. He's not married or involved with a partner of any kind, no kids—he's just a poor sap who got screwed by someone in whom he put his trust.

My mind drifts to Josephine. *What happened in her last relationship?* Did she put all her faith in him and he did something inexcusable? What exactly is she scared of, giving her the opinion that avoiding me is the safer route?

All I can recall her saying about her past relationships is something about not being with anyone since breaking it off with her ex.

Suddenly, I'm able to piece it all together without her having to fill in the blanks. The fucker hurt her, and she has sworn off men since. If this past fuck-up hinders my chances of getting in her pants again...

I'm a level-headed man—have to be in my line of work—which makes my sudden temper unjustifiable. This woman is seriously messing with my head. I sigh.

Shit, I know it's going turbo fast. It would have been easier on both her and I if she were another conquest, but my 'one and done' attitude fucking flew out the window the minute I held her. All I know for certain is I need to earn her trust by being the best man I can possibly be for her.

Before leaving Denver, we reassure Henry we'll be able to help him. Any hard copies, USB drives, or computers will be confiscated by our ground team, which I will most likely lead. Anything in a network or cloud will be deleted or buried so fucking deep it will never see the light of day.

Back on the highway, I swear my heartstrings pull me closer to Josephine. *I'll be with you soon, Pixie.*

When we pull up to our rental, the crew is already partying and it's only noon. I have six hours before I can have Josephine back in my arms. I decide to take my bike into the garage, tune it up and polish it down. Got to keep it right and tight if Josephine is going to be riding with me.

Chase comes out to the garage, grabbing two beers from the fridge, and sits by me. He hands me one of them. I pull Josephine's business card from my back pocket and hand it to him along with my phone.

"I was wondering when you would ask me to set up tracking on her," Chase says, turning towards the bench to fire up his laptop. "I know this is standard procedure for any of our crew members, but she better not fuck up my tech room in the clubhouse if she finds out about this, because I'll come after you."

I laugh out loud before returning to work on my bike. "I owe you one. Might as well gather any intel on her for me when you're running the background check. I want to know anything and everything, especially about this fucking ex of hers."

"Uh-huh," Chase mumbles as he works, his tattooed knuckles flying across the keys.

After working in silence for well over an hour, Chase clears his throat. "You're really into this chick, hey?"

It was hard enough admitting to Gauge about my bizarre feelings for Josephine, and I'm not sure if I'm ready to open up to Chase as well. I'm still trying to figure it out for myself. I look over my shoulder at Chase, who has stopped working, waiting for my answer. Chase is one of my brothers and third-in-command. I can be upfront with him.

Grinding my teeth, I look back at my bike to avoid his reaction. "Yeah, I dig her," I say, wiping the grease from my hand on a rag.

Chase snorts. "Not sure if I should say congratulations or give you my condolences."

I laugh before turning back and deciding to joke with him. "Wait 'till it happens to you, man."

"Fat fucking chance. With you out of the running, there's more pussy for me," he says with a salacious grin.

Shaking my head, I finish wiping down my bike before picking up my beer to take a long swig. I grab a seat at the work bench next to Chase.

"She's fucking hot, Atlas," he murmurs beside me.

My eyes narrow and I lower my beer, glowering at my brother.

Chase puts his hands up in surrender, pointing at his computer screen. "Don't fucking kill me for stating the obvious, man."

I crack my neck, trying to roll off my sudden anger toward Chase, and lean over to look at the screen. There's my beautiful girl in multiple pictures, no doubt taken from her social media accounts. Many are of her at the beach. There are some of her doing a road race of sorts, with a man running alongside her. Others have her posing with groups of various people, maybe family, maybe friends or coworkers.

Aside from her, there's one repeating figure in over half of the pictures—a baby-faced tool of a man who looks like he would get blown over if you breathed on him. Tall, but nowhere near my six-five, and lanky, with dirty-blond hair and dull-blue eyes. Dressed like a fucking uptight priss. Bet he has Palmolive hands, too.

Feeling pretty good in comparison to this preppy weakling ex-boyfriend of hers, I sit back in my chair and smirk. If this is who my pixie dated before, I've fucking won gold. I will give her *everything* she has been missing. I will more than make up for where he neglected her sweet body and soul.

"I didn't even need to hack into her social media accounts. She has everything public. She should make this stuff private." Chase shakes his head in disbelief. "I can do it from here, but she would eventually notice."

Concerned, my brows pull together. She really needs to be more careful with these sorts of things. "I'll figure out a way to bring up social media privacy with her." I know I won't feel at ease until she changes her settings.

Chase hands my phone back and points to the screen. "It's the same app we use for all our men."

My thumb hits the app and I see she's at home, which brings me comfort, knowing where she is. Part of me knows tracking her is wrong, but the bigger, more protective part of me justifies my actions as being sound. If I'm getting involved on any level more than my typical one-night stand, it's crucial for her safety. I'm on too many people's hit lists not to have eyes on her at all times.

Chase gives me a pointed look. "You know you'll have to tell her you're tracking her phone."

I nod. "If this shit gets serious, I'll tell her. There's no sense in having her freak out now. This is for her protection, and she won't understand at the moment."

"Probably not." Chase juts his chin out toward my cell. "I took the liberty of changing your backdrop and lock screen, too."

Swiping around on my phone, I see Chase added a beach picture of my pixie in a skimpy white bikini as my new wallpaper. Yeah, I totally know why Chase blurted out she's hot. This image alone is enough to keep me company on my future missions away from her. "Thanks, brother."

"Anytime, brother," Chase says, closing his laptop and taking a pull from his beer. "I've given you access to her private emails, social media accounts, text messages, contacts, bank accounts, medical records, etc."

"Jesus! I didn't ask for all of that."

Chase rolls his eyes at me. "You told me anything and everything. I delivered. Don't act like you're not curious and wouldn't snoop anyways. I saved you time and the risk of getting caught. It's not like you wouldn't demand to see this shit from her when this thing you two have turns out to be something. If you don't want to dig through her stuff, it's cool, but if you need to for whatever reason, you have access."

Gnawing on my lip, I'm torn with what to do with all this information. I don't need access to everything in Josephine's life, but now that I have it, I'm not going to turn it back over to Chase. I should keep it in case of an emergency. This way I keep it all in the palm of my hand—easy entrance when needed. *Yeah, this totally makes sense.*

Chase takes another sip from his beer before waving at his computer. "This shit was too easy to hack into. I'll make sure we ramp up her security in the cyber world. At a quick glance, everything in the background looks pretty normal, nothing stood out as concerning, aside from the crap that went down at her old place of employment in California. Oh, and maybe our favorite Italian mobster, Lorenzo, for who she did some work about nine months ago, but she seems to be holding her own with the douchebag."

My head snaps up from my phone. "What shit went down at her old work? Wait, don't tell me, I'll ask her." But I can't help myself. "How bad was it?"

Chase shakes his head. "Her ex, Jacob Klein, screwed her over. It's probably the reason she's gone solo in the field. If she doesn't fill you in after you ask her, I will. But I should warn you, from what I've seen, he's not ready to let her go. The guy hasn't stopped calling or texting her since she dumped him. And those messages are creepy as fuck."

I'm not surprised Josephine's ex is still hung up on her, but I don't like what Chase is implying. "Does she respond back?"

Chase shakes his head. "Not one fucking peep. She has moved on —he has not."

I'm silent, murderous feelings rolling through my veins. It's completely wild that I feel this strongly, but I do. "If he hurt her in any way, I'll kill him," I fume.

"It can be arranged, you know," Chase adds with a knowing look. "Shit, the dickwad really fucked up when he lost her."

I nod, but I'm annoyed he's referencing how great of a catch Josephine is.

Chase continues, oblivious to my irritation. "I mean with her curvy ass and pouty lips, he was lucky to score her in the first place."

Infuriated, I huff and puff like a bull ready to charge. *Chase better stop talking about Josephine's body or so help me.*

Clueless to my wrath, Chase finishes his beer. "But his loss is your gain. And it looks like she'll be gaining a lot more too, after what I saw of the dick pics he sent her."

Dick pics? Naked pictures! What the fuck?! That's it!

My vision goes red and the bottle I'm holding is launched across the garage, shattering against the cinderblocks.

I'm stewing and ready to haul Chase outside. "Were you looking at her nudes? Is that why you're talking about her body like it's a fucking playground?"

"Christ, Atlas, calm down! I swear I didn't see any nudes of *her*, only the ex. I was only referencing what I saw at the diner and through her pictures—where she's covered. The worst thing she sent him was a pic of herself in her bra, years ago. It was practically PG-13."

"Could you see her nipples in it? Could you?" I'm nearly screaming. I'll fucking knock Chase out if he got a look at them.

Deep down, I know my actions are over the top, but Josephine's the first woman who's ever made me consider having a relationship, and I feel protective as hell over her. She may not be mine yet, but I don't want another man ogling her pictures. It's bad enough her ex-boyfriend got them anytime he wanted.

"Shit, man, I don't know. It popped up and I closed out of it the next second. You guys may not have worked out the logistics of your relationship yet, but for all intents and purposes, she's your fucking woman, and I wouldn't disrespect you like that."

That's right, she's my woman. I calm some and jut my chin at the laptop. "Show me."

"Dude, I don't want to set you off again with me sitting right here."

"Chase," I warn.

"Shit, Atlas." But he doesn't fight me, and quickly gets to work on his computer.

The pic comes up and Chase quickly turns the laptop my way, staring up at the attic of the garage. I look closely at the image of Josephine, trying hard to control my rage at the unappreciative prick who was the recipient of it. I let out a sigh. Chase was right. As far as sex pics go, this is pretty mild, but damn if she isn't fine as hell in the shot.

"We good?" Chase asks, still staring up.

"We will be when you delete this shit from the fucknut's phone and cloud," I snarl.

Chase gives me a tired look, and I get it, he's on as much sleep as I am. "You know this shit is going to take me all night to bury."

My body tenses, a growl building in my throat. "I don't want the bastard eye-fucking her on his phone. And I don't want it buried. I want it fucking gone, as if it never existed to begin with."

"Fuck, fine," Chase concedes with a groan and starts hacking away. "But I get the bottle of Pappy you took from the drug bust in Kentucky last fall."

I grit my teeth. "Fine, you can have the Pappy Van Winkle, but don't go all weak and mix it with cola. You harden the fuck up and drink that shit straight like a man."

Chase grins, like a virgin getting his first peep show. *Clever bastard.* He's been after my Pappy since I swiped it, and he's finally found something I'm willing to give it up for. Good thing Josephine is worth every drop of the priceless bourbon. I'd rather drink from her, anyway.

I grit my teeth before asking my next question. "Does she still have images of his pecker on her cell or cloud?"

If I have it my way, my dick will be the only one she'll be laying her eyes on from here on out. I'm half-tempted to send her a shot right now, to remind her of this morning. The women I typically get involved with would absolutely love a digital pic of my junk, but I'm pretty confident it would turn Josephine off at this stage of our relationship, regardless of how impressive my cock is.

"You don't need to worry. She deletes every single one she receives, promptly. The vast majority were sent to her after she quit her job. Like he thought his limp dick could win her back. But he still sends them," Chase mumbles, typing away.

"Lecherous prick," I mutter, though I'm pleased with my pixie for erasing his sorry ass from her life.

Pissed off about her fucking ex, I look down at my phone. I've got her contacts. It wouldn't be hard to find his number. I start scrolling and check myself almost at once. She would be fucking irate if I called her pitiful ex and threatened him. I settle on sending her a text instead.

Two hours 'till I'm there, Pixie.

My phone pings and I smile, knowing it's her.

Can't come here since you don't know where I live. And I'm not telling.

I laugh out loud. Man, she's going to shit a brick when I show up tonight.

Wear something to show off those sexy legs of yours.

Fuck you, Maceo.

Now I'm shaking with laughter. God, this woman slays me. No one has the balls to talk to me the way she does. It's refreshing to have someone go toe to toe with me.

"Dude, she has you by the balls," Chase says, not looking up from his laptop.

"Oh, she will tonight," I tease knowingly.

"Asshole," he mumbles. We both know he won't be getting anything tonight but a five-thousand-dollar bottle of bourbon. Knowing Chase, he'd rather have pussy instead.

With a salute, I head to the house to get cleaned up for tonight. For once, the only bathroom in the rental is unoccupied, and I take full advantage. I scrub down in the shower and shave my face in the bathroom sink. I don't mind growing out a beard while I'm on a mission, but otherwise I can do without. I buzzed off my beard yesterday, as soon as we got home. I hate how it itches as it grows out, so I shave daily. Besides, I don't want any barriers when I run my face against Josephine's soft skin.

After throwing on some aftershave, combing my hair back and holding it in place with some hair clay, and thoroughly brushing my teeth, I wrap my towel around me and walk to the room I share with my three closest men to get dressed.

Fuck me if I'm not standing there, second-guessing everything I try on like some teenager. I settle on a pair of jeans without holes and a white fitted tee. I tie up my black boots and throw on my leather MC vest before grabbing my wallet, phone, and Pappy.

I almost take some condoms from the nightstand out of instinct, when I recall Josephine saying she has an implant.

"Fucking best day ever!" I sing, as I drop the condoms back in the drawer. I'm cool with her having the IUD right now, but if we decide to dive into this relationship, I'm going to ask her to get the damn thing removed. Never planned on or wanted kids before, but fuck me, I want *her* to bear my children—the more the merrier.

Heading through the house, I get a lot of smug smirks from my crew, which only strokes my ego. We all know I'm getting laid tonight.

I'm almost to the garage when Candy and her bubble-gum-colored hair sidles up to me, running her hands along my chest.

Candy is one of our MC bunnies, and she's constantly trying to get in my pants. She offered herself to me last night, and I was slightly tempted by the big fake tits shoved in my face. *Hard pass.* I don't shit where I eat. A club bunny won't do. Doesn't stop the bunnies from trying, hoping this time may be the time I take one of them to bed.

"Looking fine, Atlas. Going out tonight? I could go with you and keep you company," she offers, licking her glossy lips suggestively.

Fighting an eye roll, I shake my head. I've never had a woman on my hog. That baby is all mine, and I've never wanted to share it with anyone until a certain pixie crossed my path. Josephine will be the first to ride with me, and I can't wait to feel her body flush to my back.

"Sorry, Candy, but I'm off the market. I'm sure you'll find someone here to take you up on your offer."

She pouts, which has absolutely no effect on me. "You prefer the bitch in the pencil skirt with the stick up her ass?"

I pull her hands from my chest as firmly as I can without hurting her, and I lean to her ear. "Say one more venomous slur about

Josephine, and you'll see yourself out of this house, out of this club, and back on the street. You hear me?"

Candy shudders and gives me a curt nod before hustling her ass back into the house.

Back in the garage, I find several members drinking beers and shooting the shit while Chase works away on his laptop. I set Chase's bourbon payment next to him, and he gives me another proud smirk.

"Make good on this," I add, jutting my chin to his laptop screen. I give the rest of my crew a nod and climb on my bike, taking off to get Josephine.

I arrive at her condo nearly an hour early, but fuck if I can wait any longer to have her with me. My heart pounds like a drum the closer I get to her front door.

I ring her bell and stand back to let her see me through the peep hole. Hades is growling on the other side of the door. She must have trained him not to bark his head off.

Shuffling behind the door alerts me she's there, but it hasn't opened. I can fucking feel her through the wood, like her very presence is pulling me toward her.

I place both hands on either side of the doorframe and lean in toward the peep hole I know she's looking through, giving her a close-up of my face.

"Let me in, Josephine." It's a loaded statement which can be interpreted a number of ways, and I want every single one of them to happen.

"How the fuck?" I hear her mumble on the other side of the door. Clearly, she's trying to figure out how I tracked her down.

My inner asshole smiles. "Open the door, Josephine."

"No. You're, um, too early," her sweet voice calls out with panic, muffled by the door between us.

My nose flares in irritation. "Josephine, open the damn door."

"I'm not ready," she squeaks.

I groan. Of course, she's not ready. I showed up a fucking hour ahead of schedule. "Pixie, it's fine. Let me in, and I'll wait for you to finish up."

Nothing. No noise, no movement—and definitely no door opening.

She's seriously trying to keep me outside when I've waited all damn day to see her? *Not a fucking chance.* I need to have eyes on this woman, *now.*

Threatening to kick in her door isn't going to score me any points, even though it's the first thought to fly into my head. A hilariously evil idea pops into my mind, and I smile wickedly.

She is going to hate me.

I back up to make myself visible to all her neighbors in the surrounding condos. "Pixie," I shout, my baritone voice carrying to every open window in the complex. "Come on, don't be mad at me. Baby, if you let me in, I promise to do that little tickle thing with my tongue that you love."

"Oh my God!" I hear her shout on the other side.

A couple of heads pop out of windows to see what's going on. Josephine is going to be totally embarrassed. Well, she better open the door if she doesn't want me to make a scene.

"I'll even let you finger my ass like you've been begging me," I holler.

"Alright! You win," she shouts. "Just shut up, please."

Good. I hear the dead bolt and the lock before she opens the door. "Get in here," she snarls.

Sweet Lord in heaven!

My precious pixie is only dressed in a fluffy towel wrapped around her pretty, petite body. She holds it in a death grip, dramatically waving me inside with her other hand.

I step through the threshold and close the door behind me, never taking my eyes off of her.

"That's fucking hot," I growl in approval, my eyes sweeping over her glistening skin.

"Yeah, well, don't get any wild ideas. I'm not going out like this, obviously. Save your comments 'till I'm actually done," she huffs.

I grin. "I'm pretty content with your wardrobe choice right now."

She scowls. "Has anyone ever told you that you're a ginormous asshole? I can't believe you pulled that humiliating shit in front of all my neighbors. I'm never going to be able to look them in the face again."

I shrug. "You wouldn't let me in and it forced my hand. At least I didn't kick in your door."

Josephine looks super pissed, and I have to bite my lower lip to stop myself from laughing.

"How did you find where I live?"

"Finding people is kind of my job. And you didn't even make it a challenge. If you don't want people to know where you live, perhaps you should have your address unlisted in the directory."

Josephine slaps her forehead. "Well, fuck. I thought it was."

"Nope. You need to change it to unlisted. It's not safe."

"I get it. I'll change it tomorrow. But it still doesn't explain how you got my cell number," she snaps.

She's super cute when she's feisty. "Pixie, you gave me your cell number when you handed me your business card."

"Josephine, you stupid, stupid girl," she chastises herself, and I have to fight my smile.

"Not that I'm complaining, but why are you in a towel?"

"I was soaking in the tub when you started pounding on my door. I was trying to relax. It's been a busy day."

A soak in a tub sounds fucking amazing, with Josephine naked and covered in bubbles. "We could stay in and finish your bath together."

Josephine rolls her eyes before waving me away. "Have a seat in the living room. Hades can keep you company 'till I'm done."

My hands twitch to reach out and snag the towel off her body, but I'm trying to be the gentleman she deserves, or as much of a gentleman as I can be.

"Of course," I say with a wink while I lower myself onto her blue velvet couch. *Damn, I can't wait to fuck her on this.*

"Give me fifteen and I'll be good to go," she says before sashaying her perfect ass back to her bedroom. I hear melancholy music drifting down the hall. Bon Iver, I think it is.

"Fuck," I grumble, adjusting my growing cock. Looking for a distraction, I take in her home. It's totally her, elegant and simple, with enough bling to shine.

Hades pads into the living room. His coat is shiny and his nails look trimmed. It seems Josephine actually did have an appointment for him, although I'm pretty certain it was a last minute decision, letting her ditch me at the diner.

Hades looks at me and bares his teeth before plopping on the largest fucking dog bed known to man.

"Hades's bed is bigger than the one I sleep on at the rental," I holler.

Her laughter carries all the way to me. "It's not a real dog bed but an XL twin mattress. I have a plastic sleeve on it to protect it and a fitted sheet on top. Super easy to wash and keep clean."

"Lucky bastard," I mumble, thinking of the regular twin mattress I sleep on. I can't wait to have a giant-ass bed in the new MC house to roll Josephine around on.

"So, what are we doing tonight?" she asks after several minutes of silence.

"Nah, not gonna ruin the surprise," I call back with a mischievous grin, completely pumped with where I plan on taking her.

Her music changes to the Boss himself, and fuck if the love song doesn't have me on my feet and stalking right to her room. Her door is wide open, and I lean my head in and see a beautiful sight.

She's standing there in a lacy white bra and panties, looking at her massive bed where she has two outfits laid out for this evening. One is a practical choice of skinny jeans and a deep cut plum-colored shirt—she would be comfortable on the back of my bike wearing it.

But the second is a white cotton sundress that makes my cock spring to life.

Feeling like a creep, I'm about to pull my head out of the room to give her privacy when her head turns toward me. She jumps, surprised at my intrusion, making her tits bounce in the most delicious way. I lick my lips, eager to get my mouth around them.

She scowls, as if she knows what I've got on my mind.

"Uh, yeah, you weren't supposed to catch me. I seriously wasn't trying to sneak a peek at you."

"Most gentlemen knock before entering a lady's bedroom," she chides, her hands on her hips.

"Most ladies don't leave their bedroom doors open when changing, knowing a horny gentleman is right in the next room," I counter.

Sorry, not sorry. I don't feel guilty catching her in her lingerie, but I need to apologize for walking in on her. "I'm sorry for barging in on you, my lady."

"You're not sorry. And as you pointed out, I'm certainly no lady." She laughs, giving me a suggestive look.

My eyes narrow in on her. "Don't do that."

"Do what?"

"Fucking tease me," I growl. "I'm trying hard to behave right now, and you know exactly what you're doing. I think since you decided to taunt me, I get to pick which outfit you wear. I choose the dress."

Josephine sniggers, but she picks up the dress and slides it over her head. I come up behind her and help her pull it down her fit body, restraining myself from running my fingers along her side, proud of the fact I have enough control to abstain.

"Thank you," she whispers, stepping away to grab some earrings off her dresser. Josephine takes one last look at herself in the mirror. She has me sucking in air when she pulls the clip from her hair, letting soft brown waves cascade past her shoulders. I clench my fists to stop myself from reaching out and running my fingers through her long locks.

Quickly, she slips on cowboy boots and a light-colored denim jacket. She's hot as sin and she's going to look like a fucking dream sitting behind me on my bike. I shamelessly adjust myself again behind her.

"Alright, I'm ready for you," she says in a demure voice.

"Good, because I have plans for you, Josephine," I coo, grabbing her dainty hand in mine and pulling her from her condo.

CHAPTER FOUR
JOSEPHINE

I'm not entirely sure what I expected after I sped away from the diner, but this certainly was not it.

All the pent-up sexual energy burning between Maceo and I goes up in smoke—*poof*—I'm standing outside with a ridiculous helmet on my head, and he's sitting smugly on his motorcycle, waiting for me to climb on.

"I'm not getting on the back of that death trap," I seethe, folding my arms across my chest.

"Baby, I already told you, you're safe with me. I got you," he says.

"If you were the safest biker in the world and followed all the rules, it wouldn't make either of us safe from the rest of the population driving like asses on the road," I argue in a huff.

Maceo rolls his eyes. "Pixie, get your ass on the damn bike before I do it for you."

"Fine!" I swing my leg over the seat. I tuck my dress around my legs, angry at him for requesting this outfit instead of the jeans.

Who the hell rides a hog in a dress? Apparently, I do, right now.

Maceo reaches for my arms and brings them around him, joining my hands. I have no choice but to be flush against his wide back.

"There," he says, with obvious approval. "Right where you

belong." He revs up the engine, pulls away from the curb, and we're off like a prom dress.

I won't lie, riding on the back of his bike, holding on as he goes dangerously fast is *amazing*, but to hell if I'll admit it to him. It seems like we've only started cruising before he's pulling over to a local Moroccan restaurant. I smile, approving.

Maceo helps me off the bike and out of my helmet. I fluff out my hair, and he takes my hand and leads us to the delicious smelling environment.

He doesn't ask or wait for us to be seated. He pulls us past the hostess, who smiles widely at him with a wave, before he takes us to the last booth in the far back. He motions for me to sit and slides in across from me. I assume he picked this spot because we're far away from the rest of the crowd, giving us privacy.

Maceo gives me an infectious smile. "Hope you don't mind this place."

"Not at all. I *love* Andalusian cuisine. I've seen this place, but haven't had the opportunity to come here. It reminds me of my favorite Moroccan restaurant back in Los Angeles. I hope it tastes as good."

My comment makes his smile stretch wider. "Me too. I grew up with my *abuela* making these dishes. It's a little nostalgic when I come to eat here."

I can hear the sadness in his voice. "Your grandma?"

He nods before lowering his eyes to the menu. "Passed right before I turned eighteen. Lung cancer. She survived a fucking dicta-torship, but cigarettes got her in the end. I joined the navy right after the funeral. She was the only reason for staying, and when she died, I needed to do something to support myself. Navy was the right fit. It's where I met all my brothers, who I'm lucky to have today."

I bite my lip, curiosity setting in. "Your parents?"

"Died right after I was born. A house invasion gone wrong. My dad tried to stop it and got shot in the process. My mom too. I guess a three-month old isn't worth a bullet. I was raised by my dad's mom, who loved me like her own son. *Abuelita Lucia* would have loved you."

His story crushes me. I imagine him as a tiny baby having his parents gunned down in front of him. But there has to be more to it than what he's telling me. Perhaps another time.

Another time? What the hell, Josephine? Am I seriously thinking about a second date with Mr. Tall, Dark, and Handsome?

My eyes admire Maceo's gorgeous face. *Yes. Yes, I am.*

I shake my head at my subconscious. "I'm sorry, Maceo. I wish things were different and it never happened."

Maceo's dark eyes lift to mine, and he gives me another small smile. "It's okay, baby. It was a long time ago." His eyes go soft. "Hey, hey, don't cry."

I swipe away at the traitorous tear rolling down my cheek without warning. "I'm sorry," I say, bashful.

"Nothing to be sorry about when you're showing empathy." He reaches for my hand across the table, and I graciously give it to him. "It tells me you have a very compassionate and nurturing demeanor—which will be wonderful when we have kids."

I slap his hand away. "Not funny." This is the second time today he has mentioned having children with me. Who does that after just meeting someone? *Maceo does.*

He's laughing, but there's this look of hope in his face, and I wonder if he's being serious.

His eyes study me. "What? You don't like kids?"

I clear my throat. "I happen to love children." I always wanted kids—Jacob didn't.

Maceo's looks pleased and he bites his lower lip to keep himself from smiling too broadly.

Our waitress comes and we order our favorite dishes, but we start bickering over drink orders.

"They have a fully stocked bar, Pixie. Why are you ordering water?"

I frown at him. "I happen to like water with my meal. It quenches my thirst."

"Order a drink, Josephine," he commands, which pisses me off. He adds, "Please. I don't want to drink to alone."

"You're riding a damn motorcycle with me on the back after we're done here. You shouldn't be drinking at all," I snap.

Maceo motions at his huge muscled frame. "A fucking double whiskey isn't going to faze me. Hell, three double whiskeys aren't going to crack the surface."

"Fine," I concede, which makes him chuckle, before addressing the waitress. "Give me a Maker's, on the rocks."

"Fuck me, you're perfect," he mumbles to himself, making me blush from the compliment. Yeah, I'm not a weak drinker. I guess a former Navy SEAL—current hardcore biker—would appreciate this quality in me.

"I'll share my meal if you share yours," he offers after our waitress retreats with our orders.

"Deal, as long as you let me taste your *gazpacho* when they bring out our appetizers."

Maceo laughs. "Your Spanish accent is good. Most people butcher the language."

"*Muchas gracias,*" I say. "*Tengo pratica.*"

"Ah!" Maceo grins. "*Tu hablas con fluidez.*"

I laugh. "Well, I don't know if I speak Spanish properly or not. I only know what I've picked up from living in California. Growing up, my family didn't have a lot of money, and we lived in a lower income area of L.A. The general population at my school was Latinx. Most of my friends spoke Spanish, and I guess I absorbed it. I know enough to stumble through a conversation and it actually comes in handy in my industry."

Maceo nods with a chuckle. "*Abuelita Lucia* would beat me with a wooden spoon if she caught me using the incorrect accent. She would say, 'Maceo, you're a Spaniard! Speak correctly.'"

"So, you're all Spanish?" I ask.

"I'm mostly Spanish. My dad was Spanish, maybe some Portuguese. And my mom was half-Spanish, half-Colombian. How about you?"

"I'll just round my ancestry up as Nordic."

He nods. "Well, that explains your fighting spirit—you've got Viking in you."

"And you being a Spaniard explains why you're trying to conquer everyone," I fire back.

Maceo lets out a belly laugh, and the sound is too contagious not to join in. "Touché, but I'm not trying to conquer everyone, only someone," he says, pointedly.

I lean in. "You know, you're pretty intense and demanding."

"And you're pretty standoffish," he counters. "How about instead of goading each other, we stick to safer topics?"

I wrinkle my nose. "You're no fun."

His eyes gleam and he smiles. "Oh, trust me, I'm a hell of a good time. How was your day?"

"Busy. Stressful. A lot to wrap my head around, you know? I did take Hades to the groomers."

Maceo laughs. "I saw. Looks like you pampered yourself a little, too," he says, nodding to my manicure.

I'm shocked he noticed. "I went to get my hair trimmed, and Eduardo could tell I was out of sorts. He suggested the mani-and-pedi."

Maceo's dark eyes crinkle at the corners, appraising every part of me. "You look beautiful by the way, and not a speck of makeup on you. I like that you wanted to look nice for me tonight."

"This wasn't planned."

"Ah, but you decided to do it after I asked you out on a date," he points out with a cocky grin. I throw my napkin at him and he catches it in midair. "Temper, temper. What else did you do today?"

"The rest of my day was devoted to your build. I reached out to my general contractor, Jared, and filled him in on the project. He's stoked I landed us a huge business deal. Like me, he's trying to make a name for himself. After going over the plans and picking who we needed to get the job done, we split the job of calling in the troops."

"Sounds like a productive day."

"It was. And how was yours?"

Maceo sighs before meeting my eyes. "Long. I had a meeting with a client in Denver who is eager for our assistance. Came back and worked on my bike before getting ready to pick you up."

I'm about to ask him what assistance he provides when he jumps to another topic. "So tell me about you and your family. You said you're from Los Angeles."

"Yeah, lived in California all my life 'till last year when I moved here. My mom and dad still live in the same little house where I grew up. Dad's a retired welder and mom's the secretary at my old high school. I have a sister, Simone, who's two years older than me. She's an accountant, and she's doing well for herself in Sacramento."

I chew on the inside of my cheek, not sure if I'm boring him. "You don't really want to know all of this, do you?"

Maceo tilts his head. "I want to know everything about you."

"Really?"

He nods. "Tell me more."

"Um, I went to the University of Southern California for Architectural Engineering and Design. Worked in a big firm in San Diego after I graduated. Four years—I learned a lot and worked myself ragged. Didn't work out for me there, and I decided I needed a fresh start. Picked Fort Collins on a whim and here I am."

All our drinks, appetizers, and main dishes come out at once. No spacing out courses here. We don't hesitate. I moan around my first bite.

"It's good, right?" Maceo says with appreciation.

I steal his spoon right out of his hand, taking a hefty scoop of his *gazpacho* and I moan again.

"Here," he says, raising his fork to my mouth. "Try the *pastilla*. It's my favorite."

I allow him to feed me, and now I'm moaning around the tasty meat pie.

"I could fucking listen to you make that sound all night," he murmurs, watching my mouth. I flush from his confession.

We eat in silence for a while. I continue to moan with every bite, and Maceo groans in response. I swear I catch him adjusting himself several times throughout the meal, making me giggle.

As we wrestle over the last piece of lamb—which he allows me to steal—he clears his throat. "So, why didn't it work out for you in San Diego?"

My face puckers before I can recover. "It's not a pleasant subject for a dinner date."

Maceo smiles around his whiskey, but sets it down and looks at me expectantly. I groan and shrug my narrow shoulders. I have nothing to hide. If he's going to react anything like the people I left behind, it's better to find out before actually considering getting close to him.

"I quit. Jacob, my boyfriend of nearly eight years, worked with me at the firm. He went behind my back and took full credit for a project I worked on. He stole my promotion, knowing I was working day and night to get it for years.

"Jacob acted like it was no big deal, and he tried to play it off as if he hadn't swept the rug right out from under me. He told me I was overreacting, that I should have been happy for him and for us, saying he was more suited for the position. He truly felt it was best for our future together, me working under him.

"His betrayal was hurtful, but it was worse when I was screwed over by management. They were well aware it was my project and they gave Jacob the promotion anyway. It was a good 'ole boy system and I wasn't one of the boys. I was never going to get ahead and be an equal to any of them.

"I walked out the door and never went back. Packed up all my shit while Jacob was at work and moved out. I went home to my parents for a spell before deciding I needed a clean break from all of it. Moved out here for a fresh start. I've been working on building my solo career since, and I'm pretty proud of Holland Build and Design Solutions. Like I said, it's not a conversation to share on a first date."

Maceo beams at me. "I'm proud of you. You made the right decision for yourself. Not everyone has the balls to do what you did."

"You would be the only one who agrees with me. I ended my one and only relationship and was told I was the fool for leaving him. I lost all my friends. Jacob twisted the story to make me the unappreciative girlfriend who got jealous of his success, if you can believe that shit.

"I burned all my bridges when I left the San Diego firm. I burned all my contacts. No one in the trade would work with me after I up and left without notice. It's how I discovered my old firm had me blacklisted.

"Every time I applied to another firm I was immediately rejected. If by some miracle I was offered an interview, they would low-ball me in their offer for salary and benefits."

Maceo looks shocked. "Holy fuck."

I nod. "My parents were irate for my walking out on the job, regardless of the circumstances. They worked shit job after shit job to provide a better life for my sister and I. They looked at what I did as an insult to what they went through, not knowing my job wasn't any less shitty than theirs. I refused to settle, and my parents refused to support my decision.

"My sister told me I was being childish and unprofessional, and I should've taken it in stride because that's how business works. Fuck that, and fuck all of them. Since moving here, I haven't talked to any of them. I miss them, but I'm too hurt by how they treated me to get over it."

Maceo takes my hand and squeezes. "Damn, baby, that sucks. I'm sorry."

"Me too," I say, coy. "Sorry for unloading all my dirty laundry on you."

He shakes his head. "I don't want you to feel sorry for telling me anything. That's not how this relationship works."

I heave a sigh and try hard to ignore the delicious heat spreading through my body from his words. "Maceo, this isn't a relationship. I don't date clients."

"And look where we are," he says with a smirk, waving a hand between us. "Your rule should be you don't date anyone, because you're already dating me."

I shake my head and square my shoulders. "My other rule is I don't date shady people, hence why I'm no longer with Jacob."

"Good rule," he says, not catching my drift.

I stare at him, waiting for him to catch on. I see the light click on and his eyes thin. "Wait, you think I'm shady?" he asks, thumbing his chest.

"You're the president of a motorcycle gang. Your breed is not exactly known for following the law and doing good deeds," I state with a snort.

Maceo barks a laugh. "Wow! That's fucking stereotyping at its finest. I'll agree my crew has bent the law a couple times for the greater good, but everything is legit. Sweetheart, you have no clue what my men and I do for a living."

"Enlighten me, because I sure as hell won't consider dating you with what I know right now," I challenge.

Another laugh before he says, "What do you want to know?"

"Everything, because I'm nosy," I admit, making Maceo chuckle.

"You already know I was a Navy SEAL, served over ten years before I got out. My crew is the same way, former military of various backgrounds. All of us left after serving more than our fair share of time. For me, I was done watching my brothers being killed left and right in the desert, unable to help the refugees because of orders from above. The final straw was when I watched a child no more than three blown apart from a bomb strapped to his back. Maimed two men on my team."

I gasp, but he keeps going. "The stories of my MC members are

66

similar. We all wanted to keep serving but with actual results. There are too many politics when it comes to war to do the morally right thing. I left. Gauge, my vice president, followed me, along with Chase and Punk.

"Mercy Ravens MC is a club I formed by chance. It started with me and my three brothers buying a couple hogs and cruising all over the states, taking the occasional security job. I was named president since the club was my idea, and I led our team when we were SEALs. For the past two years, we've been recruiting former military who want to continue to serve and say fuck you to the politics."

He pauses to throw back the rest of the whiskey while I wait.

"Once I noticed how lucrative some of the jobs were, I started my own company. It's probably more accurate to say we're a security company whose employees like to ride hogs, than a motorcycle club who enjoys vigilante work. The military pensions we earned were never enough to keep us afloat, but the gun-for-hire jobs more than cushion our pockets. It let us expand the club and help more individuals in need.

"My crew and I make our money by taking on recon, security, and mercenary work. It's a legit business. We're hired by families, companies, investors, as well as the government to retrieve intel and people.

"With sex trafficking on the rise, we spend a lot of time bringing home abducted people, including children. Drug busts are another huge job we're hired for. Sometimes other governments hire us to help with illegal activity going on in their country.

"Some gigs are small, others are huge. The longest mission I've been on lasted over three months and pulled in over three million a head for our crew. Sometimes the missions are local and sometimes we're overseas. I can't talk about the details of specific cases since its contract work, and legally we can't disclose private information, but you get the drift."

Holy shit! His life is like an action movie. His already high hotness factor just blew off the charts.

"Our jobs are completely legal and come with a hefty paycheck. The shit we do is dangerous, but no more dangerous than when we were on active duty. The big difference is that we're able to cut through the red tape and complete the fucking missions. Whatever sketchy shit you thought my brothers and I were involved in, you can rest assured we aren't."

Jesus. I sit back in my seat and stare, awestruck. I didn't expect this response when I asked him to explain. And thank God he's not involved with the wild shit I had assumed.

My heart swells when it sinks in how good of a man Maceo is. He doesn't deserve to be judged by the crew he belongs to. He deserves to be judged by the moral of his character.

"Maceo, I'm humble enough to admit when I'm wrong. I owe you an apology. I stereotyped you right off the bat and I regret it. Thank you for pointing it out," I confess before leaning in, all starry-eyed. "You're like a modern day superhero."

Maceo smiles and lowers his face to hide the blush glowing under his tanned skin. "Thanks, Pixie."

"You're a good man, Maceo," I add.

Maceo's eyes narrow. "I may do good deeds, but I'm far from good. I've done things in my life that are worthy of jail time."

I don't know if he's trying to scare me, warn me, or whatever, but I'm not afraid of him or what's he's done in his past anymore. "I'm sure you only did those things because you felt it was justified. I don't get a sadistic vibe from you."

His deep brown eyes soften as he holds my gaze. "I like the way you see me."

My heart thumps a little harder. Since he's answering questions, I ask another. "Why is your street name Atlas?"

"Gauge gave it to me after our first active-duty mission. Atlas is the titan who carries the weight of the world. I carry the weight of the teams I lead. It's my load to bear."

"I like it," I admit with a smile.

Maceo gulps before looking me square in the face. "You want honesty?"

"Well, it is the best policy, right?"

Maceo sits back and looks down at his hands folded in front of him. "I don't date. What we're doing right now is completely foreign to me. I've never sat down across from a girl and wanted to get to know her."

"How are you picking up women if you aren't getting to know them? What? Do you just nod and smile at them, and they flock to you?"

Maceo glances at me, giving me an odd look. Immediately, I'm reminded there was little dialogue between the two of us before we were pawing at each other. "Never mind."

He nods. "Exactly. But if it makes you feel better, I had to put more effort into winning you over. You're not the typical woman I pick up. The women I've been involved with are in the same boat as me. They want to fuck and move on. You're all about commitment."

"Yes, but I'm not interested in getting into another relationship and getting my heart ripped to shreds. I want to be certain the relationship in going to last. Nor am I looking for a sex buddy. I know myself enough to know I could never have a 'no strings attached' hook up."

Maceo looks down at his lap. He's uncomfortable with the direction this conversation is heading. "I'm not looking for a commitment either, or at least I wasn't."

He runs his hands over his face. "Look, my life is dangerous, not as a biker, but as a mercenary. I work long hours, constantly traveling, and I have a target on my back. I'm not safe, and anyone personally involved with me wouldn't be safe either."

Hmm. Interesting. "So, your reasoning for not having a romantic relationship is the same as mine."

He frowns. "I don't follow."

"You're afraid of getting your heart broken, whether it's by your job getting in the way, hurt feelings—yours or hers—or by putting her in danger. Commitment is not your issue, but risking your heart is." I shrug. "I get it. Heartbreak sucks."

Maceo glares at me. "I'm not afraid of anything."

I fold my arms and lean forward. "Bullshit. Everyone is afraid of something. We just happen to be afraid of the same damn thing. Neither of us wants to give away our heart and risk losing the other person."

Maceo softens. "You really give it to someone straight, don't ya?"

"If you wanted candy-coating, you came to the wrong girl."

"I like that about you," he says, biting his lower lip. A big gust of air escapes him, and he looks into my eyes. "And I like how you use my real name. I like how you don't take my shit and how you give it right back. I like how you swear like a sailor and drink like one, too. I like how you take care of yourself both physically and emotionally. I like how you're not afraid to stand up for yourself. And more than everything else, I like the way I feel when I'm with you. How's that for honesty?"

"Whoa," I whisper. *Did my panties just melt off?* "Pretty awesome, actually."

Maceo pulls his wallet out and throws a wad of cash on the table. "How about we get out of here?" he says with a wink, rising out of his seat and offering me his hand. I take it without hesitation.

We get back on his bike, cruising along at a more leisurely pace than when we left my condo, like he's prolonging whatever time we have together. I rest my cheek against his back and snuggle closer.

At a red light, a car pulls alongside us with the windows down. Loud music and laughter filter out into the open air.

"Damn, Liam, check out the hot piece of ass sitting right next to us," a male voice yells over the music.

Maceo's head snaps to the car, and I'm suddenly fearful for the young men in the vehicle. I need to diffuse the situation quickly.

"Sorry, boys," I say loud enough for them to hear me. I slap my hand down on Maceo's shoulder and give him a big squeeze. "But this hot piece of ass is mine. You'll have to find another man."

Maceo breaks out into hysterics. The guys next to us stare, dumb-struck. Before they can comment, Maceo's gunning his bike down the road.

We drive on 'till he's pulling us over to a cliff edge overlooking the city. He gets off his bike and practically lifts me from it, setting me gently on my feet. Hand in hand, we walk to the edge to take in the view. I look out over the vastness in front of me and sigh.

"Beautiful," I mumble.

"I couldn't agree more," Maceo says.

I turn my head to look at him, but he's already staring at me, his free hand covering his chest where his heart is. He's too damn hand-some for words.

Maceo leans down to kiss me and I meet him a little less than half-way, on my tippy toes. Our height difference would be an issue, but he snakes his muscled arms around me to lift me up to him, and I wrap my arms around his neck. I want to go all in, but I pull away.

"Why are you holding back, Josephine? What is it?" he asks, rubbing his nose and forehead against mine.

"A lot," I confess.

Maceo sets me back down. "Talk to me."

I shake my head. "I don't know if I can explain it in a way that makes any sense."

He pulls me against his chest and kisses the top of my head. "Try me."

I take a deep lungful of air. "This morning, what we did, I've never—I don't have sex with strangers. I have no idea what you're thinking of me because of it."

"I would never fucking judge you, Josephine. I'm the last person to judge anyone. Don't forget I was as involved as you were," he mumbles against my hair.

I sigh. "But everyone else would judge what we did. I can't help but feel ashamed."

"No. Stop right there. No one needs to know what happened between us because it's *ours* and no one else's. And who gives a fuck what other people think? That's society putting ideas in your head about what they want normal to be. You need to get over this hang-up, baby. People are going to be judging you the rest of your life. Are you going to let this shit hold you back from what you want in life? Let me ask you something. Did you want me this morning?"

"Yes."

"Did you enjoy it?"

"Yes."

"Looking back on it, would you change anything that happened between us?"

"No."

He gives me a gentle squeeze. "Own that shit, Pixie. You saw what you wanted, and you fucking took it like a boss. You enjoyed it and wouldn't change a thing about it. You took a chance and that's more than what the majority of this fucked up world can admit to. There's no shame in taking what you desire as long as you didn't hurt anyone in the process. I'm fucking thankful you took a chance on me."

Tears stream down my face as I absorb his words and the freedom they offer. But there's more where those doubts hide.

"Pixie, why're you tensing up?" He pulls me away from his chest to look into my eyes, wiping away the moisture on my face with his big thumbs. "Is it the ex? Is he harassing you? Fuck, do you still have feelings for him?" he asks, panic laced in his voice.

"No," I shake my head roughly. "Whatever feelings I had for him died the day he decided a promotion was more important than me. And no, he's not harassing me. Well, he has, but it's been a week or two. It's not him, but me and my hang-ups on getting hurt again."

Maceo cups my face in his rough palms and raises 'till I'm looking into his dark eyes. "Pixie, I don't want to hurt you. Can we just see where this leads?"

Fire blazes through his dark features as he holds my gaze. I don't recall a man regarding me with such carnal need before. He makes me feel like the most beautiful woman ever.

I whimper. "I don't know how to be half-invested."

"Baby, I don't know how to be fully invested or even partially invested." He kisses my forehead. "You have to meet me halfway on this."

I sniffle and he looks in my eyes, analyzing me. "Do you like me?"

Yes. A lot more than I should. I bite my lip and nod.

"This is difficult for you, taking a chance on us," he states.

I bob my head again. "I know this isn't easy for you, either. I can't expect you to all of a sudden want to be in a committed relationship. I'm willing to meet you halfway and give this relationship a chance, but I can't promise I won't invest my heart."

Maceo looks up to the dark sky and swallows before looking back down at me, determination set in his face. "If you give me your heart, Josephine, you will never have to worry about me breaking it, at least not intentionally. I can guarantee I will fuck up at some point, but please remember I'm new to this before you decide to throw in the towel."

"You can't make that promise," I say through a weak cry.

Maceo gives me a devastating smile. "I already did, baby. And I keep my promises. I don't make them unless I'm certain I can hold them. With you, I know this promise is iron-clad."

Overwhelmed by all the right words, I launch myself at him. He catches me in his arms, helping me crawl up his body 'till I'm kissing him all over his face and down his neck.

God, he smells like newly fallen snow in a pine forest. I want to bury my nose in his neck, and breathe him in until my head is dizzy and I can't remember my name.

"As much as I loved taking you outside this morning, I really want to get you into a bed," he says. "If you don't stop what you're doing, I'll have no choice but to bend you over my bike and take you here."

I slide down his body. "Well, you better get me back to my condo and into my bed," I say in a sultry voice.

Maceo puts his hand on my lower back and hustles us back onto his bike, rocketing off through the night.

By the time we reach my condo, I'm panting, and my heart is pounding against my ribs, not from the speed with which he rode his bike, but with desire for Maceo and what tonight will bring.

We're a mess of tangled arms and tongues and fumbling legs as we attack each other all the way to my front door. My hands shake as I try to get my key in the lock, distracted by his wandering hands and mouth all over my body.

We stumble through the door and Hades woofs at our arrival. *Shit. He needs to go out.* I run to the back door and wave Hades outside, and he tears off in the backyard. Maceo continues to pay attention to my body with his velvet lips, until Hades comes back inside. He growls at Maceo.

"Hades, it's okay. Maceo's welcome here. Go lay down," I reassure him. He grumbles and clomps back to his bed.

Maceo hauls me by my ass and I wrap my legs around him, and he carries me to the bedroom. He lays me on the bed and makes quick work of removing his clothes, 'till he's standing in nothing but his boxer briefs, his erection straining against the material.

I can't stop myself from drinking him in, and I push up to my elbows to get a better look. He's both bulk and cut muscle, and the V in his hips etches deep into his skin. His chest is completely hairless, allowing his tattoos to dominate the view.

With hunger in his dark eyes, he steps forward, takes my dress in his hands, and gently pulls it over my head. It falls to the floor at his feet.

Suddenly everything slows down. The rush we started off with has disappeared, and all that's left is the two of us.

Maceo reaches behind me with one hand and unclasps my bra, freeing my breasts. He groans as his eyes float over me, making my body hum like a tuning fork. He crouches and slides my panties down my legs before standing back up. The way he fixates on me makes me shiver with expectation.

"God, you're gorgeous," he says, pulling down his underwear. He grasps his stiff length in one hand, his frenum piercing shining under the head of his cock. I knew he was huge when I felt him this morning, but I had no real visual until now. I'm panting and he's not even inside me yet.

"Josephine, I promise to worship your body the way you deserve, but right now I need to be inside you. I've been thinking about you since we were together this morning, and I can't wait any longer."

"I'm not stopping you," I say, breathless.

Wanting to entice him, I let my legs fall apart, giving him a full view of my most secret parts, dripping with my arousal. His nostrils flare and his eyes grow darker. Like a leopard, he crawls on top of me, hovering above me, as his fiery eyes burn into mine.

Wanting to touch him, I run my hands slowly up his heaving chest, memorizing every hard panel, 'till I clasp them behind his neck. "Please kiss me."

Maceo leans forward to claim my lips with the softest touch. The kiss is slow and steady at first, but it builds 'till our tongues clash together, the barbell on his tongue flicking the inside of my mouth.

I whimper when he pulls away, until I see he has grabbed his iron shaft, running it between my dampening folds to cover himself. His frenum barbell rubs over my clit, sending acute waves of pleasure deep inside of me. He lines his long erection up to my hot, damp entrance, lifting his eyes to mine before sliding little by little inside.

My mouth parts in a silent moan as he sinks himself deep enough for our pelvises brush, and I feel ever single inch of him inside of me.

"Fuck, you feel perfect around me," he whispers breathlessly.

His mouth connects with mine again and he gently sucks on my lower lip. He pulls his hips back, only to sink deeper, dragging his piercing along my sensitive walls. My legs wrap around him and I grasp his arms for support. Maceo takes his sweet time, pumping in and out. His hands caress me everywhere, on my face, my neck, my arms, and breasts. His touch ignites desire and passion so deep it bruises my heart.

"Right there," I moan. He thrusts harder, hitting the spot, and watches me fall apart under his touch.

I feel his lips curl into a smile against my throat. "If you like how this feels..." he trails and tilts his pelvis up, rotating his hips.

My body arcs off the bed, my toes curl, and my pussy squeezes tight around Maceo's iron cock. I claw at his slick shoulders as I orgasm.

He sucks in a ragged gasp. "My God, you come beautifully." His silky lips press hard against mine, until I open up for his tongue to explore.

This time, being intimate with Maceo is nothing like this morning. On the trail, we fucked—hard and desperate—both of us trying to get our fix like addicts. This time there's tenderness, longing, and an overwhelming desire to draw this out.

I don't recognize this type of sex. I've never experienced anything like it. Once I realize it, I nearly burst into tears.

We're making *love*.

Maceo brushes his thumb over the rogue tear falling down the side of my face. He kisses me firmly, affectionately, giving my tongue long fluid strokes with his own.

He quickens the pace of his hips and I fist my hands into his hair, arching my hips up to meet him thrust for thrust. My already heightened libido escalates when I hear his breathing get ragged, and the sound of his pelvis grinding against my clit.

Maceo's body glistens with sweat and it only intensifies his musky, woodsy fragrance. His scent envelops my senses and makes my blood pulse wildly.

When he brings me over the edge again, I cry out his name. Maceo thrusts up into me and stills. He groans loudly in my ear and I'm filled with warmth as he empties himself deep inside me. He rests his forehead against mine and my eyes flutter shut with satisfaction.

When I finally open my eyes, lazy, I find his, dark and adoring, staring into mine.

"Josephine," he murmurs, claiming my lips in a searing kiss. He pulls out of me and rolls us to our sides, face to face, pressing his lips gently over my forehead. He pulls me tight against him and I sigh.

His chest feels so warm against my cheek. I press my lips to his left pec muscle. The action must surprise Maceo because he sucks in a ragged breath, like I actually kissed his heart.

"I want more," I purr greedily.

Maceo gives me a sluggish smile. "Oh, baby, that was only the warm-up. I'm far from done with you. Hard, fast, gentle, and slow are all amazing with you. Christ, it's like you were shaped specifically for me." He runs his nose along my neck. "Mmm, you smell good."

I laugh. "I smell like sex."

"And if I could bottle it and sell it, I'd make a fucking killing." He runs his nose along my neck again, kissing the tender skin underneath my ear. "You're my new favorite scent."

My God, the words this man uses to melt me.

"You're mine, too." It's so easy to open up to him after he's fucked me ragged.

His big palm runs down my side, over my hip, and covers my bottom. "God, I love your ass. It's firm and round and fits perfectly in my hands. And when you walk..."

His reaction makes me giggle. "You're an ass man."

Maceo winks at me. "The things I'm going to do will make you squeal."

Eek! Is it wrong that his comment makes me ache between my legs?

Maceo kisses my neck once more, then props himself up on one elbow. He sighs and looks at me. "Pixie, you're too precious. The things you make me feel and the way you get in my head..." he shakes his head. "Can you do me a favor?"

"Sure," I say dreamily.

"You need to promise me you'll take more precautions."

"Hmm?"

He runs a hand over his face. "I need you to unlist your address. It's for your own safety. You're an extremely attractive woman, and anyone could form an unhealthy attachment to you. It wouldn't take much for someone to track you down."

"You mean like you," I grouse with a chuckle.

"Exactly," he says firmly. "I travel a lot for my job, and I would feel better knowing your home address is unlisted, especially when I'm away on a mission."

I nod, thinking of Lorenzo. "I completely agree. I've already dealt with some unwanted attention from a past client, he was sending flowers to my home. I don't want to deal with anyone else knowing where I live."

"Which brings me to another thing I wanted to bring to your attention. You do realize your social media accounts are public, correct?"

A teasing smirk spreads across my face. "Maceo Tabares, were you Facebook stalking me?"

Maceo's lips thin. "It's not funny, Pixie. This shit is serious. I already told you about the missions I take, finding and rescuing victims of sex trafficking. Everything personal about you is out there for anyone to see. Your address is listed. All someone needs is your business card to get your number. Security is my job, and right now you're a fucking safety nightmare."

I understand his concern, and honestly, his protectiveness is pretty adorable. "I will change my account settings to private. My business cards are another thing altogether. Maybe I need to get a work phone and keep my personal cell off the card."

Maceo finally relaxes. "Okay. Thank you. I'm really not trying to be an overbearing asshole, but I told you I have several people who would love to retaliate. I don't want you to be someone they come after. The more security you have in place for yourself, the better."

I cup his chiseled face in my hand, and he leans his smooth cheek into my palm, closing his eyes. "It's okay," I say. "Thank you for caring about my safety. You're too sweet."

Maceo opens his eyes and stares at me with a look of concern. "Pixie...there's more. I want to keep you safe in every way. I need to tell you—" he starts.

A ping chimes from a cell.

My first instinct would be to ignore it, but not Maceo. He pulls away from me to retrieve his MC cut off the floor. He stares at his phone screen, and his face morphs from concern to all business. Next, he's pulling his pants up and tugging his shirt over his head. He sits on the bed and does up his boots.

"What's wrong?" I ask as I sit up, pulling the comforter around me.

"I need to go, Pixie. There's an SOS." And it's the only explanation I'm given, before he gives me a chaste kiss on my lips. "Put those security checks in place, baby."

He stands and walks out of the room without a backward glance. I hear the front door close and instantly, I feel sick.

What the fuck just happened?

F ive days.

Five *fucking* days since Maceo left me naked on my bed after being whisked away by some strange text message. I have received no calls or texts in response to the several I've left him, and it's caused my emotions to tumble like a rollercoaster.

How could I have grown so attached to him after a single day? I have, and my heart aches for him. It's baffling.

Maceo said he was a solider for hire. For the first two days, I was worried sick, wondering where he was and what war he was fighting. By day three, I was having a nervous breakdown, thinking the reason I hadn't gotten a response was because he was either injured or dead. On day four, I was numb and broken inside. And when day five came to a close, I was fucking livid.

My cell rings from an unknown number, and I answer it. It may be business related. "Hello, this is Jo of Holland Build and Design Solutions."

A rough voice greets me. "Hey, this is Punk, from the Mercy Ravens MC. I've been asked to confirm if you're still planning on breaking ground in two days' time for the new headquarters."

I ignore his question. "Where's Maceo?" I ask in a whisper, fear gripping my very core.

"Atlas? He's on an assignment overseas," Punk says nonchalantly. "I talked to him last night and he said he wouldn't be back for at least another two weeks, three weeks tops."

My hand is gripping the phone so damn tight, I swear my knuckles are going to bust through my skin. "You talked to him?" I ask with malice.

"Um, yeah. He's...well, it's a shit show where he is, and things haven't been working out as planned. When shit goes south, he only has time to focus on the job," Punk says cautiously, catching on to my anger toward Maceo's lack of contact. "I'm sure Atlas would call you if he could."

"But he fucking called you," I point out, my voice raising an octave.

What the fuck is this? Did Maceo just want one more go in the sack with me before ghosting me?

Suddenly, I'm embarrassed. I've been bombarding his phone day and night with voicemails and texts, and all this time he was brushing me off. I feel so foolish. *You fucking gullible idiot, Josephine!*

"Shit," I hear Punk mumble as he realizes Maceo is in the doghouse because he let the cat out of the bag. "Look, he only reached out to me because it was related to a mission. That's it. When our team's working, we can't allow ourselves to have any distractions because it could take our focus away from the job."

Oh, fuck no! "Bullshit, Punk! I call bullshit. Stop covering for his sorry ass. He could have fucking informed me when he was going, or when his predicted return was, or he could have notified me he wouldn't be able to contact me while he was gone. He did none of that. Nothing! But he finds time to call you and fucking have you inquire for him if I'm still on schedule for breaking fucking ground on his damn project," I yell into the phone.

You fucking coward, Maceo! He had to have one of his brothers call me, instead of manning up and doing it himself.

"Fuck, Atlas," I hear Punk grumble as he curses out his friend miles away. "Look, Pixie—" he starts, but I fucking see red.

"Don't fucking call me that!" I can't stand to hear Maceo's pet name for me coming from another man's lips. It's reserved for Maceo alone.

The fuck it is! I shake my head at myself. *What the hell is wrong with you, Josephine?* Maceo has lost all pet name privileges.

"Fuck, sorry. Josephine, then?"

"Wrong again!" Only Maceo called me by my given name. Not even my family or friends called me Josephine. "You call me Jo or this conversation is done."

Punk sighs. "Jo, a lot of what we do is classified. Even if Atlas wanted to, he's not allowed to discuss it with you. He left your place and went straight to the airport where Gauge was waiting with a bag and the crew. He was in the air twenty minutes later. There was no time."

"Punk," I say with an exhausted sigh. "He could have sent me a damn text from the plane before takeoff. No matter what you say or how you try to spin it, there's no excuse for his behavior. Please stop pretending he had no option when he damn well did."

If he gave a shit about me, he would have made the effort to reach out. But I neglect to explain any of this to Punk.

"Next time you talk to your *president* tell him the project will start on schedule," I say in a cold, professional tone.

"Pixie—I mean, fuck, Jo, please don't be like this," Punk begs in frustration, but he seems to know it's futile. "Atlas is going to fucking kill me."

"I'm sorry, Punk. Please refer my message to Atlas when you next speak to him," I say before disconnecting.

Immediately after the call ends, I open up my text messages and fire off a final text to Maceo.

Fuck off, Maceo!

And then I block him.

Take that motherfucker! I've never blocked anyone before, especially a client, but I can't deal right now. I'm too emotionally flooded to make reasonable decisions.

All at once, my emotions get the best of me and I start yelling at the top of my lungs to let it all out. This of course, sets off Hades who starts tearing through the condo, howling like we're a fucking wolf pack.

After calming down my dog, I rummage through the kitchen pantry and retrieve a bottle of Eagle Rare bourbon. Popping the cork, I go to grab a glass and stop. I should save myself the hassle of cleaning the cup and just drink from the bottle instead. I take a long pull as I pace my living room. I haven't felt the compulsion to drink this much since Jacob fucked me over. The burn feels good in my chest, and I take another chug of bourbon.

How? How could I allow myself to fall for another bastard who only used me for his own needs then left me high and dry? Worst part was, I couldn't blame Maceo. I knew the kind of man he was. I could feel it in my bones—fuck, he admitted to my face he didn't date—and I allowed myself to go over the fragile edge all on my own.

You know what, fuck that! I can definitely blame him.

Maceo played me like a damn fiddle, saying my heart was safe and making promises to protect it. *Lies!* I guess the only blessing is that I didn't invest eight years on Maceo before seeing his true colors. No, I didn't invest more than twenty-four hours in his presence, only a single day. Plus, five days of mourning for him.

Well, that shit ends now.

First, I need to get my emotions in check and clear my mind. I stumble into the kitchen and set the bourbon on the counter. Flushed from the alcohol, I turn on the faucet and splash cool water on my face. After several long pulls of air, I regain most of my composure.

Emotions in check. Done.

Feeling the effects of the bourbon, I sit my butt at the kitchen island and open up my laptop for the second part of my plan.

I need to figure out how I can get this project done faster than the four-month deadline I predicted. I already have the permits in hand. The city inspectors like working with me. I know I can call after an assignment has been completed and have them out there in no time to give the all clear. But the only way to hustle production is to bring in more man power, meaning I need to hire a bigger crew.

Jared won't be happy with a little less profit, but my fucking sanity and heart are at stake. He'll get over it. I shoot off a detailed email to Jared, requesting a bigger crew for the job.

Deadline moved up. Done.

And third, I have to eliminate any contact with Maceo.

Yeah, pretty fucking impossible when he signed a contract. I could pull out, but he could come back at me and sue. Plus, this is a lot of money to walk away from. This is my business and livelihood. I can't run away this time. But maybe there's a way to minimize our encounters. The contract did not say *specifically* that I had to be working with him.

If I brought in another engineer—for consulting work, of course, since I'm not looking to share my business with anyone—I could make this work. It would be a big chunk taken out of my paycheck. It would set me back from expanding my business until I have another two or three projects under my belt. But saving my heart from further damage justifies the decision.

Consulting engineer needed pronto.

Now to decide who I can consult my work out to. My field is brutal with competition. Making friends with others in the same trade rarely happens. I could extend an olive branch to a local engineer, but I don't have time to waste negotiating with multiple candidates.

The gravity of my situation makes me sway on the barstool as the alcohol takes full effect. Not wanting to hurt myself, I get up and make my way into the living room to park my ass on the couch.

I'm not much for praying, but I'll try anything. *God, it's me, Jo, and I need an engineer.*

My cell pings.

I know it can't be Maceo since I blocked him. I pick my phone up and groan when Jacob's name flashes across the screen with a text.

I look up to the heavens. *God, you're fucking cruel.*

My attention turns back to my cell. *Please, don't be another dick pic.* I click on the picture and see it's a document—a contract to be exact.

Another text pops up.

*Wondering if you're interested in coming in from the dark.**

My eyes read through the contract. *Holy shit!*

If this is what I think it is, my work life could become infinitely better. But I pause. Is this worth having Jacob come back into the picture? It doesn't hurt me to hear what he has to offer, and I can always say no.

"Fuck," I mutter.

Jacob has been trying for the past year to get back in my good graces. I refused to answer his calls or return his emails or texts, but I know without a doubt if I call him, he will answer.

An idea starts to form in my head. Jacob is an option for my current dilemma. This could be an even exchange and would solve two problems in one go. I'm going to have to swallow my pride and put my hurt feelings on the back burner, but he's the only person who I know that would take the vacation time, fly out, and get the job done. I know he will say yes to my project if I say yes to his request.

Settling into the couch for what is about to be a very painful conversation, I dial the number I've been trying to forget.

"Jo? Is it really you?" Jacob asks after the first ring, obviously relieved.

I fight my nausea. "Yes, it's me."

I hear him swallow. "God, it's good to hear your voice," he admits.

I clear my throat from emotion. "I received the contract, but I want to hear what this entails from you."

"Of course, I would expect nothing less. As you may remember, the firm has been taking jobs in other states the last few years to expand our name. We were recently contracted for a major luxury hotel chain and have plans to break ground soon in Denver. My professional engineer on-site has left for a family emergency. I would go myself, but I'm wrapping up a project in San Diego and won't be available for another week. My other two engineers are currently tied up with their own projects. I can't stall the Denver project for a week 'till my PE is available again, and you know I can't go to the company executives with this shit."

"No, you can't," I say, understanding. The firm would crucify him if he went to the board meeting without a backup plan in place.

"My engineer already set up contractors and vendors, but I still need a licensed PE in the state of Colorado to sign off on the blueprints.

"Jo, I don't have time to shop around for someone local. This is happening within the week. Look, I know I shouldn't be asking favors from you after everything, but I'm willing to sweeten the deal. I can get the firm to stop blackballing you. All your contacts—contractors, vendors, engineers, designers, transportation services—would be available for you again."

Oh my God! This would open so many doors for my business.

"I've been following your little startup and you've done a lot in a year, but you can't tell me you haven't been struggling to find these resources."

He's right. I've been having a difficult time. I've had to look farther out to find companies willing to work with me, some over-seas, cutting into profit and extending deadlines. With all my contacts available, I would be saving money and increasing productivity.

"And all I need is a week of your time before my PE can get back. You would literally be working an hour on-site and be able to return to your own projects. Denver isn't too far from Fort Collins. It's a great deal, Jo."

This is almost too easy. Jacob's in no position to turn my favor down now. His job is on the line, and considering he sacrificed our relationship to get where he is, he will jump at this.

"Jacob, I'm willing to take this contract with the firm agreeing to take me off the blacklist—in writing—if you help me in return."

Silence. "What do you need, Keebler?" he asks with a smile in his cocky voice.

I cringe, hearing my old nickname. He thought it was clever to name me after an elf living in a tree making baked goods because I'm short. It was fucking annoying then, and it's fucking annoying now. But I'm not in a position to start chastising him.

"I'm in need of a consulting engineer for a project here in Fort Collins. I'm offering it to you, if you want it. Projected deadline is four months, but I'm negotiating with my general contractor to bring in a bigger crew. It's feasible to shave the deadline down to three months, maybe sooner if we don't run into any snags. I don't need you on-site daily. It would be preferable, but I would like you there at least three days a week, and to handle all questions and concerns from the client within a reasonable amount of time.

"You would have to tap into your vacation bank to avoid the firm finding out you're poaching projects on the side. Or you could finagle a way to come out to your Denver project and find time to work on mine. The pay will be more than worth all the trouble," I say cordially, surprising myself.

More silence. "Jo, why are you asking me to do this? After everything that happened...I mean, you haven't talked to me since you left California. You refused any contact with me when I would reach out until I sent you this deal. I get you jumping on my contract to get your contacts back, but why do you want me on your project? I'm not saying no, I'm just curious. Are you overbooked with projects or is there something else going on?" Jacob inquires, and I can hear the hope in his voice.

He wants this to be more than me wanting his help. He wants this to be me reaching out to him on a more intimate level. I need to set the record straight.

"Honestly, I'm not comfortable with the client. We have a difference of opinion when it comes to communication. I believe it's in the best interest of the client if he and I to have limited contact, which as you can understand is difficult to do while under contract. This project is important to me. Walking away is not an option. I can't risk breaking the contract and possibly being sued because of it," I admit.

"I comprehend all that. And I'm happy you thought of me when considering candidates," he says after a pause. "Tell me about the project."

After filling him in on what the build entails, he seems to hesitate. "Let me get this straight. You're building a compound for a biker gang?" he questions with skepticism.

"Yep."

Jacob laughs. "When do you break ground?"

"Two days, but I won't need you 'till two weeks out from then. I'll be able to manage for now since my client is away on business."

"What business does a biker gang do?" he questions, but quickly stops himself. "Wait, never mind. I'm pretty sure I'm better off not knowing."

A sudden urge to defend Maceo and his MC crew has me almost telling Jacob he's got the wrong idea, but I decide against it. Maybe this will keep Jacob on the straight and narrow while working around me.

"What do you think?" I chew on my thumb as I nervously wait.

Another pause. "I think I'm going to be spending a lot of time in Colorado the next few months."

I let out a slow sigh. "Thank you, Jacob."

"Anything for you, Keebler. Can't wait to see you again. I've missed working with you. I miss you all the fucking time," he says in a husky voice, making my skin crawl. *Gah, gross!*

"I'll be in touch," I say, before disconnecting. I take another deep breath and run my fingers through my hair. As far as eating crow goes that was pretty painful, but at least Jacob wasn't a dick about it. He's too eager to get back on my good side to be his typical douchebag self. I pray I can keep myself in check during this damn project.

Exhausted, I lean my head back on the couch. I've barely slept during the week, stressing over Maceo for apparently no reason at all. *Asshole.*

Talking to Jacob for the past hour certainly helped to sober me up. I'm able to stand without feeling like I'm going to tumble over.

I yawn. "Come on, Hades. Let's take a walk and get your business done for the night."

Hades hurries to me and I leash him up. As we walk, my phone rings, but I don't recognize the number and ignore it—I'm not in a talkative mood at the moment, even if it is business related. If it's important, the person will leave a message.

The same number calls again, and I ignore it. When they try a third time and I don't answer, there's a beep to notify me of a voicemail. I can't check it since I'm busy inverting a poop bag over Hades's epically huge turd.

A minute passes before my phone rings, a different number this time. *That's weird.* Two unknown numbers in a row. Another beep from the voicemail. And then my phone is ringing again. It's a different unknown number. This happens multiple times from six different numbers.

Fucking scammers. How do they get my number?

Once Hades and I are safely locked back inside the condo, I listen to my voicemails.

"*Josephine, pick up the phone. Come on, baby. Let me hear your voice.*"

"*I talked with Punk. And I get it, Josephine. I know you're mad, but please pick up your phone.*"

"*Josephine, I can't make this better if you don't talk to me. Answer the phone!*"

"*Pixie, I'm losing my cool here. Answer the goddamn phone.*"

"*Fuck!*"

"*Answer the fucking phone, Pixie! I'm not playing around anymore.*" "*Atlas, calm the fuck down. You're not going to win her back if you freak her out.*" "*Shit. I'm sorry I'm yelling, but you're making me lose my fucking head. And you better unblock me, damn it.*"

Jesus. Maceo's out of his damn mind if he thinks he can command me to do anything. I go through my phone and block all the numbers he used to call me. He must be using every single cell phone belonging to his team.

I look over at Hades, out cold on his bed, and I decide that's a good idea, heading toward my own bed. My phone goes off again, but this time I recognize the number as Punk's.

Irritated, I answer my cell. "What is it now?"

"Jo, please, I'm begging you. Unblock Atlas. Gauge called me all panicked after Atlas noticed you blocked him. He's going fucking wild over there, and Gauge can barely keep a handle on him. The team is worried he's going to compromise the mission."

My stubbornness could be putting the team and the assignment at risk. Guilt riddles me for a moment, but not enough for me to roll over. Maceo had me fucking worried for damn near a week.

"Oh, so now he tries to answer my texts? Well, fuck him! Punk, I'm sorry he's acting out, but now he gets a taste of the silent treatment I've had to deal with for five days."

Punk groans and curses into the phone. "Okay, you don't have to answer him or talk to him, just unblock his sorry ass. Ignore all the messages you want, but if he's at least able to send them to you, it will take the edge off his crazy."

I lie there for a moment, thinking about it. "Okay, Punk. I'll unblock him. I don't want to jeopardize the operation, but I'm not reaching out to him and I'm deleting everything coming through from him. Until he's back, I will only work with you on this project. Do I make myself clear?"

"Thank fuck. That's fine, Jo," Punk breathes out with relief only to immediately suck it back in. "Wait, you can't delete his shit. He'll know."

My brows pull together. "What do you mean 'he'll know?'" All at once, it hits me like a fucking wrecking ball.

"You have got to be kidding me!" I screech. "Tell me he doesn't have my phone monitored."

Maceo told me he deals in security. I already knew he was snooping into small things like finding my address and going through my social media accounts. But tracking my phone?

Soft thumping is the only sound coming through the phone speaker. I imagine Punk is banging his head against a wall somewhere. It's all the confirmation I need.

"Un-fucking-believable," I fume. "I'm getting a new number."

"No, Jo, please don't," he pleads. I actually empathize with the guy. Maceo's probably going to have his nuts for all the shit he let slip.

"How would you feel if all your shit was being monitored?" I chide.

He groans. "I get it, Jo. All of our shit on the crew is being monitored."

I blanch. "What?"

"All of our stuff is tracked. It's a way of watching out for each other if something happens to one of us. We know where everyone is at any given time. We're able to read through text messages and emails to keep track of info regarding missions," he says with a sigh.

"And what about shit which has nothing to do with the missions?" I inquire in disbelief.

Another sigh. "It's a natural casualty. Most of the guys have nothing to hide since we're not in committed relationships and it's kind of like bragging rights when, um, sexual things come through. But don't worry. Atlas is the only one who sees what comes through from you, well, him and Chase, since he's our cyber guy. Maybe don't send nudes to Atlas and it will be all good."

There's mumbling in the background before Punk is back on the phone. "Chase says Maceo was going to tell you about us tracking you if things turned serious between the two of you, but he didn't want to worry you if you guys were a bust. He's doing this for your own safety."

Punk's words trigger a memory of Maceo and I in bed. He was talking to me about taking extra security percussions and we were interrupted when he got the text for the mission. Was he trying to tell me he was monitoring my phone? Does this mean he thought our status moved from uncertain to serious?

Who fucking cares! He hacked your phone, Jo.

"I didn't fucking agree to this shit, Punk. None of this is fucking 'all good,'" I bite back. "What does Maceo have access to?" I need to know how deep this shit goes.

"Everything," he admits.

"Everything," I repeat as a cold sweat rolls over me. I drop the phone in my haste to make it to the toilet as all the bourbon I drank comes back up. I have never felt this violated in all my life.

"Jo? Jo, are you still there? You okay?" Punk's voice comes out louder through my phone speakers.

"How are you on the damn speaker phone?" I cry out.

"Um, I asked Chase to override your phone in order to check and make sure you're okay," he says sheepishly.

"For fuck's sake!" I scream and start sobbing. "Tell Chase if he unblocks access on my phone for Maceo, I will go to the police and report him!"

There's more mumbling in the background. It must be Chase. "Best not tell her we work hand in hand with the police," I hear his muffled voice.

"He can't, not without some major hacking since you blocked Maceo and you didn't block me. Shit, Jo. What can I do to make this okay?" Punk pleads, worry laced in his voice.

I collect myself before answering. "Nothing, Punk. There's nothing that will make any of this right."

Silence from him on the other end, but I can hear him typing away on his phone.

"Atlas wants to know why you made a phone call to a Jacob Klein that lasted over an hour," Punk asks, his voice all business.

Fucking controlling jealous asshole!

Of course, he would be going through all my shit since I've blocked him from texting and calling. He's probably livid, knowing I was talking with my ex tonight.

"Tell Atlas it's none of his fucking business," I spit before crawling over to the phone and disconnecting. I remove the battery, not wanting to be disturbed anymore tonight. Then I crawl to my bed and climb in before sobs take over again. Hades whines in the doorway, worry contorting his adorable big face.

"Come here, baby boy," I say through a sob and pat the sheets.

Hades launches up to the bed and lies right on top of me. I stroke his fur and continue to cry, letting the warmth from him seep into my cold body.

"You're the only one I trust, big boy," I tell him. I drift off, knowing he's watching over me tonight.

CHAPTER SIX

JOSEPHINE

True to my word, I did my job with a vengeance—to finish ahead of schedule. Jared didn't fight me on the extra manpower, sensing it wasn't up for debate. Seeing as I was barking orders at most of the crew members and making his job a little easier, he was happy to have a bigger crew.

The first week, the field was cleared and leveled. Slabs and foundations were poured and set. Framing was up on the main headquarters, and welders finished putting up the garages and mechanic shop by the beginning of the second week.

By the middle of the second week, the metal roofing, windows, and doors were installed to all the buildings. Inspectors were in and out daily, passing us on all inspections, allowing us to plow through.

I did all of this dutifully, while several different MC members stopped by to monitor the progress of the build. Punk was present among them most days, giving the thumbs-up to all my decisions. I'm sure Maceo gave him the order to allow me to make any and all design choices.

Punk was always pleasant and made sure I had everything I could possibly need. I tried not to take my anger out on any of them, seeing as my rage was reserved for Maceo, but all the MC members stepped on eggshells around me. I had no problem telling them to get the hell out of my crew's way if I felt they were overstepping.

As hard as I was being on my crew, they didn't fight me. Either they were used to the treatment from other jobs, or they could sense I was stressed over the project and the company around us. They nodded when I gave an order, and they did whatever I requested. I guess I was paying them enough to make the long hours worth their time. Every night, I apologized to them for my bitchy behavior, which only made them laugh as they said their goodbyes for the day.

Taking pity on Chase for wasting hours hacking into my phone, I unblocked Maceo's number. The next morning, I bought a burner. I used the new phone for anything unrelated to Maceo's project, including keeping Jacob in the loop on the progress of the build.

At the rate we were going, we could be done before the three months were up. Jacob was biting at the bit to get out to Fort Collins, but I was no fool. I knew his attention was much more focused on me than the actual build itself. I had to remind him every time we talked. He was not to come until the end of the second week.

Jacob came through on his end. I received a contract from my old firm confirming to stop blackballing me in exchange for a week of my PE services on the build in Denver, and I signed the deal. I went to Denver every afternoon to go over the blueprints, make changes if need be, and sign off on them. Then I returned back to the MC build site, relieving Jared of watching both crews, and working late into the evening.

The doors which had once been shut were miraculously open and it showed. Jared and I were bombarded by other vendors offering better deals on supplies. Last minute orders were delivered quickly by suppliers, and contractors were networking with us. Never again could my old firm screw me over without me suing the shit out of them. The week I invested traveling back and forth between projects was worth it.

Punk would call me on my old phone with anything regarding the build. All questions asked on Maceo's behalf regarding anything other than the project were immediately cut off. I was done with the bullshit and wanted to move on.

Putting all my focus into my work was the best therapy. As much as this project was causing me anxiety, I was living in my element. This is what I was always meant to do—build and create works of art that brought my clients joy.

Maceo continued to send text messages and leave voicemails, but I ignored all of them and left them unanswered. Thankfully, he avoided bombarding my email. It's almost like he could sense it would set me off. I would have thought he would have given up after days of no response from me, but he dutifully left me a text and voicemail every morning and every night, trying to make up for his screw up.

Too little, too late.

It's Friday of week two, and I bicker with Jared about pressing through another weekend with the second crew, giving our first crew a reprieve. Jared wants our original men on the job and is pushing for us to take the weekend off.

While we debate, a rental car pulls onto the property and my stomach drops. Though I was expecting Jacob to show up today, it still doesn't mean I'm happy to have him anywhere near me. I grab Jared's arm for emotional support—he knows how much I've been dreading seeing Jacob.

Jared sneers at the rental as Jacob parks the car. "So that's the dumb fuck who screwed you over back in California?"

"The one and only. Do me a favor and play nice with him. We need his help on this build."

I haven't told Jared exactly what happened between Maceo and I because I'm too embarrassed, bamboozled by Maceo's charm. All Jared knows is that we had a 'misunderstanding.'

Jared snorts. "No, Jo, we don't need him. We need you. That leech shouldn't be anywhere near you after what he's done."

"Do I need to remind you that 'leech' is also responsible for ending my blacklist days?"

"He's not the hero here, Jo. He may try to spin himself as one, but the only reason you were on that list to begin with was because of him."

Jared has been my closest friend since moving to Colorado. It's not uncommon for the two of us to go out drinking at the end of the week and bitch about our past partners—meaning Jared knows nearly as much about my relationship with Jacob as I do.

Eager to get on with it, I give Jared a sad smile, grab my cell in case Punk needs to get a hold of me, and go greet my ex.

Jacob is up and out of the car as soon as he sees me. I expected the happy-as-fuck smile on his face, but I wasn't expecting him to be so damn grabby. He catches me by the shoulders and pulls me into a death grip against his lean body the second the car door closes.

Jacob presses his nose in my hair. "Damn, Jo. It's good to see you," he says, and kisses the top of my head, breathing me in.

He's being way too chummy for my comfort. I firmly push away from him, but I control the revulsion on my face. "Glad you made the trip." I look down at his shoes and shake my head.

Jacob is dressed like architectural engineers—dress shirt, dress slacks, and loafers. We are in the field, not the fucking office. I dress for the job—ripped up skinny jeans, black tank top, construction boots and pigtail braids are my normal on-site attire. I'm tempted to ask him if he wants to change his clothes first, but what the hell do I care.

"Let me show you what you're walking into," I say without emotion as I hand him a hard hat and wave for him to follow me around the build site.

Jacob is openly impressed with what my crew has accomplished in two weeks. I take him around and introduce him to my crew members. Maybe it's Jacob's uppity demeanor that is off-putting, but none of my workers appear receptive toward him, Jared especially. He turns and walks the other way when I try to introduce them. I expect the hostility from Jared since he's aware of our history, but how the other members of the crew are behaving gives me pause. How will they respond to Jacob when I'm not on-site?

It probably doesn't help Jacob's case when I slap his hand away multiple times in front of my workers when he tries to take my hand. We're no longer lovers—hell, we aren't even friends. This is a business deal only. Why the fuck is Jacob acting like there's more between us? It's unnerving.

After a full tour of the project, I'm about to take him into the trailer—which Jared and I are using as our on-site office. I'm going to show him the plans I refused to until he was here—call me protective about my work all you want, I wasn't going to give the asshole an opportunity to steal any more shit from me—when I hear the roar of a motorcycle pulling onto the property.

Expecting to see one of the MC members rolling in, I turn toward the approach. My heart completely stops as I take in the glorious figure on the bike.

Maceo rolls up to the trailer in black tactical clothing and aviator glasses, hiding his dark eyes, which I'm sure are glowering at me right now. His hair has grown as well as his beard, which is very full after being away for three weeks. He looks hot as hell as he climbs off his bike and stalks toward me like a lion approaching his prey. He rubs his massive chest with one of his hands as he makes his way, like his heart has been hurting as much as mine.

Well, boo-fucking-hoo. The alpha asshole stepped all over my heart first!

I hoped for one more week before he returned, like Punk originally told me. Alas, it looks like Maceo's team was able to accomplish the mission early. He's dressed like he wrapped up the job and immediately boarded a plane home without changing out of his gear.

My heart squeezes back to life, painfully, with each step he takes toward me. Time away from him has done absolutely nothing to steel me against his aura. A sinking feeling grows in the pit of my stomach. I'm nowhere near over him. Hell, is it a lost cause?

Maceo doesn't stop until he's standing over me. He pushes his sunglasses over his thick hair. "Pixie," he purrs, making a fire to burn low in my body.

"Atlas," I say evenly, hypnotized by his dark gaze.

Jacob looks between the two of us, as if finally realizing this giant man is the client. The one I told him I was having issues with. "Hi, Atlas," he says with a cheery voice, holding out his hand. "Jacob Klein. Really excited to start working with you on this project."

Maceo glares at Jacob like he's an insect to squash. He looks down at Jacob's hand, which he lets hang there. "Yes, I'm well aware of who you are."

Jacob's swallow is audible.

Maceo turns his fierce gaze on me. "What the fuck is this?" he says nodding toward Jacob.

"Atlas—" I begin, but I'm cut off.

"I've fucking told you that you, only you, call me *Maceo*," he spits through his teeth.

"Mr. Atlas, please, let me explain. Jo asked me here to help with —" Jacob tries to clarify his presence using his most confident voice, sensing I'm in the crossfire of Maceo's rage.

But Maceo interrupts by raising his hand and unleashing his fury on him. "Was I fucking speaking to you?"

Jacob's mouth clamps shut instantly. This kind of hostility from clients is brand-spanking-new for him.

Maceo's upright hand forms into a fist before he extends his index finger and shakes it, warning Jacob to stay silent. The cords in his thick neck are strained, and Maceo tries to control his rage. "Excuse us a moment, Jake," Maceo says in a condescending tone.

"Oh, it's Jacob," Jacob corrects.

Maceo takes me firmly, but not painfully, by the elbow and leads me a good fifty feet away. He rips off his sunglasses from his head and hangs them on his shirt, then leans into my personal space, practically engulfing me with his frame. "Care to explain why your fucking ex is here on my property?"

I inhale through my nose, squaring my shoulders and looking up at him. "I've asked him here to consult on this project in my absence."

Maceo does a double take. "What the fuck are you talking about?"

"Given the current circumstances between us, I believe it is in the best interest of the project to bring in a third party as acting engineer to avoid further confrontation. He will be present from now 'till completion of the build," I say.

"Over my dead body!" He seethes, making me nearly jump out of my construction boots. "I didn't hire that loafer-dick. I signed a contract with *you*. You, Josephine! If I wanted a different engineer, I would have hired a different one. I *gave* this to you. You don't get to make the call of passing it on to someone else now."

"I'm well within my rights of the contract to bring in anyone I want to help consult on this build," I say, in a slightly louder voice.

He runs a shaky hand through his hair, panic taking over his face. "Did he sign a deal with you? How long has he been here?"

"No. We haven't done any formalities yet because he only showed up today, but this is happening," I yell back. *To hell with professionalism right now.* I'm too livid to give a shit.

"Nope, not going to happen. I will fucking pull the plug on this whole operation, if that—" he shouts while pointing a thick finger over my head at Jacob. "—fucker stays on this job. It's you or nothing. This is not negotiable, Josephine. Send the prick back to San-fucking-Diego or I will personally take him there myself."

Fear washes over me. Maceo's within his rights to back out of the deal as long as he pays for material and services rendered. If it was just me I would tell him to go ahead, but I have a general contractor and two different crews relying on this job. I can't do this to them.

"Are you seriously threatening me right now? You know my crew needs this job. Take your anger out on me all you want but leave them the hell out of it. You're being fucking unreasonable," I scream at him.

"I'm being unreasonable? How the fuck should I react after not hearing back from you for two fucking weeks? Rolling up to *my* land to see that prick hanging all over *you*? Eye-fucking you like you're still his when you're damn well mine. Tell me what *man* would fucking sit back and allow that shit to fly. I'm not fucking threatening. I'm making a damn promise. It's either him or the build, you choose," he snarls.

I'm literally shaking with fury. The nerve of him to call me *his*, claiming me like a fucking cave-man, pisses me off like nothing else. He fucking had me and threw me away.

"I was fucking worried sick about you for five days. I barely slept, hardly ate, and then I find out you were ignoring me. You deserved the silent treatment. Ugh! You're such a hypocritical asshole!"

"You're goddamn right I am! Now send the fucker on his way or God help me, Josephine, I will throw his ass out and you know I will," he thunders. "Nobody, and I mean nobody, can have what's mine. And that's you, Pixie!"

Blood rushes to my head. *That's it!* "I'm not a fucking possession, Maceo!"

Maceo anger slips and he looks regretful. "Of course, you're not a possession, but did you give me your heart or not?"

"I—" I try to deny it and can't.

Maceo sees me hesitate and his ebony eyes fill with relief. "You see? You're my woman and that dipshit is trying to weasel his way into your life again. I fucking refuse it."

"Everything alright here, Keebler?" Jacob says with a bounce in his step as he approaches us, acting completely oblivious to whole situation.

Maceo's eyes narrow and his nostrils flare. He turns his whole body to face Jacob, forcing me behind him. *Yeah, this isn't going to be pretty.* Now I'm the one grabbing onto his elbow, suddenly panicked with how Maceo will respond to Jacob.

Maceo's fists clench at his sides. "What the fuck did you call her?" I yank helplessly on him, anything to shake him out of his rage. But Maceo doesn't budge.

Jacob's eyes widen and his hands go up in surrender. "Man, take it easy. It's only a nickname," he says in a slightly higher voice, and lets out a nervous laugh.

"Well, it fucking sucks. Does she look like an ugly cartoon to you? Don't call her that again. It's fucking disrespectful. She's Jo to you, and only Jo," he snaps, shaking his head angrily.

Jacob looks at me with wide eyes. "O-kay."

"You alright, boss?" one of my crew members calls out.

My attention was completely focused on keeping Maceo from strangling Jacob. I didn't notice the little militia of my construction workers forming around us, ready to swoop in and help me. Over half my crew members have stopped working and are slowly easing their way toward us, tools in hand. Jared is among them with a hammer in tow.

I need to do damage control, stat.

"It's all good gentlemen, just a misunderstanding. Please, return to your duties. I'll be around shortly to go over details and answer questions about the project," I say diplomatically.

My crew doesn't move on, not until I give them all a little nod of reassurance. Jared is the only one to keep pushing toward us till he's standing beside me. With how tense the current situation is, I'm grateful for his presence.

"Name's Jared," he says nodding to Maceo and Jacob. "I'm Jo's general contractor. Wanted to make sure we're all on board going forward."

"Hi, Jared. I'm Jacob, the consulting engineer," Jacob says, leaning forward to shake hands.

"The fuck you are," Maceo growls at him.

Jacob looks up in surprise at Maceo. He eyes up Maceo, suspiciously.

Jared looks between the two men then down at me, giving me a shrug. "You're the boss," Jared says to me with a sympathetic look before looking up at Maceo. "But Atlas is the client, and if he's not happy with the arrangement then we can't move forward."

I all but bare my teeth at Jared. *Traitorous bastard!*

I should have known Jared would pull something like this. In his eyes we got what we needed out of Jacob when the blackball was lifted. He wasn't on board with bringing on Jacob in the first place, but he doesn't know the full story behind Maceo and I either.

I fold my arms over my chest and roll my eyes skyward before looking back at the three men in front of me.

Maceo has relaxed and is grinning at Jared like he found a new best friend. Jared tries to hide his obvious relief, kicking Jacob off the project, but he doesn't conceal his smile well. And Jacob looks to be in shock. This is probably the first project he's been fired from, and he hadn't even started.

Jacob turns his stunned face to me. "I guess since my services are no longer needed, I'll be on my way," he says. "Jo, can I have a word?" He walks ahead not waiting for me to follow.

Fuck. I glare at both Maceo and Jared. Seeing Jared and Maceo acting all chummy together, I'm sure Jared's figured out something sexual happened between us. He's mentioned many times I needed to get back on the horse and find a new man—well, apparently Maceo is that man.

Turning on my heels to follow Jacob to his rental car, I can still hear the two of them talking.

"What's your poison?" Maceo asks.

"Scotch," Jared replies.

"I owe you a case."

"You don't owe me shit. I was happy to get rid of the fucker. He doesn't deserve to be anywhere near our Jo. But please don't fucking set her off anymore today. I'm trying to make her take off for the weekend. We all need a rest. Seal me the weekend off for all of us, and we're square," he says.

"Done," Maceo states.

My jaw ticks with annoyance.

Once at the car, I find myself eating crow. "I apologize, Jacob. I didn't expect this big of a backlash. I'll reimburse you for travel expenses and your time."

"Don't worry about reimbursement. I'll stop at the Denver project in the next few days and write it off as a business expense. But I see why you called in for some help. I totally get your communication issue with the dude. He seems fucking violent. Are you sure you're okay doing this solo? I don't want to leave you here if you're unsafe," Jacob asks, with an edge of hostility, or maybe concern, in his voice.

I shake my head. "I'm fine, Jacob. Yes, he can be an asshole, but I've dealt with assholes before. Trust me, he's harmless."

Yeah, he's only ripped out my heart after he told me he wouldn't—completely harmless otherwise.

"I don't know, Jo. The way he looks at you and yells...it seemed pretty possessive," he says with an icy tone as he glares over my head at Maceo.

You have no idea. "Atlas is very particular on what he wants and who works for him. I'm sorry this didn't work out," I try to pacify.

Jacob's cold blue eyes focus back on me before softening. He takes one of my hands in his. "I'm sorry it didn't work out either. I was looking forward to being on a team with you again. You know, you can always come back. After how you helped me and the firm out the past week, they wouldn't fight me if I said I wanted you on my team again."

"Not needed, but thank you, Jacob. I'm right where I need to be." *There's no way in hell I would return to the company and work under you.*

Still holding my hand, Jacob gives me a crooked smile. This smile would have had my stomach fluttering only a year ago. It does nothing for me now.

"I'm staying at the Hilton. Maybe we can see each other before I head back out, catch up and maybe talk out some of our issues," he suggests.

I cringe inwardly. *Hard pass.* "I can't, Jacob, and you know why."

His brows furrow, but he nods once. Before he releases me, he bends down to kiss me. I turn my head and his lips brush my cheek instead. Jacob backs away with an angry grimace, but he says nothing else as he climbs in his rental and circles out of the build site.

When I turn around to give Maceo another tongue-lashing, he's already striding toward me. He hauls me over his shoulder like a Neanderthal. My hard hat hits the ground with a thud, and I'm instantly kicking and punching him.

"Goddamnit, Maceo! Put me the fuck down."

There's a loud slap, and my ass is burning.

Oh! Why did something painful like him spanking me make my lady-bits tremble? I shelf my arousal and focus on my anger.

"Ow! How dare you fucking spank me, you dickhead!"

Another slap follows, stinging. I squeal in protest. "Fuck you, Atlas!" *Christ, my panties are soaked.*

Suddenly, I'm back on my feet in front of Maceo and his bike. He swings himself over the seat, pointing for me to get on.

Defiant as always, I turn on my heels to walk away, but he grabs me before I can take my first step and hauls me over the back of his bike. I barely have time to grab hold of him before he's revving the engine and speeding away.

I have no idea where he's taking me and I don't even care, because as mad as I've been with him over the last three weeks, I can't deny the fact my heart is too fucking happy, pressed against his back.

Maybe Maceo plans to make the past three weeks up to me. Maybe—and it's a big fucking maybe—I'll let him.

CHAPTER SEVEN
MACEO

G oddamnit, this woman infuriates me like no one else. I can barely contain my anger to control the speed of my bike, racing away with Josephine at my back where she belongs.

I admit it. I fucked up when I left on my mission. I was working on autopilot like I always do when on an assignment. I had every intention of spending the night with Josephine before Gauge's text came through.

Gauge wasn't exaggerating when he texted SOS. We reserve that message for the worst of the worst missions. It means grab your shit and go. You find out the details as you head to the destination.

In my head, I thought I explained it well enough to her, but I forgot she wasn't accustomed to the ways of the MC. There's no explaining needed for other MC members. We all know the drill.

I've never had to explain the who, what, when, where, and how of the itinerary to a woman. Telling her I had to bounce and giving her a kiss goodbye without explaining what was happening was a complete failure on my part. I should have taken a minute to fill her in. I was leaving for a serious job where I would be unable to contact her.

Of course, I saw her text messages come through and I listened to her voicemails. They were some of the sweetest things I've read or heard in my entire life, especially coming from her. My reasoning for not responding was simple. I knew if I called her and heard her sweet sing-song voice, I wouldn't be able to get off the phone, or focus on the task at hand. I knew if I sent her one text message, it would lead to more texting, taking me away from the mission.

The more distractions I indulged in, the longer it would take to complete the mission, which in turn would make it take longer to get back home. But reading and listening to those messages was something I took comfort in each and every day. And I was an asshole for not returning those comforts.

In hindsight, my lack of a response was the worst thing I could have done. If one of my brothers did what I did to a woman they cared for, I'd be the first to call him out on his thoughtlessness. Why the hell was it acceptable for me to do it? Simple, it wasn't.

When her final text rolled through on day five of the mission, it completely threw me.

Fuck off, Maceo!

It was the moment all the pieces came together to show me my mistake. I quickly sent a text and it immediately bounced back.

She fucking blocked me.

There's nothing scarier than the moment you realize everything you never knew you wanted is slipping through your fingers because of your own fuckup.

I started calling her, but it wasn't going to work, for the same reason as the text not going through. I yelled across our shitty hideout house for Gauge to give me his cell. But she wouldn't answer it. Probably screening her calls like a good little girl should when receiving unknown numbers. I called two more times and was greeted with her voicemail each time. Doing the only thing I could, I left her a voicemail, hoping she would listen to it and call back.

When Punk called to tell me he inadvertently spilled the beans about talking to me the night before, I understood why she snapped. I hung up and grabbed Triple's cell next and it was more of the same, her voicemail and me trying to explain myself.

Hoping for better odds, I grabbed all of my team's cells and tried calling her from each one of them. But she didn't answer. Message after message came pouring out of me. I was hoping and praying she would listen to one.

I'm not proud to admit it, but I started losing my shit in front of my whole damn team. They were already on edge over the disheartening mission we were working. I flipped the room, screamed, and pounded on my chest as my worst fears were sinking in. I finally found the woman of my dreams and I fucked it up.

My God, she must have thought I just fucked her and left after we finished, because I never explained why I was leaving. It would have taken a minute—a fucking minute—and I wouldn't be in the position of losing her. My stomach rolled and I raced to the bathroom, vomiting.

Gauge did everything he could to console me, but I was far past calming down. I needed to comprehend what she was going through the last few days for her to give me the middle finger. Maybe there was more to it. I needed to know if there was. I didn't want to invade her privacy, but she wasn't giving me any other option.

I found my cell and accessed her accounts, going through her recent emails. All business and nothing else. I did the same with her texts and it was similar, aside from what she had been sending me. There was a recent text sent from Jacob, but she hadn't responded to it. I disregarded it as I'm sure she had. But it was when I went through her call log that my heart stopped.

She had called her fucking ex not thirty minutes after sending me her last text and then blocking me. Her call with him had lasted an hour. *A fucking hour!*

No. No. No. This could not be happening. I fucked up, and she was running back to her ex-boyfriend? *Fuck no!*

I fired off a text to Punk since I knew she was communicating with him, and he would ask her about the prick if I ordered it. Things went from bad to worse.

Josephine's a smart woman. It wasn't entirely Punk's fault he

108

asked her not to delete my messages and she connected the dots, but as soon as I inquired about Jacob, she realized I invaded her personal life without consent. *Fuck me!*

My fury was being an equal-opportunity cunt and taking it out on everyone.

Punk was able to convince Josephine to unblock me, at least. I took full advantage by bombarding her with texts and voicemails. I was such a sap in all those messages, confessing my feelings and hopes for us in the future.

For two weeks I left her messages. And for two weeks, I got no response back. I finally understood what she was going through those five days I hadn't responded. The worry and heartache she had for me matched mine for hers exactly.

At least I took comfort in the fact Josephine hadn't reached out to her ex again. Perhaps it was something she needed to do for closure in order to move on with me. Yes, that *had* to be the reason for her calling him.

With renewed energy to get back to my woman and make her see, make her experience my feelings for her, I went into full focus. Listening to my gut on a high-risk gamble was how we ended up finding the little girl and bringing her home. Gauge took over lead to finish up formalities, allowing me to hop on the first jet back home to Josephine. There was no time for stopping, eating, sleeping, or changing. I couldn't afford to waste another second without her.

Now I'm pushing well over a hundred racing us back to her place to pick up where we left off three weeks ago. I'm not a fool. I know I can't charm my way between her thighs before we hash it out, but I have no shame admitting we will be having some long makeup sex afterwards. As soon as I pull up to her condo, she jumps off and races to her front door.

Where the fuck is she going? I'm off my bike, bolting to shove my boot between the door and frame before she can slam it in my face.

"Josephine, please let me explain myself," I beg. She shoves harder against the door, but she gives up when she sees it's no use.

I shoulder my way into her entryway, only to have Hades pinning me against the door, snarling and barking against my chest. Her dog is no joke. He will do anything to defend his *mamá*. But I'm not anyone he needs to fear. I only want to love her.

The dog hates me. I need to win him over, pronto. "Easy, Hades," I say in a soft voice. "I'm not going to do anything to upset your *mamá*."

He barks four times, like he's bitching me out, trying to communicate 'you've already upset her.'

I nod and rub a hand down his black coat to calm him down. "I know I've already upset her. I never meant to. I wasn't thinking like a boyfriend. I've never had a girl to explain myself to before."

He cocks his head and grumbles up at me, as if saying 'then why did you do it?'

I nod again, as I keep rubbing my hand down his back, well aware Josephine is standing behind Hades, watching the whole exchange. *Good, I want her to hear all of this.*

"In my head I thought I explained it. I said I got a text and had to leave. I never considered for a second I needed to explain myself more, but I forgot my norm is not the same as your *mamá's*. My work is time sensitive, and I was in the zone. SOS usually means a child has been abducted. I'm not supposed to disclose any of this, but you and your *mamá* need to understand exactly why my mind was closed off."

Hades growls and bobs his head at me.

"A governor's eight-year-old daughter was kidnapped right from her bed along with her twenty-three-year-old nanny. He and his wife were at a gala. The assailants, who are affiliated with a drug cartel down in South America, killed all the security on site. I left your *mamá* and went straight to the military airport and was briefed by the governor's security team on the flight out.

"First day we spent on the ground gathering whatever intel we could from the locals and authorities. Second day we were busy setting up headquarters near where we believed they were located.

The third day was the hardest. Governor received a video message. I'll spare you the details of what they did to the nanny."

Josephine gasps, but I don't look up as I talk. I keep my attention focused on Hades who has now dropped from my chest to my feet, watching me closely, waiting to hear more.

"The video was a warning. The same thing would happen to his little girl if the governor didn't back out of a bill he was pushing to pass. It would make it harder to bring in illegal drugs to the state. On the fourth day we made a bust on the house where we thought the little girl was being held, but the tip was bad, and we blew our cover. It spooked them into moving her to a different location. Day five was a shit storm of surveillance and collecting info, working to track down her new location. That was when the last text from your *mamá* came through," I explain.

I'm not good at this. I don't know how to show my emotions or say what I'm feeling without hearing a nagging voice in the back of my head telling me to 'stop being weak.' Subconsciously, I slap the shit out of that voice. If I can't be man enough to own what I'm feeling for Josephine and express it to her properly, I don't deserve her.

I shut my eyes and hang my head, feeling tears running down my face, and I can hear Josephine crying, too. With Hades sitting back on his haunches now and no longer a threat, I direct my conversation to my pixie. She deserves this.

"I knew I fucked up, but I didn't know how badly until Punk called and said he told you I talked to him. You saw it as me having time for him and not for you, and that was never my intention. Punk had been leading a team in Denver in my absence. He had wrapped up and I wanted a run down.

"Since I had him on the phone, I asked him to check in on my woman and use the excuse about breaking ground. I had him do it because I knew if I called or texted you, my attention would be completely focused on you, and not on the little girl I was there to help. The more distractions, the longer it would take for me to get back, and I didn't want to waste a second away from you. Any time with you is too precious to fuck around with. I did what I had to do and brought the little girl back to her parents," I admit.

Josephine sucks in a ragged wet gulp of air, and I finally grow the balls to lift my head and look into her sad weeping eyes. Those fucking gorgeous blue pools bring down the last of my walls.

"I don't want you thinking I only wanted one last time with you before moving on, because I can never get enough of you. I don't want you to believe I was ignoring you, because I wasn't. I read every single text and listened to every message you left as they came in. Your words, your voice, they were what gave me the fuel to move faster and push harder to get the job done and come home. They meant everything to me even though I couldn't respond. I failed you, because as much as I needed those messages from you, you needed them from me, too.

"I have no excuse. I fucked up, and I was an unworthy asshole. And I'm sorry Josephine, so fucking sorry," I cry, sinking to my knees at her feet, wrapping my arms around her torso and burying my face against her.

The only times I've shed tears in my life were when my *abuela* passed and when I lost a brother-in-arms. I cry when I experience loss, but not like this. I'm full on sobbing. Even though I'm putting everything I have into winning her back, I may still lose her if she decides not to forgive me.

This short, feisty, ill-tempered temptress has snuck up on me and wrapped herself around my frozen heart, warming it and bringing it back to life. I have lost so much in my life, and now I could lose the one person who gave me hope for something more than a lonely existence. I cry harder when I feel her fingers run through my hair.

"Maceo," she whispers with a shaky voice. "Taking off and not being in contact with me is only half the issue."

I choke down my sob and nod. "I know I overstepped my bounds when I asked Chase to hack into your phone and track you without your consent. It was wrong of me to gain access to your public and private accounts. I had no right viewing your call lists, texts, or emails. Everyone involved in the Mercy Ravens has open access to everything. It's how we look out for each other. But we enter the club knowing this. I didn't give you the option, and for that I'm sorry."

"But why did you do it in the first place?"

"I told you my work is dangerous. Just because I complete a mission doesn't mean shit can't follow me home. I've had death threats, assassination attempts, and I've been caught and tortured. Do you honestly think I would consider getting involved with someone knowing I hadn't put necessary precautions into place to protect them? I did it for your safety. As wrong as it sounds, I wasn't going to tell you unless we decided to pursue a relationship. I didn't want to freak you out. You wouldn't have given me a chance if I requested this from you before we had our first date. It doesn't justify my actions, but it's the reason why I did it. I tried to tell you before I left."

She sighs heavily. "I know you did, but the text interrupted you. Are you still monitoring everything?"

I swallow hard, afraid of her reaction. "All monitoring has stopped except for tracking your location. I will not end that unless you tell me to, or if you tell me we are over." My nerves take over and I start to tremble.

Hades is on me, licking my head, nuzzling against us while he whines. *Well, I guess I won over her hellhound. Can I win her over?*

Taking a risk in my pride, I look up to her face and find her watching me with silent tears rolling down her delicate face. "Have you read my texts or listened to the voicemails?"

She shakes her head and looks regretful. "I—I didn't read or listen to them," she says.

I nod. I thought as much. Had she at least listened to one, she would have reached out to me. "Do you want me to tell you what my messages and texts were about?"

Josephine sniffles. "Yes."

Man up, Maceo. Look her in the eye and tell her everything.

"I talked about not being able to wait to hold you in my arms and grovel at your feet for your forgiveness. I talked about how you had every reason to be pissed off at me after I hurt you and how pissed I was at myself, too. I talked about how I made a promise to you before I left about your heart being safe with me, and I how I hated myself for having broken it. I begged you to give me a second chance, so I could spend every day putting your heart back together and making it stronger than before. I confessed how much I fucking need you, and how you couldn't begin to comprehend how hard I've fallen for you."

Josephine quivers as tears tumble down her rosy cheeks.

"The moment I laid eyes on you on the trail you caught my attention. But that night when we had dinner and we finally talked...I knew that everything in my life was going to change. You've woken something inside me I never knew I had. I can't imagine living with this feeling if you're not by my side. I don't care if we hardly know each other. I don't care if this whole situation is coming out of left field. I care about you. Josephine, I love you. *Estoy jodidamente enamorado de ti.* Please, let me prove it to you, *mi amor.*"

Next thing I know, she's sliding to the floor through my arms and she's sobbing against my chest. I have no idea if her tears are a good sign or a bad sign. I hold her and the air in my lungs, waiting for a signal to let me know either way.

After several minutes of her crying and me holding her, I take the risk and I cup her face 'till she's staring into my eyes. "This isn't only lust between us. It's complex and overwhelming, but I'm certain of what I feel for you. You own my heart, baby. You're the first and only one to receive it." I slant my mouth over hers.

The first touch of her trembling lips against mine is like being welcomed home. *I need more.* I deepen the kiss till she's moaning in my arms and fisting my shirt. I run my hands down her lithe body and start tugging her tank out of her waistband and over her head. Entranced, I stare down at her slender form and the swell of her small but round breasts hidden behind a black bra. My mouth waters with anticipation of when I will suck them into my mouth and palm them in my hands.

Her hands start yanking on my shirt, but it won't budge. I chuckle as I help her pull it over my head. She runs her slender fingers up my bare chest and over my nipples. I groan as she pulls on them. *Fuck, that feels good.*

My cock is growing painfully hard in my pants. I wrap my hand around both of her braids and tug 'till her neck is exposed to me, letting me run my nose along her soft, citrus skin. She squirms and giggles under my touch.

I pull back. "What's so funny?"

She reaches up and pinches my beard. "It tickles."

I smile at her wolfishly. "I can't wait 'till it tickles you in other areas." She squeals with laughter as I attack her with kisses and abrade her skin with my facial hair.

As much as I want to continue, I need to know where her head is at. I've thrown a shit-ton at her. Even in my own head, I know this is wild. But my head doesn't decide who I love, that's all my heart, and she's the keeper of it.

"Pixie, tell me what you're feeling," I ask between kisses.

Josephine's hand reaches out to cup my face and her brows pull together. "I'm scared," she admits in a whisper.

I shut my eyes for a moment, letting her worries wash over me. I'll store them for her, and she'll never have to worry again.

My eyes open back up. "I know, Pixie. I'm scared too. But I'm more scared of walking away from the greatest thing to ever happen to me, all because I fear having my heart crushed. I'd rather have my heart broken by you, if it means having one day with you, than to walk away now and never have the time at all."

Tears trickle down her cheeks. "Fuck, Maceo," she chokes as she gathers her composure. "You're the most overbearing, controlling, and riveting man I have ever met. You both frustrate and inspire me. I've tried to ignore you and your demands, but I don't want to, I never wanted to. If you're in, I'm in, too."

Hope swells inside me and I can't hide the shock on my face at how fucking lucky I am. In one swift movement, I'm scooping her in my arms and heading to the bedroom. We're past the doorway when Hades comes bounding into the room and hops up on the bed.

I freeze, unsure how to continue. I've been aching for this woman since I first laid eyes on her three weeks ago, and I don't want an audience while I claim her, regardless if it's only her dog.

"Sorry, he's been my bed buddy the last two weeks," she explains.

She doesn't need to say more. I broke her heart and Hades has been holding her together for me. Can't blame the dog for thinking he's right where he needs to be.

With a small smile, I place her on her feet and approach the bed to address Hades. "Brother, I need you to be my wingman right now and give me the room with your *mamá*."

Hades cocks his head and woofs, jumping from the bed and padding out of the bedroom. *Holy shit, that actually worked!* Quickly, I cross the room and close the door before turning back to my pixie, who's smiling ear to ear.

"It's funny how you talk to him like he can understand you," she mimics my words from our first encounter.

"Well, a very sassy pixie told me he understands everything," I say with a sheepish grin. I amble slowly toward her, watching the blush of her arousal grow on her cheeks, down to her neck toward her cleavage. As I reach her, I take her by the hips and gently walk her backward to the bed 'till the back of her knees hit the mattress and she sits.

Josephine gives me a look of pure adoration. "Maceo," she whispers.

My name on her lips winds me up. I can't wait to make her scream it as she orgasms.

Sinking to my knees, I take her feet and unlace her work boots, pulling them off and peeling her socks away. I quickly unlace my own combat boots and kick them off before standing again. I cup her cheek and bend to take her lips. The kiss grows and she sucks on my bottom lip, causing a growl to grow in my chest. I break the kiss, and gently push her down and up the bed.

My hand reaches out for her jeans, undoing them. I hook my fingers into the loops of her pants and tug gently. She helps me by raising her hips, letting me pull them down over her slender legs. Staring at her sprawled out on the comforter, all soft skin and toned muscles, looking sexy as fuck, makes my heart beat like a humming-bird's wings.

I lean forward 'till I'm hovering above her body on my hands and knees, and float my lips down, under her ear, down her neck, and along her collarbone. Josephine's bright blue eyes roll back into her head as she gasps in anticipation.

"So fucking sweet," I purr against her skin. My tongue snakes out to taste the citrus flavor of her flesh. "Mmm."

My hand slips around her back to unclasp her bra, pulling it slowly away from her body, prolonging my agony, until her perky breasts are bare, revealing the most perfect rose buds. They pebble into hard diamonds under my gaze.

Unable to resist, I run my tongue around one hard pink nipple before sucking her breast into my mouth. My barbell piercing flicks around the tender peak while my hand fondles her other breast. Josephine moans and withers underneath me, making a groan rumble in my chest.

I release her breast from my mouth with a wet pop, trailing my tongue down her body to swirl and dip into her belly button. Josephine giggles as my beard rubs against her stomach. I chuckle about how much more I'm going to tickle her. I nip at each of her narrow hips, making her lift off the bed each time.

"Maceo," Josephine moans when I sink lower down her body.

I trail my lips down her thighs and over the apex of her sex. I inhale deeply, my blood rushing through my veins with expectation. God, she smells so fucking good, making my mouth water. I inhale again and commit her scent to memory, it's euphoric. My fingers slide inside her black panties and I slowly pull them down her smooth legs, her scent hitting me in the face, and working like an aphrodisiac.

When she's finally lying naked before me, I stand and allow my eyes to feast on her, memorizing every hill and valley along her slender frame. Her chest rises and falls quickly, telling me she's as worked up as I am. I push her knees apart with my calloused palms to see her in all her naked glory. Her hairless sex is glistening with arousal, ready for me to claim her.

Josephine bites her bottom lip as I get up close and personal with her perfect little pussy. Her hands starts to roam over her breasts, and she tugs at her hard nipple while the other hand slides down to her engorged clit, making tight, slow circles.

"Fuck, baby," I say as I watch her play with herself. She purrs and rotates her hips to seek her pleasure. My hand automatically gropes myself through my pants. My cock is already dripping, and my boxer-briefs are going to be as soaked as the panties I peeled off Josephine.

Deftly, I undo my belt and pants before shaking them down my legs and stepping out of them. Josephine is on her elbows as she watches me in anticipation. I tug my boxer-briefs off in one swift yank, making my dick hit me in the stomach. My pixie's eyes go wide as she takes in all of me. I pump my cock twice and my fingers run over my frenum barbell.

Not wasting any more time, I drop to my knees and grab her legs, pulling her toward the edge of the bed. I hike her legs over my shoulders, with me sandwiched in between. Josephine groans in approval as she lays her head back and closes her eyes. I run my tongue along the insides of each of her delicate thighs but avoid her hot center folds, teasing her with nips and licks to ramp her up.

"Josephine," I murmur, as I line my tongue up with her center and look up her body to her face. "Watch me as I pleasure you. I want to watch you come."

She whimpers, opening her eyes and looking down her body at me. My eyes stay locked on hers as my tongue snakes out and licks her from her entrance to the pearl of her clit. Her hips buck against my mouth and I chuckle before doing it again.

Damn, she tastes delicious, like fucking sugar and cream.

"So good," I mumble against her sex with pleasure, lapping at her addictive fluids.

Eager for more goodness, I point and dip my tongue into her entrance, savoring her sweet juices before bringing my tongue back to her clit, circling around it, but avoiding her triggering tip. She moans and twists her hips to direct me where she wants, but I pull back with a possessive growl before spreading her thighs apart farther to allow my wide frame to get in and feast on her.

If she wants more contact, I will definitely deliver. Nothing would bring me more pleasure.

My tongue flicks wildly at her sensitive clit, my tongue piercing hitting her receptive nub with more force, and she screams out in pleasure. Her slender hands tug on my hair, making me groan, causing vibrations against her pussy.

"My God, your tongue piercing," she moans raggedly.

I want to high-five myself for giving her what she desires.

Her legs squeeze against the outsides of my shoulders to try to block off the increased sensitivity. She thrashes her head when I take my hands and spread her legs all the way, preventing her from cutting me off. Part of me wants to remind her she wanted this, but there's no way I'm going to stop when she's close to peaking.

"Please," she whimpers. "It's so intense."

Fuck! I stop, unsure if she wants me to continue.

"Why did you stop? Don't stop!"

Okay, good, she wants more. I continue my relentless pace and her legs begin to quiver.

"Come," I rumble against her sex as I watch her, knowing she's close. My hot mouth surrounds her needy clit, my cheeks hallow as I suck her into my mouth. Her body practically levitates off the bed.

"Maceo!" she screams with bright eyes as her core pulses and her juices run down my beard. My lips smack noisily as her arousal continues to cover my face. Her orgasm goes on and on while I continue to flick my tongue against her, refusing to let it die quickly, making her lust thicken the air around me.

"Maceo, please," she moans. "I need you inside of me."

Fuck yes! She doesn't need to ask me twice.

Licking the rest of her off my lips, I crawl up the bed, snaking an arm around her waist to pull her further up on it with me.

Josephine grabs both sides of my face and draws me in for a kiss. I eagerly oblige, swiping my tongue into her mouth to tangle with hers. *Damn, she knows how to kiss me the way I like.*

We both groan as I settle myself between her slick thighs, her wet, molten core pulsing against my steel cock. My dick is fucking eager to be in her again, a snail trail runs down its length. I grab my shaft and run it up and down between her glossy, needy folds to coat myself with more of her precious lubrication. I tease her like this for several seconds before Josephine has had enough.

"Maceo, fuck me!" she growls.

Well, fuck me if those words aren't my undoing. My muscles tighten, my pulse races, and my cock jumps with need.

"As you wish, beautiful," I hum. I line myself up with her pussy and thrust myself inside.

We both moan in unison, before I slowly pull all the way out and slide back home to the root. I stay still for several moments, allowing her extremely tight center to loosen and relax around my girth.

Slowly, I rotate my hips as I pull out and back in again, and again...

Christ, this feels way too good. I'm a fucking lucky bastard because she's letting me do this to her body.

Needing her closer, I wrap my arm tighter around her body, bringing her flush against me. I kiss her languidly and swallow each of her mewls while my hips continue their torturously slow pace. I know she told me to fuck her, and I will, but right now I need to love and worship her body. She wraps her tiny legs around my waist, or as much as she can, seeing as I'm much larger than her.

It's not long before her breathing becomes labored and her legs are a trembling mess. Eager to lose myself in her while she lets go, I pick up the speed of my hips, grinding my pelvis against her clit. She meets me thrust for thrust. She's moaning and crying noisily, turning my libido into overdrive, and pushing my pace faster.

Shit, I like to fuck hard, but I've never met a woman who could keep up with me until now. Her whole body tenses up in my arms, like the most coiled spring, and I know I only have seconds.

"I. Love. You," I grunt between thrusts.

Josephine screams and detonates around me, wringing my cock hard, and giving me no choice but to let go. "Fuck, Josephine!" I continue to drive up into her, filling her up with my come to the point it leaks back out of her and onto us.

Spent, I fall onto her chest. I know my weight is probably crushing her, but she literally fucked me ragged. She wraps her slender arms around my neck and runs her hands into my hair, holding me to her. We remain connected for several minutes in a utopian state.

She takes this blissful moment to surprise me.

"I love you, too, Maceo."

Fuck, my cup runneth over.

My heart swells to twice it's size, knowing this beauty loves me back. I raise my face to hers, and tears prick my eyes. I honestly don't know what I've done in this life to deserve the woman in my arms, but fuck if I won't do everything in my power to keep her in them 'till my dying breath.

Speaking of swelling. No words need to be said between us. With a smile plastered on my face, I pull back and thrust forward into her for the second time today.

CHAPTER EIGHT
JOSEPHINE

Sated, I lie with my head on Maceo's expansive chest and lean over to kiss the spot where his heart is located. He hums when my lips make contact with his skin, and I smile. My body curls around his warm muscular form, and he traces small circles along my spine.

I in turn run my fingers over his tattoos. He has several—the Navy SEAL insignia is across his right pectoral, a conspiracy of ravens floats down his entire right arm to the cuff of his wrist, the Greek Titan Atlas holding the world on his shoulders dominates the left bicep, and several of Poseidon's tridents run up and down around his left forearm like a Greek band. I look up into his handsome face and it's like looking at a real-life demigod, a son of the sea.

My eyes return to his tattoos and my hand comes to the side of his torso where I see a long list of names in small script. I run a finger down the list and count sixteen names in all.

"They're the names of people I've served with who died in the line of duty," he answers my unasked question.

"There are a lot," I whisper, afraid this may be a very sensitive subject for him.

He squeezes my side gently. "That's how it is as a SEAL, and as a hired gun. You go in prepared, but sometimes fate has other ideas. This is how I grieve for them. Tattooing their names into my skin means I'll always have a piece of them that'll live on."

His words haunt me, and I stiffen. My mind races back to the horrors of his work.

Sensing my uneasiness, he rubs my back. "It's okay, baby."

My head is swimming with questions, but I decide to ask the one bothering me the most. "Did you get the men who took the little girl and her nanny?"

Maceo sighs heavily. I lift my head to gauge his reaction. Maceo looks like he's warring with himself. His dark eyes look down at me as if he's decided. "Yeah. We got them all, except the mastermind. But he will be dealt with."

It's not what I meant, and he knows it. "Did you kill them?"

Maceo's eyes flicker but never leave mine. "Yes."

I press for more. "Did you personally do it?"

Maceo's jaw ticks for a moment. "I was point. We went into the rat-infested house where the child was being held. I, *myself,* took out half a dozen assailants who got in our way before we were able to grab the little girl."

He pauses, as if debating how much to say. "When we rounded up the remainder who weren't killed, I went through and pulled aside the ones I could identify from the video—the ones who raped the nanny. Three out of the five were unlucky enough to have survived the siege. I fired a round into each of their dicks, giving them pain in the weapon they choose to hurt that poor woman. I finished them off with a bullet to the back of their skulls—the same way they did to the security team at the governor's mansion. A message needed to be sent. There were no survivors."

I'm paralyzed by his confession. Truly, I should be horrified with what he did to those men, but they got off easy. Maceo could have been more brutal with them and I'd still justify his actions.

I press my body into him. "Good." I'm glad they're dead and

unable to hurt someone else. And I'm glad the man I'm clinging to is the man who sent them all to hell.

Maceo lets out a breath of relief, reassured I won't freak out over this knowledge.

"I know you said you brought the little girl home, but *is* she okay?" I ask in a fearful whisper.

"She's a strong child. Physically she's fine, not a scratch on her, but emotionally—with what she witnessed—it will take time. Hope the governor gets her a good counselor to give her a fighting chance as an adult," he confides.

"Thank God she's okay, and thank God you were the one sent to save her," I say genuinely, as I snuggle more into his side.

Maceo's eyes grow darker, more menacing, as he looks at nothing in particular. "The threat is still out there. Esteban Moreno will make another move—anything to smuggle his drugs into this country and fill his pockets. It's only a matter of when. The fucker keeps coming back."

Worry grips me. "Who is Esteban Moreno?"

Maceo's arms constrict around me almost agonizingly. "Esteban Moreno is a kingpin of a Colombian drug cartel, and the most powerful drug trafficker in the world. He's a villain in his own country—kidnapping, raping, and murdering to control the Colombian people. The fucker has been a thorn in my side my entire life. And I will be the one to end him," he growls.

Jesus! Now I'm actually terrified. "Maceo?"

His dark eyes focus back on me and soften with worry. "Am I scaring you, *mi amor*?"

"Yes," I answer without hesitation.

Maceo rolls us till he's hovering over me, his eyes never breaking contact. "Don't be frightened, Pixie. I protect what I hold most dear and fight for what I love. You never have to fear me."

I shake my head because he's misunderstanding. "I'm not afraid of you, Maceo. I'm afraid *for* you. You seem hell-bent on taking this guy out. I don't want anything to happen to you," I express, cupping his chiseled face with one hand.

Maceo leans into my palm before taking my hand and bringing it to his lips for a kiss. "You don't need to worry about me, Pixie," he reassures me with tenderness in his eyes.

"Maceo, I *do* worry about you. Don't tell me not to worry when you admit a goal in your life is to take down a drug lord you have some vendetta against. It's a fucking *drug lord* for crying out loud, not someone selling crack on the corner," I spit, suddenly pissed at him.

Maceo grin's at me. "You're too fucking cute when you get all riled up."

"I mean it, Maceo. Don't you dare do anything stupid and get yourself killed, because I will never forgive you if I have to live without you." I try to push him off me. He doesn't budge an inch. He's ridiculously massive compared to my scrawny ass.

He chuckles and leans in to run his nose along my neck before bringing his lips to mine. "No worries, baby. I'll be completely methodical and calculated when I take him out, like I was with everyone before him. I won't be leaving your sassy ass until we're both very old and gray."

"Maceo—"

"Let's get cleaned and go out," he says, interrupting me and pulling me up with him. Maceo said this Esteban guy has been a torn in his side all his life, but what does he mean? I want to argue, to find out where this long-lasting feud stems from, but my stomach is growling and I hope 'go out' translates to 'get food.'

Maceo playfully slaps my bottom, making me giggle as we hurry into the bathroom. Once we enter, Maceo lets out a low whistle and spins around, taking in the oasis I created.

"Now, this is what I'm fucking talking about," he says appreciatively of the spa. "How many shower heads are in this thing?"

I turn the shower on to blast hot water. "One rain shower head and eight body spray jets. I couldn't afford much when I moved here because I was investing everything into my business. Hence, I'm in this tiny condo. But the one thing I insisted on was an updated kitchen and bathroom. I gutted, framed, dry walled, and installed everything myself. Anything to save a couple bucks without compromising on luxury."

Maceo smiles as he pulls me into the shower. "I love it when you talk shop."

We make quick work of getting clean, but as I get out to towel off, Maceo remains under the water, soaking in as much pleasure as he can.

"I can always update the presidential suite to something like this if you want. I can help you install everything if you don't want to invest any more money," I offer.

Maceo smiles to himself while still in the shower. "'Presidential suite.'" He chuckles.

"Let's stop by the build site after we're done here. I need to walk you through everything and see if it meets your standards. Punk has been very useful while you were away, calling the shots when I needed a decision to be made, but you should go over it yourself. The further we get in the build, the harder and more expensive it gets when you choose to make changes. I also need to grab my purse and car anyway," I suggest. "Oh, and no more spanking me in front of my crew. It was humiliating."

Maceo looks over at me, amused. "Did you enjoy it, Pixie?"

I blush. "That's beside the point. I don't want to make anyone uncomfortable on the job."

Maceo's eyes darken. "What? You mean make them jealous of what I have and they don't?"

I point a finger at him. "Now you're being possessive again. You need to cut it out. And no, I don't mean 'make them jealous.' I don't want anyone to feel like our displays of affection are offensive."

He gives me a deadpan look. "Baby, if I act possessive it's because I feel like another dude is challenging me."

"No one is challenging you, Maceo. It's in your head."

He snorts. "Clearly, you can't see how every male looks at you.

But I will do my best to refrain from paddling your glorious globe while you're at work. I'm gonna be honest though, you may need to remind me not to slap your ass in public. When it's there in front of me, my hand just wants to reach out and grab it or spank it. And I'm sorry for embarrassing you. I don't want you to think I don't respect you when I do. Clearly, I was out of line."

Good. I'm glad he's at least acknowledging he was wrong and apologizing.

Maceo's eyes roam over my body. "But back to my original question, did you enjoy me spanking you?"

"Yes. No. I mean, yes, but not in front of others." *Are we actually talking about this?*

Maceo grins mischievously. "Would you let me do it again?"

Embarrassed, I cross my arms to fold in on myself. "Is spanking a fetish of yours?"

Maceo's response is a wink.

Oh boy. I think back to how if felt when his hand slapped my ass. It hurt a little, but it did turn me on. "Fine, yes, I would let you do it again, but I'm not into S&M. I'll let you get a little rough, but I draw the line at welts."

Maceo turns off the shower and steps toward me in all his naked wet glory. Shakily, I hand him a towel, which he takes and starts drying off. "Hmm. I think our safe word should be 'ice cream.'"

I snort. "Seriously? 'Ice cream' is my safe word? Why don't we use the word 'stop?' It's pretty clear what I want when using it."

He shrugs. "It's both of ours', by the way. There may be things I don't want you to do to me. And what's wrong with 'ice cream?'"

I put my hands up in surrender. "'Ice cream' it is then." I really could care less. I'm just happy we have a safe word established.

Maceo finishes drying off. "I'll go along with you to the MC clubhouse and have the tour if you promise to take the weekend off. I know you've been working your crew 'round the clock and you'll be with them if they're on-site. I've been away from you for far too long, and I want some time alone."

I lean back on the counter and admire the giant raven wings tattooed on his back. "Yeah, I heard Jared working his magic on you. It's a deal, as long as I get to pick where we eat lunch."

"As long as it's not Brazilian, Colombian, or anything from South America." He cringes. "I can't stomach any more of it."

"Good 'ole American then, burger food truck by the university perhaps?" I suggest with hope.

Maceo smiles and bright white teeth take over his handsome face. "Perfect."

Thirty minutes later we're back on the build site with me towing Maceo by the hand, showing off everything we've completed. I'm not oblivious to the smiles and sniggers of my crew members behind my back as we pass. They're not very discreet with the winks and appreciative nods they give Maceo. A couple of them fist bump him as we walk by. I'd glare at all of them if I wasn't beyond blissed right now.

Jared is practically jumping when I give the all clear for the weekend off. He gets out the megaphone to inform everyone, and the relief is evident from the crew as they erupt in cheers.

Maceo's pleased with everything completed so far, and he's on board with what's in the works. We go into the trailer where I add the upgrades he wants done in his bathroom, as well as a security gate he wants installed at the approach where you enter into the grounds. Once it's done, I take a final walk around the site to check on everyone and answer questions for my team.

Saying goodbye for the day, I grab my bag, get in my car, and follow Maceo toward Colorado State University where a variety of food trucks are parked and feeding patrons. I pick my favorite burger truck and we both order the same mushroom and swiss Angus burger, with a side of fries for one and onion rings for the other.

I slap his hand away when he tries to pull out his wallet. As soon as my palm cracks against his hand, his pupils blow out with lust.

"Mmm. Again," he purrs at me with a devious smile.

Whoa! I choke down a laugh. "Maybe later. But seriously put your wallet away. This is my treat."

We find a shaded spot under some Gambel oaks and dive in to our flattop grilled burgers.

"So goooooood," Maceo says around his food.

I laugh as I snag another onion ring from him. "It's all the grease."

Maceo nods through a mouthful of food. "I definitely needed this. I know it was only three weeks, but I missed American food. We were limited in what we could eat on the mission. It's not like a group of foreigners can just walk into a restaurant without raising some red flags. We ate what we could get from the local food vendors, meaning a lot of local cuisine. It's great for a week, but you grow tired of it and lose your appetite. I probably lost ten pounds."

"Well, maybe after this we should get frozen custard. I ran ten miles this morning. I could use the extra calories, too."

Maceo's eyes grow bright as he looks at me. "I fucking love you," he mumbles around his food.

After, lunch we walk around downtown chatting, that's it. Getting to know each other like any normal couple would, the only difference between us and the general population is we do everything backward. First, we fuck. Second, we confess our love for each other. And third, we get to know each other. It's not for everybody and I definitely wouldn't recommend it to anyone else, but for us it worked out that way.

Toward afternoon, we finally grab the frozen custard I promised him. We find a park bench along the river and enjoy our desserts.

"Will you stay with me tonight?" I ask as I finish my cone.

Maceo grins. "I was planning on it," he admits with a wink. "But I need to stop by the MC rental and get some clothes. Gauge brought my bag back from the mission. I have nothing on me but the clothes on my back."

"I can go with you," I offer, smiling up at him from where I'm leaning on his shoulder. "That way if you wanted to pack a bigger bag, you could throw it in my car."

The grin on Maceo's face grows wider. "Oh, I would like that very much. I definitely need the alone time with you. I'd offer for you to stay at the rental but you would need to sleep on top of me in the twin bed, and we would have three other roommates, not to mention the potential of them bringing a bunny into the room."

"A bunny?" I question. "No offense, but you don't come across as a group of guys who would keep rodents as pets."

Maceo throws his head back and laughs. "A bunny is what we call the girls at the MC. They aren't members, they only comfort the guys."

I pull away with revulsion. "Seriously, Maceo? You better not have anything to do with those women or, God help me, you'll be stuck in your twin bed without me."

Maceo's body quakes with laughter. "God, I love how you take no shit."

I respond by punching him in the arm making him full-on belly laugh. "Okay, okay, I'm sorry. You have nothing to worry about with the MC bunnies. I've never been involved with any of them in any sexual way whatsoever. Those women can be pretty clingy, and I was a content bachelor till you ran into my life. They think because one of the guys had a night with them, suddenly he belongs to her and she can still hop around from member to member. It's fucked up. So, thanks, but no thanks. I got the best woman right here, chewing out my ass for shit I haven't even done."

I huff, eager to believe him, but refusing to give him an easy win.

Maceo wraps his arm around me and pulls me into his lap, rubbing his angular nose against mine. "I love seeing you get all jealous and territorial. My little kitten with her claws out. It's hot as fuck."

I warm a little, but I'm still not satisfied. There are eager-to-please women living in the house with him. "I'm not happy about this, Maceo. How would you feel if I were living with several horny men?"

Maceo scowls then sighs. "I get it, but Pixie, you have nothing to worry about. I'm not going anywhere. And the bunnies aren't bad people—okay most of them aren't bad people."

I roll my eyes, but he continues.

"Like Opal, she's probably the sweetest girl out of the bunnies. She takes care of the guys when they're sick, makes birthday cakes for us, washes laundry for the guys as she has time—she's a really nice person. She's sweet on Gauge and is exclusive with him, although he doesn't return the favor. Not everyone in life gets a fair shot. Opal ran away from home as a teenager because her mom's boyfriend kept sneaking into her room at night.

"We found her stripping in a club and could tell she was miserable. We asked if she wanted to come back to the club 'till she got on her feet. No one asked her to have sex for room and board and no one was allowed to touch her until she consented. As far as I know she's only been with Gauge," he says.

I stop and mull it over. It isn't fair of me to judge any of these women until I meet them. And I'm confident Maceo wouldn't lie to me. If they're nice people, who am I to look down my nose at them, or on how many people they sleep with?

"Come on. Follow me home." He helps me to my feet, and off we go.

The Mercy Ravens MC rental is small. *Understatement!* It is micro, making my tiny condo look like The Buckingham Palace. How the hell a dozen men and, *ahem*, a handful of bunnies live in this place has me scratching my head.

As we pull up to the ranch, I can see the detached two-car garage, open and overflowing with Maceo's crew. A fire pit has been set up in the driveway and is blazing away.

Men are laughing loudly, and several meagerly clothed women are hanging all over them. I'm barely out of the car before a beer is placed in my hand and I'm being pulled into the middle of a group of men. I have only seen them a handful of times dropping by the build site. Maceo is off to the side talking with two other men, but his eyes are focused on me as he listens and nods to his crew members.

"Ravens!" Maceo shouts at his brothers as he approaches me. "Behave yourselves around my pixie or I'll have your balls."

Most of the men nod or say "yes, sir," but not Punk. He comes up and throws his long-tatted arm around my shoulder haphazardly, with a cocky grin planted on his young but handsome face. "Ha! I knew it! I knew you always wanted my balls," he jokes.

Maceo shakes with laugher before slapping Punk's face playfully. "Sorry, but I can't take them if you don't have them," he jokes back, making everyone laugh, including Punk. "Watch my woman for me while I debrief with Chase and Gauge about the mission."

Punk nods, and Maceo gives me a wink before walking into the garage with Chase and Gauge.

Encircled by the MC, I decide to take in my surroundings while nursing my beer. Punk stays right by my side, similar to how he is on the build site, as the other members come over to our group to say hello. I suspect they're only being friendly to check out their president's woman.

Other than feeling multiple sets of eyes running up and down my body, making me lean into Punk for security, they all seem decent. Two of the guys are cracking me up as they debate over the official version of the poem *There Once Was a Man from Nantucket*. My vote is for the inappropriate version.

Everything seems fine until a pack of women saunters into the circle. A dark-haired vixen with russet skin loops her arm through two of the guys in the group. A tall redhead walks up to one of the burlier looking dudes, and he immediately puts his arm around her while she whispers in his ear. The redhead walks by, winking at me as she pulls along the MC member by his cut and into the house.

I try to act as nonchalant as I can, but I'm incredibly uneasy. It escalates when I see a pink-haired statuesque woman with boobs that defy gravity staring me down with cold brown eyes. I look away from her, and a blonde bombshell with rainbow streaks in her hair comes right up to me.

"Hi, you must be Jo. I'm Opal," she says sweetly, and holds out her hand to me.

Oh, she's cute! I smile at her and shake her hand. "Nice to meet you, Opal. Maceo told me you're the nurse around here."

Opal smiles brightly. "Well, someone has to take care of them. You know, man-flu is no joke," she giggles.

"It's a legit cold, Opal!" one of the members argues, which makes us both laugh.

Opal looks at the beer in my hand. "Ugh, gross!" She pulls the bottle from me and pushes it onto Punk. "Let's get you a real drink." She grabs my hand and pulls me toward the house.

In the small yellow kitchen, Opal makes us Moscow Mules. It's a giant leap up from the crap beer. She hands me my drink and raises hers to clink with mine. "Cheers."

"Mmm. I've always liked these," I say, and take another sip.

"Me too!" she says with a laugh.

I look at her curiously. She's gorgeous, but young. I have a sudden urge to protect her. "Are you sure you're old enough to serve me?"

Opal gives me a sheepish grin. "I realize I don't look as old as I am, but I'm twenty-two. Legal enough to serve alcohol, and legal enough to be here."

I raise an eyebrow. "You sure you want to be here?"

"The club took me in and protects me. I can't imagine being anywhere else," she admits.

My heart goes out to her. "Don't settle. You owe it to yourself to reach for the stars." She smiles brightly and I smile back at her.

"So how are things going with you and Atlas? I mean, you're here, so I'm assuming things are better than when he and the guys were on mission. It was not fun around here by the end of that first week. I thought Punk was going to have a stroke. He was totally worried he messed things up between you with his big mouth. And Chase wasn't much better—trying to do God knows what with his computers to help Atlas out. The whole club was on edge."

I nod, remembering that night all too well. "Things are good between us. We needed to have an honest conversation with each other about what we expect going forward."

Opal's pretty face lights up. "I'm relieved to hear it. Honestly, all the members seemed happy to see you show up with Atlas tonight. No offense, but he's kind of an asshole when he's not having sex regularly."

I burst out laughing because I can totally see it. The two of us are in stitches when the pink-haired girl and the dark-haired vixen walk into the kitchen.

"What's so funny?" the pink-haired woman asks in a snide tone, twirling a lock of hair between her manicured fingers.

"Nothing," Opal says quickly with a smile over the brim of her cup, looking at me. "Jo, this is Candy and Ebony. Red is the other girl here, but she's, ya know, busy."

Yeah, I know what 'busy' means. I look over at the other two girls.

"Hi." It's all I say because I can't help but feel hostility rolling off of Candy. Ebony seems playful, she sings along to the music blaring outside. I look between all three. "So, your club names are in reference to your hair color?" I guess.

"Yes," Opal says excitedly. "Well, sort of. Red was actually nicknamed Big Red, but she didn't really like it. Anyone who refers to her as Big Red ends up getting the tip of their dick flicked, and not in a pleasant way either."

I laugh again. Ebony walks over to me, looking in my cup. "What are you guys drinking?"

"Moscow Mules," Opal chirps. "You want one?"

Ebony's face lights up. "Hell yeah!"

"Have the rest of mine. I have to drive back home," I say placing the cup in her hand.

"Sweet," Ebony says, before throwing back the last half of my drink.

"Oh, you're not staying?" Candy asks sweetly, hiding a sneer.

Obviously, this woman doesn't like me or my presence here. Maceo told me I have nothing to worry about when it comes to the MC bunnies, but I get the sense Candy feels some sort of ownership over the men. Does her ownership extend to Maceo himself?

"Nope," I say leaning against the counter to make it appear like I'm more relaxed than I really am. "Maceo and I are spending the weekend at my place to, ya know, *catch up* on lost time." I watch her to see if I can gage her reaction. By the way Candy's eyes narrow and her hands fist, I would say she definitely feels some sense of possession over Maceo.

"Oh, that sounds romantic," Opal's voice swoons. "I wish I could have a getaway spot with Gauge. I feel like we're constantly being rushed to finish before one of the other guys comes into the room."

Ebony rolls her eyes. "How many times do I need to tell you? If you would let the other guys watch, or be in the room while you fuck, you wouldn't have to rush. Hell, you should try a threesome or foursome with his roommates, they're fucking amazing."

Opal wrinkles her nose. "I'd rather not. Gauge would never allow it. I'll stick with my man." She's too innocent for all of this.

"Oh, please," Candy patronizes. "You act like you're his old lady. He doesn't want a fucking commitment with you. The sooner you jump on one of the other guys, the sooner you'll get over it."

The kitchen falls silent. Opal's face crumbles, and Ebony and I stare at Candy in shock.

"That was fucking cold and uncalled for," I say in a menacing tone. Opal is clearly intimidated by this bitch. If she can't defend herself, I sure as hell will—hell, I'm not afraid of anyone.

Candy glowers at me. "It's the fucking truth, and she needs to hear it. He sure as hell hasn't stopped getting his dick wet—with Red or me or any number of the bar bitches he picks up when he's out. She's a fucking bunny. She needs to stop saving the goods for only one guy and start spreading the love, or she's out."

I straighten myself the way I always do when I'm challenged.

"Opal doesn't have to spread anything for anyone if she doesn't want to. From what Maceo told me, you guys choose who you want to have sex with, when, and how much. He doesn't fucking care if you do or don't have sex with anyone. It's not a requirement to be here at the club. No one here forces any of you to do shit. So stop pressuring her to do stuff she's not comfortable with."

"What the hell is with this *Maceo* shit? His name is Atlas. And a bunny isn't monogamous. We fuck the lot. If she isn't doing it, she's not a bunny. What the fuck is she good for?" Candy snaps back, getting up in my face.

"You're right, she's not a bunny. She's a Mercy Raven MC *woman* who everyone loves. What she provides to all of them, they appreciate, and she doesn't need to spread her legs to earn it. This twisted idea you have in your head about having to sleep with them is simply not accurate of what the crew expects from you. Lay the fuck off of Opal," I seethe.

"What the hell do you know about any of us, or this club? What? You think because you gave Atlas what you have between *your* legs that you suddenly know him and what his club represents? You don't know shit," she shouts, jabbing her finger into my chest.

I smirk. I'm going to hit far below the belt, making Candy's head spin. "At least I know he wants what's between my legs."

"Daaaaaamn!" Ebony crows with a grin, raising her cup up high. "This girl came to dance!"

Candy looks like she's ready to combust before an evil glint shines in her brown eyes. "I said I'm a MC bunny. I've serviced *all* of the Mercy Ravens MC."

I snort at her absurdity. "I know for a fact you've never serviced Maceo. He told me as much."

Her smile is vile. "Then he lied to you."

Now this woman is being a straight up cunt. I won't stand by and have her insult my man by calling him a liar. *Enough of this shit.* "Okay, let's go confront Maceo together. Let's hear it from the club's president."

The panic in Candy is subtle, but it's there. She's not use to women challenging her back. "Atlas is busy with Gauge and Chase going over the last mission. He's not going to be happy if we interrupt him."

I smile, because I'm kind of a vindictive bitch that way. "I guarantee he will not be upset with the intrusion because he's *always* happy to see me. Come on, let's go ask. It will take one minute, tops. It's a yes or no question." I coax with my hand, waving at her to follow me outside to the garage.

Candy sneers at me, clearly heated for me calling her out on her shit. "You might be willing to piss off Atlas when he's working, but I know enough not to bother him."

"Okay, fair enough. How about we settle it another way?" I push down the maniacal laugh bubbling in my chest. "How big is his dick?"

Opal chokes on her drink. Ebony is losing her shit behind me.

I have no intention of actually divulging this information to Candy and the other girls, but I do want to make Candy squirm.

Candy takes a moment to collect herself and shrugs. "It's big, of course."

Ebony rolls her dark eyes before looking over at me. "The guys brag about their dicks all the time. Her guess is from what she's picked up in conversation, and not what she's seen firsthand."

Candy shoots Ebony a disgruntled look that screams 'shut the fuck up.'

"Okay, different question. What does he have tattooed along the inside of his left thigh?" There's nothing tattooed there, but she doesn't know that.

"Um, I only focus on his dick. I guess I never paid close attention," she says, flustered.

"What about which penis piercing? Prince Albert or Apadravya?" I'm not actually revealing anything personal, but none of the girls realize this. The answer is 'neither' because it's a frenum piercing. Doesn't matter if she jacked him off, sucked him off, or fucked him, she would know by feel alone.

"Uh, it's, it's the PA," she guesses in a stutter.

"Neither! But for argument sake, what color is his penis when he's hard?"

Opal looks between us like a deer in headlights and Ebony bounces in place like she has a bet on the fight.

Candy looks at me, confused. "It's red?"

"Wrong!" I say. I get up in her face and smile. "It's every shade of my lipstick."

Opal squeaks and covers her mouth, and Ebony slides to the floor, cackling.

"You're a fucking liar, Candy. The president isn't going to be happy when he hears you're spreading lies about him," I threaten.

Candy huffs and hustles past us, slamming the front door on her way out to the party. The three of us start cracking up.

"Damn, girl! You're my new favorite person. That bitch has been overdue for being put in her place," Ebony cheers.

Opal looks gleeful. "I can't believe you did that."

I shrug. "She had it coming when she attacked you. She lied about Maceo to me. She could easily be lying about Gauge to you." I don't say any more because I don't want to upset her. I don't want to give her false hope, but she should hear it from Gauge himself.

A throat clears behind me and I turn to see Maceo leaning against the doorjamb to a side door I hadn't noticed before. He's grinning from ear to ear.

"You heard all that, didn't you?" I ask, already knowing he did. He's puffing out his chest like a proud peacock.

"Atlas, you got one badass bitch," Ebony clucks.

Maceo saunters into the tiny kitchen to wrap his arms around me. "I most certainly do."

CHAPTER NINE
MACEO

M y cock has never been more aroused in my life. I watched the fight go down between my pixie and Candy. I just told Josephine about the bunnies and that she had nothing to fear, but I still worried she'd be insecure around them.

Understandably, most women would be. But I'm not into insecure women. Jealous women, yes. But insecure women, definitely not. If Josephine were to show insecurity, I would take her to bed until I stripped those insecurities away.

Much to my pleasure, Josephine took what I said to heart and she was interacting with Opal. I watched them through the kitchen window laughing over a drink, and I smiled. I wasn't too concerned until I noticed Candy and Ebony come in.

Worried, I walked to the screen door off the side to see what was going on. Josephine graciously offered her drink to Ebony, which pleased me. Ebony and Opal are great girls, super nice. I was happy when I saw Josephine giving them a chance to prove how sweet and harmless they truly are. But all hell broke loose when Candy started ripping into Opal.

Ready to get involved, I stopped when Josephine took the reins. Here my girl was, defending Gauge's girl after just meeting her. With a proud heart, I smiled because she believed me when I talked about Opal. My pixie was like me, defending those who couldn't defend themselves.

Everything was good until I heard Candy telling Josephine she serviced *me* all the time.

Fucking bitch! Who the fuck does she think she is?

I know Josephine believed me when I said they were no threat, but I didn't want to have the theory tested so soon. I just got back on Josephine's good side, and if Candy fucked this up for me, so help me God, I would be throwing her out on her sorry ass by her pink hair.

My heart doubled in size for the second time today when I watched my girl shut Candy down, not only defending me, but the whole MC. *God, I love this woman.*

I nearly gave myself whiplash when I heard Josephine ask Candy to prove it by asking her how big my dick was. My girl wasn't pulling *any* punches tonight. She was calling Candy out on her shit and doing it in front of the other bunnies.

Damn, this woman was meant for me.

But the sucker punch was when Josephine said my dick was colored with all the shades of her lipstick. I nearly clapped my hands in applause. Fuck, my girl was claiming me right there, in brazen detail. Goddamn if I didn't love her possessiveness. Made me feel like my feeling of ownership over her wasn't totally out of line.

After Candy runs off sulking, I decide to make my presence known. I open the screen door and leer at my overprotective woman. I lick my lips, taking her in. When we get back to her place, I'm going to reward her devotion by shoving my head in between her thighs and staying there all night long.

"You heard all that, didn't you?" She folds her arms over her small chest, as if daring me to question her.

Tickled pink, I break out into a smile from ear to ear. It wouldn't matter what I thought. She did what she believed she needed to do and fuck me if it wasn't hot as sin.

I kiss the crown of her head. "I'm done talking with the guys. Why don't I grab my bag? I'll be right out."

Quickly, I throw a bag together, packing way more than a weekend's worth of clothing. I fully intend on staying with her well after the weekend. I grab my toiletries from the bathroom and throw them in my bag too.

In the kitchen, I find my pixie still giggling with the two bunnies. I hold out my hand and she takes it, waving goodbye to the girls.

Outside, I nod goodnight to my crew as I walk Josephine back to her car. I open the back door, throw my bag in, and open my girl's door and help her inside.

After I have her buckled in, I bend down and give her a chaste kiss. "Race you home, Pixie."

Josephine gives me a mischievous smirk and starts her car. "Last one home has to pick up Hades' poop," she calls as she peels off.

Oh, it's on. I love how competitive my woman is—makes for exciting foreplay.

Pumped, I race to my bike and gun it. There's no way I can lose this bet. I've seen the size of her dog, and I'm guessing his turds are the size of my damn forearms. Josephine is relatively new here, I'm willing to bet she's unaware of the back roads she could take to shorten her commute. I gamble on it and head that way to her place, praying I get there first.

I roll up as she's pulling in behind me. "Oh, come on!" she gripes from inside her car.

"Sorry not sorry, baby." I laugh and get off my bike.

She's grumbling as she climbs out, but she's laughing as well. I love how I can mess around with her and she gives it right back to me. Gauge was right. I needed a woman like her to challenge me.

I pull my bag from her car and heft it over my shoulder, and I follow her to the condo. Hades is howling as Josephine works to unlock the door.

"Hey, buddy. Mommy missed you, yes I did. Look who came back. Yeah, Maceo is going to stay with us for a while, okay? Good boy," she says and grabs his leash hanging on the hook by the door, attaching it to him. "Let go take care of your business."

I throw my bag on the floor by the door before locking up and following her outside. I don't want to be away from her for any length of time.

We walk hand in hand with Hades leading us. I swear he stops at every tree, every leaf, every noise—all must be investigated. I'm starting to like this dog more and more. He's attuned to his surroundings, and his devotion to my pixie makes me feel good she has him.

As suspected, Hades's turds are no joke. A grown man couldn't lay anything that large. "What the hell are you feeding him?" I ask, pointing at the waste bag.

She laughs as she throws the bag out in a nearby waste disposal. "Impressive, isn't it?"

We're both laughing as we make our way back to her place when Hades suddenly freezes on the walk, looking up at the house. He stands at attention, hackles up, baring his teeth. We both jump when he starts barking frantically and pulls against the leash. I try to grab the leash from Josephine before Hades rips her hand off, but he breaks loose and charges to the front door, jumping against it and snarling.

I bend down and quickly pull my Glock 19 from my ankle holster before turning back to Josephine. "Go back to the car, Pixie. Lock yourself in. Don't come out or let anyone in until I say it's okay. You got it?"

Josephine's eyes swivel between me and her dog. "What's going on?"

"I don't know, baby. I'm going to find out," I say, rubbing her arm.

"But you and Hades—" she starts.

"Pixie," I say, grabbing her arm and shaking her a little. "Go."

Josephine's eyes are blown wide with fear, and I'm afraid I'm going to have to manhandle her into the car myself. Thankfully, she runs to the vehicle and locks herself in.

With her secure, I make my way to the door with my gun

ready. Hades is barking and scratching at it like rabid animal. The doorjamb appears to have been tampered with—judging by the large gouges of wood taken out along the knob. "Easy, boy," I say to Hades, and I move my hand to the handle. To my utter horror, the door swings open as I turn the knob. I know I locked this door when we left for our walk. Someone definitely has forced their way in.

Hades rushes inside and straight to the bedroom, acting like he did at the front door. I aim at the door as I approach it. I count to three and kick the door in, with Hades on my heels. The sliding door to her deck is wide open. *Fuck.*

I rush out to the yard and catch a glimpse of someone jumping the fence. Charging ahead, I hurdle it and take pursuit. Hades barks behind me, close to my heels. *Holy shit, he cleared the fucking fence.* The thing had to be at least six feet tall.

I try to make out details of the assailant, but it's dark, and he has a head start. I follow him up the ridge where I see him jump into a car and take off without headlights. It's impossible to catch a glimpse of the license plate. All I know is it's a newer, dark-colored sedan, but not enough details to determine make and model.

Coming to a stop, I gasp in and out as my lungs adjust back to normal. Hades continues to run down the road after the car.

I whistle for him, and he comes right back to me. Thank God, because I have no more sprint left in me to chase after a dog. Hades pads up to me, his gold eyes nearly glowing in the dark. He leans his big head into my open hand. I rub him behind his ears.

"*Buen perro.* Let's go back to *mamá.*"

I jog back to the front of the condo with Hades at my hip. Josephine is still locked in her car, staring up the front door, when I tap on her window. She screams and grabs at her chest before unlocking the car.

I cradle her in my arms and kiss her head, comforting her, while Hades jumps up on us and licks at her face. "It's okay, baby. I'm sorry I scared you. The guy is gone, but I want us to go inside and look around to see if anything was stolen. Then we're going to call the police to report the break-in."

"O-okay," she stutters.

As we walk through her apartment, we start with the front, checking the living room and kitchen. Her laptop, tablet, and all her other expensive devices were still where she left them. But she stops in front of her laptop, cocking her head.

"What is it?" I ask.

She looks up me. "Did you touch my laptop when I was in the car?"

I shake my head. "No. Why?"

"It's open. I always fold the screen down when I'm not using it." She reaches out to it.

"Don't touch it. If someone tried to get into it, they may have left prints," I say, halting her hovering hand. "Do you keep it locked?"

"Yes. I have a very complex password, and I change it regularly."

I nod in approval. "Is there anything on it someone would want to access?"

She shakes her head no. "Everything, all my work, bank accounts, spreadsheets are backed up on a hard drive. I don't store anything on the laptop." She turns to the kitchen and pulls a decorative flower magnet from the fridge, opening it to reveal her mini drive.

My eyebrows go up. She's very protective with her laptop's contents. I would be too, if someone had stolen all my work. "Let's check the rest of the place."

Behind the kitchen is the laundry room followed by a powder room. All is good.

As we make our way to the end of the hall where her bedroom is, she gasps and covers her mouth.

"I did that," I admit. "I'll fix it later."

We enter the bedroom and we both start to panic. All the drawers in the nightstands and the dresser are open. The lights are on in her bathroom and her walk-in closet. Josephine freezes and looks around the room, taking it all in. Her shoulders move up and down with silent sobs before I hear her cry.

I pull her into my arms. "Shh. It's okay. I'm here," I coo into her sandy hair. "I don't want you to touch anything, but I want you to look and see if anything is missing." She nods and I let her go.

Josephine starts in the bathroom and closet. Nothing appears to be missing, but she notices the cap is off of her perfume and a box of photos she keeps on the top shelf is on the floor. I'm starting to see she's incredibly anal about where her things belong and the state she leaves them in.

In the bedroom she peers into her nightstands' drawers—again, nothing is missing. At the dresser she pauses and starts to cry again.

"My underwear...some are missing, I think," she says through her sobs.

Motherfucker! Some sick pervert was in my woman's room and fucking swiped her damn panties. *Enough of this shit.*

I pull out my phone and dial 911. I give our location and explain the situation. I make a second call to Chase. He answers on the first ring. "Prez?"

"I need a security system installed in Josephine's condo. I also want cameras installed at all the entrances. I want motion sensor lights everywhere. I need a new front door, preferably steel with several deadbolts. And send two men to watch over her place tonight," I order.

I hear him starting up his computers. "Okay, but what the fuck is going on?"

I explain what occurred this evening at the condo, and the guy who got away with her lingerie.

"Shit," Chase says angrily. "That's fucked up. How's Jo doing?"

I look over at my woman, sitting on the floor with her knees to her chest, crying with her head buried in her arms. "How do you think?"

"I'll be over with a team shortly. The door may have to wait till morning, but if one of our men is out front and one is in the back, we should be okay." He hangs up and I go to my pixie and pull her to her feet, taking her into the living room to wait for the police.

For nearly two hours, the police comb through the crime scene, dusting for prints, taking pictures, and interviewing Josephine and I. I'm grateful the police were all guys I know and worked with in the past on various missions or from my SEAL days. Luke Quire, a good friend of the MC, is lead detective on this case and he's taking it very seriously, as he should.

He approaches me after talking to his guys. "Atlas, this doesn't look good. This wasn't some home robbery. Hell, I don't even think it was some panty snatcher," he says in a low whisper.

I know there's more to it, but I want him to confirm my thoughts. "Go on," I say.

He looks over his shoulder at my woman before turning to me. "The guy was digging, Atlas. He tried hacking into her computer. Luckily, it shut down after too many attempts. He snagged over half her underwear, the lingerie from what Jo said. He was browsing through her personal photos. God only knows what he may have taken from the box.

"But the thing that gets under my skin was the perfume cap being off the bottle. He was *sniffing* her perfume, like he was trying to smell *her*. Whoever he is, he not only interested in her sexy lingerie. He wants parts of her. Personal photos, panties, private information locked away on her computer, even her fucking scent," he says, grimacing.

Anger rolls through me and I close my eyes to control it. I had my suspicions, but Luke brought it all home. My pixie is being *stalked*.

Luke presses for more info. "Has she mentioned anything happening like this before, or seeing someone more often than what seems normal?"

I shake my head. "Not that I'm aware of."

We both walk over to where Josephine is sitting, huddled in the corner of the couch. I walk behind her and put my hands on her shoulders for comfort while Luke sits next to her.

"Jo, can you tell me if anything like this has happened before?"

She shakes her head. "No. Never."

"Have you noticed anything odd moved around in your apartment, or deliveries you never ordered? Have you noticed seeing a person more often than coincidence?" he asks.

Again, she shakes her head. "I'm fairly anal retentive. Everything in my house has a place and I have a routine by putting things away immediately."

She points to a vase of roses on the kitchen island. "The only deliveries I've received that I haven't ordered myself are flowers every Friday morning from Lorenzo. It started nine months ago after I finished a build for him. At first, when he sent them there was a card asking me out, and I refused every time, but now he keeps sending them with a card wishing me a beautiful week—which is code for him asking me out, but not having to deal with my rejection."

"Lorenzo?" Luke asks.

"Bianchi," I finish with a snarl. Thankfully, Josephine doesn't flinch by how I know this.

Luke's eyes go wide. "Lorenzo Bianchi, the Italian mob boss?"

My pixie bobs her head and sighs. "Yep. But I wouldn't waste your time on him. He's not the kind of guy to break into a woman's home and run off. It's not his style. He would break in and be in my bed waiting for me, but not running."

My eyes roll skyward at the image she described. "She's right. It's not him," I grimace. He wasn't the perp, but I'm definitely going to pay him a little visit over this business of sending my woman flowers. That shit is going to end.

Luke pulls out his notebook from his coat pocket. "Who have your past clients been in the last year?"

Josephine gives him the names and numbers of her clients. On the list are some shady people. Slumlords, mafia, drug dealers, and a fucking cult. Explains why she never bat an eye when I said I was president of a motorcycle club. She had already been dealing with the worst of the worst. Most people would decline immediately if they thought our club was a gang, but she was building her company from the ground up, meaning she was not in a position to be picky.

Luke's eyes kept getting bigger and bigger the longer the suspect list became.

"You're wasting your time with that list," I tell him.

"How so?" he questions.

"She hasn't had any issues with her past clients—indirectly or directly. This has to be something more current, someone who recently came into the picture."

"Like who?" she asks with a quizzical look.

I sigh. "You've hired a second crew to help on the build. They aren't people you know, like the crew you've been working with for the past year. You've been working them real hard and they've been around you a lot. Maybe, tonight being the first night off since starting the build, maybe one of them took a shine to you and followed you back here. Maybe they've been waiting for you and Hades to get out of the house, giving them an opportunity to break in."

Josephine's mouth falls open. "I'm good to all of my crews. I may have been working them hard the last two weeks, but everyone knows I have an open-door policy and if they have a gripe, they can come straight to me. Not one has approached me on this project, and people have on past ones."

"I didn't say any of them might have a vendetta against you, but maybe one formed an unhealthy crush or obsession," I counter.

Josephine shivers while Luke nods his head in agreement. "It would explain why they haven't tried anything 'till now," Luke says before handing Josephine the notepad. "Can you write down the names and numbers of all your crew members, new and old?"

Josephine shakes her head vigorously. "I'm not getting Jared or my crew involved with this. I don't believe it's any of them, new or old. I finally got the manpower I need for my projects. I don't want to piss any of them off to the point they choose to leave for another job," she says stubbornly.

I rub her shoulders gently. "Luke is tactful and I'm sure your crew will want to help out in any way they can," I say in the most reassuring voice I can muster.

Her fear of upsetting her crew to the point of negatively impacting her company is justifiable, but at the end of the day her safety is in jeopardy and I'm not willing to compromise.

With a huff she takes the notepad and goes through her phone, writing down every crew member's name, number, position, and how long they have been working with her.

"Anyone else you can think of who may have an unhealthy attachment to you?" Luke asks Josephine.

My teeth grind together because I know I'm going to set Josephine off. "Yeah, one more. Her ex-boyfriend, Jacob Klein. She hadn't talked to him for over a year until two weeks ago. He showed up today on my property," I say with spite.

Josephine's head swivels around on me. "I called him, Maceo!" she half yells, half growls, before turning back to Luke. "Jacob reached out via text and offered to give me my old contacts back if I helped with a project in Denver. I agreed and asked him for help in return as a consultant on my project. I did my week on his job and he showed up today to start helping on mine. He left as soon as Maceo made it clear he didn't want him there. He's no longer on the project."

"Did things end amicably between you two?" Luke presses.

"Well, no. He hijacked my work and I left him over a year ago. He wasn't pleased when I told him it wasn't going to work out," she admits.

Luke raises his eyebrows at me. I know the look. He's thinking the same way I am. "His rental is a black BMW 5 Series Sedan. The prick is probably still in town. I would interrogate him first."

Luke nods before looking back at Josephine. "Do you know if he was staying in town for a while?"

Josephine sighs. "Jacob is a prick, but this seems...extreme. He invited me to visit him at his hotel tonight. I declined and told him I was not interested and never would be. I assume he would have headed out to Denver to check on his other project instead of sticking around. But I know he was planning on staying at the Hilton in town."

I snarl. "Fucking loafer shoe bastard." Who the hell does he think he is? Inviting my woman to his fucking hotel room? If I see the pencil dick again, I'll strangle his ass.

"How did he seem after you turned him down today?" Luke questions.

Josephine's head falls into her hands. "Angry," she murmurs. "He's not used to rejection. Pretty much, if he wants it, he gets it or takes it."

Luke closes his notebook and gives Josephine's arm a gentle squeeze. "We're going to look into all of this. In the meantime, you should stay somewhere else."

Josephine, stubborn as ever, shakes her head. "I'm not going to be run out of my own home. Where the hell would I go with Hades?"

"You'd stay with me at the club. It's the best place for you. All my men are there to protect you. It's the perfect solution," I say, running my hand over her hair.

Josephine's purses her lips before she turns to glare at me. "I'm not staying anywhere near that bitch, Candy! I can't trust myself not to let Hades loose on her. Plus, Hades hates men. Hence, why he's locked away in the laundry room right now, barking at all these strange guys here," she chides.

My jaw clenches in frustration. I don't know why she's riding my ass right now when I'm trying to reason with her. "Pixie, we're staying at the rental, and we're implementing some serious changes."

She pushes her elfin chin out at me. "Yeah, like what?"

My hand twitches to spank her ass for her sassy attitude. "One of my men will be with you at all times. If I'm not with you, one of them is. And when I mean all times, I mean *all times.* Your morning run will no longer be only you and Hades. Working on the site, you will have a man with you. At night there will be a man outside your door, as well as one in front of the condo, and one in the backyard. Grocery store, bank, gas station, doctor appointments, client appointments, everywhere and all the above, you will be escorted by at least one member. Until we get this settled, you are watched. Do I make myself clear?"

Josephine's scowling at me. Her glare could put any of my men to shame with how deadly it is. She can't say no. I'm the security expert, for fuck's sake, and know far more on the topic.

Annoyed with her for not answering me, I ask again, "Do I make myself clear, Josephine?"

"Yes, *Atlas*," she spits back.

Oh, she's definitely going to get her ass smacked now for calling me by my club name.

"Good," I say firmly. "But tonight, we're not going to get any rest here. After the police are finished, which may take another hour, my men are coming in to install the security and surveillance equipment. And a new front door. I'll ask Chase to add a new bedroom door to the list, too. We're going to pack up your stuff and you and Hades are coming back to the MC rental for the night. I'll kick the other guys out of the room if you want."

Her safety is my number one concern and I will take all the necessary precautions. Speaking of precautions. "Did you unlist your address and make your social media accounts private, like I asked?"

She glowers at me. "Yes, I did, like the good little girl I am. Am I allowed to pack my own shit or are you going to dictate how that's going to go down too?" she snaps.

Before I can respond, she's off the couch, and storming past the cops to get to her bedroom. I watch her retreat and shake my head. Her sass is going to get her two slaps on the ass tonight.

"You got yourself a real firecracker, Atlas," Luke says, grinning. "But seriously, how did you land her? She's drop-dead gorgeous."

"Watch it, fucker. She's mine," I growl.

Luke chuckles and shakes his head. "You're a lucky *sonofabitch*. But I need to ask you something and I didn't want to do it in front of your girl. She's upset enough right now. We've gone over who may have done this and who she knows, but what about the people you know?"

My job alone puts me on a lot of people's lists. If I were to make a perp list for Luke it would trump the one Josephine gave him. I groan aloud. Luke better have another notepad on hand because I'm about to fill it up.

Luke hands me his notepad. "Right, how about you narrow your mental list to your top five."

Never one to skimp, I give him my top ten. Esteban Moreno leading the pack.

CHAPTER TEN
MACEO

"Holy shit! What the fuck is that thing?" Triple yelps when Josephine and I walk in the door with a snarling Hades. Ebony, who's sitting on his lap, takes off into the kitchen screaming something about a Chupacabra. Hades starts pulling against his harness and growling through his muzzle, trying to heave his way toward Triple.

"Hades, NO!" Josephine shouts and yanks him back. He comes back to her obediently, but continues to growl, staring down Triple like a giant rawhide.

"Play it cool. Talk to him like a human and you'll all be good," I say confidently.

"You want me to act cool when that thing wants to go for my jugular? Fuck that!" Triple shouts. This sends Hades into another snarling fit right as Punk and Gauge enter the living room, making them jump back when they see Josephine's beast.

I get down on all fours in front of him. "Hades, you're scaring my men. You've gotta cool it, buddy. We need to stay here tonight and will be back home tomorrow. I know you're scared of these guys, but trust me when I tell you they're more scared of you," I say, in as calm a voice as I can. It's kind of hard when I'm shout-talking over his growls. He settles some, but positions himself in front of Josephine, not trusting anyone to come near her. *Good boy.*

"I'm going to take off your muzzle now if you promise to stay a good boy," I tell him. He stops growling and sits back on his haunches, waiting.

"Dude, Atlas, don't do it. The dog is looking at me like I'm dinner," Triple pleads.

"Agreed. It's not a good idea," Gauge says, holding onto Punk like a human shield.

Josephine rolls her eyes. "You guys are such babies."

"Are not!" Punk defends. "Only concerned citizens."

Again, my woman rolls her eyes. "Hades was an abused animal used for dog fighting before I rescued him. I'm sorry if he doesn't like any of you, but it probably has more to do with the fact that you're men. You need to earn his respect and trust."

I go to take off his muzzle and all three of my men protest in panic. "You guys," I shout over them. "This is happening. The dog doesn't deserve to be muzzled in the house. Grow a pair, why don't you."

This time, I remove the muzzle and all my men suck in air. With the muzzle gone, Hades immediately starts to lick my face. "I know. I don't like you wearing it either," I say, petting him.

Chase walks in through the front door, back from setting up the team over at the condo, and notices Hades. He gives a low whistle which catches Hades's attention. "Now he's a big dog," he says in an appreciative voice before getting down low. Chase lets Hades sniff his hand before running it down his dark coat. "You sure are a handsome fella."

Hades woofs in approval and tries to crawl into Chase's lap, knocking him flat on his back. Chase laughs as Hades lies across him, lapping at his face.

"You see," I say, waving my hand at Hades to my men. "You be good to him and he'll be good to you. Now, hand over your tough-guy cards to Josephine."

Josephine and Chase laugh while the other three grumble. Peeved, Gauge backhands me in the chest. Hades lifts his head and growls at him, making Gauge put his hands up in surrender. "Good boy," I say to my new favorite dog.

Josephine yawns. "Well, this has been fun boys, but Hades and I need our beauty sleep." I escort her to the bedroom and point out my lower bunk.

"I'm going to go over everything with the guys first. I'll be in with you after." I lean in to kiss her soft lips. She kisses me back but not as enthusiastically as I would like. She's still salty with me for calling all the shots right now. I know it's hard for someone as independent as her, but my top priority right now is keeping her safe.

I'll hold her tonight, and I'll whisper all the sweet nothings in her ear while she drifts off to sleep—'till she forgives me.

Chase has gathered everyone in the garage, aside from Ziggy and Butch who are at the condo doing surveillance. "How is it going over at Josephine's?" I ask.

"Good. Floodlights are being installed along with the security system, and they will be activated by doors and windows. I got a guy coming out tomorrow to fix both doors and the cameras are already up on the outside. It should be good to go by noon tomorrow."

"Roger that. But one more thing, I need to know if you were able to delete the image of Josephine from that asswipe's phone and cloud." I don't think I'll be able to rest until her picture is erased from his life.

Chase gives me a thumbs-up. "All gone. I went a step further and deleted *all* the pictures of her. The fucknut won't be able to look at her digital image again."

My hand drops on his shoulder in appreciation and I nod before gathering everyone's attention. "Ravens, listen up!"

"HOOYAH!" they shout as a squad. The SEAL way dies hard with this group.

Having their undivided attention, I give them the rundown of what happened tonight, what action is being done on the local authority's part as well as on our end, and what the plan is going forward. As I suspected, my men are enraged. An attack on their president's woman is an attack on the club itself.

Reaper throws his fist down on one of the tables. "Let's go find this ex of Jo's now! We know where he's staying. Let's go pay the fuckhead a visit and put the fear of God in him."

"It's not so simple. We don't know for sure who it is right now. Whoever the fucker is, I want him caught. The bastard sniffed her perfume and swiped her panties and who knows what else—I want him alive and to be able to make the choice when the time comes as what to do with him. But the cops are aware of her limp-dick ex and they're not going to be happy with us getting involved with any of the suspects," I say with regret because I would love to go and fetch Jacob myself.

"What I want is recon. I want eyes and ears all over the fucking city. Chase is going to focus on our past assailants who show the most potential to come after us. Ziggy and Butch will be helping him once they come back. Punk is going to lead Eagle and Stage on surveillance at the build site. Josephine doesn't believe the assailant would be one of her original crew members, but there's been a second crew hired. Focus your attention to the new crew but interview them all.

"Gauge will lead Triple and Flay's surveillance on Josephine's past clients. Gauge, when you go to question Lorenzo, I want to be present. Reaper and Brass, you will do surveillance on Jacob Klein and report to me. You will go civilian and not wear your cuts—I don't want this fucker to know we're watching him. She will not be allowed to be alone at any time. I will do protection detail. If I'm not available, one of you will fill my spot."

Punk raises his hand, an amused smirk spreads across his face. "Is Jo all on board with this whole operation, or is she going to give us all hell every step of the way?"

Asshole. He already knows that Jo's going to be a handful. He's just enjoying my discomfort. All I can do is glower at him.

Punk snorts. "Got it. All is good with team J-aceo."

I roll my eyes as there rest of my brothers laugh at my expense.

"You have your assignments. Report anything suspicious no matter how minor the detail. Oh, and be good to Hades or he'll make your balls his chew toy. Meeting adjourned."

"HOOYAH!" they shout before dispersing.

My phone buzzes with a text from Luke.

Talked with the ex-boyfriend. Claims he was at the hotel all night, but he seemed nervous.

The fucker should be nervous. I'm certain he's our number one suspect. I respond.

He's hiding something.

Agreed. Keeping an eye on him.

I pocket my phone and head to the bedroom. Josephine said she had no problem sharing the room with the guys, as long as I was with her. Off to bed, my roomies and I go to catch a couple hours rest.

As I come down the hall, I watch as Chase lets himself in with a yawn, but Gauge and Punk stand outside the door. I can hear Hades growling from the inside.

I chuckle. "My pixie was right. You guys are babies."

Gauge glares at me. "The dog is fucking guarding the door and showing his teeth. Sorry if I don't want to step over him and have my nuts exposed." Punk nods in agreement.

"Gauge, baby, are you going to come and keep me warm or not?" Opal calls from his bunk.

Like a siren's song, Opal is impossible for Gauge to resist. With a deep breath, Gauge enters the room. Punk hesitates a second more before following, hopscotching over Hades to get to his bed. Everyone settles in and I go to crawl in next to my sleeping beauty.

I stop and stare down at her sleeping form. She has taken out her braids and her hair is all over the place in gorgeous waves, one arm up by her face and another across her stomach. Her perfect rose lips are parted, and her face looks peaceful.

I look at her body and see she has removed her bra. Her nipples are poking through her tank top. If we were alone, I would lean over and bite them. She removed her jeans and is only covered by her thin panties.

Ah, shit! My woman could pass for a centerfold the way she looks right now.

Possessive as I always am with her, I make sure my brothers aren't checking her out. Their eyes focus everywhere else as they climb into their beds. They've learned quickly I'm territorial.

My attention returns to her. She's so fucking beautiful, it hurts. I rub my chest to ease the pain.

In my moment of bliss, Hades takes the opportunity to hop into my bed. Subconsciously, Josephine rolls to snuggle against her beast.

"No, no, no," I whisper to him. "She's my cuddle partner."

Hades only looks up at me with a raised eyebrow, saying 'you snooze, you lose.'

With a surrendering sigh, I concede. The dog has been through hell tonight. He deserves to sleep with the person he feels safe with. I grab an extra pillow and blanket from the closet and lay down on the floor next to my pixie. I could take the couch out in the living room, but I want to be as close to Josephine as possible.

Plus, if any of the bunnies haven't found a bed to share with one of my men tonight, the living room is theirs. I'm not about to go out there and lay on the couch, only to have Candy roll in and try to climb on me. Sleeping on a carpeted floor definitely beats some of the places I have slept in my life. With that in mind, I settle in.

Exhaustion takes me, but I wake when I feel something lay across my chest. On instinct my arms go up in defense, but I stop short when I see it's my pixie sprawled over me.

My heart squeezes knowing she woke up and purposely crawled out of bed to be with me on the hard floor. Loving how she molds against me, I wrap my arms around her. She snuggles up to my chin and a moment later, she's out. I lay in the dark holding her to me, listening to the soft sounds of her breathing, lulling me back to sleep.

Five in the morning rolls up fast when you've only had two hours of sleep. I've been awake for maybe ten minutes, rubbing my hands up and down Josephine's body.

Holding her last night was one of the single most wonderful moments of my existence. I've had plenty of sex in my life, but I've never once slept with a woman. I've always fucked them good and went on my merry way. Waking up to Josephine lying across me was more pleasurable than I would have guessed.

Josephine stirs against me. This would please me, since I want her to get up and run with me, but the way she's moving is waking up more of me than I'm comfortable with—in a room full of people and a dog.

My cock was already teased enough from having her warm body close by, but now it feels as if it's going through torture. I wouldn't be the first of my roommates to fuck a girl in the room while others were in it, but damn if I'm going to have any of my men watch, best friends or not, as I ravish her sweet little body.

Groaning, I move her to the crook of my arm, my cock cursing me out for moving the sensation of her body away. She snuggles in deeper and her eyes flutter open to look at me. She smiles sweetly at me and I grin wide at her.

"Good morning, beautiful." I lean in to kiss her soft lips.

She rubs her eyes. "Good morning? It can't be morning yet?"

My arms tighten around her. "Sorry, but it is. Want to run with me?"

"Mmm," is her only response. She leans over to kiss my heart over my chest and rubs her tight little body against mine.

"We could visit a certain boulder, if you want," I purr suggestively.

She swats at my chest but otherwise giggles. "I'm going to be a crap running partner today. All the emotional flooding from yesterday is catching up to me. I'll be happy to sleep in a bed tonight."

I rub my own eyes then. She's probably right. Working out today isn't going to do us any favors. Might as well make this my one day off this week. "Let's get dressed and grab breakfast instead. We'll find a café where we can sit outside and have Hades with us."

"Will we be able to go back to my place after?" She yawns. My poor pixie. She could use more sleep. We both could, actually.

"The new doors should be in by noon. We can go there after they're installed. I actually have an errand which is overdue, and you can both escort me." I give her a chaste kiss before sitting up with her in my lap.

I look over at my bunk and see Hades sleeping belly side up, dead to the world. He's not going to be fun to wake up.

Josephine stands and reaches for her bag, yanking out some cute denim shorts and a billowy floral top. I quickly look around the room to make sure the guys are still out. She strips and puts on her fresh clothes.

My eyes rake over her petite body. For someone who runs as much she does, she has great curves and a nice full ass. It has to be genetics.

Quickly, I throw on my own ripped up jeans and gray T-shirt.

"I'm gonna go brush my teeth," she says, heading to the bathroom.

"I'll be right in to do the same." I make quick work of putting the extra pillow and blanket away before trying to pull Hades from the bed. While I'm playing tug of war with him, I hear a scream. I practically trip over Hades as we both race toward the bathroom where Josephine went.

She's by the sink, staring in the bathtub, clutching her toothbrush. She turns when she hears me rush in and points to the bathtub. I look in and find Red completely naked and passed out.

"Is she a-alive?" Josephine stutters.

Shit will hit the fan when Josephine finds out Red being naked in the rental is a normal occurrence. I don't say anything to my pixie and pick up Red's clothes from the ground, shaking her awake. "Red. Come on. Let's get you dressed, okay?" I slide her tank top over her head before helping her into her underwear and mini skirt. She's barely able to hang on when I stand her up.

"Is she sick?" Josephine asks, worry in her voice.

I help Red out of the tub. "Self-induced. She thinks she can drink as much as the guys because she's tall. Apparently, she hasn't figured out weight has something to do with it. Come on, Red. You can crash on my bunk."

I tuck her in and grab a bucket in case she gets sick. Josephine hands me a bottle of water she retrieved from the kitchen and I place it next to Red in the bed.

"Thank you," Red murmurs before falling asleep again.

I stand from the bed and see Josephine shaking her head as she walks back to the bathroom with Hades close to her side. A couple seconds pass before I hear her again. "You've got to be kidding me!"

Quickly, I make my way to the bathroom, stepping over Hades in the hall. This time it's not Red naked in the shower, but Candy butt-ass naked peeing on the toilet. A very angry Josephine is standing in the middle of the bathroom.

"The fucking door was closed, but she waltzed in and sat her ass down anyway," Josephine rages.

I run my hand down my face. It's bad enough Josephine found Red naked in the shower. She could have brushed it off as a heavy night of drinking, but having a completely *sober* and *nude* Candy invading her privacy is not going to fly under the radar.

Candy sneers. "Calm down, Pencil Skirt. I'm only peeing. Finish brushing your teeth and ignore me."

"I don't give a shit that you're in here pissing. I do fucking care that you're naked," she seethes at Candy, but her laser eyes are on me. *Yep, my pixie is super pissed now.*

Candy finishes and flushes the toilet. "God, you're such a prude!"

"And you're a bitch," Josephine retorts.

Time to step in. "Alright, that's enough, ladies."

Josephine whirls around on me. "Fuck off, Maceo. Just fuck off! I'm in no mood for your alpha male ego bullshit right now. *'Oh, look, two girls fighting over me. I better assert my dominance and let them know who's boss.'* Well, fuck that! I swear to God, if you try to brush this shit off as nothing, I'm fucking done."

Okay, my mistake. My pixie is not pissed. She's fucking livid. And, as much as I hate to admit it, she has a right to be.

I put my hands up in surrender. "I'm not defending shit. I get why you're pissed and I hold nothing against you for being angry. I'm sorry you had to see any of this when you woke up this morning."

I turn my gaze to Candy. "Get dressed. I don't care that you live here rent free or sleep with anyone you want, but I do care if you're walking around here naked. Keep that shit to the bedroom. This garbage is not going to transfer when we move into the new clubhouse. If I catch you or Red running around here like this again, you're out, you got it?"

Candy stares at me with her mouth hanging open. "Are you for fucking real?"

"Don't make me repeat it," I say in a much more ominous tone, which makes Candy shiver. Candy gives me a nod and hustles her ass out of the bathroom.

Josephine pushes past me. "Pixie," I call after her.

She grabs her bag and whistles for Hades to follow her. *Shit. She's running again.* I block her exit by filling the hallway with my body, spreading my legs and arms. She swings her bag right at my crotch and connects with my balls. I go down like a lead balloon and she steps right over me. I'm sucking wind, trying to keep the nausea down, before I follow her outside.

She's throwing her stuff in the car with a lot of force, making Hades too nervous to jump in. I grab her arm and pin her to her car. She tries to kick and swing but I block it.

I wait until she settles down before leaning my lips in toward her ear. "I'm sorry," I apologize softly. It's getting easier to be this open with her, but admitting I'm sorry is still difficult.

Anger radiates out of her and she struggles against me once more. Again, I wait for her to calm before continuing. "That shit will end, I promise. No more naked girls running around. No more lewd behavior for all to see. I can't undo the past and what has already happened here, but I will make damn sure you are shown the respect you deserve. You're my queen and you will be treated as one by all."

Josephine huffs, but she doesn't kick out. I know she's no longer angry. She's only upset we have to deal with this type of shit. I may need to send all the bunnies packing if they don't get on board with some changes, and quick. My men won't be happy about having to catch tail at bars every night instead, but I'm the fucking president and what I say goes.

I wrap my arms tight around her and wait. Slowly, Josephine wraps her arms around me, too.

"You promise me shit will change?" she asks with a small voice.

"Cross my heart," I swear before leaning down and kissing her. I wince and adjust myself. She got me good.

Josephine looks ashamed. "I'm sorry I busted your nuts."

I chuckle and help her into her car. "I'll live. Not gonna lie, I'm pretty pleased you can bring a grown man down. Makes me feel good that you can defend yourself."

Josephine follows me in her car as I ride my bike downtown. We leave Hades in her car with the windows down while we walk into the local café and order our food to go.

It feels a little surreal to be walking into one of these joints holding hands with the woman of my dreams. Less than a month ago, I would have been making fun of all the tools in the same situation. The idea would have bothered me before, and now I simply don't care who sees me eating at a prissy joint like this with my pixie.

Josephine has a hard time hiding her exasperation when all the baristas strip me down with their eyes. I laugh and pull her in for a good long kiss in front of the whole café, letting it be known to all I'm taken, and that Josephine is fucking mine.

With scones and coffees in hand, we retrieve Hades and sit outside at one of the many small tables. Scones are fine for a breakfast snack, but I'm in real need of protein.

"We'll get you a big lunch, I promise," she says around her coffee while petting Hades's head on her lap. The poor dog is muzzled again since we're out in public, which bothers me since it's still early and no one's around.

"Take it off of him, baby," I beg. "It's only six in the morning. Nobody is going to be here this early on a Saturday."

She shakes her head and pulls apart her scone. "I know he's harmless. But all it takes is one person calling the police and I could lose him. Be happy I didn't get him the muzzle shaped like a duckbill."

I stop mid sip. "There's such a thing?"

She nods with a smile. "It's adorable, too."

Oh, hell no. "Don't you dare make my boy wear anything like that."

Josephine cocks her head, the breeze catching a couple strands of her wavy hair. She gives a teasing smile. "So, he's your boy now, hey?"

God, she looks fucking good with her hair all wavy and full from her braids yesterday.

"You're both mine now," I say with the utmost seriousness as I drink my coffee, watching her over the brim.

"Is that so?" says a snide voice from behind us.

I turn around in my seat and glare at Jacob. *What the fuck is he doing here?* Is he following my woman now?

Hades is up on all fours, snarling at Jacob. I run my hand down Hades's back and feel his muscles shaking. The dog clearly dislikes Josephine's ex-boyfriend. Was Jacob the intruder last night and Hades recognizes his scent?

"Jacob? You're still in town? I would have thought you'd have already left for Denver." Josephine asks with surprise, pulling on Hades's leash to make him stop growling, but he doesn't stop. I take the leash from her since I'm able to restrain him better.

Jacob smiles tightly down at her. "I'm staying near here, remember? Came here to get my morning coffee and breakfast. I was hoping to have some company last night and stayed in town."

Having heard enough, I stand from my chair with Hades in front of me, making Jacob step back a pace. *Good, a line needs to be drawn in the sand.*

"Sorry, but Josephine will not be keeping you company again. She's mine."

Jacob gives me one of those polite smiles which really means 'fuck off.'

"Didn't realize you speak for Jo," he chides before addressing Josephine. "So, what, you're into bikers and bad boys now? Are you going to let him control your life? Seriously, what would your parents say if they knew?"

I bark a laugh and thumb at Josephine. "If you think she could be controlled, you really never knew her." Josephine snorts in agreement.

"It doesn't matter who I'm with, Jacob, as long as the person is decent, which Maceo is. He's honest and compassionate, and all things I deserve in a relationship. And don't bring my family into this. I'm done with their negative opinions anyways. No one, especially you, has the right to judge who I date," Josephine chides back.

I frown because 'date' isn't the word I would use. It simply isn't strong enough for what we have together. I will address it later with her when dickhead is gone.

Jacob's face puckers and his eyes narrow at her. "I won't be leaving for Denver until after the weekend, maybe, and I'm not sure when I will return to San Diego. I have lots of vacation days I plan on using while I'm here," he says in a possessive tone.

My fingers twist into the Velcro of Hades's muzzle. Jacob just needs to give me a reason to unleash our hellhound.

Josephine sighs, like she's exhausted with Jacob pushing himself on her. "You'll be wasting your time sticking around here. I would head to Denver now or go back home if I were you."

Anger is clearly etched on Jacob's boyish face, and he takes a deliberate step toward Josephine.

Hades, suddenly free and clear of his muzzle and off his leash, takes a running leap at him. He jumps against his chest, snarling and gnashing his teeth near Jacob's face. Jacob shrieks like a little kid.

"Whoops! He must have got away from me," I say unapologetically, pulling Hades back to me by his collar. Hades continues to bark at Jacob, yanking hard. I hook him back up to his leash. "Wow! He really doesn't like you. Almost as if he senses you're a threat."

Jacob's eyes are bulging. "I'm the threat? He attacked me!"

I shrug my shoulders and hand the leash back to Josephine, who is looking as wide-eyed as Jacob. "He's a guard dog. He protects Josephine with his life. He doesn't attack anyone unless he senses a threat. Are you a threat, Jacob?"

Jacob straightens out his shirt and throws me eye daggers. "I don't know what you're talking about."

"Really? Because I think you do. I think, when Detective Quire came and questioned you last night, you lied to save your own ass," I taunt.

Jacob glowers and looks to Josephine. "Jo, I'm here for you if you want to get away from this asshole. Call me and I'll be there."

I laugh maniacally. "She won't be calling you. And trust me, I'm taking great fucking care of her, *exactly* how she likes it." It's low and dirty, but I've never been above it before and I'm not going to start now with this asswipe.

His eyes flash and I see him clench his fists at his sides.

Oh, Oh, OH! Please bring it. I would *love* for the loafer-dick to take a swing at me. I would end it all right here, right now, and be within my rights of self-defense. To my great displeasure, he looks once more at Josephine begrudgingly and stalks into the café.

Josephine shakes her head. "You just had to poke the bear, didn't you?"

Wanting to show my ownership of this woman, I scoop her out of her seat 'till we stand chest to chest, clasping my hand at the nape of her neck, demanding she look up into my eyes. I claim her lips in a crushing blow, forcing my tongue past her teeth. I don't stop kissing her until she's practically mewling.

166

I hope the loafer-dick is watching. I hope he sees how much she belongs to me. I hope he fucking covets what I have, and what he will never have again.

"Mine," I growl, as if it explains my behavior.

"Geez, Maceo. Glad I'm not wearing yellow like a fire hydrant or else I'd be scared you'd mark me with your piss," she says breathlessly.

I grin impishly down at my slip of a woman. "I've never been into urolagnia, but for you I'd make the exception."

"Eww, gross!" She giggles.

"Don't knock it till you try it," I tease with a laugh of my own.

"Hard pass," we both say at the same time and laugh in unison.

Her smile fades. "Can we not stay here? I don't feel comfortable with Jacob close by."

"Of course." I kiss the crown of her delicate head. "Come on. We can walk to my next errand." I take Hades's leash and give her my arm.

I give her a serious look. "Oh, and we aren't dating."

Josephine looks crushed. "We're not?"

I stop walking and kiss her hard for a moment before looking directly into her aqua eyes. "You're mine. My woman. My pixie. My baby. And I'm your man. That's enough of this dating nonsense. We're more than that shit and you know it."

Josephine smiles and blushes hard. *God, I love this woman.*

Five minutes later, we're walking into Lloyd's Barbershop, a modern and edgy spin on the classic barber joint. The place is packed, usual for an early Saturday morning, with many guys wanting to get cuts before a new week begins.

I'm in desperate need of cleaning up. Since I'm on guard duty, I don't have a choice but to bring *mi amor* along. On one hand, I'm happy as fuck to show her off to all the guys in here. But on the other hand, I'm ready to fucking deck anyone who's going to look at my woman in a pervy way. Keeping myself in check will be second to watching over my pixie.

"Atlas, my man," Lloyd says, greeting me with a bro hug. "You're overdue, *hombre*."

"Don't I know it." I run my hand through my unruly hair. "I need an undercut and straight razor."

"You don't want me to trim the beard? It would look good on you, man," Lloyd suggests.

I shake my head and look at Josephine. "Nah, shave it clean. I want to be able to feel my woman again." A few heads whip around to look at my pixie.

Lloyd does a double take and homes in on Josephine, appraising her for the beauty she is. "Damn, Atlas, when did you pick up this fine woman?" He reaches out for Josephine's hand and takes it in both of his. "Are you in trouble, miss? Do I need to sneak you away from this guy? Seriously, how did you get mixed up with this asshole?"

Josephine laughs. "I'm good, but thanks."

"Josephine, this is my Colombian brother, Lloyd Martínez. We served together on a couple missions back in our SEAL days. He's one of the best guys I know."

"Nice to meet you, Lloyd," she says sweetly.

"Likewise." Lloyd's eyes drop to Hades. "Oh, man! A Cane Corso. Damn, he's a big boy." Hades sniffs at him, wags his stubby tail, and backs up to Josephine.

"This is Hades," Josephine introduces. "He's a little protective. We're going to hang out over here while we wait for Maceo."

Lloyd's eyes bulge. "Oh, man, she's calling you by your birth name. You have fallen hard, *hombre*," he hoots. "Come on dude. Let me make you look good again for your woman."

Now, few guys will admit they like getting pampered, but we all fucking love it. A hair wash, a haircut, a good shave. They're all things that help me relax. But as relaxed as I am, I continue to watch Josephine in the mirror sitting in the waiting area behind me. She watches me back with a cute smile.

Fuck, I want to have her right now.

168

Hades is a little restless as he waits. More than once he creeps over to where I'm sitting and lays his head in my lap. I pet his velvet head and he scoots back over to his *mamá* where she kisses the top of his nose.

"Man, Atlas, she's a real *belleza*. I've never seen you this fucking happy before," Lloyd says as he works.

I smile because he's right, I've never been this happy in my entire life. "Well, eyes and hands off. She's mine."

Lloyd laughs. "How did you two meet?"

Now it's my turn to laugh. The asshole in me would have told everyone I knew I fucked her out on the trail, fifteen minutes after meeting her. But the part of me which protects Josephine will always win out. "She's the architectural engineer for the new MC clubhouse."

Lloyd's eyes pop. "She like, designs buildings and shit?"

"Yep," I say, holding as still as possible when he's shaving my neck with a straight edge.

"She's reasonable?"

"Yes. You got something you want built?"

Lloyd shrugs and finishes up. "I'm thinking about expanding, but I want to do it right, ya know."

"Pixie," I call. She comes up to me, and I reach out and take her hand to my face, rubbing skin on skin.

"Looking good, baby," she coos, and I kiss the back of her hand.

I grin wickedly at her in the mirror. Her calling me 'baby' is the sexiest thing I've heard come out of her mouth—apart from screaming my name, or the moans she makes when I'm making love to her.

"Could you leave a business card here for Lloyd? He's thinking about expanding."

Josephine goes into full business mode, and next thing I know, Lloyd is planning on sitting down with her next week to go over plans for his new barbershop. I have to give Josephine credit, she knows how to sell her business.

We walk back to the car and my motorcycle arm in arm. I can't help but scoop her up half a dozen times to kiss her all over. I'm loving how much closer I am now that my face is shaved. We take Hades to the trails to run off his energy before heading back to her condo.

The new door has finally been installed. Wanting to be alone with Josephine, I tell Ziggy and Butch to head back to the rental and get some rest. Hades bounds inside and over to his bed where he plops down and starts snoring.

I grab Josephine by the hips and kiss her long and deep. There are many things I want to do with this woman, but right now I want to take her for a long ride on my bike. Give her a break from all this break-in shit and spend time with her doing something I hope she'll grow to love as much as I do.

"Go get on some jeans. We're gonna go for a ride." I better be careful with how handsy I get right now, or the only place we'll be going is to her bedroom.

Josephine's eyes shine and she bounces excitedly. "Okay," she squeals with delight. I smack her ass as she runs to her room.

I go to grab my bag when I hear Josephine's purse ping. "Babe, you got a text," I call out.

"Can you check it for me? I want to make sure it's not a delivery for the build site," she answers back.

"No problem, baby." I dig around in her purse. I pull her phone out and there are no messages. That's weird. But I hear another ping. What the...?

I dig in her purse and pull out a simple black phone. I touch the screen and it lights up with a text from loafer-dick.

I meant what I said, Keebler. Call me if you need anything. I'll be waiting for you.

My fingers wrap around the seemingly harmless device as my vision goes red.

CHAPTER ELEVEN
JOSEPHINE

"W hat the fuck is this?" Maceo's fire and brimstone voice says behind me.

I spin around with my shorts shucked and see Maceo holding up my burner. *Well, fuck.*

"It's the burner I picked up when I found out you hacked into my phone." I answer honestly. "I was pissed and I thought I wasn't getting back together with you. I knew you were not settling on me walking away and weren't going to stop tracking me.

"I felt violated and betrayed and I wanted control of my life again. I bought the phone to keep you from spying on me. I probably would have told you about it sooner if the past twenty-four since you came back hadn't been so hectic."

Maceo closes his eyes and grinds his teeth. "You have every right to be mad about me hacking into your phone and everything else. I understand why you got it, but I don't understand why loafer-dick is communicating with you on it. How many times did you have contact with Jacob on this phone?"

"It was how I communicated with him about coming onto the project. I knew you were angry when you saw that I talked to him the night I blocked you, and Punk told me you needed to focus on your mission, so I used the burner instead. Check for yourself. It's all right there. I believe it was three times I called him to update him on the progress of the build. He would text a lot, but I never responded to anything unless it was related to the project," I say evenly and unashamed.

As pissed as he is right now, he has nothing on how furious I was the night when everything came to light. For Christ's sake, he hacked into my life and was spying on me. I shouldn't need to defend myself in this situation at all.

Maceo nods, accepting my reasoning but clearly displeased. The next thing I see, he's crushing the phone in his hand like it's an aluminum can. I gape.

Holy shit! How is that humanly possible?

He throws the broken phone into my bedroom trash can and stalks toward me, eyes coal-black and smoldering.

Before I can respond with words or move my body, he grips me by the waist and spins me to the bed where he forces me to bend over, my chest flush against the comforter.

What in the world is going on?

He bends to whisper in my ear. "I recall you giving me permission to do this."

Oh my! I'm instantly moist between my thighs, knowing what's about to happen.

His body moves away and I feel the slap of his palm on my ass. It stings and I suck in a ragged breath. He cups my sore cheek with his massive hand, massaging away the pain.

My body shivers in response to his touch. He slaps my other cheek with a loud smack, harder than the first. I yelp in surprise and struggle to stand. He uses his free hand to push me back down into the mattress. Again, he rubs the sting of the burn deeper into the curve of my ass, causing a trail of heat to go straight to my clutching sex.

My brain is discombobulated as it tries to make sense of my reaction, being forced into submission.

"The color red looks amazing on your ass," he whispers.

It seems like Maceo's done, but suddenly he gives me five more rapid slaps on alternating cheeks. I cry out. But worse than the pain or the humiliation is how turned on I'm getting from the punishment he's inflicting on my bottom. My thong is soaked through and I bet my money he knows it too.

Both of his palms are massaging my burning ass cheeks and I hate how good it feels. I whimper at the contact and fight myself from pushing my butt up into his open hands, begging for more.

"I've wanted to spank your ass from the first day, when you took off after I fucked you on the trail. And every time since, when you've done something to piss me off, I've been visualizing having your bare ass exposed to me," he says in a husky, deep voice.

Maceo stands behind me rubbing my ass cheeks. His fingers lace into my thong and he slides it down slowly, sinking to his knees behind me. His hand cracks over my ass again, and he quickly runs his hand over my sensitive skin. I bite back the moan working its way out of my throat.

Again, he slaps my ass, but this time the massage comes from his mouth—sucking, nipping, and kissing my hurt cheek. No longer able to hold back, I moan embarrassingly loud.

He smacks his hand over the other cheek and repeats the kisses. I'm practically purring, and my resolve weakens.

"I love how fucking responsive and wet you are for this. I love how much my punishment turns you on. I love how you're taking this like a champ," he murmurs between kissing both sides of my ass with his soft lips.

He pulls my ass cheeks apart and inhales. "I love how fucking good your excitement smells," he growls before diving in to feast on my pussy.

The sensation is intense and I cry out, pulling myself up on the bed. He grabs me by the hips and yanks me back.

"Nu-uh, Pixie. This pussy is *mine* to enjoy and you're going to take *everything* I give you. Unless you say 'ice cream,' I'm not stopping" he growls before spreading my legs wide, giving him more access to my pulsing sex.

His thick tongue licks me from clit to ass crack before circling around my anus, making me squeak in surprise. I've never had my salad tossed before and the sensation is not one I can place, both erotic and weird, but not unpleasant.

Right, like I'm going to say 'ice cream' when he's about to make me come? Not happening.

Maceo repeats the process using the broad side of his tongue so the barbell presses firmly into my most sensitive areas. He continues this till I'm grinding my sex against his mouth.

Christ, that tongue piercing is going to be the death of me.

He quickly stands and lifts me up on the bed, 'till I'm on my hands and knees on the edge. I hear him fumbling with his pants and ripping off his shirt before he lines himself up behind me.

We're at the perfect height for each other in this position. His tall frame rests his iron pipe up perfectly against my sex. He swipes the head of his engorged penis over my pussy, collecting my overflowing juices before running it over his very long shaft. My insides quiver with anticipation.

"Hurry, Maceo. I need you inside of me," I moan.

He nips at my shoulder. "Wait for me, baby."

In one swift thrust, he's sheathed all the way inside me, nearly making me come on contact. He starts a slow rhythm, pushing in and pulling out. When fully seated, he rotates his hips in the most delicious of ways, his frenum barbell hitting my G-spot, intensifying the sensation in this new position. I haven't climaxed yet, but my pussy is already clamping down on his cock to pull him deeper.

"Fuck, you feel amazing. Your tight little pussy was meant to take my thick dick. Like it's the snuggest glove ever," he says in low, strained voice.

I try to respond in agreement, but only an incoherent garble comes out as I take the pleasure he's giving me.

My God, this man is going to ruin me!

Maceo grabs my hips and starts to slam harder, hitting my cervix, and making me moan and cry out in ecstasy. With one hand he snakes around to my clit and catches it between his thumb and forefinger, working it as fast as he's working me from behind.

Usually, I can feel my orgasm come on before it happens, but this one catches me by surprise. My pussy clamps down vigorously on his cock, making my vision go white. I squeal deafeningly as my climax goes on, with him relentlessly pounding away behind me, showing no signs of letting up.

His fingers release my clit before grabbing my hips with both hands again. "Shit, baby. You squeeze me so fucking tight. You're making it tough for me to keep this up," he says breathlessly.

His hips pick up the pace, slapping loudly against the back of my thighs. "Wring me dry, Pixie."

Within seconds I'm climaxing again, my pussy trying desperately to milk him. "Maceo!"

"Take it. Take it all," he growls, his balls slapping into my clit from behind. *God, it feels good.* I can already feel myself building up a third time.

His fingers go to my anus where I can feel him circle it before applying pressure. I feel a digit, his thumb maybe, pinch and push past the rigid muscle barrier. I feel incredibly full this way and I never knew it could be this pleasurable.

"I'm going to fuck this ass one day. I'm going to fill all your holes up with me and every other dickhead out there will smell me saturated on you. They'll know you've been thoroughly fucked and belong to me," he growls, pumping faster and harder.

Sweet Jesus! His dirty mouth is enough to make me orgasm. I'm beyond worked up and my arms begin to shake from trying to hold myself up. I fall forward on my face with only my ass sticking up in the air. Somehow this angle allows him to go deeper and I'm screaming with pleasure.

"Fuck me. Fuck me. FUCK ME!" I yell as I have the most powerful orgasm yet.

Maceo pumps twice more with enough force to dent the wall before I feel the warmth of his come shooting into me. If I didn't have this IUD, I would swear I'd get pregnant.

"Fuck, Jo. Fuck!" he roars through his own powerful release, pumping me full of his hot seed.

Spent and overloaded with sensual feelings, I don't notice he's pulled out and is spooning me on the bed until several minutes have passed. I feel his seed slowly seeping out of me and down my thighs. I should get up and wipe myself off to avoid getting the bed wet, but I'm too far gone to care. I'll strip the bedspread later. I burrow deeper into his embrace. "I love you, Maceo."

Maceo rumbles his approval before kissing the back of my head. "I'll never grow tired of hearing you say those words. I love you, too, Josephine, so fucking much."

Needing to see his handsome face, I spin in his arms. "Does this mean you're not mad at me anymore?"

His dark eyes hold mine and he smiles crookedly. "Oh, I'm still mad as hell, but I guess it's what I get for being overbearing and over-protective. My concern is focused of this panty-snatcher issue. I'm not going to lie. I don't feel comfortable if you're not included with the rest of us being tracked."

"You're trying to protect me," I state. It's not a question, I know the answer already.

He nods. "I know it's unconventional, but baby, I'm going to freak out if I try to call or text you and you don't respond. And I'm well aware I can't expect you to respond immediately when you're working or with a client. Tracking your location, like my brothers and I do for each other, would put my mind at ease. I realize this is one-sided, and I'm willing to allow you to be able to track me as well."

Whoa! Does he mean...? "I'll know where you are when you're on a mission?"

He nods.

Jackpot! No more wondering where he is on assignment may be the ultimate compromise. He's laying out what he needs from me in our relationship and giving me something huge in return.

"I have nothing to hide. I'll allow it, but only tracking. Everything else is a hard limit. You can't overstep these boundaries again."

Maceo looks relieved. "I'll make sure Chase removes everything from our system—aside from location monitoring, and we'll have him install the software in your phone for tracking me. I'm going to respect all of your boundaries."

"Punk said not to send you nudes because it could come across Chase's screen," I say sourly. It annoys me how Chase sees and hears everything that's private between us. I may only have location monitoring, but everything of Maceo's is accessible.

Maceo stiffens. "I should probably tell you we came across a lingerie pic you sent loafer-dick of yourself."

"Of course, you did," I grumble.

"I had Chase delete the image from the fucker's phone and his cloud. He will never be able to see you posing seductively again."

"And now neither will you. I can't send you shit without having a third party involved," I say snidely.

Maceo's face light up like a kid on Christmas day. "You'll send me nudes?"

I sigh. "Correction. I would have sent you nudes, especially if you were gone on a mission. I almost did when you were gone because I was desperate to get a response out of you."

Maceo drums his fingers over my thigh, gears turning in his head with all the sexting that could have been. "I'll have Chase block himself from seeing any digital images you send me. There's got to be a way he can do it."

I laugh. His enthusiasm is over the top. "Well, don't get your hopes too high, dirty boy. I guess if it doesn't work out, I can get used to the fact Chase will be the only one who sees me naked outside of the two of us," I tease, knowing full well I will never send a nude that will be looked at by anyone other than Maceo.

Maceo's nostrils flare and his dark eyes turn ebony. "The hell you will. I threw a beer bottle at Chase's head when he saw the one picture of you. I don't want to think of what I would do to him if he actually saw you naked."

"I was joking, Maceo!"

"You better be," he grumbles, rolling me on top, and making me straddle him. "You and this sweet little body of yours are all mine. I'm not fucking sharing any of it with anyone else, regardless if it's only a fucking picture. For my eyes only."

I lean forward and kiss his lips and then his chest where his heart beats. "Yes, dear."

He chuckles before sighing. "I need another thing from you, Pixie. I need you to block the asshat on your phone. I don't want you calling or texting him, or vice versa. I want him gone and out of our lives. I realize we've both had past sexual partners, but the fact I had to be face to face with another man who's had you fucking infuriates me. The way he was eye-fucking you, and how he put his pretty boy lips on your cheek, it makes me want to hunt him down."

Okay, I get the jealousy. I felt the same this morning with two girls walking naked around him. I climb off him and walk to the living room where I dropped my purse. I fish out my phone and block Jacob. Maceo follows me out of the bedroom and watches carefully.

"Done." No more chance of Jacob reaching out to me by phone.

Maceo looks pleased and juts out his chin at me. "Come here."

Obediently, I saunter right up to him and let him wrap his hands under my ass before he hoists me up to straddle his waist. I don't need to wrap my legs around him. He holds up my weight like its nothing.

Maceo's lips find mine and he kisses me feverishly, thrusting his tongue into my mouth. He swipes his tongue against my own, his piercing teasing my senses.

Without a word, he walks us into the bathroom before setting my ass down on the cool marble countertop. A shiver rolls up my spine, and I'm not sure if it's from the cold surface or the excitement I'm feeling. He yanks my blouse over my head and undoes my bra, springing my breasts free. He quickly sucks one of my nipples deep into his mouth before releasing it with a wet smack.

"You've got perfect fucking teardrop tits." His eyes rake over me before his mouth is on mine again. "I'm going to fuck you from behind one of these days facing this bathroom mirror," he says between rough kisses.

Holy moly, am I worked up! "Why wait? Let's do it now."

He sniggers against my lips. "Because right now I want romance with you, and the tub looks big enough to fit me and have you rest between my legs."

I hum my approval. A bath with him would be magical. He turns around to crank the hot water and I pull out orange-ginger bath bubbles.

Once the tub is full and brimming with bubbles, Maceo steps into it and sinks down. He moans and holds his hand out for me. I let him help me step into the tub before I seat myself in front of him and lie back across his muscled chest.

Maceo's fingers entwine with mine. Content, I let my eye lids drift closed. I've never taken a bath with a guy before, and I'm happy to discover it's much better than taking a bath alone.

Today was a day of many firsts. Should I say anything to Maceo about it? Would he care?

"Damn, woman your thoughts are loud. Tell me what you're thinking, Pixie." He lifts our hands to study them laced together.

"I'm thinking of all the things I've done with you which I've never done before," I admit, feeling very inexperienced in comparison to him. As a grown woman, it's embarrassing to admit this.

"Oh!" Maceo clucks with interest before becoming demanding. "Tell me."

I should have known better than to question whether he wanted to know or not. Any little intimate detail about me, he wants to know, especially if it's sexual.

"You have given me a lot of firsts," I say. "I've never had sex anywhere but in a bed. Never outside in the open, like a fucking exhibitionist and not caring if anyone watched. Never felt a tongue piercing on my clit before. Never fucked someone with a dick piercing either. I've never been eaten out from behind. Hell, I can count on one hand the amount of times I've been eaten out and I begged for it. I've never had someone finger my ass before, let alone rim it. Never fucked while being held upright. I've never been thoroughly fucked from behind to the point I lost my balance and face planted on the bed.

"I've never soaked through a pair of panties until I dripped down my legs or soaked through my outer clothes 'till meeting you. I've never had more than one orgasm during sex before you. And I sure as hell never saw the white light behind my lids while having the most intense orgasm of my life—until you made it happen."

Maceo groans and I can feel he's fully erect again. "Jesus, baby. Look what you do to me."

I bite my lower lip, both excited for what's to come and nervous about what he thinks of everything I revealed.

Maceo flips us around 'till I'm on my knees, gripping the edge of the tub with him seated behind me. He runs his fingers through my folds till he's toying with my clit and my eyes roll back into my head.

"How many, baby? How many men have been inside your sweetness?" he asks in a low, edgy voice.

I'm thoroughly super charged for him. I sigh, "Only one before you."

"Jesus!" Maceo groans above me. "I can't believe the prick never tried to claim *all* of you. Should I be fucking thanking him for leaving it all for me? Did he know how to love you properly?"

All I can do is shake my head no. I'm mewling and gasping too much for my words to be coherent.

Maceo inserts two fingers into my dripping pussy. "Have you been finger fucked from behind?" he asks, his lips at my neck and his fingers working me from behind.

His dirty words undo me and I come hard around his fingers. "NO!" I moan loudly in admission.

Maceo is practically growling as he pulls out and sucks me off his fingers. "Damn, you taste delicious." He grabs my hips and drives into me with his thick shaft. "Tell me more, baby."

My pussy clenches down on his member. "Before you I never fucked without a condom," I scream around his thrusts, water splashing over the tub and onto the floor.

"I've never fucked bareback before you, either," Maceo snarls as he continues his assault.

"I've never been spanked before," I whimper, my legs start to shake.

Maceo slaps my wet ass cheek, as if to remind me of how much I liked his open palm on my bottom. He twists my hair in his hand and yanks me up into a kneeling position, and his hard cock continues to pummel me. He lets go of my hair as both his big hands cup my breasts.

I don't have big boobs, not by any stretch of the imagination, but I have enough to fill up his palms, or to give him more than a mouthful if he desires. He traps my nipples between his fingers as he squeezes them, pounding into me from behind. His frenum piercing is more intense from this angle, hitting deep against my hidden ball of nerves.

"I will give you all the firsts you deserve, and I'll be the last," he says, biting down on my neck. He licks the mark with his sensual tongue. "Now come, Pixie."

And I do. Again and again, 'till I'm practically a rag doll he's fucking.

"Pixie!" He grunts raggedly, shooting his load into me in one hard final thrust.

We sink to the tub and groan in unison. He pulls me into his arms, and we sit in sated silence for a long time.

Maceo breaks the stillness. "I'm the first one to *really* have you. You're *all* mine!"

Yes, I most certainly am.

Two weeks go by in a blur of maddening bliss and controlled chaos.

Maceo didn't just stay the weekend with me. He still hasn't left, which I kind of suspected. He's been slowly moving things over here, into my dresser and closet. He thinks he's being sly, bringing his items over when I'm at work, but I notice everything, regardless if it's the slightest move. What I'm not doing is complaining about it, because I'm ecstatic he's meshing our lives together. I'll never call him out for moving in without asking me.

In some ways, we're like an old couple where we have a routine and hardly deviate from it—we get up early, usually with his head between my legs, run with Hades, fuck, shower, and get ready for the day. Breakfast at the MC's diner with the rest of the crew, he drops me off at work, goes and does his recon job, and we have lunch together if our schedules allow, maybe squeeze a quickie in. We go back to our jobs and work late, he picks me up and takes me to dinner, or I cook for him, we take a long walk with Hades, make love, shower, and maybe make love again before falling asleep in each other's arms. It's comfortable and lovely.

In other ways, we're like two naughty teenagers who are fucking like rabbits—on the couch, *a lot* on the couch, the kitchen island, my car, the floor, on the washer, in the shower, on the trail, over his bike, the build site, once in the public library—literally everywhere. If it's a clean surface, we'll probably fuck on it if we haven't already.

Maceo keeps pushing the boundaries of what we do together to see how far I'm willing to go. I worried my lack of experience would turn him off, but it seems to have the opposite effect. He wants to be the one to introduce me to everything sexual, to be the teacher and I his pupil.

In the short period of time I've been with Maceo, I've had more orgasms than I had in eight years with Jacob. We fuck multiple times a day with multiple orgasms each time. Every single day.

One day we had sex five times. FIVE TIMES! And I came more than once each time. I could barely walk around the build site the next day, and I'm sure all of my crew members knew why, but I didn't care. To hell with what others may think. I'm deeply in love with Maceo, and nothing could make me stop feeling this feverish for him.

One thing I was not expecting in our relationship was to be spoiled by Maceo. It was definitely a pleasant surprise. Not only did he shower me with love, affection, and backrubs, but gifts—particularly lingerie.

Boxes and boxes were delivered each day from Victoria's Secret. I think Maceo was trying to replace my stolen panties. I told him he was sweet for thinking of me, but he didn't need to. He was pretty insistent on pampering me—honestly, I got the impression he just liked me modeling skimpy, sexy underwear for him—so I let it be.

There's a certain level of security you need to have in order to be completely honest, and I'm thrilled we have it together. I can tell him how I feel when I'm feeling it, without worrying about repercussions, and vice versa. We can get mad and it's okay because we know the other is going to hear us out. He's still a little hesitant to talk about his parents' murder, but I can't blame him. I'm not pushing for it either. He will tell me when he's ready.

But as great as our sex life and relationship are going, there have been some unsettling occurrences. Going back to the construction site after someone broke into my condo has posed some challenges. As soon as the police questioned Jared and my other crew members, I was bombarded with questions.

Are you okay? When did this happen? Is it a past client? Is it your ex? Do you feel safe where you are? Why are there a shit ton more bikers here watching us? Does this have anything to do with Atlas? You don't think it was one of us, do you?

All of them seemed considerate, at least from what I could gather, and all of them wanted to know what they could do to help, but I was very leery of accepting help from any of them, aside from Jared. He didn't fall into the suspect pool for me. He's always been respectful and professional, never showing any interest in me other than being friends and business partners. He seemed more upset than the rest that this happened to me. His supportive hugs never felt weird, only brotherly.

Still I walk around the build site with Punk trailing me everywhere, and for once I'm grateful for the shadow. Punk takes protection detail very seriously. A couple times I had to tell him to ease up. He was starting to scare delivery drivers away. Something about a ripped six foot two walking tattoo ad scares the shit out of people, when he approaches them and questions their intentions.

Outside of work, I received a few anonymous phone calls. The kind where you answer and no one says anything on the other end, you know the creepy-as-fuck kind. Chase was all over them, but he said they were never on the phone long enough for him to trace. Scared the shit out of me to the point I started to screen all my calls again, including during business hours, which is a bitch when it turns out to be work related.

Lorenzo must have been talked to by the police, because the flower arrangements grew in size and frequency. His cards promised protection for the price of a date.

Maceo went through the roof when I showed him. I worried when he stormed out of the condo, but he came back later with a huge triumphant smile. Why he was smiling I'm not entirely sure, but if it had anything to do with Lorenzo's busted nose, I have a good guess. Maceo may have hoped Lorenzo would stop pursuing me, but the flowers kept coming, only now without a note, almost as if to say he was still there—without being in my face about it.

Unfortunately, the cult priest reached out to me too, begging me to join, so the alien spirits could protect me from the dangers of my world—or some weird shit like that. He or one of the few members called me often enough, and I ended up having to block them.

The whole intruder issue was bringing out everyone's crazy.

Maceo calmed down some after Chase found out Jacob returned to San Diego the Monday after our last confrontation. However, the serenity was short lived. Jacob was blocked on my phone, but he was blowing up all my social media saying the meanest shit you could imagine.

Are you too good to talk to me now, or is Atlas holding you back? You sunk to a whole new level dating the president of a biker gang, haven't you? Bet he passed you around to his entire crew, you little whore. I'm sorry I tried to help you. I would have treated you like a fucking queen had you stayed with me. Why can't you see you're supposed to be with me?

The rage which built up inside of me from his words was near intolerable, but somehow, I did tolerate it.

Chase blocked him on all my social media accounts, but the damage was done, and it wasn't long before other people were commenting as well. I begged Chase not to show Maceo because I knew his reaction would not be good. Chase understood, but he said he was ordered to give all information on Jacob to his president.

After Maceo found out about Jacob's cyber bullying, Chase wished he had buried it. Maceo was fucking irate—like '*Hulk smash*' irate. It took both Reaper and Brass—two of the club's biggest guys — to hold him back from jumping on his bike and heading to San Diego to snap Jacob's neck.

According to Gauge, Maceo's the most level-headed person he knows. But when it comes to me, all his rationality flies out the damn window. But Maceo wasn't the only one who wanted to vindicate me. Punk, Ziggy, and Eagle were ready to ride to California with Maceo to put Jacob in his place too.

Who would have thought a tough MC club would have these many softies willing to defend me?

I made Chase delete all my social media accounts. I didn't want to, because it seemed like Jacob won, but it was necessary. Maceo assured me anyone who truly knew me would never doubt me for a second.

A nice distraction was sitting down with Lloyd and going over the plans for his new barbershop. He absolutely loved it and signed on the dotted line, exactly like Maceo. As soon as I'm done on the MC build, Lloyd's new barbershop is the next project for me and my crew. Jared is super pumped. He was practically doing back flips. It isn't too often that we have back to back jobs, especially as big as these.

On days when tension is high and my emotions are out of whack, I bring Hades with me everywhere. He's like an oversized therapy pet for me. He behaves well at the project site, and eventually I trust him enough to take him off his muzzle and leash. He still won't let any of the men come near me, but at least he isn't trying to attack them. Punk is able to come up to him now and pet him on his big head. As much as it's comforting for me to have my dog with me, Hades is getting as much out of it if not more.

Opal and I are growing closer. She's sweet and beautiful, but Gauge is reluctant to claim her as his own for reasons unknown. She gives everything and gets nothing in return aside from sleeping in his bed. It breaks my heart. She deserves more, and I told her as much.

I must have planted a seed, because the next day she asked me to help her get her GED, and I run with it. I help her fill out the registration paperwork that allows her to start online courses. She was only one semester away from graduation when she ran away from home. So she's able to obtain her degree in three months if she's really motivated. I told her to come out to the build site to use my computer for her studies, which she does every other day.

Maceo is rarely far if I need him for anything. Other than boxing or lifting weights at the gym or doing recon jobs close to home, he's with me most of the time. When he isn't, I'm with Punk and, on occasion, Gauge.

At least the build is going well. Installation and siding are on all the buildings. Interior framing is done. Plumbing and electric are being installed throughout, and as soon as that's done, drywall will be in the works. I'm pretty pleased as I make my rounds around the construction site each day. By the end of week four, the rock paver patio and walk ways are being laid out, as well as the outdoor pavilion and grill station.

Maceo loves coming to pick me up at the end of every day and seeing the progress. It also makes me feel safer when he's with me. Jared keeps pestering him about going out for drinks with the crew. He knows I won't go without Maceo, but Maceo is more interested in getting me home and underneath him than getting wasted. I'm not complaining.

It's the start of week five of the build and I'm running around checking in with my crew when one of my men pops up behind me, making me jump.

"Sorry, boss, but there's a car up the road, sitting at the entrance. Wasn't sure if you were expecting any visitors," Cliff says, pointing to the location.

I scratch my head, trying to figure out what kind of delivery guy would be driving a flashy black car. *Is that a Lamborghini?* Definitely not a delivery driver. Is it someone that Maceo knows?

"Do you know where Punk is?"

Cliff thumbs the mechanic shop. "Taylor was asking about some kind of preference on where to install the built-in tool cabinets. You want me to go fetch him for you?"

I nod. "Him or Eagle or Stage. I'm going to head up there and check it out."

"Sure thing boss," he says before heading off to the mechanic garage.

I hike my ass up the hill toward the car parked directly across the approach. It dawns on me as I get closer that I should have grabbed Jared or any of the other guys. I back-pedal at the last possible second before freezing in place, staring at the dark tinted windows.

"Jo!" Eagle hollers at me, but I don't take my eyes off the car. Something is off, I can feel it. The window rolls down, but I can't see the driver from this angle.

"*Josefina.*" A dark foreign voice beckons from inside the dark car. "*Toda sola.*"

"Jo!" Eagle calls louder this time. He must be running up to me.

"*Ven aquí, quiero hablar contigo,*" the faceless voice purrs.

187

"Who are you?" I ask with a tremble in my voice I desperately don't want to show.

"JO! Get away from the car!" Eagle roars with panic.

The car revs to life, startling me. I back-pedal again, worry building in my gut. *This is bad.* I do an about-face and start running down the hill at full tilt with Eagle hauling his long lean frame toward me.

The car peels off when I reach Eagle, who traps me against his side. Punk and Stage hop on their bikes and speed off in pursuit. A tremble works its way up my body. Jared and my crew members all hustle over to check on me, fear etched into their faces.

Eagle yanks out his phone but refuses to let go of me. He hits a button and puts it to his ear. "Build site now! Tell Chase to check traffic cams in search of a black Centenario Lamborghini. Yes, I got her. Punk and Stage are in pursuit, but they won't catch him."

Ten minutes later Maceo comes barreling onto the property in a huge black SUV. He skids on the breaks before slamming it into park. He jumps out, wearing the black tactical attire he wears when on a job and runs over to where I sit on the steps of the trailer, huddled against Jared.

"What the hell is going on, Atlas?" Jared questions angrily, rubbing his hand up and down my arm to soothe me. It's not helping. Only Maceo's touch will do.

"I'm going to find out," Maceo growls at him, hauling me into his arms and cradling me like a child. He brings me around the vehicle and buckles me into the passenger seat. He climbs in behind the wheel and speeds off with Eagle tailing us on his bike.

We don't stop until we reach the MC rental. Maceo climbs out and comes to my side before yanking the door open and sweeping me back into his muscled arms. He marches us into the garage with Eagle trailing. Chase and Gauge are inside, deep in discussion, both in tactical clothing—they must have rushed over from their recon job.

Gauge's eyes narrow when he sees us. "What do we know?"

"She's going to tell us." Maceo sets me on a stool next to Chase and brings another one around to sit in front of me. My attention is fully on him when he takes my hands in his.

"Pixie, what happened?" Maceo says in a rough voice, which contrasts the soft circles he draws on the back of my hands with his thumbs.

"Cliff came and asked if I was expecting a visitor because a car had been sitting at the entrance for a while. I knew it wasn't a delivery driver, and I asked Cliff to go grab one of your crew. Not thinking, I started to make my way up the hill toward the car because I figured it had to be someone you knew. I stopped before reaching it because it felt...off. The windows were tinted, and I couldn't see who it was. The window rolled down a little, but I still couldn't see in. I heard a man's voice. Foreign. He spoke Spanish."

"What did he say?" Gauge presses.

I scrunch my face trying to recall. "'*Toda sola*,' I think."

Maceo squeezes my hands tight. "Are you sure? Are you sure it wasn't *tutto solo*? They are very close and mean the same thing, but the second is Italian."

My face twists up in memory. "I'm not sure," I admit.

"What's it mean?" Eagle asks.

"'All alone,'" Maceo translates.

"Did he say anything else?" Gauge asks.

I nod. "'*Ven aquí*', something, something, something."

Maceo's eyes narrow with fury. "Are you sure it wasn't *vieni qui*. Again, it's Italian and means the same thing, but you could have misheard and thought it was Spanish. It's important to know which one because it would eliminate or point to a suspect."

"Okay, again, what does it mean? Not everyone here speaks more than one language," Eagle gripes.

"'*Come here*,'" Gauge offers, looking as stressed as Maceo.

I shake my head and start to cry. "I—I don't know," I stutter on a sob.

Maceo grabs me from the stool and holds me to his chest, kissing the top of my head and shushing me softly. "It's okay."

"This doesn't rule either of them out. We need more to go on," Chase says to no one in particular before looking at me over his thick black framed glasses. "Did he say anything else? The smallest detail could help."

Choking back my tears, I recall more. "He said my name, but it wasn't right."

"What do you mean?" Gauge questions with furrowed brows.

"He called me '*Josefina*.'"

Maceo stiffens around me, his arms constricting like a boa. He's shaking, really shaking, and because I'm in his embrace, I'm vibrating right along with him. It takes me a moment for me to register he's angry, *no*, he's furious.

"I'M GOING TO KILL HIM!" he roars.

CHAPTER TWELVE
MACEO

"**E**steban is a dead man!" I holler at no one in particular and everyone at once.

Everything Josephine has said about the encounter could only point to Esteban. I wanted to believe it was Lorenzo. The fucker would be easy to take care of, a bullet to the head while he was sitting at home or in his restaurant, and *bing, bang, boom,* done.

But no. Lorenzo was squeaky clean aside from showering my woman with love notes and flowers. I thought after I cracked his nose open with my fist he'd stop, but he still sends her them. Gauge looked into him and there was nothing to connect him to the break-in or this recent encounter.

This was Esteban trying to strike fear in my pixie and in me.

Josephine whimpers in my arms and I hold her closer. *No one touches my pixie.* The very thought of Esteban within grabbing distance of her makes my blood boil. I will hunt him down and torture him slowly for attempting to be near my woman.

Gauge yanks Josephine out of my grip and pulls her behind him. My reaction is to snarl my possessiveness for her, lunging at him. I've got five inches on him, but the fucker is strong and gets a hold of me.

"Chill, Atlas! You're scaring her," Gauge yells, shaking me by the shoulders.

That snaps me back to my senses. I look at my pixie. She's staring wide-eyed back at me with tears in her bright blue eyes. My heart crumbles.

You fucking idiot, Maceo!

"I'm sorry, baby. I didn't mean to frighten you. The fact the bastard got so close to you, the person I treasure most, kills me. All I can think of is what his intentions might have been," I apologize and pull her back in my arms, holding her tight.

She wraps her tiny arms around me and buries her tear-filled face into my chest, my apology accepted.

"Am I the only one who still thinks this is Lorenzo?" Eagle states. "The douche was driving a fucking Lamborghini. That has Lorenzo all over it."

"Gauge has already ruled him out. This guy was speaking Spanish, not Italian. Plus, I have eyes on Lorenzo. He's at the restaurant right now. There's no way he could have made it from the construction site and back to his restaurant without me noticing. Yes, he has a Lamborghini registered, but it's yellow. I'm agreeing with Gauge, and saying no, it's not him," Chase says robotically while working on his computer, video surveillance tapes taking up most of his screen.

"Have you tracked down Esteban?" Eagle asks.

Chase shakes his head. "I lost him once he got onto I-25 heading toward Denver. I'm hoping Punk and Stage have something to report."

As if on cue, Punk and Stage roll up on their hogs. Punk is off and running inside the garage toward us. "Please say you were able to follow his ass through traffic cams," Punk growls.

He curses up a storm when we all shake our heads and inform him it's Esteban.

"We need to check all exits surveillance footage from here to Denver. I'd bet money he got off the highway before he left the city. He didn't come here to poke the Ravens. He came to dance. He's here in the city, I know it," Punk says angrily, running a hand over his shaved head. He looks over at my woman, worry consuming his face. "Fuck, Jo, are you okay?"

Josephine's response is a whimper as she clings to me.

Punk nearly growls, reaching out to brush her hair away from her face, tenderly. I practically bare my teeth at him for touching my woman, but he ignores me, and deep down I know it's innocent. He's who I've assigned to her as a guard when I'm not available. Aside from myself, he's the closest to her out of my men. His concern is genuine.

"We'll catch him, Jo. Don't worry. But no more going off on your own, you hear me? Goddamn, nearly gave me a heart attack."

Josephine gives a curt nod, agreeing. I'm confident she has learned that lesson.

"Esteban broke into Jo's condo?" Stage asks, scratching his thick beard, and bring us back to our dilemma. "It seems a bit below his station."

"Maybe he assigned it to one of his men?" Gauge suggests.

"Or maybe it's two different perps?" Chase says with a raised eyebrow. "I'm not ready to rule out Jo's ex-asshole. He may not be here right now, but he's constantly harassing her."

All of us curse. That would be the worst possible scenario. We cannot afford to split our team on this.

Gauge looks directly at me. "We may need backup on this, Prez."

I thin my eyes at him. I know where he's going with this and I don't like it. "We're not taking Lorenzo's offer. The fucker wants to get in my woman's pants!"

"We use it to our advantage until the prick is caught. He has the men and the fire power. We cannot afford to go at this half-assed if it's Esteban," Gauge challenges.

"Maceo?" Josephine asks with a weary face. "Esteban is the guy who coordinated the kidnapping of the governor's daughter, right?"

"Yes." I know where her mind is going. I had hoped to put this conversation off until I was ready for it. Time's up it seems.

She looks up at me. "Why is he coming after me, then?"

And there it is. The question I had hoped to never have to answer. I sigh and look at my brothers. They don't need to be told I want the room cleared. They walk away silently, giving me the privacy I need. They know the story, some more than others, but they know enough.

Once alone, I turn to her and take her hands in mine. "I need to give you the story about my parents. You know they were killed in a home invasion. My father was an active Navy SEAL. My mother was an American nurse who worked for Doctors Without Borders. They met when my dad was stationed in Colombia for an assignment, trying to infiltrate a drug ring. My mom was there providing medical services to people in need. She was half Colombian and spoke fluent Spanish, like my father. My mom was a real beauty and my dad fell hard. It was love at first sight."

My throat is thick with emotion and I have to swallow before continuing.

"Neither of them knew my mother had caught the attention of the fastest rising drug lord, Esteban Moreno. What Esteban wanted, he took, but he wasn't fast enough to get my mom. He tried to win her heart, but she outright refused him, seeing him for the criminal he was, putting the people she treated in medical need to begin with.

"Then my dad came along, this badass SEAL who was there to hunt Esteban down, and my mom fell head over heels for the hero he was. They had this whirlwind romance—guess it's where I get it from. She left for the states to marry my dad once his recon assignment was complete. They were extremely happy from what my *abuela* told me, full of hope for a new future together as husband and wife. Shortly after they married, my mom found out she was pregnant with me and they were excited to start a family."

Josephine grips my hands to comfort me. She knows how difficult this is for me to talk about, otherwise I would have already told her.

"Word somehow got back to Esteban that not only had my mother run off, but she had married a man who was trying to bring

Esteban's establishment to its knees. He tracked them down and saw my mom was pregnant. He tried to convince her to leave my dad and go with him. She rejected him. He approached her a second time after I was born in the hospital, offering the world, but she said she already had the world with me and my dad. He left before my dad could take him out."

My heart rate escalates and my breath stutters.

"When I was a couple months old, Esteban sent a team to kill my parents. I guess he thought if he couldn't have her, no one else could. Why I wasn't put on the hit list, I'll never know."

Josephine chokes on a sob and I pull her into my arms, hating how she's crying for me. I kiss the top of her head and rock us. "Please, baby, don't cry."

"This is why you're obsessed with taking him down," she states, understanding.

I take in a shaky breath. "Yes. He killed my parents, and he has been fucking with me ever since."

"What do you mean 'ever since?'" she asks on a sob.

"He's been watching me over the years. He would send birthday gifts every year when I was a child, to remind me of what he had done. On the anniversary of my parents' death there would always be a huge flower arrangement delivered to my mother's grave from him. He would on occasion sneak into the country and come watch my baseball and soccer games when I was kid living in Florida. My *abuela* would curse and scream at him. I always knew when he was there. It's like he wanted to taunt me, to scare me and *abuela*.

"As I got older, he was more reclusive, but he would call my school to find out how I was doing in my classes. He tried to give me a scholarship for some college in Colombia to play soccer. It was fucking weird, like he felt guilty for what happened and grieved for my mom.

"The last straw for me was when he sent flowers to my *abuela's* funeral. I snapped. The fucker was taunting my poor *abuela* even in death. I joined the Navy and became a SEAL like my old man, wanting to have something in common with him. I wanted to become a machine capable of taking Esteban down and making him pay for what he did to me and my family."

"But why did he approach me?" my pixie asks with worry laced in her tone.

"To fuck with me, of course. I have personally stopped his drug advances into this country for the past two years. I was so fucking close to nabbing him the last time I was in South America," I say, lifting my fingers to show an inch. "This fucking close. He thinks he can get to me through you. Well, the fucknut has another thing coming. He will *never* touch you. As close as he got to you today, he will never get anywhere near as close again. No one is taking you from me."

Josephine shakes her head. "Maceo, I want you to stay the hell away from him. He's not worth losing your life over," she pleads.

"You're right, he's not. But *you* are. Now that he has shown interest in you, I need to stop being on the defense and go on the offense. I will lay my life on the line to protect what is mine, to protect you, and keep you safe by my side always," I murmur into her hair.

She pulls away from me hastily, new tears streaming down her face. "I don't want you dying for me, Maceo!"

I reach for her, but she backs away and runs out of the garage.

Fuck. She's running again.

I sprint after Josephine, knowing she may have the endurance to go on and on, but she doesn't have the speed I have to run her down. I catch up before she hits the road and grab her by the waist. She shrieks and kicks and slaps at me, but I hold onto my little hellcat until she peters out. She cries and leans forward and I lower us both to the ground on our knees where I hold her from behind.

Slowly her tears come to an end. A voice in the back of my head yells at me to reassure her all will be alright, but another part of me worries she may be better off without me involved in her life. I never was close to a woman until Josephine. My short rendezvous with the opposite sex is what kept them all safe from Esteban. Josephine is the first woman I've ever loved, who I have completely given myself to. Of course this would make her a target for Esteban.

A small part of me thinks of letting her go, but a bigger part of me is too selfish to consider it, and it argues she's safer with me since Esteban would know she still holds my heart even if I let her go. My mind is settled. She's mine for the keeping.

"I'm sorry this is happening. Please, don't leave me now. I need you by my side, always," I whisper to her.

"You can't risk your life, Maceo. If you die, I'll die, whether it's by Esteban's hand or a broken heart," she whimpers.

I groan at the thought of my little pixie dying of a broken heart without me. This woman slays my soul time and again. I make the one promise I know I shouldn't. "I promise I won't die."

Josephine sniffs but stops crying. She rotates in my arms 'till she's facing me, and she pushes me on my ass where I hit the ground with a huff. She crawls into my lap and straddles me before throwing her arms around my neck, leaning her head against my chest. My arms lace around her body, holding her snugly against me.

"You promised, now you have to keep it," she murmurs, kissing the spot where my heart is.

I nod. "I know." And I will do everything in my power to hold that promise. I want a long life with this woman. I want a family with this woman. I want to burden her with my soul. But if it did come down to it, I would gladly lay my life on the line to save my pixie from death. It's what you do when you love someone, you sacrifice for them, and sometimes you pay the ultimate price to ensure their safety.

We're interrupted by a convoy of my men rolling in on their hogs. I pick her up and she wraps her legs around my waist. I carry her inside to my bedroom where I set her on my bunk, tucking her into bed. She may not recognize it yet, but she's crashing. I want her comfortable while she slips into a long sleep after the adrenaline subsides. Slowly, her eyelids close and I lean over to kiss her soft lips.

Once I'm confident she's asleep, I leave the bedroom and close the door behind me. My crew is waiting in the garage for me to address our new issue. Opal stops me before I make it outside.

"Atlas, you're going to take care of this right?" Opal asks with worry, and by 'this' she means Esteban.

I give her a hug for reassurance. "I will handle it, and I will make sure no one else on our crew is harmed," I say. She's asking me to take out Esteban and not assign it to one of my other men, like Gauge. I don't mind getting my hands dirty. I clean up my own messes.

In the garage, I find all my men waiting to hear what I will order when it comes to Esteban. Gauge comes up to me before I address the rest of the crew. "We need the men, Atlas," he tries again, more firmly this time, his green eyes almost pleading with me.

I nod begrudgingly. He's right. We need men. Lorenzo is offering assistance with 'no strings attached,' whatever the fuck that means. Maybe he does care about Josephine and hopes to walk away the hero in this, or maybe he doesn't want Esteban taking over his territory with new merchandise. Either way, he's offering help. I'd be a fool to turn him down. "Set up the meeting."

Relieved, Gauge nods and looks over at Chase, who nods back before returning to his computer to send Lorenzo a message.

I clear my throat and all my men stare at me, waiting expectantly for some grand plan. "Ravens," I address.

"HOOYAH!" they shout.

"We're going up against my arch-nemesis again. Esteban has made contact with Josephine today at the MC clubhouse build site. We've lost sight of him and have no clue if he's in the city or state. We're going in without info. Not the ideal situation, but not one we haven't done before. It's time we stop our defense and go into offense. We need to make the first moves from now on. Once we have a location on him, we go in. We're going to be working hand in hand with the devil for a spell 'till this situation is resolved. Lorenzo Bianchi has offered men and firepower. We will take his men. We don't touch any of his stolen goods. We use our own weapons. There's only so much I'm willing to take from the fucker."

A murmur of approval ripples around the garage. None of us want to get our hands any dirtier than we have to.

"Chase," I address him specifically, "I want you to inform the Feds Esteban has been seen here in Fort Collins. See if we can be granted access to their database. Maybe they will be generous with us for once. Contact Detective Quire from local law enforcement and update him as well."

Chase nods and grabs his cell, heading outside to make the call to the FBI and Luke.

"Punk, you will take Eagle, Stage, Flay, and Triple and supervise the build site—one of you must be with Josephine at all times. Gauge is setting up a meeting with Lorenzo to assign tasks to his crew. Chase will continue to monitor all things here with help from Butch. Reaper, I want you to stay on surveillance for Jacob Klein—he hasn't been removed as a suspect from the break-in at Josephine's condo. After Brass and Ziggy finish up the recon job in Aurora, Brass will work security detail and Ziggy will work with Chase. I will be with Josephine at all times until the threat has been removed," I say with authority before clapping my hands. "Meeting adjourned."

"HOOYAH!"

Exhausted, I go to Punk and give him the keys to my SUV. "Hades trusts you. I need you to go fetch him. Take Opal or Ebony and have them pack up a bag for me and Josephine. We're staying here until we handle the situation."

Punk takes the keys and nods. He whistles at Ebony, who is sitting outside in an Adirondack chair soaking in the sun. She hops up and bounds over to him. He snakes an arm around her and helps her up into the SUV before taking off.

Rolling my shoulders, I make my way back to Josephine. She's sprawled across the bed with the covers kicked off and her jeans tossed on the floor. I run my hand down my face and groan.

My girl likes to sleep in her skimpy panties and tank tops. How the hell am I supposed to control her subconscious behavior while we stay here with my men? I can't stop her from stripping naked in her sleep and expect my brothers not to ogle her.

I look again at my sleeping beauty and know that if I was in the position of any of my men, I would be drinking in her image. She looks like a fucking goddess in her sleep, her lithe body on display, her soft lips slightly open, and her ash-brown hair sprawled out like a fan across the pillow.

Fuck, I'm getting hard. With a groan, I adjust myself through my jeans but realize it's fruitless.

Unable to resist, I strip out of my clothes, down to my boxer briefs and crawl in next to her. I pull her body against my chest and rest my chin against the back of her head, breathing in her citrus scent.

I yank the flat sheet up to cover us, but Josephine immediately thrashes around until it's off of her—not having air conditioning will make you run warmer.

No covers it is then. I'll punch any of my roommates who look at her if I have to.

Josephine is restless in her sleep, mumbling and whimpering, saying my name while gripping my forearms. I nuzzle closer and whisper, "I'm here. I love you. I'm not going anywhere."

I feel like I haven't been asleep long when the bedroom door opens. Hades comes clomping in and hops up at the foot of the bed to lie across my legs. He licks Josephine's foot, making her jolt in her sleep. I grin because she does the same thing to me when I lick her feet.

Punk comes in next and drops our bags against the wall. He gasps when he takes in Josephine's half-naked body. He turns away quickly to head out the door. "Fucking lucky bastard," he mumbles as he closes the door behind him, making me chuckle.

Don't I know it. His confession is enough to make me not want to bust his nose for peeping on my woman.

The rest of the week is rough. And by rough, I mean Josephine is working like a dog to get the MC clubhouse finished as soon as possible. She's barking orders around the build site to her crews, having deliveries rushed, and calling in every favor she has to get the clubhouse off the ground and running.

Though work has been pushed forward, she's not skimping on quality. If she's not happy with something, she gives the order to tear it down and start over. At least her crews recognize why she's suddenly in bitch form, but Punk's team is getting a rude awakening to Josephine in full turbo mode.

More than a handful of times, I've witnessed her scream at them when she was feeling smothered. She hates having people hovering over her. Unfortunately, that's the order I gave my men. Punk is already used to Josephine acting this way from when she gave me the silent treatment for two weeks, but the rest of the guys are not. Her crew thinks it's hilarious when she starts bitching out one of my men, and I have to agree.

When a sprite of a woman brings down any man over six feet tall with a verbal thrashing, it's absolutely comical. The time Flay tried escorting her to the Port-A-Potty has been hands down the best thus far.

Josephine was in a rush to use the bathroom—two cups of coffee —and Flay made her wait so he could check out the toilet stall. It was fine until he lifted to lid on the toilet, sending my woman into an ass-chewing tizzy.

"Who the fuck is going to crawl their dumb ass into the bowl? Fucking no one ever! Now pull your head out of the shitter before I lose my shit!" she bitched.

I nearly pissed myself laughing. I make my men check it before she enters, but not the inside of the toilet.

Things have been flying along at the construction site. When Josephine cracks a whip, it's all hands-on deck. Plumbing and electrical are done and have passed inspection. Interior walls, mudding, trim and doors are finished. Central heating and cooling have been installed. Acid stain is complete on the basement and the first floor. The kitchen is finished. The garages are complete and the workshop is getting final touches with paint.

I know why she's acting this way, and it guts me. She wants the clubhouse up and ready, prepared for battle. She's been hounding Chase nonstop about what he needs for his state-of-the-art tech room, demanding that he order everything he needs and she'll worry about the budget.

She also went over my head and decided each of the bunnies should have a room. I argued, we needed the room to grow our crew. Josephine went ballistic on me about treating the bunnies like some kind of sex-for-free trash, good enough to sleep with my men but not good enough to get their own bed. Doing anything and everything to get back in her good graces, I bowed out when she said they should at least get two rooms and share with another bunny. The girls were ecstatic, even Candy was slapping Josephine on her bottom as kudos.

Friday is finally coming to an end. Josephine worked her crew ragged and consents when Jared says they should take the weekend off. After her crew has left, she throws on some knee pads and goes to work, installing tile in four of the bathroom showers on the second level, snapping at me and my brothers when we try to help, or if we get in her way.

It's nearly midnight when I make her quit. She throws off her head lamp and cusses me out the whole way to my bike.

My men are dying because they've suffered her raff all week, and they love how she's ending the week by going after me. If this were any other woman, I would be putting her in her place, but this is Josephine.

"Pixie, you're killing yourself! You rushed breakfast, skipped lunch, and forgot about dinner. My men are hungry, and you need to eat something. Work is still going to be there on Monday," I try to reason with her, putting the helmet on her precious head and clipping it in place.

"Exactly, Maceo! The work is going to be there on Monday. It won't get done any faster unless I put in the extra hours. This project needs to be done now! Not tomorrow or the next day. Right fucking now!" she screams at me.

Jesus, she's flipping out. I grab her by the shoulders and shake her, not hard, but enough to snap her out of her tantrum. She looks up at me, wide-eyed, before she breaks down in big sobbing tears.

Damn it, Maceo, you fucking jerk!

My pixie is stressed and filled with anxiety because of all this shit with Esteban and the panty-snatcher. She's trying to control the one thing she can, which is her work. And here I am losing my cool because she's trying to stay busy and keep her mind from running wild.

Way to fucking break her, you asshole!

Cursing myself internally, I look over at my men who are all shaking their heads. None of them have had a real relationship before either, leaving me to navigate this shitshow by myself.

Shit, shit, shit! What do I do?

My pixie needs a hot meal, a bath, and a good long sleep. My cock screams at me '*she needs to fuck,*' but I beat it down—now is not the time. Josephine needs TLC and lots of it. And by the amount of sobbing, she needs it stat. I know for a fact she will not get any of the above at the rental. I could take her back to the condo, but I want my men around for another set of eyes and ears.

My girl needs privacy, somewhere she doesn't need to rush if she takes a soak in a tub. Someplace I feel comfortable enough not to drag in my whole crew. *Hmm.*

Throwing a Hail Mary, I pull my phone and make the call. He answers on the first ring.

"Atlas. To what do I owe the pleasure of hearing from you at this hour?" Governor Warner asks.

"You still have security at your cabin if you're not there?" I ask, not wasting time.

"Yes, there's always security there. Why?"

Thank fuck. "Calling in a favor. I need to use the cabin this weekend for myself and my woman."

"It's yours. I'll call ahead and let them know you'll be arriving. When?"

I look over at my girl who is still bawling. I would rather drive the thirty miles to Loveland in the morning, but she needs this pronto. "Right now."

"Then enjoy," he says before hanging up.

I pocket my phone and motion for Josephine to climb on the bike behind me. She does, but I can tell she's shot. We will have to take the SUV there, which is a shame because I would have loved to take her for a road trip on my bike. I pull out onto the road with half my crew. We make it to the rental, and I escort her to the SUV, setting her inside. She looks at me confused, with a red face and puffy eyes.

"I'll be right back." I place a kiss on the end of her ruby nose then run inside the rental.

On a mission now, I make quick work of our bags and haul them out to the SUV. Hades watches from the garage where he has been hanging out with Chase most days when Josephine is working. He whines, worried about being left behind.

I never asked the governor if I could bring a pet, but fuck it, the man owes me big time, and I'm not riding the hog. I whistle for Hades and he pads to my side. After loading our dog and throwing our bags in the SUV, I wait when Gauge approaches.

"Atlas?"

"Tell the men they're off duty this weekend. Party, get lit up, but stay smart. We'll be back Sunday evening."

"Do you need any backup?" he asks, scratching his face and eyeing Opal. He's already thinking of what he's going to be doing first.

"Governor has it covered," is all I say and jut my chin out at Opal. "Go get your girl. Call if anything comes up, otherwise leave us the hell alone."

"She's not my girl," Gauge denies, but we both know he's lying.

"Right, like Josephine's not mine, either," I counter and give him a pointed look. He can lie to everyone else, including Opal, but he can't lie to me.

Ignoring me, Gauge grins wickedly as he eyes Opal. When he finally turns to me, he nods before leaning in to give me a one arm hug and a slap on the back.

Josephine is eyeing me wearily as I climb in and pull out onto the road. I take her hand and kiss each knuckle. "We're taking a little vacation," I say with a playful smile.

"Maceo, I need to work this weekend. I need to finish—" she starts to argue, but I put my finger to her soft, warm lips.

"No, Pixie, you don't. We're on high alert for Esteban. FBI is watching him. The governor knows he's been in the state and the authorities are ready. Lorenzo has his ear to the ground and will alert us immediately if he catches wind of anything in the criminal under-world. Esteban's not going to do anything with this much heat on him. My men are keeping an eye on everything else. You are ahead on the build. So we can take the weekend to get away from all the crazy shit and enjoy each other. I need you relaxed and at peace before we start next week," I say simply, running my hand along her thigh.

She shakes her head heatedly and looks out the passenger window. Well, it's not the reaction I wanted, but at least she's not crying anymore.

I turn on the radio and stumble across the Killers, Josephine's favorite. I turn up the volume for her, when it's loud, she likes to sing along. She thinks I can't hear her, but I can and I love it. Her voice is the sweetest thing when she lets loose. It's not long before she's bopping her head and singing. I stare ahead, grinning like a fool, feeling pretty proud of myself.

Thirty minutes later we're pulling up to the governor's cabin. They let us through the gate after I give my name and we cruise right up to the, *ahem*, cabin. The only thing *cabin* about it is the logs. The rest of it is all high-end.

Josephine looks out at it with awe. "This is what you call a cabin?"

I shake my head. "This is what the governor calls a cabin. I call it a mansion."

Josephine looks up at me with an excited smile. "We're really staying here this weekend?"

I grab her chin and kiss her plump lips. "You bet your sweet ass we are. And best yet, we have security all over the property, a chef, maid service, all the bells and whistles. There's a pool out back. Hiking trails right off the property. A little bit of paradise not far from home. I hear there's a big soaker tub in the master suite, too."

Josephine's face lights up like a firework. Enthusiasm bounces in her bright smile and costal blue eyes. She jumps out of the SUV and opens the back door for Hades. I climb out and grab our bags before taking her hand and leading her to the massive front door. Before we can knock, a security guard opens the door and ushers us in.

"Mr. Tabares, welcome. I'm Brian, head of security here. If you need anything, please ask. We hope everything meets your expectations. The master suite is upstairs and to the right. Chef Jordan has prepared you two a spread to help you relax. Please enjoy."

Brian's eyes go a little wide when he takes in my pixie. He tries to hide his attraction to her with a quick swallow, but I see it. Even dirty with a tear-stained face, she's a fucking knockout.

I shake his hand and squeeze firmly in warning. "Thank you, Brian. This is *my* girlfriend, Josephine, and our dog, Hades. Don't worry about the growling, he does it with everyone until he's comfortable. Please, don't let anyone disturb us 'till morning." Hades bares his teeth at him, enhancing my threat.

"Understood." He gets it—keep your eyes off my woman, and don't bother us because we're going to be fucking all night long, or else I'll break your neck.

Possessive as always, I wrap my arm around her shoulder and guide her upstairs with Hades trailing behind.

Two huge oak doors lead us into a massive suite with a balcony overlooking the backyard and pool. The room is decorated in all-natural earth tones which seem fitting for the environment. The massive bed will work great for my size and all the wicked games we will be doing in it this weekend.

In the center of the room, a bistro table has been set up with candles, wine, and a huge antipasto platter. *Thank fuck, because I am starving.* Hades makes himself at home on an oversized loveseat in the far corner of the room. Dropping the bags, I walk to the bathroom and flip on the light to see a massive tub which will be perfect for later.

Patting myself internally on the back, I walk up and grab my pixie by the hips before leaning down and claiming her rosy lips, still salty from her tears. I pull her up in my arms 'till we're on the same level, deepening the kiss. She slants her mouth and opens like a flower to me, allowing me to brush my tongue against hers. Her lungs hum with approval.

We haven't had sex at all this week because of all the drama and tension. Plus, she and I are not willing to do the deed with three other guys in the room. I plan on making up for lost time, but first I need to fill my belly and hers.

Gently, I set her down and break the kiss. She groans in complaint which pleases me and my cock—to know she wants me as badly as I want her.

"Do you want to eat first, or get cleaned up and then eat?"

Josephine looks at the spread and her stomach answers for her.

I chuckle. "Chow time it is then."

I pull her to the table and pick up the bottle of red wine. I don't typically drink the stuff, but I know Josephine does on occasion. If it's good enough for her, it's good enough for me. I make quick work of unscrewing the cork and pouring a hefty serving for both of us. Josephine takes a long gulp and I do the same. Yeah, I'm not a fan of the dry flavor, but it will do the trick.

"I hate Merlot," she confesses as she takes another drink. "Makes me feel like I'm sucking on a cotton ball."

I laugh at her accurate concierge interpretation. "Will it get us drunk?"

She nods. "Most definitely, with that high of a proof. It's a fucking expensive-ass bottle."

"Liquid cotton balls it is then," I say, slamming it back before digging into the food, which is way better than the wine, fortunately.

Josephine joins in and moans as she eats. I love the little noises she makes, whether it's from making love to me, eating or drinking something she loves, taking a warm bath, or when I rub out her achy muscles. Those little noises all have the same effect on me, having me sigh with satisfaction, my heart pounding, and my cock growing. This time is no different, my dick fights against the zipper in my jeans. I adjust myself, but it's no use. My dick wants out of my clothes and inside of Josephine.

An empty bottle of wine and a cleared platter half an hour later, we are full and sprawled out on the bed. My hand is running up and down her side, warming her to my touch. She's making those little noises again and it's like a fucking siren call to my cock. I claim her mouth and duel with her tongue as my hands swiftly take her pants off, followed by her tank top.

Eager to be skin on skin, I pull away from her and pull my own clothes off, but I leave on my boxer briefs to control my urge to take her.

Josephine's jeweled eyes hold mine as her hands trail up my abs, and rest on my pecs where she toys with my nipples. I fucking love it when she grabs them, love the feel of her hands all over me. My body responds with shivers and goosebumps from her featherlight touch.

I undo her lacy bra and lay her out across the bed where my eyes soak her in, entranced by my little temptress. Eager to taste her citrus skin, my lips run up her legs, over her mound, along her narrow stomach and between her breasts before claiming her soft lips.

Her melodic moans are becoming heavy pants and I have to remind myself to slow down. I'm too used to calling the shots and taking control, and if I don't lay off, I'm going to forgo my original plan. I'm giving her what she needs tonight, not taking her like the beast I am.

Quickly, I back off and pull her matching lacy panties down slowly to prolong my arousal, and the musky scent of her lust wraps around my head and dizzies me with need. She uses her pointed toes to push my boxer briefs down my legs, and they join the pile of our discarded clothing.

She spreads her legs for me, which is an invitation hard to refuse after not being inside of her for the past week. I crawl over her body like a tiger ready to pounce.

Taking her by surprise, I roll us, having her straddle me instead. Her blue eyes fly wide open and I smile exultantly up at her. My pixie wants to be in control—needs to be in control—after all the pandemonium over the past few weeks.

It's why she's been walking around like a little dictator with a Napoleon Complex on the build site. She feels everything is falling through her fingers and she's trying to have some stability over something in her life.

As much as I like to be in the dominant role, Josephine's not that breed of woman. She'll let me take control in the bedroom, but outside of it, she's her own boss, and I wouldn't want her any other way.

I want her to know she can take control over me, right here, right now. I will relinquish my alpha role if only for tonight, to give her the power she desperately needs. I will give her everything and more, and she will never need to ask because I will always know what she needs. Our souls are linked and tonight she's going to know I read her loud and clear.

CHAPTER THIRTEEN
JOSEPHINE

Oh my God! Did hell freeze over or is Maceo handing over the reins of his own accord?

Maceo has never given me the opportunity to be on top. He usually wants to be in control of the pace, the pressure, and all of the pleasure. But here I am, straddling his waist, and he's giving me a roguish smile of approval. His hands are on my hips, ready to help me out if need be.

If he's giving me the green light, I'm going to take full advantage of the situation. He always works me over till I'm a moaning mess. It's time to repay the favor. I will have him sexually frustrated to the point where he will be second-guessing himself for putting me in charge.

My lips claim his and he kisses me back with the same intensity. My tongue tangles with his. I take his bottom lip and suck it into my mouth before releasing it with a wet pop. He groans and his fingers dig into my hips greedily.

Moving into one of his erogenous zones, I capture his earlobe with my teeth before I nibble and suck on it, making him growl. His hips bow up, desperate for his cock to make contact with me.

Running my tongue down his hairless chest, I make sure to kiss where his heart pounds wildly before I move on to bite and suck on each one of his nipples. He groans and fists his hand in my hair. I pull his hand away gently, running my tongue down his ripped torso where I sink my teeth into each side of his hips.

Fuck, he tastes good. I want to taste more of him—and I will. He sucks in a ragged breath and again is trying to fist my hair. I swat his hand away.

Maceo has always gone down on me, and not once have I been allowed to return the favor. I will tonight. Tonight, he's the one who is going to have multiple orgasms. Tonight, I will do to him what he always does to me—I will blow his mind.

My lips blow cool air on his long, thick member and it jumps in approval. Maceo's breathing is heavy with anticipation. I smile cruelly, because I'm going to get him back for all the shameful things he made me experience, just to watch me blush with embarrassment.

Maceo mentioned once that he never had a decent blowjob, blaming it on the size of his penis choking girls out. Normally, I would roll my eyes hearing a guy say that, thinking his ego was too big for his head. But I'm very familiar with the vast size of Maceo's penis, and I have to admit he's probably right—his junk would gag any woman.

Well, *almost* any woman.

Little does he know, I have no gag reflex. Granted, I've only gone down on one other guy. He wasn't near Maceo in size, but I'm more than confident I can handle him. Taking him to the back of my throat will not choke me in the slightest.

"Watch me, Maceo," I purr up at him.

He hums with eagerness as he folds his arms behind his head, propping himself up and looking down the length of his long body with hooded eyes.

I give him that sultry smile of mine he loves before taking him in my hands.

Maceo finally catches on to what I have planned. "Baby, you

don't have to do this. I told you before I don't want to make you ga-*ah*
—" is all he gets out.

To shut him up, I run the tip of my tongue from the base of his
cock to the slit of the tip.

He moans. *Fucking moans.*

I repeat, and run my tongue back down to his shaved balls,
sucking each into my mouth, one at a time.

"Fuck," he growls, fisting his hand in my hair.

"Nu-uh," I say, prying his hand from my head. "No touching."

He groans and thrusts his hips up to my mouth.

I giggle at his keenness, before running my tongue back to the
bulbous tip already leaking precome. I swipe at it and taste him on
my tongue for the first time. He's salty and bitter and all things
manly. Exactly what I want from him.

My mouth sucks the tip of his cock into my mouth, and he hisses
in consent. I swipe my tongue around him multiple times, driving
him wild with need, before I take him all the way into the back of my
throat where he bottoms out.

"Holy shit," he sputters, seeing what I can give him that no one
has before.

That's right big boy. I'm one in a million.

I'd smile victoriously if his thick dick wasn't in my mouth. Instead
I start the steady rhythm of pulling nearly all the way back 'till I feel
his frenum piercing on the tip of my tongue, and pushing him back
down my throat, taking extra care to suck him hard when I pull back.

"Jesus!" he pants, throwing his head back, enthralled.

My pace picks up, and I add the tip of my tongue to the bottom of
his shaft to massage the sensitive veins underneath. He bucks his hips
and groans with pleasure. Perspiration builds around his temples and
down his neck, making him glisten like an oiled bodybuilder.

More than once I have to whack his hands away when he tries to
take control of the situation. But I refuse to relinquish what he
handed over willingly to me.

I pick up my tempo, and I can tell he's getting close to blowing his load. One of my hands runs up to his tightening balls. I pull down gently but firmly to stop his release. He tosses his head, growling over being denied the right to come. I give myself a mental pat on the back.

I'm shamefully aware I'm soaking wet between my thighs. His arousal is spiking mine in the most blush-worthy ways.

"I can smell you, baby." He inhales deep through his nose and groans. "Fuck that's hot. My dirty little pixie get's off on sucking my cock."

I release his balls and continue my tortuous pursuit. I bring him to the edge before pulling down on his balls again.

This time he nearly cries out and grabs hold of my head, but I won't give in and he will wait 'till I allow him to come. He releases me with a snarl and falls back against the bed.

Again, my mouth, throat, and tongue work him to the edge. When I sense he's close, my fingers snake past his balls to the soft flesh right behind them, next to his anus. I brush the lightest touch against his taint.

He gasps with surprise, his hips bucking up till his cock is all the way down my throat, and he shoots his load into me. I suck and suck as he continues to shoot ropes of come inside me. I don't let up until his groans turn to whimpers, and I slowly pull him out of my throat with a wet pop.

The smile I give him puts his devil grin to shame.

"Come here, you," he growls, pulling me up to his eager and hungry lips.

He kisses me with such passion that my head is swooning with lust. His tongue swipes against mine. Can he taste himself on my tongue the way I taste myself on his?

"If I knew a mouth like yours existed, I would have searched to the ends of the earth to find you." His words stir something in me—I feel powerful, beautiful, and extremely wanted.

"Well, buckle up, biker boy, because I'm far from done with you." I reach between us and grab his already growing cock. He groans with need as I work his thick shaft roughly in my hand the way I know he likes it.

When he's fully erect and firm as a board in my hand, I position myself over him. I know Maceo is worried about dry fucking me, because he always heavily coats his cock in my juices before taking me. But the wetness between my thighs is more than enough, and my eagerness to feel him inside me makes me bypass the step.

I slide right down onto him and don't stop until I'm on top of his groin. We both groan as his length stretches me, the tip of him pressed against my cervix. We wait a heartbeat, and my pussy relaxes to accept him.

Testing the waters, I rotate my hips to see if I'm loose enough to begin moving. I feel like I'm ready to burst into instant orgasm in this position, panting with need. I work my hips again and watch as his dark eyes roll back into his head. It gives me a little power trip, to surge forward as I slowly begin to rise and fall on his shaft. I lean back, resting my hands behind me on his thighs, my breasts thrust out into sharp peaks, and I work us both into a tizzy.

I moan. "God, you feel so good inside me."

"No place I'd rather be," he groans, licking his full lips. "I would stay here inside of you forever if I could," he breathes, making my head swoon with want.

Maceo sits up and sucks one of my breasts into his mouth before he moves onto the next. I moan and thrust my hips forward before throwing my arms around his neck to help me get leverage. He meets me thrust for thrust, his arms snaking around my body.

Suddenly, he's pistoning up into me, trying to take the lead again. If I wasn't power hungry right now, I would let him finish us both off. It feels too damn good to have him this deep. But I'm directing tonight.

I push him back down against the bed and pull myself off of him, straddling his waist. He roars his frustration and clenches his teeth, forcing himself to calm down. I smile cruelly at him.

"You're enjoying my discomfort far too much," he says in a deep husky voice, making my toes curl.

I give him a salacious grin. "I don't enjoy your discomfort. I enjoy making you wait to come, like you do to me."

He groans at my admission. "Don't go fucking abusing the power. I may take you instead, if you tempt me enough."

"Payback's a bitch, isn't it." I giggle before sliding back down on him and rotating my hips forward.

His breath catches, and I like the sound he makes. I repeat the motion again and again. It's not long before I'm fucking him as harshly as he fucks me. My legs are shaking, and I need to splay my palms across his chest to hold myself up. He grips my hips tightly and I know I will have marks on them tomorrow. The way his dark brown eyes watch me with wanton need as I take him has me hurtling over the edge.

My orgasm has me screaming his name as my pussy grips Maceo's cock, but I don't stop when my climax continues and I'm spent. I know he's getting close. He grunts more and tries hard to speed me along.

But I have another ace up my sleeve.

I've never tried this position before, but he seems too far gone to care if I mess up or I'm awkward. I pull myself off of him and quickly spin around to a reverse cowgirl before I slide back down.

He's told me he's an ass-man. This position should be his undoing.

Surprised, he sucks in harshly before his hands are on my ass. I lean forward, resting my hands on his shins, giving him a better view of my bottom.

"Fuck me! Pixie, you're driving me out of my damn mind."

Oh, oh! Ooh, his frenum piercing is hitting me perfectly in this position. I can feel myself quickly building toward another orgasm. Guess we'll both be having multiples tonight.

My breathing is labored, but I'm determined to see this through. I will bring him to orgasm before I allow myself to get lost.

Suddenly, Maceo grabs me by the hips and starts thrusting furiously. I guess he's had enough of me being in control, and I'm okay having him help bring us both over the cliff.

"Maceo," I beg, for what, I'm not sure. I need more of him and his words. "Oh my. Mmm, oh," I pant as I feel myself reaching the edge. So damn close.

"Tell me you're mine," he moans as he claims me.

My pussy grabs hold of him and won't let go as I inch closer to my release. "Fuck, Maceo, I'm yours, I'm yours, I'm yours..." I cry out.

"Damn right you are!" He roars, reaching his own release, and filling me with warmth.

His orgasm triggers my own. My pussy clamps down harder on him, sucking him deeper into me, milking every last drop he has to give. I'm moaning loud enough that I'm sure Brian is downstairs getting an earful. I will be beyond embarrassed walking around here tomorrow, but right now I'm too damn happy to give a shit.

Maceo pulls me backward and off of him till I'm cuddling against his chest. His lips are all over my mouth, my face, my throat. All I can do is feel the love he's giving me and kiss him back with as much as I can give in my sated state.

I love this man in front of me. Head over heels, fucking falling forever, in love with him.

"Christ, that was good," Maceo crows as he lies on his back, rubbing me against him with his calloused hand. "I may need to give you the wheel more often."

Kissing his wild heart, I nuzzle in to his side and purr with delight. "How did you know I needed that tonight?"

Maceo gives me an unwavering smile and I melt a little inside. "Because I know my woman and her needs. I can read you like an open book, Josephine. You've been stressed. No, scratch that, you've been going crazy with anxiety over everything. I know why you've been a workaholic this week and it has everything to do with Esteban. I wanted to give you the control you needed tonight, only over me instead of work."

"Only tonight?" I tease, my hand reaching down to stroke his cock still wet from our romp.

Maceo dark eyes are ablaze with hunger and he rolls on top of me. "It's my turn now. Let's see if I can make you scream loud enough the outdoor security comes to investigate," he taunts, sinking into me.

I don't know how long I've slept, but I know it's longer than it's been the past six weeks. Maceo took me two more times last night—once in the tub and again in the bed—and each time was no less intense than the first. He wanted to work my body into a coma. *Mission accomplished.*

I roll over in the big bed to find Maceo, but he's not there. I sit up and hear someone singing in the bathroom. *Maceo?*

I've never heard him sing before, and damn his voice is fine as hell. It's Spanish, and I have to listen closely to grasp the meaning of the words. It's a love song and my heart suddenly swells to twice it's size. Could this guy get any hotter if he tried?

Drawn to his voice, I crawl out of the bed and sneak into the bathroom. He's singing away in the shower with his back to me. I tip toe inside and lean against the wall, listening to him. I hate it when Maceo catches me singing. I get bashful as hell when he tries to coax me on, but I get it now, listening to him in his deep baritone voice. It's sinfully erotic.

Unexpectedly, he spins around and snatches me by the waist, making me squeal with surprise. He pulls me into the shower and pins my body to the tiled wall where he rubs his slick frame against mine, singing the last verse of the song in my ear. My eyes flutter closed, letting his words wash over me in his protective arms.

"I fucking love you, Josephine," he whispers against my ear, making me sigh. His lips capture mine in a searing kiss. I'm gasping for air when he finally breaks it.

He has a feral gleam in his dark eyes, holding my gaze. "Do you have any idea what you do to me? You make me want to be a better man. You make me want things I never knew I wanted. I fucking need you by my side, always. I can't live without you. You're my life force."

My heart is skipping with happiness. "Oh, Maceo," I coo.

He sinks us to the shower floor, and I sit straddled in his lap, kissing him like my life depends on it. Maceo pulls back a little till he's looking deep in my eyes.

"Marry me, Josephine," he whispers.

Whoa! What? I couldn't have heard correctly.

"Pardon?" I squeak, bewildered.

He gives me a panty dropping grin. "I said *marry me*, Pixie," he says more clearly. There's no mistaking him.

My mouth drops open. "Are you serious?"

His smile grows wider, showing off those pearly whites of his against his russet skin. "Never been more serious about anything in my life."

My eyes practically pop out of my head. *Holy shit! Where is this coming from?*

I know the sex was good last night, but it's great every time. Does he want this, or is he saying this in the heat of the moment?

He laughs at my reaction. "Yes, I want this. I want this with you."

"Jesus! Are you reading my thoughts now?" *Is he reading my facial expressions?*

He chuckles darkly, wrapping me closer to him. "I've always been able to read you, baby. Your emotions are like a textbook written all over your face."

My cheeks flush with embarrassment.

"I love that color on your face," he admits, kissing my nose. "So, what do you say, Pixie? Will you make me the happiest man in the world by becoming my bride?"

"Uh, uh, uh, oh my God! This is insane! We've known each other for less than two months!" I scramble for reason.

He chuckles. "And we fucked fifteen minutes after meeting each other and look how awesome that turned out. For comparison's sake, six weeks versus fifteen minutes is like years of dating leading up to this point."

It's a little hard to argue with his logic, as frenetic as it is, because I get it. *But this is fast.* Real fast. Marriage is forever. If he's only doing it for shits, kicks, and giggles, I will be crushed.

He runs a big palm along my cheek. "Marriage means forever for me too, Pixie."

"Shit, you could read that on my face, too?" I peep, frightened.

He shakes his head and laughs. "No, I didn't need to. You said it out loud."

Nervous about saying anymore of my thoughts out loud, I bit my lower lip.

"Careful baby. You're going to bite the damn thing off if you clamp your lip any harder. That's my job," he teases before turning serious. "I know this is fast, but I promise you I'm not doing this on a whim or for a wild ride. I would *never* be reckless with your heart. I want you as my wife, to have and to hold forever. I want to be your husband and show the rest to the world how fucking lucky I am to have your love. I want this with *you*.

"I promise you will never regret saying yes to me. I will treat you like the queen you deserve to be and I will never let you doubt my love for you. You will be my first and last thought in everything I do; hell, you already are. I want to make it official in front of the people we care the most about it. You can make Hades the ring bearer if it pleases you. Say yes and I promise to make all your wildest dreams come true."

My heart is sprinting.

Maceo grabs both sides of my face and kisses me with a feverish passion I've never experienced. All his love, all his hopes, all his dreams are sealed in that kiss, along with the promise of forever.

"Say yes," he commands in a murmur against my swollen lips. "Say you'll marry me. Say yes to me, to us."

I listen to the little voice inside of me that pushed me toward him the first time. I listen to my gut doing somersaults in anticipation. I listen to my heart pounding for Maceo. And more importantly, I listen to Maceo himself.

Everything points me to where I was always meant to be, by him forever and always.

"Yes," I whisper against his lips.

Maceo gasps. He takes my lips to seal the deal in a long scorching kiss. "Oh, thank fuck," he cries with relief. He presses me into the shower floor, and sinks into me.

My legs wrap around his torso, my arms hold on to his broad shoulders, and my lips claim his. He kisses me back softly, gently. One of his massive hands cups the back of my head, and the other slips behind me, pressing into my back. He's cradling me in his embrace, treasuring me like I'm priceless.

Maybe it's because I'm wound tight with emotion that I'm sexually overcharged, but he's only glided into me a dozen times and I'm coming. I scream my release, grasping on to his back, digging my nails into his skin. He roars, thrusting once more, as my body pulls his pleasure from him.

I lie panting against the shower floor. "Geez. I've never come that fast."

"Not since I was teenager," Maceo confesses. He chuckles before standing up, hoisting me to my feet.

Dizzy from all the passionate sex, he holds me a few moments till I'm steady. He grabs the hair soap, working it into my hair, massaging and running his fingers gently through my snarls. I moan at the contact, making him groan.

"You keep up those little noises and I'll take you again," he warns, washing the suds from my hair.

I smile and make him bend down so I can wash his hair. He groans with satisfaction when I press my fingers hard against his scalp, massaging the soap in. "Right back at you, handsome," I giggle.

He runs the conditioner through my hair and then his own hair. We rinse and fight over who gets to soap the other's body first. He wins by using his brute strength, but he better be nice, or else he's going to get another reminder of how payback's a bitch. His hands make quick work of cleaning my body, paying extra attention to my butt cheeks, biting each cheek when he runs the wash cloth over them.

I go a little slower with him, letting my fingers roll over each hard panel on his taut stomach. I trace the deep V of his pelvis, moving lower till I'm running the cloth over his growing penis. He groans and pulls me to him, holding me close.

We jump out and dry off quickly. This somehow turns into a towel snapping party. I race around the bedroom, screaming with giggles, and he tries to crack my ass. He tackles me on the bed, and we both roll around, kissing zealously.

Hades whimpering at the bedroom door is the only thing that pulls us apart. Maceo throws on a shirt and a pair of jeans, sans underwear, and rushes out of the room. Hades barks and gallops after him.

Laughing, I roll out of the bed. I dig through my bag, finding lots of revealing clothing, and shake my head. That's what I get for letting Maceo pack my luggage.

I settle on the white cotton dress he loves and white ruffled low-rise bikini panties. I forgo the bra since it doesn't do much for the little I have on top. I'm perky enough to pass it off. Maceo will probably get all riled up knowing I'm bare on top.

I'm nearly done with French braiding my hair when Maceo returns with Hades. "Breakfast is waiting downstairs," he says, smiling.

Maceo's eyes home in on my outfit, paying extra close attention to my chest where my nipples stretch out the fabric of my dress. He grabs himself through his jeans and mutters a curse. "Wicked woman," he groans, making me giggle. "You seriously want me walking out there with a hard-on?"

"I have no clue what you're talking about," I say innocently, trying hard to hide my smirk. I tie off the end of my braid.

Maceo comes up behind me and kisses the back of my neck, making me purr. "The hell you don't," he murmurs into my flesh.

With lightening speed, he twirls me around, throws me over his hulking shoulders, and slaps my ass, making me yelp. Laughing, he walks us downstairs to the main level.

"Morning, Brian," Maceo chirps, waltzing past him. Brian probably got a full view of my ruffled ass since my dress is hiked up. I nearly die of embarrassment. Doesn't help that I recall screaming through my orgasms, and Brian undoubtedly overheard.

"Mr. Tabares," Brian greets, swallowing roughly. "Ms. Josephine."

"Hi, Brian," I mumble against Maceo's back, thankful my face is hidden from view.

Maceo's shaking with laughter by the time he sets me down in the kitchen. I slap his chest. "You did that on purpose, you alpha asshole."

"If I'm going to be walking around here with a giant boner in my pants, they sure as shit are going to see why I've got it." He gives me a salacious grin before kissing me on the top of my head. He pulls me to the breakfast nook.

A delicious-looking quiche is in the center of the table with a platter of fruit and a giant bowl of crispy hash browns next to it. The delicious aroma makes my stomach growl.

A middle-aged man with an apron and a jolly look comes over and pulls out my chair for me. "Ms. Josephine, good morning. Would you like coffee? Tea? Mimosa?"

This must be Chef Jordan. I smile back at him. "Good morning. I would love some coffee, but could I have a mimosa too?" I ask shyly.

He laughs and nods before turning to Maceo. "And for you, sir?"

"I'll have the same," Maceo says, his eyes focused longingly on me.

"Very good. I'll be right back." Chef Jordan rushes back toward the kitchen.

Maceo takes my left hand and brings it to his mouth, kissing my ring finger. "I want to go shopping today."

My heart jumps. "If you're thinking of taking me ring shopping, think again. Call me old-fashioned, but I want you to pick it out."

He looks up from my hand and gives me a wolfish grin. "Oh, don't worry, baby. I got it covered. I want to do something a little...different."

I cock my head. *What does 'different' mean?*

Chef Jordan brings our beverages, and we dish ourselves breakfast, complimenting the chef for another delicious meal. He sucks up our praises. I excuse myself to feed Hades. He's been at my feet, drooling all through breakfast. After Hades has gobbled up his meal, I take him to the bedroom to nap while we're gone. I meet Maceo outside by the SUV, and he helps me into the vehicle, climbing in beside me, and taking us into town.

Twenty minutes later, I'm scowling in the beauty department of Walgreens. Maceo pulls tube after tube of lipstick out, trying to match one to my lips. "Um, why are we doing this?" I ask for the millionth time.

Maceo smiles and shakes his head. "I'm not telling. It's a surprise."

My scowl deepens. "I thought the point of wearing lipstick was to color your lips a different shade, not match it."

"All will be revealed in time, Pixie," he says with a chaste kiss to my cheek. "This is the one." He walks to the check-out and purchases the cosmetic.

"Are you sure? I mean, you skipped a whole row right there," I goad, sarcastic.

"Nope, this is definitely it," he says with a smile, ignoring my slighting. He hands me the lipstick. "Here, put it on."

I read the name and snort. "*Toasted Rose.* What's it supposed to be? A sun burnt flower?" I apply the lipstick, rolling my lips together to smooth out the nonexistent color difference.

Maceo pulls out a piece of white paper from his pocket and slaps it against the wall. "Kiss it," he commands.

"You fucking kiss it," I hiss back.

Sometimes his authoritative behavior is sexy, and other times I want to kick him in the butt. Right now, I'm ready to swing my foot into his ass.

He chuckles. "You're damn cute when you're feisty. Please, humor me and kiss the paper."

Sighing, I pucker my lips and kiss the piece of paper, leaving behind an impression of my lips.

"*Perfecto*," Maceo says. He nods for me to climb back in the SUV. I huff and puff and plead for him to fill me in on what he's planning, but he won't budge. He wants to surprise me. And surprise me he does when he pulls up to a tattoo parlor.

I roll my eyes. "Really, Maceo? We're having a romantic getaway, and you want to get new ink that will take God knows how long," I bitch, climbing out of the SUV. I slam the door with a little more force than necessary.

Maceo is full-on belly laughing which chaps my ass. "Trust me, Pixie. This will be worth it."

Like a stubborn child, I fold my arms and stomp into the parlor. Inside it's way more sterile-smelling than I imagined and very clean. At least he picked a good place to have work done.

A burly looking Black dude with full sleeves and big gauges in his ears approaches us. "Well, look what the devil dragged in," the Black man says with a smirk. He comes up to Maceo and gives him a huge brotherly hug.

Maceo smiles. "Hey, Darnel. Good to see you."

"Man, you didn't tell me you were coming into town. I would have taken the day off," he says with regret.

"I'm actually here with my fiancée, and I wanted to get a special piece done for her," he says, nodding at me. "Come here, Josephine, and meet one of my SEAL brothers."

Shocked he addressed me as his *fiancée,* I come to his side and hold my hand out to Darnel. "It's nice to meet you."

Darnel takes my hand and pulls me into a big hug. He's a great hugger. He steps back to look at me. "Hello, beautiful," he says with a bright smile. He looks back at Maceo. "'*Bachelor for life,*' huh, bro? Yeah, fuck that when a beauty like this walks your way."

"She definitely flipped my switch," Maceo admits with a proud smile, eyeing me.

Darnel slaps Maceo on the back. "Congrats, brother. I can't wait for the big day. When is it?"

"He proposed today. There's no date set," I answer, but Maceo goes over my head. "End of the month if I get it my way."

"The *hell* it is, asshole. I'm only getting married once, and it's not going to be some half-ass rushed shotgun wedding. You will wait until I feel like it's fucking perfect," I snap.

Darnel barks a laugh. "She swears like a SEAL! Oh man, I can see why she's got you hooked. Okay, okay. What's the ink you want done?"

Maceo pulls out the lipstick mark and holds it out to Darnel. "I want my pixie's lips on my heart. It's her favorite spot to kiss me, and I want her name tattooed underneath."

My head whips to attention. "Say what?"

"I also want a wedding band on my left ring finger, with the name *Pixie* on it," he continues, ignoring my surprise.

Whaaaat? I grab the sides of my head. Tattooing me all over his body is definitely an upgrade in the relationship department. I guess it hasn't sunk in my head we're *engaged* and getting married in the very near future.

Why wouldn't he want to have a piece of me tattooed on him? Thinking about it, I can definitely say this is very fitting of Maceo's character.

"Oh, this shit will be easy," Darnel says, waving us back to his station, ignoring the other patrons who have been waiting patiently for his services.

Maceo pulls his T-shirt over his head, and I catch my breath. I don't think I'll ever grow tired of seeing Maceo shirtless—ripped torso and bulging muscles galore. He sits back in the reclining chair, handing Darnel the paper with my lipstick. "I want it this shade since this is her natural color."

"No problem," Darnel says, getting the gun ready.

Maceo nods for me to come to him, patting his thigh. "Sit with me, Pixie."

Eager as always to be close to him, I crawl in his lap and lean my head against his right shoulder, giving Darnel an unobstructed work space. Maceo rubs his hand up and down my back while Darnel works on permanently attaching my lips to his chest.

Darnel has me sign my name on the paper so he can match my penmanship. If Darnel ever needs a new career, he could easily be a forger—he copies my signature perfectly.

My eyes well up seeing a piece of me going over the spot where Maceo holds my love.

Once Darnel finishes, Maceo sits up and looks at it in the mirror. He turns to look at me and gives me a wink, dissolving the clothes right off of me. He sits back down, inclining the chair, and leans his left hand over the table in front of Darnel.

I look on in amazement. "How long have you been doing this?"

Darnel doesn't look up from his work. "Eight years. Maceo was the first one to let me work on him. I've done all his ink since."

"He does the entire crew. Only Darnel is good enough for us," Maceo adds.

Darnel gives Maceo a simple band around his finger, with *Pixie* on top in calligraphy. I'm suddenly jealous Maceo has all these personal things of me on him and I don't have anything.

"I want a tattoo," I announce.

"No," Maceo say.

"*Excuse me!*" I say, putting my hands on my hips.

"No, baby," Maceo repeats, shaking his head.

Darnel sniggers, shaking his head as he works.

My arms fold over my chest. "I'm sorry, but I wasn't asking for permission."

"Not that I want to get in the middle of a lover's quarrel, but Maceo doesn't want you to cover up your perfection when you're already a work of art," Darnel adds, winking. "Sucks for my business, but I get it."

"Exactly. I love how her skin is flawless," Maceo tells him. "It's fucking pure, like an angel."

"And you're the devil covered in your marks," Darnel finishes for him.

Well, that pisses me off! I huff my disappointment, trying not to let either one of them see how flattered I am by their comments about *perfection*—which I'm far from—but hell if I'm going to point it out to either of them, especially Maceo.

"All I would have gotten was your name inked across my ring finger like you did," I whine.

Now we look weird with him having an inked band and me having nothing. Perhaps I'll come back without Maceo to have it done. But seeing Darnel is in cahoots with my man, I may need to go somewhere else.

Maceo takes my left hand and kisses my ring finger. "I love you the way you are. If you really want a tattoo, I won't stop you, but don't get one because I'm getting one. Tattoos should not be made rashly. Think it through to see if your heart is set on it, and take your time picking out exactly what you want. I'll bring you back to Darnel if you're hell-bent. The only reason I got my first one was to cover up a stab wound from a sting operation gone South. Now, every one I pick is symbolic."

I pout. "I think a ring is pretty symbolic."

Maceo smirks, like he's got a big secret, and kisses my hand again.

Darnel wraps up and swats Maceo's hand away when he tries to pay. "Make it up to me by having an open bar at the wedding," he says with an impish grin.

"Well, there'll definitely be open bar," Maceo says, giving me a pointed look, daring me to argue. I shrug—hell, I'm all for open bar; no argument from me.

Darnel laughs and sweeps me up in a crushing hug. He give Maceo a brotherly hug as well. "Now hurry up and marry her before she comes to her senses," he teases Maceo.

"On it," he says with a chuckle, pulling me out of the parlor and back into the warm sun of late morning. He kisses the top of my head, swings his arm around my shoulder, keeping me close. He walks to the SUV and helps me in before driving us to Flatiron Reservoir.

Maceo helps me from the SUV and keeps me snug against his side, walking to a rocky beach. It's beautiful out here and hardly a soul in sight.

Out of the blue, Maceo drops to one knee and takes my left hand. I'm caught off guard since he's already proposed. He pulls a ring out from the front pocket of his jeans.

"Let's make this official, shall we," he says with a wink, sliding the ring onto my finger. "Thank you for making me the happiest man alive." He stands and takes me by the waist, pulling me against him, and kissing me amorously.

When we finally come up for air, I'm panting and clinging to his biceps. He spins me till my back is to his chest, and he holds up my left hand, letting me finally see my engagement band.

I gasp. It's the shape of a flower—a solitaire round clear diamond is in the center, with six black diamonds surrounding it. It has me written all over it.

"The center diamond was from my mother's engagement ring and the black diamonds are from a crucifix belonging to *Abuelita Lucia*. I wanted you to have something from all the people who've made me who I am. And I wanted it to represent us.

"You're the clear and pure one who is the center of my universe, while I'm the dark and wicked one surrounding you completely in my love. I thought the flower pattern was very *you*," he explains with his chin resting on my shoulder.

"It's perfect," I murmur, tears rolling down my face. "It's more than I could have hoped for."

Maceo turns my chin 'till I'm looking up at him. "You love it?"

I nod and smile. "Almost as much as I love you." I reach up on my tippy toes and kiss him.

Maceo lifts his arm in front of us and snaps a picture on his phone.

"Proof I got you to agree to marry me," he says with a wink. He snaps another picture of the two of us laughing, holding up our ring fingers proudly.

CHAPTER FOURTEEN
MACEO

"She said YES!" I holler out of the SUV's window, pulling up to the rental after our weekend away.

My crew charges the SUV and yanks us both out, cheering and whistling like fucking frat boys at a rush party. Hugs and kisses for Josephine, and I get harassed and back slapped.

Hades jumps out of the window, barking and growling at all my men, defending me like the good boy he is. I rub his head to calm him down, and off he runs to the backyard. I'm swarmed once again by my brothers.

They all know I've been planning on proposing for weeks. It was a matter of finding the right place and time to pop the question. When Josephine asked when I had the ring made, her jaw dropped—I had it made the week after I got back from our mission, only three weeks after we met, but I've been planning it since day one.

Once I had the idea to take Josephine away for the weekend, I knew operation pop-the-question was a go. Apparently, all my men did too because they're prepared, pulling out a beer keg, starting up the grill, and setting up tables. The bunnies fill them with platters of food to celebrate our engagement.

All the MC girls surround Josephine, examining her ring and

asking how I popped the question. I smile at how sweet she is with all of them, including Candy.

One thing about Josephine I love is she gives everyone the benefit of the doubt, and that extends to the woman who has tried for the past year to get in my pants. It takes a lot for her to push someone away. I guess it's why she has given me chance after chance to prove myself to her.

I smile and turn to Gauge. "This is cool of you guys. I appreciate it and I know Josephine does too, but how did you know I asked her?"

Gauge grins. "Chase. He saw you took some pictures on your phone of the two of you with the ring on her finger."

"Hope you don't mind, but I uploaded that picture of you guys to our company website. I cropped it to only show your hands, but I thought showing a more domesticated side to our crew would maybe help our image and the business," Chase says, shrugging.

I smile and nod. I like the idea of showing the world my bride. The fact it's only our hands makes me feel better. I don't want our faces out there. Keeping her safe will always be my top priority.

"Which reminds me, Atlas, you went to Darnel to get the new ink and didn't ask me to go?" Punk points at my ring finger.

I fist my hand and show it off proudly. "Fuck yeah, I did. Got my woman branded all over me," I say smugly, lifting up my shirt and showing off my chest with her lips.

"That's fucking sweet," Gauge says, admiring the originality of my new tat. He looks over at Opal and back at me. "I may steal your idea if I find myself as lucky as you and Jo."

I smirk. "We'll make it a club thing. Have our old ladies' lips tattooed on us."

"You will not use that fucking awful title when talking about me," Josephine yells from across the yard where she's still hanging out with the bunnies.

Gauge and I bust a gut. *Oh*, she's going to be hearing it a lot, maybe not from me, but from others. I will not call her that if it truly offends her. Right now, I'm proud as punch calling her my fiancée.

Damn. Josephine is my fiancée. How did I get so fucking lucky?

I look at my best friend with a smile. "Gauge, we've done everything together since boot camp. Care to follow me again as my best man on my biggest day?"

"Honor as always, brother," Gauge says, clinking his beer cup with mine. We both down them in one gulp.

I nod at Chase and Punk to get their attention. "You two are standing up in the wedding as groomsmen, and I don't want to hear no bitching. If Josephine says we're wearing monkey suits, we're wearing the fucking monkey suits."

Gauge laughs at both of them because now he won't be alone in dressing up. Chase folds his arms and curses, but Punk smirks. "Monkey suit or not, I'll still look better than all of your sorry old asses. I'll be like fucking James Bond up there next to you all. And it's going to land me all the available pussy," he says.

"You're only three years younger than me," Chase snorts. "Old asses my ass."

"Whatever! Women want a man not a boy, Chase," Gauge barks out in a laugh.

"I'm fucking twenty-four. Man enough to give it to them all night long while your thirty-year old ass will be a one-and-done," Punk fires back.

Next thing I know, Gauge and Punk are in a wrestling match on the ground. The rest of my brothers are taking bets and egging them on.

Chase swings an arm around my shoulder, pointing to our two best brothers. "You know how you know if you've had a successful party? When a fight breaks out," he chuckles.

I roll my eyes skyward and get in the middle to break up my brothers. A beer is placed in their hands. They laugh before bickering about which of them was winning the wrestling match before it got broken apart.

Josephine's retreating figure catches my attention and I jog over to her. She's staring at her phone with a frown. "Pixie, baby, what is it?" I ask, wrapping my arms around her. She holds her phone out to me. The name 'Dad' is displayed on the screen.

Well, shit just got interesting.

Josephine told me on day one she hasn't spoken to her parents since she left California. The fact he's reaching out to her now seems unusual.

"Did you, like, call up my dad and ask for his blessing, or some shit?" she asks, confused.

"Fuck that tradition! You're a grown-ass woman who makes her own decisions. I don't need his blessing. Plus, you were already mine to begin with. I don't give a fuck if your parents don't approve."

To be honest, I never gave a thought to asking her father. In some ways Josephine and I are old school, but for the most part, we're pretty progressive. I can't help but feel maybe I should have reached out to her old man.

Josephine and I are about to get married and, regardless of the hurt feelings she is harboring toward her family, she would want them there on our wedding day. Maybe this would be a way to rebuilding the bridge between them.

I rub the back of my head in frustration. "Fuck. I should have asked your old man for his permission and blessing."

"No, Maceo. You're right when you say you don't need their approval to marry me," she firmly defends me.

But I'm not sure anymore. I don't only want Josephine. I want everything that comes with her too, crazy ass family and all.

"No, it's important. *Abuelita Lucia* was very traditional. She would have demanded this. I mean, what if we have a kid someday? I would want their partner to ask me for my blessing and not whisk them away right out from under our noses," I say, gnawing on the inside of my cheek.

My mind is made up—I'm going to have to correct this. I've still got all of Josephine's contacts in my phone. Maybe I should call her parents later.

Wait, Josephine hasn't spoken to them in a year. If I call them out of the blue and they have no clue who I am, it could set the two sides into another fight. *Fuck!*

Josephine snaps her fingers in my face. "Maceo, focus! My dad called me and I have no idea why."

I shelve my trepidation for the moment. "Did he leave a message?"

She shakes her head. "No."

"Maybe he butt-dialed you?" I suggest, scratching my five o'clock shadow.

Her phone vibrates in her hands with her dad's number. "Fucking hell!" Josephine whimpers.

"Okay, um, answer it?" I ask, unsure. "Maybe it's important."

Josephine gulps and answers the phone. I quickly take it and put it on speaker. I'm a nosy bastard who wants to be involved in all things Josephine.

"Hi, dad," she says with a tremble in her voice.

"Jo?" her father asks with disbelief.

"Yep. It's me. Um, what do you need?" she asks, trying to keep her voice neutral.

Her dad shutters a sigh on the other end of the line. "I'm sorry. I'm a little shocked you answered."

"Makes two of us," she admits.

He laughs nervously. "It's good to finally hear your voice."

Josephine blinks away tears and swallows. "It's good to hear yours too. Is everything okay at home? Are mom and you good? How's Simone?" she asks in rapid succession.

"All is good here. Simone's still traveling a lot for her job. Your mom is keeping busy at the school. I've been tinkering around the house. Put a new tile floor in the bathroom and kitchen, making your mom happy."

"Oh, I bet she is. She always hated that yellow porcelain," Josephine says, growing more comfortable.

Her dad snorts. "Oh, yeah, she sure did. Got sick of her complaining about it. I decided to finally do something. I'm retired and bored out of my mind. She wanted this fancy tile, all flowery and black and white, looks busy as hell on the floor, but she's happy. Could have used your help installing it, seeing as you know all about this kind of stuff."

Josephine looks at the ground with a tight mouth. I know she's thinking she would've loved to have helped her old man and make her mom happy. She probably feels robbed of the chance.

"I'm sure you did a fine job. I learned how to work from you after all," she says instead of what she's feeling.

Her dad sniffs on the other end of the line. Crying perhaps? "It still would have been nice to have you home."

Josephine lifts her face to the sky, forcing her tears to stay in. I can tell already she's a lot like her old man. Both of them downplaying their emotions. Both of them stubborn as hell. Neither one brave enough to come out and say they miss the other one.

My crew is getting a little rowdy in the background, and her father catches their laughter. "You at a party or something?" he asks.

"Yes, actually. It's sort of my—" I stop her from saying engagement party, shaking my head. Breaking the ice tonight is enough. Let's not drop that bomb on him yet. "It's a party my friends are throwing," she settles on.

"Ah. I won't keep you long. I was wondering if everything was okay. Your mom and sister noticed you unfriended them or something on Facebook," he says.

"I didn't unfriend anyone. I deleted my social media accounts," she corrects.

"Oh. Why? Your mom was pretty upset. She thought maybe whoever this new guy you're dating was making you isolate yourself or something."

Oh, hell no! I look down at my pixie and she's fuming. *This is bad, really bad.*

"And how would mom know if I'm dating anyone?" she snaps into the phone.

"Well, she saw the comments Jacob was posting, how hurt he was that you weren't giving him another chance. She felt bad and reached out to him. He told her you're trapped with some dangerous biker who controls everything you do, and you're too proud to ask for help. He's worried about you. And now we're worried too."

I swear lighting strikes are going off behind my pixie's blue eyes. She's reached her fill and all hell is going to break loose.

"If mom was fucking worried about me, maybe she shouldn't be reaching out to the ex-asshole who broke my heart in the first fucking place. If she reached out to me, then she'd have a fucking clue Jacob's a whiny little shit who fucking can't take the hint and move on. I fucking quit social media to avoid his toxic, stalking behavior. Do you actually want me to be with a man who calls me a 'whore' because he's pissed off I'm in a relationship with someone else? How fucking messed up is that shit?!"

"Jo, I didn't mean to offend—" he tries to explain himself, but Josephine cuts him off.

"Maybe if mom called me, she'd learn how fucking successful I am with my own design company, or how I landed my first multimil-lion-dollar project. Maybe if either of you fucking said you were sorry for driving me away, you'd find out I'm doing great and engaged to the man of my dreams who—yes, is a president of a biker club, a retired decorated Navy SEAL, and has his own personal security company, and then you'd fucking understand how I struck gold by landing his sweet ass.

"We didn't know—" her dad tries again.

"Do me a favor, next time you get the itch to call me, fucking don't. I've got a new family who loves me, would do anything to keep me safe, and doesn't tell me my dreams are shit. Feel free to adopt Jacob's sorry ass. I'm out!" she shouts into the phone before hitting the 'end' button.

Holy fuck! I'm speechless.

Josephine is trying hard to calm herself down, but it's clear that it's going to take more than just counting to ten in her head.

It's dead silent behind us. I turn to look at my crew. They're all staring at Josephine with their mouths hanging open. Josephine must sense the silence too, because she turns to face the party. She stares at all of them and they stare back at her.

The air crackles between them as all my men start smiling. Smiling turns to laughing. Laughing turns to clapping. Clapping turns to cheering and whistling. My woman showed everyone she fucking owns the title of *First Lady*.

Gauge starts applauding. "That was fucking awesome!"

Eagle laughs with disbelief. "Did you say all that shit to your pop?"

Ebony giggles. "And I thought I had daddy issues."

Punk comes running up and bear hugs Josephine. "I always wanted a sister with a filthy mouth."

Chase breaks out the Pappy and pours a tumbler, handing it off to Josephine and toasts her. "To the fucking Queen of Bitching. That was epic."

Everyone is super proud of her, myself included, but Josephine is far from happy. She throws back her drink and smiles politely at everyone, but her heart is in pieces. She puts on a brave face and pretends she's unaffected by what went down, but there's no way anyone would react the way she did on the phone if it didn't affect them.

Her parents may be wrong, but things will never change if Josephine never gives them the time of day. I foresee a road trip in my near future by myself to Los Angeles. She's going to be one angry hellcat when she finds out, but this is something I can do for her and them. If her family is truly toxic, I'll back off, but coming from someone who lost all his family, I can say family means everything.

Pulling my woman close to me, I shower her with kisses, but she seems unresponsive. She looks at me with unreadable eyes. "I need to see you out back," she says before walking to the backyard.

I rub the back of my neck, watching her slender form retreat. For once, I'm not exactly sure how to read my pixie. I set my beer down and follow her.

I 'round the corner of the back of the house where it's completely secluded except for us. If there was a time for my girl to talk undisturbed, this would be it.

I reach for my fiancée to comfort her, but the little vixen grabs me by waistband of my jeans, spinning me against the house using all of her weight. My back hits the house with a thud, and her tiny hands work to undo my pants.

Hot damn! How could I not read this on her?

My woman is in need of angry, get-my-fuck-on, wild sex. Right here, right now, in the fucking wide open, where any of my brothers could come walking by any second. The idea both thrills and petrifies me. Her hands are already working my cock to full mast, making my mind up for me.

I spin her 'till her back hits the house, and move us into the shadows where the moonlight doesn't touch us. My fingers hike up her skirt, sliding her panties to the side.

Normally, I like to take my time with Josephine, savoring everything, but my nerves are on high alert. I don't want any of my men watching me ravish her. She's mine and I treat her with respect. Having anyone witness us fucking would be giving away a piece of her, and I can't allow that. All of her belongs to me and me alone.

Eager to please, I yank her up to my waist. She wraps her toned legs around me and I take her hard, impaling her on my long, thick cock already leaking with precome. She cries out but I swallow it with my mouth over hers. I thrust my tongue into her sweet little mouth the way I thrust my cock into her tight little pussy. My thighs are smacking against the backs of hers and my balls are flying up, flicking her in the ass from the force of my thrusts.

She whimpers and moans as quietly as she can, but when my tongue can't silence her, I clamp my hand over her mouth. Something about this is turning me on more, but also unnerves me.

I realize I've taken away her verbal communication. "Smack me in the face if you want me to stop." My hips pick up speed and my thrusting becomes more violent. My girl wanted an angry fuck and I'm going to deliver. I will rut her for all it's worth.

Josephine's fingers dig into my shoulders, and her legs begin to quiver the closer she gets to her climax. My own balls begin to tighten and I feel her wetness drip down my sack, making wet *whacking* noises when they slap against her beautiful ass. It sends my hips into overdrive.

When her pussy clamps down like a fucking vise grip, I detonate like a bomb, shooting my come like shrapnel all the way up into her womb. That fucking IUD is going to have its work cut out for it tonight.

I don't pull out of her. I keep her perched on my cock against the house, leaning my forehead against hers. I remove my hand from her mouth, kissing her swollen lips.

"My God, baby, you're fucking incredible. I love how you take what you want, when you want," I whisper.

"Mmm. I want more," she says, licking at my bottom lip.

I groan from the stimulation. This woman fills all my wildest dreams.

Just then I hear two of my men walking toward the backyard. I look over my shoulder and see Reaper and Brass shooting the shit, making their way to the fence line to piss.

Slowly, I lift her off me and pull down her skirt. Come drips down her thigh and I wipe it away with my hand. I push my flaccid cock back into my pants and zip up.

Walking us out of the shadows, I hold her to me and kiss her. Yeah, I'm a guy who likes fucking pillow talk and cuddle time with my fiancée.

Barking interrupts our make-out session. We see Reaper and Brass running full tilt towards us. Hades must have scared them mid-piss because Reaper's junk is still hanging out when they run back to the safety of the house.

"Call off Cujo! Call off Cujo!" Reaper hollers, Hades hot on their heels.

I'm fucking dying and Josephine—my better half—runs after Hades to get him to calm down. Brass laughs too once he sees Josephine has got Hades under control.

"Aw, fuck!" Reaper fumes, shaking his head in disgust. "I pissed all over myself!"

Brass and I double over on the ground. Hades crawls all over us, licking at our faces.

Josephine only looks skyward. "Reaper, would you mind tucking your goods away?"

I slap at the side of his leg, avoiding the piss, thankfully. "Put your shit away."

"Afraid she may like what I got more?" he teases, tucking his dick back into his pants.

"Not a chance. I've got a good two inches on you, man," I joke back.

"Nu-uh, no way. Fucking pull it out and we'll do a side by side comparison," Reaper challenges.

Calling his bluff, I start to undo my pants. "Do you want us to judge when we're soft, hard, or both?"

"Eww!" Josephine shakes her head. "Brass, will you please take me back to the party and away from this sausage competition?"

Brass throws his head back laughing, giving Josephine his arm, and escorting her back to the front yard.

Reaper and I follow behind laughing. "It was a joke, Jo," Reaper tries to defend, grabbing at his side, in stitches.

I run up behind Josephine and grab her by the waist, flipping her over my shoulder. I waltz back out to the group with her giggling. "Let's get this party started!" I roar.

"HOOYAH!" everyone shouts.

Monday morning would have been awful if Josephine hadn't cut me off as early as she did. I always used to grimace at any man whose woman told him enough was enough, but with Josephine, I get it. She's like my little hangover preventer.

Needing to touch her, I roll over in our shared twin mattress and pull her against me. Suddenly, I'm being licked aggressively in the face.

"Aw, Hades!" I sputter, pushing him away and sitting up in bed. I run a hand through my wild hair and find Josephine standing in her bra and panties, pulling her work clothes out for the day.

The thing about Josephine that's refreshing is she's not afraid to get her hands dirty. She doesn't go in suits to the build site. No, she puts on the same clothes as all the rest of the construction workers, regardless of the fact she's the engineer and boss.

When push comes to shove, she will throw on the hard hat and safety glasses and jump in to help out. She would never ask one of her workers to do a job she herself wouldn't do, like I would never ask one of my men to take a job I wouldn't do. It's one of many things I admire about her—another thing we have in common.

"Mmm. Bring your sexy ass over here," I whisper to her, not wanting to wake the others.

Her megawatt smile takes over her lovely face. "Not a chance in hell. I love your brothers but not enough to give them a show. Plus, I need to get to the site. I have a crap load of deliveries coming in today and I want to be there early to oversee everything. I want to run later this evening when it's cooler, if you don't mind."

"I don't mind at all." Seeing as she's in a decent mood, I decide to ask her about last night. "How are you feeling after talking with your dad yesterday?"

Josephine grimaces. "I'm not ready to talk about it."

My jaw ticks. I don't want to push her before she's ready to talk, but I also get the feeling she won't talk about it if I don't bring it up— she internalizes too much.

"I understand. It's still fresh. But I'm here if you want to talk about your parents. You have every right to be upset with them, but I feel like they're only reacting this way because they're only hearing one half of the conversation. Maybe if you tried talking to them again—"

"Maceo, please, I know you mean well, but I can't deal with them right now. Last night was about us, and my dad put a huge damper on it with that bullshit about Jacob. I'm not shutting you out, I'm not trying to bury it, I just want to focus on the positives in our lives," Josephine says, tears brewing in her costal eyes.

Wanting to comfort her, I get up and wrap her up in my arms, kissing her head. "Okay, I'm sorry. I'm only trying to help."

She leans into my chest. "I know, thank you. You could help me with something else. Do you have a chain?" She backs away to finish dressing.

"What kinda chain?" I ask, confused as I let my eyes continue to roam over her gorgeous goods.

My pixie pulls off her engagement band. "I can't work with this on my finger. One, it's a safety hazard. And two, I don't want to damage or lose it. I want a chain to wear it around my neck," she explains.

Ah! I get it now. I walk to my dresser where I keep a spare chain for my dog tags and hand it to her. She slips the ring on it and pulls the chain over her neck. It's long and nestles between her delectable cleavage, next to her heart.

I scratch my head, not happy she's not wearing her band. I understand her reasoning, but I want people to fucking see she's mine when I'm not around. Her engagement band was one way to show others she's taken. I look down at my ring tattoo and can see why Josephine wanted the same thing, but I don't want her skin stained.

Grinding my teeth, an idea comes to me and I grab my phone. I look up silicone ring bands for women and order a multicolored pack of them for her. My woman *will* wear a ring to represent me.

Satisfied, I quickly throw on some clothes and join Josephine in the bathroom to brush my teeth and comb back my hair. I watch in the mirror as Josephine makes quick work with a loose braid. I like how she knows many different hairdos. If we have a little girl some-day, Josephine will be able to help her do her hair all cute.

I've been thinking about kids a lot. Well, maybe it's not a lot, I don't know. I do know it's a shit ton more than I thought before.

I'm thirty years old and I'm not getting any younger. Now that I finally have the woman of my dreams I never knew I wanted, I want to add kids into the mix and I don't want to be an old man when I have them.

Josephine is twenty-seven. I know she will want to be married first before we start a family. But after Opal told me planning a wedding could take up to a year, I started doing the calculations in my head.

A year from now, I'll be thirty-one. If we get pregnant right off the bat, it's another forty weeks till the baby comes, meaning I may as well round up to thirty-two. Josephine is not going to want back-to-back pregnancies, and two in diapers will be rough, which means we wait another year and another forty weeks.

I'm looking at thirty-four before I have two kids. And I want way more than two kids with Josephine—I want a fucking bus-load.

Okay, maybe not a bus-load, but three to four sounds like a nice number to me. I could be nearly forty when our final kid comes into the world.

Fuck, that's too long.

I throw my comb down on the counter in frustration. "Josephine, I want you to get that IUD out now!" I growl.

Josephine looks at me wide-eyed with her mouth open and her toothbrush hanging out.

Okay, that could have come out better.

But fuck, I want to start a family. I want to go to the courthouse, have a judge marry us, and start the next phase of our lives. She deserves the wedding of her dreams, I agree, but I want the family of our dreams. I don't want to be fucking forty when it's finally complete. I need to explain to her where my head is at.

She spits in the sink and her eyes flash. "Excuse me?" she questions with a hand on her hip.

Shit. I need to explain fast before she takes my comment like a demand, which it kind of is, but if I play nice and beg, maybe she'll go along with it. "Let me explain," I plead.

"Oh, please do," she says frigidly. I'm on thin ice right now. I better think before I open my damn mouth.

"I want kids with you, now," I blurt.

Yep, let that shit fly. Think before speaking, my ass.

Josephine's eyes are narrowed, but she sighs and calmly looks at me. "Maceo, I'm going to give you the benefit of the doubt and assume there's a lot more going on in your head than what you're revealing. Why don't you start again from the top?"

Thank you, sweet baby Jesus!

Before spilling myself open, I try to relax. "I know you want to be married first. But Opal said it may take a year to plan a wedding. It could take a long time to get pregnant too. And then it's forty more weeks of waiting. And that's only kid number one! What about kids number two, three, and four? Each one forty more weeks, plus time between each one. I don't want to be a geriatric man throwing the ball around with my kids and not being able to keep up because I'll need a knee replacement. I want to be alive when they graduate or get married," I ramble, staring at her with my hands flying into my hair, my voice raising an octave.

Shit, shit, SHIT!

Josephine grabs me by the shoulders. "Maceo, I want you to take a deep breath. Okay? Can you do that for me? Breathe in, breathe out."

I mimic her breathing and my hands fall away from my hair.

"Now I want you to listen to me, okay? I know you want children. You've pretty much wanted me pregnant since the first time we had sex. And don't think I didn't catch how unhappy you were when I told you I had an implant. You've been dropping hints left and right about wanting a family. I'm not opposed to having kids. We need to discuss how many we'll be trying for, because four seems like a lot, and I don't see you as the type of dad who's going to be okay driving a minivan," she says in a reasonable tone.

Wrong!

"I'll drive a minivan!" I say quickly. If that's the way I get the amount of kids I want with Josephine, I will fucking *rock* the minivan. Of course, I'll still have my bike to keep me cool.

Josephine holds up her hands to stop me. "Okay, the amount of kids isn't the important part here. Maceo, you're being dramatic. You're acting like you're going to be an old man tomorrow and you will not be old until decades from now, not a decade, but decades. You're still going to be alive when our kids graduate and get married. Christ, you're still going to be running around and throwing a ball when we have grandchildren because that's the kind of man you are."

My ears perk up on the word 'grandchildren.' "You think we can convince our kids to get married and have kids early?"

Josephine rolls her beautiful blue eyes. "If I say *sure* will you settle down?"

"Maybe," I admit before sighing. "I'm sorry. I know I'm freaking out about this. Since I've found you, I see myself wanting the whole package. I want a *big* family with a house full of loud kids. Maybe I feel this way because I never had my parents or any siblings, I don't know. All I know for sure is that I want to have this family with you, and I don't want to wait any longer."

Josephine nods. "I'm not agreeing to anything right now, but I will put your mind at ease on some of this. One, I don't need a big fancy wedding, only a nice one. Two, it won't take a year to plan because I like late summer or fall and that's coming up. Three, if I get the build done in the next month, we could have the wedding there. It will be big, spacious, everyone will fit and no one will have to travel. Four, I'll remove the IUD after we get married, so we can start trying for kids. And five, I may be kicking myself later for mentioning this to you, but my mom was a natural twin, and her grandmother

245

before her. We have a real chance at killing two birds with one stone and having multiple babies at once."

My heart fucking leaps. *Twins.* We could have twins. That's two babies in one pregnancy. Two pregnancies have the possibility to produce two sets of twins. That's four kids right off the bat. The fucking family of my dreams will be complete all before the age of thirty-four. *Fucking GOLD!*

With my heart jackhammering, I haul Josephine in my arms, cheering like a wild fan at a sporting event, not giving two shits if I wake the entire house. Josephine is a gift from God, created specifically for me.

All my dreams for us are within reach. But first we need to finish the build. Throwing Josephine over my shoulder, I race out of the bathroom and down the hall.

"What the fuck is going on?" Gauge say, stumbling out of the bedroom with his gun drawn, mistaking my excitement for danger. Chase is right behind him, yanking on his boots.

I swing around and face my brothers. "We're having TWINS!" I scream at the top of my lungs, banging on my chest like fucking King Kong with his woman.

"Holy shit! Jo's pregnant?!" Punk calls out from the bedroom.

"No, I'm fucking not!" she screams back to the whole house.

Giddy, I spank her juicy ass since it's right there next to my face. "She will be soon," I promise the entire house before remembering the agenda. "Shit. Can't talk. I've got to get her over to the build and finish the damn thing, now." I'm running out of the house to my bike.

Josephine's screaming at the top of her lungs, but I honestly can't hear a thing she's yelling at me. I'm too jacked up. I finally put her on the ground, kiss her full on the lips, and hop on my bike, waiting for her.

"Maceo, I don't have my work boots on. I don't have my keys to the trailer and buildings. I don't have my laptop, which I definitely need. And you're completely barefoot," she says in a rush, probably afraid I'll haul her over my bike if she doesn't hop on.

I look down at myself. Sure enough, I'm barefoot. I laugh out loud because I'm slap happy. I probably would have driven off and not felt the difference.

Quickly, I get off my bike and run into the house after Josephine to finish getting dressed. My mind keeps racing, thinking about everything Josephine revealed.

A wedding at the new MC clubhouse this fall would be fucking awesome. She's right when she says it will more than meet our needs as well as any guests invited. The kitchen is big enough for a catering company. There are bathrooms galore. The backdrop outside will be fucking stunning for an outdoor ceremony. If she's okay with doing the wedding at our new home, I'm all for it.

We'll be married by fall. IUD comes out after the honeymoon—hmm, maybe I can convince her to remove it before the wedding. We could try to conceive during our honeymoon. Either way, we'll be pregnant with twins by Christmas for sure!

"You know I can hear you, right? You're talking out loud," Josephine says, walking back outside. "And just because twins run in my family, doesn't mean it's a for sure thing with us."

"Oh, it's happening. We're *totally* having twins. And I'm going to get you pregnant again and it will be another set of twins. I feel it right here," I say confidently, pointing at my chest where my new tattoo is.

Josephine chuckles. "You'll get what you get and won't throw a fit."

"I'll get what I give you, which will be two sets of twins," I say proudly.

As I climb on my bike, I'm hit with a conundrum. "Oh my God, where are we going to put them all?"

"I told you, we'll get a minivan if it comes to that," Josephine says, calmly, strapping on her helmet and climbing on.

How can she be fucking calm right now? *This is serious!*

"Not the vehicle. I'm talking about the clubhouse. Where are we going to keep four kids in the presidential suite? It's not going to work, Pixie. You need to add a fourth story to the building," I ramble, panicked.

Josephine sighs. "You really want to raise our children in the Mercy Ravens MC clubhouse?"

I'm not opposed to it. I mean, the guys are all there to help keep an eye on them and the bunnies could help...*Oh my God!*

Between my men and the bunnies fornicating like they currently do, and how much they plan on doing more once we move into the bigger space, there's no way we can allow our kids to live under that roof. My God, it would be a nightmare once they hit puberty.

"What are we going to do?" I ask miserably.

"Relax, future hubby. I got this. You have a hundred acres."

"*We* have a hundred acres," I correct, rubbing her hands around my waist.

"Yes, we've got *a hundred acres*," she says again more slowly, and her words finally sink in my thick head.

"You could build us a house on the property!"

"Ding, ding, ding! Yay! We have a winner," she teases.

"Where would we build it on the property?" The wheels in my head start rotating with ideas.

"Wherever you want, baby. If you want it right next door, I can do it. If you want to move an acre or two away, I can do that too. If you want it on the other side of the property, I'll make it happen. Let me finish the clubhouse first. Next, I can plan the wedding. I can draw up a couple drafts of a house we can agree on after the wedding. We'll build the house and work on babies after we're settled," she says causally.

I shake my head. The timeline is too long for my liking. "Wedding planning and house drafts together, followed by babies. We can live in the clubhouse with the babies till the house is done," I counter.

Josephine huffs. It's her trademark gesture when she's pissed off. "You expect me to plan a wedding in two months' time, and work on house drafts, all while continuing my regular job? And don't you dare tell me to quit my job."

I snap my mouth shut because it's exactly what I was going to suggest, and I would be a damn fool if I let it slip. Josephine's job is important to her and of course I want her to keep working if it pleases her.

Part of me wants to make her aware she doesn't need to work anymore if she chooses. I'm set for life with the work I do, and she and our future kids will be well taken care of if anything were to happen to me. Best to keep it to myself until another, more appropriate time comes along.

"I would like to have our house done before we bring our babies into this world. I deserve it, as do our children. I want our memories to be in our own home and not the headquarters," she adds.

Annoyed, I chew on the inside of my cheek. I hate to admit I agree with her. I want our kids' first steps, first words, first everything to be in our forever home. I groan and look up at the early morning sky. "Fine," I concede, begrudgingly.

She squeezes me tightly. "Thank you, hubby," she says sweetly.

I smile hearing her say 'hubby' a second time and turn to look at her. "I like my new pet name, you know."

She giggles and her eyes sparkle. "I do too. Now hurry up and get me to work."

Eager for her to crack the whip and finish our build, I start my bike and pull away at a more controlled pace than what I thought myself possible of earlier.

Fifteen minutes later, we're pulling onto the property. None of the other workers have arrived yet, which is exactly the way Josephine likes it. Her routine involves using the next thirty minutes to go over everything, helping the day to run smoothly.

And that was the plan until we come to the trailer where she keeps her office on-site. The door is partially open and beat to shit. I climb off the bike and grab my gun from my ankle holster.

"Stay outside. Call Gauge," I tell her and make my way to the trailer. I push the door wide open and stare in shock.

The whole place has been tossed. Blueprints and drafts are ripped and thrown about. The desks and chairs are on their sides. The filing cabinet's drawers have been yanked out and its contents are scattered on the trailer floor. Jared's computer looks like it was bashed with something substantial, like a hammer or something bigger. Good thing Josephine takes hers home every night, otherwise hers would be in as bad of shape.

But none of this bothers me as much as what I see spray painted across the wall. My heart drops in my stomach and I have to count down from ten before I fly into a rage.

"Maceo, what's going on?" Josephine asks behind me. She gasps as she reads the words on the wall.

BIKER WHORE.

CHAPTER FIFTEEN
JOSEPHINE

There are no words to describe the terror I'm feeling. I run out of the trailer and rush to the main house, sick to my stomach about what else might be damaged. I run and examine everything. Maceo runs after me.

"Pixie, stop! What are you doing?" he asks, clearly panicked.

"My fucking job, that's what. I need to make sure this fucker didn't damage anything else on the property," I spit, checking all the windows, doors, and siding. All looks to be intact. Thank fuck for that. I sprint to the garages and do the same. Everything is fine.

I run to the mechanic shop and see the side door is wide open. Of course, the one fucking place on the property which was complete would be the spot this fucker chose to wreak havoc.

Maceo reaches me and stops me from advancing. He doesn't say anything but gives me a look which I'm quickly learning means to give him the lead. I watch him go inside, cursing up a storm.

"*Sonofabitch.* I'm going to fucking kill whoever did this!" he roars from inside. I feel queasy, but I go in to assess the damage.

Maceo had every right to scream his head off, but unlike him, I want to weep. Looks like the asshole took a sledgehammer and went to town on the hydraulic lift. It's bent in impossible ways. All the built in cabinets took a hit too.

Oddly enough, the prick left the painted walls untouched as well as the concrete floors. Small thanks for that. But between the lift and the cabinetry, the budget took a ten thousand dollar hit. I had been dropping the majority of what was left of the budget into the high tech intel room for Chase, and now I have no way of making this up. I'm going to have to come up with the money from somewhere.

Everything is going topsy-turvy. First, was the fiasco with Jacob being kicked off the project and throwing Maceo over the edge. Second, was the panty-snatcher and being forced out of my condo. Third, was the Esteban encounter that freaked the hell out of everyone. Fourth, was the phone call from dad where he showed he and my mom still side with Jacob—I'm still angry as hell about it and frustrated knowing Maceo isn't going to let me stew over it for long. I love my parents, even after everything, but I will not tolerate them talking negatively about Maceo when they haven't even met him.

And now this shit with the MC build being vandalized is one too many things on my shoulders. Moisture starts to build in my eyes.

Maceo grabs me and holds me to him as my tears spill over. "It's okay, baby. We're going to catch the fucker and I will take care of him," he says, running his hands over me comfortingly.

"What the hell?" Jared says, walking into the shop. "W-what, why?" he stutters with anger.

"If you think this is bad, don't go in the trailer," I mumble.

Jared looks ashen and he sinks to the floor, surveying the damage. "I saw it. Who did this?"

"We don't know," I say, choking on a sob.

Jared is suddenly jumping to his feet. "Your men installed the outdoor security cameras after that man approached in the car. The bastard has to be on video!"

Maceo releases me and pulls out his phone. "Chase. Bring up the footage of the build site. Start with Saturday morning around one."

Maceo walks out of the garage to the thunder of motorcycles coming on the property.

Jared comes up to me and pulls me into a hug. I lean into his chest and he lets me go ahead and ruin his flannel button-down with my tears. "It's okay, Jo. We're not going to let anything happen to you. Between Maceo's crew and ours, you're safe. The Ravens are going to find who did this and they'll make him pay."

"This is going to set us back a lot of time and money. Fuck!" I cry.

Punk comes into the shop with Gauge, and spots me falling apart on Jared. Punk's eyebrows rise up and he gives Gauge a look. He then marches up to Jared and pulls me gently, but firmly, from his arms before swinging me up and cradling me to his chest. Without a word, Punk carries me out of the shop.

I hear Gauge speak to Jared in a low voice. "Don't let Atlas catch you comforting his woman."

"Josephine's my best friend and business partner. Atlas can deal with it," Jared grumbles.

"I'm Atlas's best friend and that shit wouldn't fly if I tried it," Gauge retorts.

I want to chastise Gauge and apologize to Jared, but I don't need to. Gauge wasn't threatening Jared but warning him. With the mood Maceo's in, having something as blasé as Jared giving me a hug would throw him over the edge.

Maceo is going to have to get over his jealousy of other men especially since my best friend is a man, I work with men, and Maceo's family is made up of all men. It's not acceptable, and Jared is right— Maceo will need to learn to 'deal with it.' However, today is not a day to test him.

"Jesus, Jo. You need to eat a sandwich or something. Do you even weigh a full Benjamin?" Punk teases. I know he's trying to lighten my mood, but it can't be salvaged.

"Send me the feed," Maceo barks into the phone. He turns to see Punk bringing me to him. His eyes narrow at Punk, but he trusts his brother and he trusts me. The courtesy would not be extended to anyone outside of the club, regardless of how close of a brother Jared is to me.

Maceo gives a chin nod at my computer strapped to my back in its backpack. Punk sets me down and helps me get it out. Maceo takes the computer and pulls up the surveillance video.

Early this morning around two, a black car pulls along the road near the property and a hooded dark figure with a backpack gets out with a baseball bat. He rushes the fence, scaling it easily, and jumps to the ground on the other side. He races to the trailer and starts beating on the door with the bat till it busts open. He disappears inside for some time before reemerging. We all know the destruction he did in there.

The vandal takes off across the property toward the shop, and bangs the shit out of the one garage door till he's able to yank it up enough to roll underneath it. Again, we know the damage he did in there as well. He emerges through the shop door as opposed to crawling under the garage door again. He jogs over to the house, but can't find an easy way in the steel and stone structure.

As if admiring it, he runs a gloved hand over one of the windows and peers inside. He backs off and assesses the building, almost like he's debating if it's worth the effort. He obviously can tell the windows are bullet resistant. A baseball bat would bounce off and probably hurt the vandal in the process.

He pulls off his backpack and yanks out what looks like a can of spray paint. He shakes the can but duck's down when headlights sweep across the house—a car must have driven by on the road. It's enough to spook the intruder, and he takes off up the hill to the fence along the road and climbs back over.

I blow out a sigh of relief. "This could have been much worse. He could have destroyed the house. Thank God I take my computer and flash drive home with me. I have backups to all the work in the trailer. We're set back ten grand and at minimum two weeks with the shop, but we can move forward with everything else."

"Did you see how he was analyzing the buildings? He knew all the weak spots to gain excess to them. He either knows construction sites or is a construction worker," Punk says to Maceo.

"He's not a crew member of mine," I say, matter of fact.

Maceo turns to me. "Why do you say that?"

"My crew was all here when your crew came in and set up the security cameras. My workers know where all the check points are and avoid them when they want to slack on the job or piss somewhere in a corner. If it was one of my crew, they would have used the spray paint to obstruct the camera lenses."

"This was an outsider or at the very least someone who may have been on the build site and was familiar with it, but unaware of the cameras," Maceo says.

"Can you play it again?" I ask. Maceo hits the button and the videos pop up. I watch closely as the guy runs between the structures. *Hmm...*

"What is it? What do you see?" Punk asks.

I cock my head. "I'm watching his running form. It's kind of like a fingerprint, allowing you to know runners based on their stride patterns. This guy keeps his gait real short, like he's marching, and he holds his arms high, meaning they can get stiff quickly if not stretched out. It explains why after he took out the trailer and shop, he backed off from the beating on the outside of the house. He was already too worn out," I say, watching the video.

Maceo looks over at me with something resembling pride. He likes how I'm observant.

My face puckers watching the video. "His form looks familiar to me, like I've seen this person before. He's definitely got the build of a runner, long and lean. The upper body on an average noncompetitive runner is typically shit, because the upper body is not given the same attention as the lower body.

"Competitive runners work their upper bodies too. He had enough to scale the fence no problem. And the damage he did in the trailer and shop was significant. He had a hard time scaling back over the fence, but this could be because his upper body is tighter.

"He definitely is a competitive runner or was a competitive runner who's still committed to the exercise. But his gait...the marching form is similar too—" I stop, my stomach falls.

"Pixie?" Maceo asks, watching me intently.

I close my eyes and sigh heavily. I should have known who it was from what was written on the inside of the trailer. I've seen it written a lot lately from one particular source.

What was he thinking? I open my eyes and glare at the computer.

Maceo bends down to me and lightly turns my face to him. "Who is it?"

"It's Jacob," I whisper. "It took me a moment to recognize his form; it's been over a year since I watched him run. We ran track together at USC, we didn't stop with our workout routines after graduation. He's done more road races than me, but he never did like how I was a more successful racer than him. Everything was a fucking competition with him. I cannot believe this shit."

Maceo's dark eyes grow darker. "The way he scales the fence in the video is the same way the perp who broke into your condo scaled the back fence of your yard. It had to be him that night, too."

"That's why you couldn't catch him when you pursued him. He's a middle distance runner. He's got the speed and the endurance to make a quick get away," I explain, shaking my head.

"We got him!" Punk cheers, his fists flying above his head. I wish I felt his enthusiasm, instead I feel cold.

Maceo shakes his head. "We've got nothing. We have a video showing *someone* doing this shit, but we've got no smoking gun. There's nothing to connect Jacob to this. He wore gloves and was completely covered head to foot. The fucker was wearing a mask, for Christ's sake. The police are going to see this and say this could be Jacob or anyone else who fits his build," Maceo says clinically, pacing back and forth. He paces a lot when he's thinking, or stressed, or both.

I rub my temples. "Speaking of police, we need to contact them and report this. I have to file a police report to see if we can reclaim anything through insurance."

"Already done," Gauge says, walking toward us with Jared. "They should be here any minute."

Overwhelmed and feeling pretty shitty about myself, I pull away from the group. I walk toward the outer edge of the construction zone where there's only acres upon acres of wilderness. It's here I break down, again.

Maceo must have followed me, because as soon as the tears start falling, his arms are lacing around me from behind. He spins me around and holds me to his broad chest. "Pixie, what's going on?"

"This is all my fault," I blubber. "If I had ignored his text about taking me off the blacklist and never called him, he never would've come here. He never would've formed this unhealthy attachment to me if I hadn't invited him. I fucked it up by contacting him back for this consulting job, which backfired. It's my fault he did all this damage."

"Absolutely fucking NOT," Maceo says, vehemently. "Loafer-dick already had an unhealthy attachment to you prior to any of this. The fact you invited him has no bearing on the choices he made to break into your condo and fuck with my MC clubhouse.

"Jacob made the decision to break into two private properties. He made the decision to steal your items. He made the decision to vandalize my property. His decisions are his alone and haven't one fucking thing to do with you inviting him here."

"But I put the temptation back in his face," I argue.

Maceo shakes his head and holds me tighter. "The temptation has been there for him since you left. You think I haven't seen the fucking dick pics or the smut texts he sent you months after you left his sorry ass? He hasn't stopped harassing you. This shit has been ongoing. Stop thinking this has anything to do with you calling him while I was overseas. He would have made his way here eventually with or without you reaching out to him. It was only a matter of time."

He kisses me so hard and deep I can barely think. I know he's doing this to distract me, but damn if it isn't working. It makes me imagine us alone in a bedroom with a large bed, and him totally naked...

Maceo breaks the kiss and smiles naughtily down at me. The way he's appraising me, I could swear his mind is in the exact same place mine is. "Soon," he promises, kissing the crown of my head.

Damn, maybe he can read my thoughts as well as the emotions on my face.

He tugs us back over to the group and looks at Punk. "Have Chase look into loafer-dick. I want confirmation he was in the state. Check credit cards, cash withdrawals, cell towers—everything to nail the fucker. The police can't use it, but we can," he orders.

Punk nods and walks away to make the call as sirens scream in the distance.

The cops investigate nearly all day, causing a shit storm of traffic when my crew and delivery drivers arrive on-site. I have nearly all my workers inside the main house to avoid disturbing the police investigation. It's a clusterfuck in there, but at least they're all working and keeping busy.

Jared and I can't shut down production today and expect our workers to return tomorrow, as if going a day without pay is something they can afford. If we stop work, we run the risk of crew members jumping ship for paying jobs.

Detective Quire questions me and Maceo again. Maceo fills him in on our suspicions that it's in fact Jacob, but Luke agrees there's not enough to bring him in with what little we've got and our suspicions alone.

My attention is being tugged in multiple directions with the build, my crew, Maceo, and the cops that I can feel my fragile sanity starting to rip.

Maceo is on the phone with Chase and growing angrier by the second, which isn't good because he's already in full alpha asshole mode. Tipping him over the edge may cause a nuclear explosion to go off around him. I feel bad for Chase having to deal with him right now.

Punk follows me around like a human shield, though we could probably stop having him do it. Jacob is the panty-snatching fence-jumping vandalizer. Yet, I know Punk would give me the 'Maceo's orders' or 'Esteban is still out there' speech. Conceding, I let him guard me to keep the peace.

Jared and I crunch numbers and try to figure out a way to recoup ten grand. I call our insurance company, and Jared tries to hash out better deals with venders.

By the end of the day, I'm asking Jared if he's reconsidering our partnership. I've brought such a fucking headache to this job, and I wouldn't blame him for bailing. Jared does everything he can to reassure me that he's with me all the way, but I can't help but worry about it.

Maceo is busy investigating Jacob with Chase and Gauge, so Jared and I stay late after our crews leave for the day, and sort through the mess of papers in the trailer. I categorize stacks, while Ziggy and Jared tag-team putting things in chronological order. Butch helps by reprinting all my torn blueprints at a local print shop. Punk, Flay, and Eagle remove all the broken furnishings and file sorted paperwork.

Ziggy rush orders a new laptop for Jared. He sets it up on the make shift desk of two saw horses and an old door that Punk threw together—Ziggy is even kind enough to walk Jared through his new computer. By two in the morning, the file cabinet is back in order and the floor is clean. All that's left is a stack of papers a foot high, but I call it a night.

Maceo takes me home and we fall into bed fully clothed. Hades crawls on top of Maceo and the three of us go to sleep.

In the morning, Maceo and I go for a run with Hades. Our asses are dragging but we need this. I drive to work with Hades since Maceo wants to lift weights. Opal accompanies me. She needs a place to study and prefers to do it away from Gauge—he's too much of a distraction for her. Punk escorts us to the site, and I attack the last pile of paper, having it all sorted before the rest of my crew shows up.

My workers are happy to spread out again and get right to work. Jared comes with a can of paint to cover the spray-painted wall of the trailer—Ziggy even offers to help him paint, making Jared a happy camper. Cliff makes a new door for the trailer and installs it. By lunch time the trailer looks new.

Two of my crew members remove the built-in cabinets and garage door in the shop. The metal is scrapped to recoup some money. I rush order new ones and they will be in by next week. The hydraulic lift is a big budget hit, but Maceo says to go ahead and order the new one and he will foot the bill. Relieved, I cry in Maceo's arms. As the day comes to a close, we are working as if nothing has happened and everything is on track.

By the end of the week, I'm ready for the weekend. Jared and I are determined to finish the build before three months are up, and we brainstorm nonstop to figure out how we can make it happen.

We buy pizza for all our employees to thank them for all their hard work. Sometimes all you need to do to let your workers know you appreciate them is surprise them with food. Lunch goes a little over, but spirits are high afterwards.

By four o'clock in the afternoon, the insurance company calls back to inform us our claim has been accepted. It's enough to cover the rest of the expenses. I'm locking up shop and shooing the rest of my workers home, waiting for Maceo to arrive and drive me back. I double-check the new security system Chase installed and make sure all the cameras are functioning before walking over to my security detail.

Punk nods at me to get on his bike. I guess Maceo isn't coming after all. I don the helmet Punk hands me and crawl up behind him, wrapping my arms around his mid section gingerly.

Punk laughs and yanks me flush to him. "I don't bite, Jo."

It feels weird being this close to Punk when I'm Maceo's fiancée, but I don't have another option of getting home.

"Where's Maceo?" I ask.

"Atlas has been working with Chase and Gauge all day after he finished at the gym. Chase has found a lot of damaging evidence against Jacob, but none of it can be used since it was obtained illegally," he informs before starting his bike. "Hold on tight, Jo."

Eagle and Ziggy lead the caravan with Punk and I in the middle and Flay and Brass taking the rear. It always seems like overkill to have this many men watching out for me, but I'm not going to argue anymore with Maceo. He's made it clear I'm top priority and the Ravens are protecting their first lady.

We get to the MC's rental and I see Maceo in the garage with Chase and Gauge, huddled around one of the computers. I climb off Punk's bike and remove my helmet. Maceo stands from his stool and makes his way toward me, Hades padding alongside him. When Maceo is toe to toe with me, he bends down and gives me a deep kiss, making my toes curl in my steel-toed boots.

Maceo raises a dark eyebrow at Punk. "Thank you for bringing my fiancée home. I trust you were on your best behavior?"

"Didn't touch or hit on her, I swear," Punk says quickly.

I slap Maceo on the chest gently. "Stop being a bully. Punk is always a gentleman to me."

Maceo laughs and Punk relaxes. "He knows I'm fucking with him, Pixie."

I look at Maceo expectantly. "Punk said Chase found the mother lode on Jacob?"

Bright white teeth take over Maceo's smile. "He sure did. Come have a look." He takes my hand and pulls me gently to the garage where Chase and Gauge are working. Punk follows and goes to the fridge in the garage to grab everyone beers.

Maceo sits his fine muscled ass on a stool and sits me on one of his tree-trunk legs. "Chase, why don't you give my woman the run down?"

Chase gives me a knowing grin. "The fucker is smart, I'll give him that much. He's avoiding using his credit cards because he knows they can be traced, but he took out a large cash withdrawal from his savings a week before he vandalized our turf.

"I hacked into surveillance videos around the area and caught him on camera entering a motel Monday morning around four, on the outskirts of Fort Collins. He paid with cash, we assume, since his credit shows nothing. Video footage shows him leaving around three in the afternoon.

"We believe he avoided buying a plane ticket because that could be traced. He drove here in his own vehicle. You would be unfamiliar with it since he purchased the black Volvo after you two had split. He probably thought he was safe traveling around town because no one would recognize it.

"The surveillance video outside your condo clearly shows him staking out the property in his car, probably waiting for you to return. We got him driving by our rental, too, but he was smart enough to keep driving and not stop.

"The fucker left his cell off or didn't bring it because his cell plan shows nothing. More than likely he bought a burner to use for an emergency."

A cold shudder runs through me. The idea of having Jacob stakeout my condo gives me the heebie-jeebies. "In other words, we've got nothing we can turn over to the cops?"

"We've shown them the videos from our properties, but I can't turn over the motel surveillance video without getting myself arrested for hacking. This is unfortunate since it's the only video with actual confirmation of him being present in Fort Collins," Chase answers.

"Why can't we go to the motel and ask for it? Maybe they would be willing to hand it over without a warrant," I suggest.

All the men shake their heads.

"Not gonna happen. The motel is a corrupt hot spot and the

owner is as crooked as they come. He's been burned one too many times and won't work with cops. Anyone who knows our club knows we work with local law enforcement. We already told police we thought we saw Jacob enter the motel, but without a warrant, the owner isn't handing over anything. Police can't get a warrant since there's not enough evidence to merit one," Gauge explains apologetically.

"There's no other surveillance video around town showing he was here? What about a gas station or a restaurant? He needs food and fuel," I try again.

Again they all shake their heads.

"He never left the motel once he arrived. He visited your condo, our rental, and the build site before checking into the hotel. I couldn't pick up his license plate in either video, but it's his car, I'm certain. City surveillance cams show his car cruising around town, but he's got fake plates. Says it's from Nevada. No luck seeing inside the car since the windows are tinted. As far as food, he probably didn't eat or brought it all with him in the car. Fuel can easily be transported as well in the trunk of a vehicle." Chase says.

I shake my head and fight the tears stinging the back of my eyes. "He planned this. This was thought out and calculated. On his credit charges, did it show him buying any of his supplies, like the surplus of gas, or the spray paint and baseball bat?"

"Nothing comes up. Cash transactions at stores don't have a name attached. You're right, he did plan it all out," Gauge says.

"Like I said, he's smart," Chase murmurs, staring at his computer screens.

"Yes, he is. He swiped all my work right out from under my nose without me knowing. And he's a smooth talker. All of my family and old friends believe I'm the one who had the issues in the relationship because he was able to con all of them," I admit with angry tears. I could kick myself for having dated a fucking manipulative genius.

"Well, he may be smart, but we're definitely smarter," Chase says with a wicked gleam in his brown eyes. "You see, every time he's acted out it's because he's provoked. He broke into your condo after you turned him away from the job. Atlas marked you as his in front of him. He could have been planning this second attack for a while like you say, but he sprung into action after I uploaded the picture of you two to our security company website. I posted the picture on Saturday around noon, giving him plenty of time to make the seventeen-hour commute by car with time to spare."

"What picture?" I ask.

"Atlas took pictures on the two of you after he proposed. I cropped the picture of you two holding up your fists showing your rings, and posted it on our website saying 'the prez is getting hitched,'" Chase explains. "I thought it would be a good marketing tool and help our image."

"Well, if he's been stalking your company site the way he was stalking my social media, he would've definitely seen it and lost his shit," I declare.

"Exactly. Every time something big happens with you, he attacks. He started slowly with inappropriate texts and dick pics when you refused to have contact with him. He upgraded to busting into your condo after seeing you. He probably got angry because all his digital images of you in his cloud, phone, and both your guys' social media accounts were deleted by *moi*," Chase adds.

My hand flies to my forehead and I jump off Maceo's lap. "My photo box in the closet! He was trying to find pictures of me because he didn't have them anymore."

"More than likely why he was trying to break into your computer as well," Maceo grits through his teeth. "And he probably took your sexy panties because he didn't want me to benefit from them."

Gauge busts a gut. "Is that why you got a Victoria's Secret credit card? To buy Jo new underwear?"

Maceo blushes hard, snapping at his best friend. "Dude! That was supposed to stay between the two of us!" Maceo's numerous surprise lingerie gifts start to make sense to me now.

Punk looks impressed. "That's actually a brilliant idea. That way you get your woman to wear what you want."

Maceo rubs the back of his neck, self-conscious. "I thought so. They've got a great reward program."

Maceo's brothers laugh at his expense.

"Fuck all of you. Don't come crawling to me to reap the benefits of my free shipping and monthly perks." It's pretty adorable seeing my fiancé embarrassed.

"Oh, come on, Atlas! You promised I could use it to splurge on Opal," Gauge protests. He slaps a hand over his mouth quickly, surprised.

Say what? Did Gauge let something slip about him and Opal?

Chase and Punk look just as shocked as me—not shocked that there's something more serious between Gauge and Opal, but that he let his guard down around the rest of us. I can see that Gauge is more open about his relationship with the pretty girl when it's just him and Maceo shooting the shit.

Maceo gives him a look. "I'm starting to think Opal could do better." We all laugh again.

"Anyways," Gauge says, returning the conversation back to me. "Jacob knew something was going on between you and Atlas, and it was his way of saying 'fuck you.' He was harassing you on social media since he was no longer in town after the confrontation you guys had with him at the café after the condo break in."

"We put his next action into play when you and I announced our engagement; then the build site was vandalized," Maceo points out.

"Getting back on point," Chase speaks up. "This shit only happens when something big takes place with Jo which isn't in loafer-dick's favor."

Maceo gives Chase a stern look. "No."

"I'm telling you, Atlas, this will work," Chase fires back.

"And I'm telling you as club president, no! I will not be using my bride to bait the fucker."

Chase throws his hands up in frustration. "It's not like she'll be in any fucking danger. Your woman has more security than the British royal family. Let's put out something to grab Jacob's attention and be ready and waiting for him. If he sneaks onto our property again, we can get him for trespassing. If he damages any of our stuff, we can get him on vandalizing. If he gets into the building, we can get him on breaking and entering."

"And if he gets a hold of Jo then what? We get him on assault or rape or murder? The perp is escalating," Gauge argues back, shaking his head in disgust.

"It won't get to that," Chase defends.

"Because we aren't fucking doing it!" Maceo roars. "Gauge is right. The fucknob is not going to be satisfied breaking in or damaging property. He's been there and done that. He's only going to step up his game and go to the next level."

I'm listening to all of this in stunned silence. I'm scared, *real* scared.

Gauge mentioning that Jacob's behavior is escalating terrifies the shit out of me. Jacob wants me back and thus far, nothing he has done has worked. Now he has turned to scare tactics and threats, showing he's extremely dangerous.

But as scared as I am, a bigger part of me doesn't want to be. A bigger part of me wants to fight back and hold Jacob accountable for his actions.

Cops can't do anything to help right now. I could get a restraining order, but a restraining order doesn't do shit if the other party ignores it and takes what they want from you anyways. Too many women have fallen victim to a false sense of security when it comes to a restraining order.

No, something needs to be done and it needs to be done now, while Jacob is emotionally overloaded and is most likely to fuck up and get caught.

"Chase is right," I blurt.

Maceo and Gauge look at me like I've grown a third head. Punk scowls—putting me in danger goes against his bodyguard instincts.

Chase slaps his hands down on the work bench. "Thank you, Jo!" He says with renewed energy. "See, she gets it."

Maceo's massive form grows larger, hovering over me, shaking his head and pointing a thick finger at me. "This isn't fucking happening. I'm not putting you in jeopardy."

"It's not your call. It's mine," I snap back.

"The hell it is! My club, my rules, and we're not doing shit to provoke the fucker," Maceo snarls. "I'll fucking lock you up before I let the cocksucker try to pull anymore shit on you."

Defiant, I square my shoulders. "Go ahead and hide me away in a bunker but use me to pull the prick out first. I don't have to be anywhere near the situation. Hell, none of you need to be near the situation. We can bring in local law enforcement to handle it."

"And what's going to bring his sorry ass in? We had no clue when he was going to attack us before. What the hell is going to prompt his next attack?" Maceo barks at me in challenge.

I smirk because it's obvious. "A wedding, of course."

CHAPTER SIXTEEN
MACEO

I swear to God, I'm going to spank her ass 'till it's beet red. Her fucking challenging me, *ugh*! Taking on Jacob by using herself as bait, and fucking schooling me in front of my brothers on how to reel the fucker in, has got me pissed off to the point I see red.

I'm both livid and turned on. Angry she would want to use herself as a pawn in the take-down-Jacob scheme, and riled up with need over how fucking cunning she is.

My pixie is like a fucking black widow and I love it—enticing her prey and then trapping them. She reminds me of Stage that way. He has the name for a reason. He can set a trap up to capture perps better than anyone on our crew.

But I can't let her know this. I can't let her think I'm on board with this hare-brained idea of taking him down by throwing a mock wedding, because I sure as shit am not on board.

"Are you fucking crazy?" I shout before thinking.

Josephine's nostrils flare. "I'm not crazy, you alpha asshole. This is a perfect ambush."

Feeling a migraine coming on, I pinch the bridge of my nose.

"Think about it. We have Chase put on the Mercy Ravens Security website how the prez will be marrying on a planned date, at a planned location. If he's cyber stalking us like we assume, our names will come up with all the details. Hell, we can say we're getting married at the courthouse and have the whole police force there," Josephine explains. Excitement gleams in her coastal eyes, the kind of excitement she reserves for the bedroom.

Is she getting turned on by this? Fuck, I think she is. Seeing Josephine get aroused over taking down her ex is enticing as hell. I will my cock down to half-mast. Now is not the time to lead with my dick.

"I don't want to think about it," I spit through my teeth. "Pixie, I'm not okay with pissing him off more and having him snap. You can plan everything, but it doesn't mean shit will go down the way you want."

"I hate to admit it, but it's not a bad idea," Gauge says to me.

Motherfucker! "Go suck a bag of dicks, Gauge! You telling me you'd be on board with this shit if it was Opal who was sticking her neck out?"

Gauge's green eyes go nearly black. He hates when I publicly point out that Opal and him are a thing. Well, tough shit! He needs to get over that hang-up and see how when you love someone you don't gamble with their life. And it's exactly why I'm not willing to mess with Josephine's.

Chase tries to justify Josephine's reasoning. "Now wait a sec. Jo could be onto something here. The fucker will definitely want to stop your marriage. We'll be there as security. You will be with Jo. The police will be right there to make an arrest. You know his desperate ass is going to come with a weapon. The fucker will get thrown away in jail for a long time if he walks into the courthouse with it. This might be the best way to get him put away."

"The best way to deal with him is putting a bullet in his head," I snap.

"Well, we can have that arranged if you want to get your hands dirty," Gauge says in all seriousness. Gauge thinks like me on how to deal with problem people. I know he would be there with a shovel if I tried to take matters into my own hands.

The idea of ending Jacob's life and putting him in a hole to rot is very tempting, and growing more so the longer I think about it. I have a silent exchange with my closest brothers. All three of them nod in agreement.

Punk gives a vile smile. "Fuck yeah! Let's put this bastard down."

"Nobody is killing anybody," Josephine protests with alarm.

"Dammit Punk!" I bark. Chase and Gauge groan in agreement. The kid never knows when to keep shit on the down-low.

Josephine gives me a pointed look. "You need to look at it from a third party point of view. You know if this involved anyone else, you'd be all over my idea."

"But it's not anybody else. It's you! I'm sorry if I fucking care too much to put you at risk, but it's the way it is, so deal with it," I fume.

Why the hell is she pushing on this? I'm trying to keep her fucking safe and unharmed.

"Remember what you told me after Esteban confronted me? You said it was time to stop doing defense and go on the offense, which is exactly what we need to do now. Your words, not mine. So either what you said is true or it isn't. Which is it?" Josephine challenges.

Fucking hell! Frustrated, I roar and flip one of the work benches. Hades cowers behind Chase, making me feel awful, but not bad enough to apologize to him right now with the state I'm in.

How the hell am I being outnumbered right now? *It's a fucking mutiny!* And Josephine throwing my own words in my face, pisses me off like nobody's business.

Josephine grabs me by the arm and yanks me from the garage. I go with her because I follow her everywhere like an eager puppy, because I do everything and anything for her, including when I'm fucking boiling over with rage.

In the backyard, Josephine spins on me. "You need to calm down."

"I am fucking calm!" I snarl like the beast I am.

"Your actions speak otherwise!" she shouts.

Oh man, my woman is peeving me off to high hell. How the fuck can I argue my point to show her reason?

I run my hands over my face. "Pixie, you freaked out on me when I told you I would put my life on the line for you. How the fuck should I feel knowing you want to do the same for me?"

"You told me I needed to trust you and you promised me you wouldn't die. I *do* trust you, Maceo. Now I'm asking the same from you. You need to trust me on this. I promise you nothing will happen to me," she states firmly.

I feel my resolve slipping and it freaks me the fuck out. Does she not understand what she's asking of me? Does she not see how much this goes against what I feel is best?

No, she doesn't and I'm incapable of refusing her.

"Baby, please don't make me do this," I beg. I don't beg, ever. This woman has me wrapped around her finger. I'd fucking bend over backward like a contortionist for her.

Josephine's eyes go soft and she reaches up to cup my face. "It's going to be okay, Maceo, I promise."

My eyes squeeze shut and I fall to my knees at her feet, wrapping my arms around her wispy frame. I hate myself for what I'm about to agree to, what I'm about to order.

"Okay. I'll trust you."

My happy-go-lucky demeanor has fucking evaporated since agreeing to entice Jacob into an attack. I'm in 'full alpha asshole mode' again, according to Josephine. I don't give a shit if I am. Regardless if I'm on board with this operation, I'm not happy about it.

After a week of strategic planning, we've finally agreed as a crew how to handle this monster. Chase posts a news update on our website informing readers the club president will be marrying Miss

Josephine Holland in two weeks time in a civil union ceremony at the court-house here in Fort Collins.

Punk notifies local law enforcement there may be an issue with Jacob Klein acting out during our wedding. Luke will be present along with several of his men. If Jacob tries to pull anything, they will be there ready to make the arrest.

Chase was right about helping our image with uploading all the personal shit about me getting engaged. We're getting more requests for jobs and having a hard time passing. Thankfully, most are local recon jobs or at least in the state, and only require three to four guys per job.

Unfortunately, this means we're asking Lorenzo's men to play guard duty at the job site way more than I'm comfortable with. Granted, they're more worried about Esteban moving in on their territory than the threat Jacob is imposing on Josephine, but Lorenzo is willing to offer more to assist anyway. I'm firm on keeping their involvement to a minimum. It's bad enough seeing Lorenzo himself dropping by my property to check out my woman.

Fucking hate that fucker in his fucking tailored suits. Ugh! I want to throat punch him every time he tries to talk to my pixie. I already broke the sleazeball's nose for propositioning a date from her. Luke was able to talk Lorenzo out of pressing charges, stating I was protecting my woman from a potential stalker. Lorenzo didn't want Josephine thinking he was a threat, so he backed off. But still he hangs around like a bad cold you can't shake. Fortunately, Josephine is too busy to pay him any notice.

Josephine is in micromanager form and is too preoccupied with completing the project, so I've recruited Opal to keep Josephine on track. Sham wedding or not, we still need to keep up appearances, meaning doing some actual wedding stuff, like finding a wedding dress and picking out flowers. Opal comes to the build site and drags my bride-to-be away, giving her construction crew a much-needed break from her nitpicking.

There are definite moments where it feels like we're truly plan-

272

ning our wedding. I catch myself getting excited watching Josephine flip through wedding catalogs or Pinterest, setting things aside I know she intends for the *real* big day. More than once, I hear her mumble to herself about how it isn't fair to have to plan two weddings.

"Let's make it a real one," I say. If I had it my way, we would already be married.

Josephine doesn't look up at me as she shakes her head. "Two weeks is not enough time to plan all the things I want. Sorry, but the answer is no."

Annoyed, I grumble to myself and sit next to her on my bunk, surrounded by all things wedding. It's late and my fingers have a life of their own, grazing up and down her naked thighs. Josephine is wearing her typical braless tank top and tiny panties for bed, practically making me swoon. Who would have thought these simple clothes would look like the sexiest lingerie to me?

I may start buying her tank tops from Victoria's Secret along with the underwear I can't seem to stop ordering. Is there such a thing as having a lingerie shopping compulsion? Nah, it's just seeing my woman in skimpy undergarments that's my real compulsion. Not being able to have sex with her in the house is definitely starting to drive me up the wall.

At least my brothers have learned not to make direct eye contact with Josephine when they step in the bedroom. They've all gotten a peek at her in her bikini panties or thongs, and they've all gotten death glares or verbal threats from me about keeping their eyes to themselves. The only thing making it worth them gawking at her, is knowing she's mine and they're all jealous she belongs to me. Or maybe it's because they're jealous of what we have together.

"I found the dress," Josephine says, not looking up from her phone.

My fingers continue to draw patterns into her sun-kissed legs. "Good. One thing off the sham wedding list done."

Her sparkling blue eyes finally look into mine. "No, not *that* dress. I'm talking *the* dress."

Oh, man. My heart pounds in my chest imagining her in a white dress walking down an aisle toward me.

What does it look like? Is it simple or glammed up? Is it white or ivory or some other color altogether? Is it puffy like a princess-dress or something more formfitting? *I've got to know.*

"What does it look like? Tell me now," I command eagerly.

"Like hell I will. It's bad luck," she rebukes.

I shake my head. "No, no, you got it wrong. It's if I *see* you in it before the wedding, it's bad luck," I plead my defense. "So tell me. Better yet, do you have a picture of you not wearing it?"

Josephine sighs. "You'll have to wait. It's being rushed over from a different vendor who has it in the right size. It should be in next week."

Dammit.

"What about the fake dress?" I ask, still envisioning the real one.

"I found it today, too. The seamstress was in today when Opal and I picked it out, and she was able to take all the fitting measurements. I go next week for the final fitting, and if all is good, it comes home with me."

"Good."

"Before I go to my next fitting, you should talk to Lorenzo's men," she says, looking back at her phone.

I'm suddenly alarmed. "Why?"

Josephine rolls her eyes in frustration. "They're getting a little— what's the word?—*restless*, I guess. They pretty much harass all the construction workers on-site who come near me, which is bad enough. The crew knows what's going on and tolerates it. But today when Opal and I came out of the wedding boutique, one of Lorenzo's personal bodyguards, Tiny Tony, was hauling this man out of his van. He pulled his gun on him and interrogated him about his California license plate and why he was carrying a camera. The poor guy was practically crying when he explained he was on vacation."

Groaning, I rub my hand down my face. *Fucking Lorenzo and his hounds.* They did the same shit to a delivery driver who came to the property this week too. "I'll have Gauge reach out to Lorenzo."

"Thank you, future hubby," she purrs, which goes straight to my loins.

Looking for a distraction, I pick up one of several wedding bags scattered about and peer inside.

Josephine snatches it away. "Nope! No peeking."

"Is it for the real wedding or the fake wedding?" I ask, greedy to get a better look at what I saw in the shopping bag.

Josephine pauses. "The fake wedding," she admits, finally.

"Then it doesn't matter." With a winning smirk, I yank the bag back and pull out what I had only caught a quick glance of. I hold the silk garter between my fingers.

At first, I'm super turned on to see this lacy white piece of material, but I frown. "I know we agreed to do some things for appearance's sake, but I sure as hell won't let Jacob get close enough to see what you have under your dress."

Josephine shrugs. "If I don't wear it for this fake wedding, you may want to keep it for practice."

My brows pull together. "Practice?"

"Mm-hm. You know, practice. Pulling it off my thigh with your teeth for the garter toss," Josephine says, pinning away on Pinterest.

Come again?! Using my teeth anywhere near her thigh sounds right up my alley, and acts like an electrical current straight to my junk.

Grinning, I sink to my knees in front of the bunk, grabbing hold of her leg and sliding the garter up her thigh.

Josephine looks shocked. "What are you doing?"

"Practicing," I answer with a roguish grin, my head working between her thighs closer to her hot center. I nip at her mound through the thin fabric of her panties, making her to buck her hips in my face.

The bedroom door swings open and Punk saunters in. He takes stock of my face full between her thighs.

"Oh, fuck!" Punk shouts, spinning around and slamming the door shut, before pleading on the other side. "I swear to God, I didn't see anything, Atlas. Don't fucking rip my dick off, please!"

I bark out a laugh from between Josephine's legs. Josephine reprimands me with a shoulder slap.

"It's okay, Punk. There's nothing going on. Come on back in," Josephine apologizes. My pixie tries to push me away, but instead I straighten up on my knees and remain situated between her slender thighs. It's where I'm fucking meant to be, and I have no intentions on budging.

The door cracks open slowly and Punk creeps into the room. He looks us both over to make sure we're indeed dressed. Well, I'm dressed. Josephine is in her underwear. He clears his throat. "Chase asked me to find you," he addresses me wearily.

"What about?" I pull Josephine by the hips till she's flush against me. I snap her garter on her thigh like a rubber band for added effect.

She slaps me on the chest this time. "Stop trying to make Punk uncomfortable. It's bad enough all your brothers believe you're going to murder them if they look at me the wrong way."

I chuckle. "Okay, I'll behave."

"What's that?" Punk points at Josephine's leg.

"It's my practice garter," I say pompously.

Punk cocks his head. "A practice garter?"

"Yeah, you know, when I get to go under her dress in front of everyone at the wedding to take it off with my teeth," I say, smirking, and lick my lips.

Punk's eyes go wide, drinking in my words. "That's fucking hot. I want one of those! Where do I get one?"

Josephine snorts. "You kind of need a fiancée to practice on."

"Hard pass," Punk says before shouting over his shoulder to the living room. "Ebony, do you have a garter?"

I try to reel him back in. "What does Chase want?"

Punk looks back at us. "He says we've got activity on Jacob's end."

276

"*Sonofabitch*," I mutter, pulling myself away from my sweet woman's body.

Striding past Punk, I hear him addressing Josephine. "Fucking hell, woman! You need to cover your curvy ass up if you're going to follow Atlas outside."

"You walk around in your damn boxers," she spits back, insubordinate as always.

"Yeah, well my ass cheeks are covered. No one wants to see me in a thong, but they sure as hell will want to see you in yours. Atlas is going to kill everyone out there if I let you past this door," Punk insists.

"Cover up, Pixie!" I growl out, making my way through the house and outside. Ultimately, it's her choice, but Punk is right, and I'd probably go into a rampage if she leaves the bedroom in only her underwear. I know she's eager to come out to the garage to see what Chase has, but she should hide what's *mine* from everyone else. It's bad enough Punk got another fine look at her backside. I don't need any of my other brothers drooling over her.

I enter the garage to find Chase working. "What do you have?"

He drops what he's doing on one computer and spins to another, waving me over. "We definitely caused a stir. He's getting sloppy. He's still taking out large amounts of cash, but I went over his most recent credit card transactions, and it seems he made a recent trip to a hardware store. Tape, rope, gloves, even a Bowie knife. He's planning something and the fact he's using his credit card means he doesn't care if he gets caught."

"Fuck," I mutter. This is the shit I was worried about, that we would push him over the edge, and he would become extremely dangerous. "He's planning on making a grab."

Chase nods. "It appears that way."

"Too bad for him he won't get me," Josephine says with defiance, making her way through the garage with Punk in tow. Thankfully she listened and put some shorts on.

I spin to face her head on. "You're on lock-down starting now," I order.

Her eyes nearly pop out before narrowing to slits. "I'm not going into hiding, Maceo."

Oh, how I'm going to love finally using her own words against her.

"I do believe it was you who suggested I stow you away in a 'bunker' as long as you were used to draw him out. Well, guess what buttercup, you played your move and now it's my turn. This is what I do, it's my fucking job, and I'm the fucking best at it. You will do what I say from here on out. Am I clear?" I say with all the fucking authority in the world.

Josephine glowers. "Crystal," she bites back, but says nothing else, folding her slender arms over her perky chest. I stare her down, waiting for her to challenge me like she always does, but thankfully she doesn't test me on this. I don't want to have to be an asshole to my pixie, but if push comes to shove, I most certainly will. I nod when I feel confident she's bowing out of the fight.

"Keep tabs on Jacob. Get Ziggy and Butch to help you. I want to be informed of anything and everything," I tell Chase before addressing Punk. "I want you out scouting the whole damn city. Take four men to help you. I'll tell Gauge when he gets back to talk to Lorenzo's men about being on alert for Jacob's appearance. Esteban is not the current threat we need to worry about."

"Where's Gauge?" Punk asks, finally realizing he wasn't in the garage with us.

Chase smirks. "He's *busy*."

Punk lets out a low whistle. "Shit's getting serious between those two."

"It's always been serious. The dumb ass is finally waking up. If he wants to keep Opal for himself, he needs to fucking man up and commit," I say honestly.

"Fuck. First you, prez. Now Gauge. It's like a fucking disease is spreading around here," Punk jokes. "I feel like I need a damn immunization shot or something."

"One, two, three, not it!" Chase chants while touching his nose.

"Oh, hell no! I'm not the next sucker to get tied down to some pussy," Punk fights back before realizing what he said out loud in my presence. "No offense, prez."

Josephine cocks her head and attitude at Punk.

He lowers his head in shame. "Sorry...sis."

Josephine clutches her chest. "Aww, Punk!"

Punk's smile practically splits his face in half. "Really? You're okay with that name? Not going to bite my head off like all the other times I used the wrong name?"

Josephine sniffs and her eyes grow misty. "No, I really like it... little bro."

Punk guffaws. "I am not *little bro*. Big bro or bro, but not little bro."

"You are so *little bro*," she giggles.

"Yeah, anyone tell you it's uncool to pick your own name, little bro?" Chase jabs. "That's almost as bad as Stage and his obsession with John Wayne and going around referring to himself as the Duke."

Now that was fucking hilarious. Stage will never live that one down, mostly because our crew won't let him forget it. I push aside my amusement. "Brothers, let's focus."

"I'm taking Triple, Stage, Eagle, and Flay for my team," Punk says, all joking gone.

"I'll put Reaper and Brass on patrol duty between all the properties. I need to notify Luke at the station that Jacob will be making a move soon. I'll have Gauge ask Lorenzo to station his men at the MC build site as well as Josephine's condo," I say evenly. "In the meantime, I will stay with Josephine."

"We should inform the construction crew and Jared that something is about to go down. They need to be on alert," Chase suggests.

"I can do it," Josephine volunteers.

I look at her and consider it. "I'll allow you to call Jared since you are close with him, but let's have him fill in the crew as a whole, that way all of them know at once and have the same information."

She nods her delicate head and I can't help but reach out and grab her, holding her to me and resting my chin on the top of her head. Time is running out for Jacob, and soon the threat of him will be a bad memory. But until then, I won't be letting her out of my sight.

Preparing for battle is always a sobering moment. You've been trained for this line of work. You've conditioned your body for all the emotional, mental, and physical shit about to come your way. You have all the tactical gear which will keep you protected when push comes to shove. And you have the knowledge and capability to wield the weapons given to you.

For all intents and purposes, you should be ready, but that's not necessarily the case, because there's always the fear.

The fear of the unknown is one big bitch. It fucks with your head. It fucks with your sleep. It fucks with your appetite. And it fucks with your concentration. Fear can only be bottled up so much before it overflows onto everything else.

I deal with this fear by working out. I run. I go to the gym and lift weights. I punch the bag around for hours. And it helps, but it doesn't conquer all my worries.

The only thing that does the trick is being with Josephine. When I hold her in my arms at night close to my chest with our hellhound sleeping on top of our legs, my fear subsides. But I need more. I need to bury myself deep inside of her to fucking silence the fear that grows each passing day as we approach our fake wedding. Unfortunately, it will have to wait.

We're three days from operation-take-down-Jacob and the pressure is getting to everyone. Chase has been practically living in the garage—the asshole hasn't slept more than an hour or two at a time and even then, it's only because he accidently fell asleep at the computer. Punk and his team come home to shower and sleep, but not much else. Gauge has been going back and forth with Lorenzo and he's ready to throw in the towel on the fucker. I'm trying to keep all these pieces together and none of them want to stay stuck.

But Josephine, she's been acting, *different*. I thought she would go stir-crazy during lockdown, but she has been unnaturally calm. She has been handling all of her work from the rental, using FaceTime to communicate with her crew and see what's going on. Work is flying along and they're doing their best to help with the project.

With more free time on her hands, my pixie has been joining me at the gym. The women who always ogle me are furious to see my fiancée in tow, but I'm relieved to have her in my presence. One, I don't need to worry about where she is. Two, I get to work out with the love of my life. Three, I get to watch her walk around the gym in her hot shorts and sports bras. And four, all the fucking predatory women are backing the fuck off, finally. No means no, but it doesn't stop half these women from reaching out and grabbing my arms, pecs, or ass. That shit ended as soon as Josephine walked through the door.

We leave the gym and head downtown to grab some lunch. I'm starving and I'm sure Josephine is too, seeing as we skipped breakfast at the diner to go for a long run on the trail. Not our fault we ended up against the same boulder that bonded us nine weeks ago—a little nostalgic sex was definitely what we both needed to relieve the stress Jacob has added to our lives.

"I want tacos," Josephine pipes up as we walk along.

"Sounds good to me." I take our linked hands and raise her hand to my lips for a peck.

"Okay, but we need to hurry and get back to the house. I need to shower before my fitting," she reminds me.

"No problem. We'll get home, clean up, and I'll take you."

"Um, no, you will not take me. You can't see me in my dress."

"Fake wedding, fake wedding dress. The rules don't apply," I say with finality. There's no way in hell I'm going to separate myself from her.

She stops walking and drops my hand. "I'd be fine with the

arrangement if it was only the fake dress, but this includes the *real* dress, too."

I groan and rub both my hands up my face and into my hair. The rule is she must have someone with her at all times. All my men are on assignment. "You know this means I have to ask Lorenzo for a guard for you then, right?"

Josephine mimics my actions by running her own hands over her face. "Gah! Why? Can't I go in by myself, and have you stand outside keeping watch?"

I give her the deadpan look I usually give when I mean business. "You know it isn't an option, right? You need someone there at all times."

Josephine's eyes roll to the back of her head. "I fucking hate Jacob. This is all his fault," she whines.

"Damn right it is," I agree. "How about we grab Tiny Tony and I go with. I'll be outside waiting, while he goes in with you."

Josephine's face puckers. "Can we use someone other than Tiny Tony?"

"I thought you liked Tiny Tony?"

"I do. Out of Lorenzo's goons, I like Tony the most—he's a decent guy. But I don't want another incident where he threatens an innocent bystander."

"Lucky Luca?" Our options are limited with Lorenzo's henchmen. He will only use his personal best as security for Josephine. I guess I should be grateful for it, but I question his ulterior motive.

Josephine shivers. "Um, no, he's worse."

Yeah, he is worse. "Pretty Paolo then."

"What the hell is with all the awful mafioso names? No, I don't want Pretty Paolo. He scares the living daylights out of me."

"Tiny Tony it is then," I say pulling out my phone.

CHAPTER SEVENTEEN
JOSEPHINE & MACEO

J osephine
    "All clear," Tiny Tony says in a deep voice after he checks
out the dressing room, now allowing me to enter.

The sales clerk is more than a little uncomfortable having him
back in her shop after the last time he visited. I can't blame her. She
goes to hang the dresses in the changing room and shivers when she
passes by his massive body.

Tiny Tony is definitely a joke of a name. He's the largest man I've
met, even bigger than Maceo, which is saying something. How he's
able to move stealthily with his bulky frame is a paradox I haven't
figured out yet.

"Thanks, Tony," I say, entering the dressing room. He seems to
soften when I address him like this. I'm guessing he doesn't like the
oxymoron name his mafia family gave him. He smiles and closes the
door so I may undress.

The bridal boutique is completely empty at this time, aside from
the clerk, Tiny Tony, and myself. Probably because it's the middle of
the day on a Wednesday—no one's around. It's kind of nice to have
the whole space to myself. As soon as I walked in the door, I had a
glass of champagne in my hand and all the attention of the sales clerk.

But I don't want to dawdle with Maceo waiting outside. I'm as eager to be back with him as he is with me.

Nervous and excited all at once, I can't wait to try on my dream dress. I step into it and zip it up as far as I can. I exit the dressing room and climb on the step stool in front of the mirrors.

Tiny Tom steps forward and zips me the rest of the way before I appraise myself in the full-length mirrors.

"You look stunning!" the clerk gushes.

"Beautiful," Tiny Tony agrees.

"Thank you, both of you." I smile at my reflection.

There are a lot of women who have been dreaming about their wedding dresses their entire life, but I'm not one of them. I had no clue what I liked and didn't like till I started shopping with Opal. I definitely wasn't a princess-dress kind of girl, nor was I into heavy beading or tulle on any level.

The dress I picked is a swag-sleeved trumpet dress with layered lace appliqués and a sweetheart neckline. The lace is ivory on top with champagne underneath, and it's formfitting, hugging my bottom, but the goblet skirt and chapel train definitely make it feel less restrictive. I feel like the most beautiful woman in the world standing here.

"I'm glad we ordered you the size two instead of the size zero. Your lovely backside wouldn't have fit in it," the clerk says, admiring me.

Excuse me? I put my hands on my hips. "Is that a nice way of saying I have a fat ass?"

Tiny Tony lets out a thunderous laugh. The clerk looks mortified.

She's quick to apologize. "Oh my goodness, no, Miss Holland, I certainly didn't mean to insult."

Tiny Tony is still laughing. "She's saying you got the goods in the back. A size zero is for someone who has no ass at all. You got a bottom most women would kill for. Work that shit."

"Well, okay then!" I say, feeling better with the explanation. "This is the one!"

The clerk claps her hands together excitedly, probably because she made a huge commission. Tony helps me down from the stool, unzips me, and opens the dressing room door before closing it behind me. I step out of the gown and put it back on the hanger with a huge smile before handing it off to the sales clerk. She scurries away to the back room to put it in a garment bag.

With a sigh, I slip the other dress over my head. It's not like I don't like the fake dress—I do, but it reminds me of what will be a very tension-filled day with Jacob on the prowl.

This dress is more of an A-line, straight-across neck, knee-length white wedding dress with lace. It's simple and elegant and, above all, it's cheap. My hands spread down the fabric and stop at the waist when I feel a fold in the material.

No way! Pockets! How did I not notice this before?

I must be making a lot of excited noises because Tony starts chuckling. "What are you squealing about in there?"

"Pockets, Tony! My dress has pockets and it's lovely."

"If you say so," he murmurs.

Clearly Tony is not convinced and I need to defend my stance. "Imagine if you had to wear dress slacks without pockets."

Tony is silent for a moment before answering. "That would be fucking horrible."

"Exactly. Hence, my excitement over pockets in my dress is justified."

I do a little happy dance and spin around to find my purse. "Where is it? Ah, there you are." I pull out my phone and slip it into one of the pockets, where it sinks deep into the dress. *Score!* A dress with pockets is the best ever. Seriously, it should be mandatory. I may like this one better than the *real* wedding gown now.

I'm still admiring the dress when I hear a loud thud and some groaning followed by another thud. I step out of the dressing room to see Tiny Tony in a heap on the ground.

I rush to his side. "Oh my God, Tony! Are you okay?"

My mouth opens to cry out for Maceo, but a strong hand comes down over my mouth while another snakes around my body, hoisting me into the air. I scream against the hand, but my voice is too muffled to alert Maceo outside. My arms are pinned down, making them useless in a fight. I frantically kick out with my legs and buck my body against my abductor, but nothing connects.

He grunts as he drags me to the back of the store. I catch a glimpse of Maceo through the windows in the front room. Tears prick my eyes. He's right there but doesn't see me as he talks on his phone, no doubt to one of his men about Jacob.

My eyes dart around the room frantically to see how I can sound the alarm. I struggle against my abductor and try to knock over everything in my wake. I manage to reach a rack of veils and turn it over but the veils fall silently to the floor, buffering the impact of the rack hitting the hardwood. It's not enough, and I try to reach for more, but now he knows what I'm up to, and he yanks me backward quickly and out of reach of anything else.

Desperate, I cry out against the hand over my mouth when I'm pulled through the double doors to the back room. I pass the sales clerk, gagged and tied up in a pile on the ground. Tears stream down my face when I cry out to her and she cries back to me.

My abductor pulls me out the back door toward a dark van. The door slides open, and Jacob is there, waiting with open arms.

Fear spiking my blood, I fight with all I have against the man restraining me. I step on his foot, and he grunts in pain, but his hold stays solid. I try to bite his hand, but I can't move my jaw enough. Jacob sees the guy struggling and comes to grab my legs.

No, no, no! I know if they get me in the van, I may never get out alive. I take my head and snap it backward against the man holding me and make contact with his face. He drops me with a howl.

I scramble to my knees only to be kicked in the gut by Jacob. There's an excruciating snap in my ribs as the air rushes out of me. I roll to my side, gasping for air. *Shit, that hurts!*

Jacob climbs on me and slaps a piece of duct tape across my mouth before grabbing my wrists and taping them together. I shake my head forcefully side to side and try to raise my knee to nail him in the balls, but he's straddling me too high to make contact. He slides down my legs and quickly tapes my calves together before I can break a leg free to kick at him.

Frantic, I scream against the tape, tears pouring from my eyes. Jacob's hard face softens as he looks at me. My gaze pleads with him, but he shows no sign of empathy. Smiling jubilantly, he leans forward to kiss the tape across my mouth before climbing off me and hauling me into the van.

The man who abducted me looks familiar but I can't place him. He sits in the driver's seat, holding the bridge of his nose to stop the steady flow of blood.

"She fucking broke my nose!"

"I'm not paying you to nurse your own fucking injuries. Now drive!" Jacob hisses, lying down on top of me in the back seat.

The man curses, but he starts the van and takes off.

Jacob wraps his arms around me in an act of possession. "You're safe now, Keebler. I won't let anyone come between us again." He wipes my tears from my eyes. I cry harder as his lips trail kisses all over my neck and down to my cleavage where my heart pounds with fear.

Maceo

Resentfully, I agreed to let Tiny Tony take over my role of bodyguard and escort Josephine into the bridal store. I peek through the windows occasionally, hoping to catch a glimpse of my blushing bride, but the dressing room is to the left side, and it's impossible to see into it from this angle.

I pace anxiously in front of the store, waiting for her to finish up. I won't be calm till she's by my side again.

My phone buzzes. I pull it out to see Chase calling. "Yes?" I answer.

"Atlas, we may have a problem. I started digging because I was uneasy with the lack of activity on Jacob's end for the last three days. I hacked into the firm where he works and saw his request for vacation has been approved," Chase rambles.

"Not surprising. He probably plans on driving out this way before the wedding, like he did before."

"That's not the issue. His request for time off started yesterday! He could be—"

Springing into action, I pull my piece and burst into the store. "Pixie!" I shout, running to the dressing room area. I see Tiny Tony on the ground with what looks like a cracked skull, a baseball bat next to him. I quickly check for a pulse. It's there, but Tony is seriously fucked up.

I race back to the front room and look down the corridor to the back of the store. A rack of tulle and lace is on the ground. I raise my gun and push through the double doors. A whimper catches my attention and I see the sales clerk bound and gagged. I race to her side and yank down the gag.

"Where is she?" I growl.

"He took her out the back," the clerk cries, nodding at the back door.

Frantic, I run out into the alley behind the building. I spin in a fast circle and see nothing. Going into full SEAL mode, I search the area for any clues. I look at the ground, and my blood runs cold.

Several blood splatters are on the pavement. If the fucker harmed one hair on her head, I will kill him.

I yank my phone out and call Chase. He answers immediately. "Chase, he has her. I need visual from traffic cams around Bellezza in Bianco Bridal Boutique. Check for his car or any odd vehicles fleeing from the site. And I need an ambulance, stat." I rush back into the store and make quick work of releasing the clerk before running back to Tiny Tony.

He moans on the ground, and I rush to his side. "Easy, Tony. I got you. Help is on the way."

"It's him," Tony mumbles in pain.

"I know it's Jacob." I grab a dress from the rack and rip it to wrap around Tony's head.

He moans. "No, the other guy."

"Who?" I ask. *Is he concussed?*

"The guy I confronted the first time I brought Jo here."

My heart sinks. "The man with the California plates?"

"Yes," he cries.

I call Chase and put him on speaker. "I need you to listen to Tony." I put the cell near his face.

"Black minivan. Older model. California license plate—6TRJ547," he grits out. "It's what he drove last time I saw him."

"Got it," Chase says. "I'm not picking up any van on street surveillance footage; he must be staying off main streets."

For fuck's sake. "Track her phone; she still has the app." *Please, please, please baby. Please have it on you.*

"Tracking now. I've got visual confirmation on her app. They got onto Interstate 25 heading south. Surveillance footage from an entry ramp onto the highway shows it's the black van."

Thank God! "I want Reaper and Brass to head south now. Have Gauge get in touch with Luke at the station. Tell them we have an abduction. Get Punk and his team to come in from the north to try to cut them off."

"Done," Chase answers quickly. "What are you going to do?"

"I'm going to go save my pixie." I end the call.

"Ambulance is here," the clerk informs me in tears.

I jump to my feet and hold the door open for the paramedics before running out to my SUV.

Josephine

My stomach roils as Jacob's hands and lips crawl over my body. I shake my head fretfully when I feel him pull the hem of the dress up till it's bunched around my waist.

"I've missed your sweet little body," he croons into my ear and nibbles on the lobe. I yank my head away in disgust. He fists my hair in his free hand, yanking on my scalp till I'm crying out against the tape in pain.

"Why are you fighting me? Has the fucking dirty bastard gotten into your head?" he growls before taking his other hand to rub against the placket of my panties. I weep and plead with my eyes for him to stop.

"Has he touched you? Has he spread his disease all over you like the parasite he is?" he snarls, ripping my panties from my body. I scream against the tape and try to buck him from my body.

"Hey, man, not cool. You said you weren't going to hurt her. It's the only reason I agreed to take this job and your money," the driver says angrily over his shoulder.

My head swings to the man, and I scream through the tape, praying he has some sort of conscience and won't allow Jacob to molest me. The guy looks back over his shoulder, and his eyes actually look remorseful.

I know him. I've seen him recently outside the bridal boutique when Tiny Tony manhandled him. But I know him from when I worked at the firm. He worked as a custodian at night and only started there right before I quit. I'm not used to seeing him with his long hair shaved off; perhaps that's why I didn't recognize him that day outside the bridal store. Jacob must have recruited him for this job and paid him big bucks to do it. The driver turns his attention back to the road, and my hopes are dashed.

"Mind your own fucking business, Jesse," Jacob snaps before returning his attention to me. "We're finally back together. We're going back home to San Diego, where we can continue our life as it was always meant to be. I'll even let you keep this little business of yours. I'll give you the fucking kids you always hounded me about. I'll give you everything you need. This past year will be a wash, and we will never talk of it again."

Dread washes over me when I see the feral look in his eyes. I clamp my thighs together right before he tries to pry them apart, using my bound hands like a battering ram against him.

With a growl, he grabs my taped hands in one of his and hoists them above my head, while his other hand works to undo his pants. I scream harder against the tape when I feel his erection spring from the confines of his boxers and rub against my legs.

"It's been too long, Jo. Too fucking long since I've been inside of you," he says, trying again to pry my legs apart.

He kisses each of my breasts through the dress and bites at my nipples. I screech, but it's no use with my mouth covered. It must annoy him because he backhands me hard across the face. My head whips to the side. I see stars, and my vision goes spotty. He takes my moment of weakness to open my legs, but is stopped by the tape binding my lower legs together.

He growls in frustration, pulling a knife from his pocket and cutting the tape. It snaps me out of my haze, and I start kicking at him with all I have, knocking the knife to the floor of the van. My legs are probably the strongest part on my body from all my running, and I'm going to use them as a weapon. I pretend I can hear Maceo in my head, chanting, coaching me on how best to crush Jacob with my legs.

Fight, Jo. Harder. Kick harder. Don't stop.

I get him good—several times in the chest. He snaps and grabs for my neck, putting his full weight on my body.

"You will learn to love me again," he snarls and squeezes my throat.

I try to hit him with my bound hands, but my hits grow weaker because my airway is blocked.

I see images of my handsome fiancé flash through my mind. His million-watt smile. His deep baritone laugh. His strong arms wrapped around me, protectively. The smell of his woodsy scent consuming my senses. The steady beat of his heart under my hand.

If I have to die, at least I die with memories of Maceo flooding my oxygen-depraved mind.

Maceo, I love you.

My vision blurs until everything goes black.

Maceo

I race south down I-25, going over a hundred miles per hour in the SUV. I know it's only a matter of time 'till I reach the van. This guy may have sped out of the city, but he'll do everything he can to not draw attention to himself on the interstate. Luke has already informed interstate police of my pursuit, and they will not chase me, only the van.

I hear the roar of motorcycles and spot Reaper and Brass in my rearview mirror. My brothers have come to fight beside me. I press down on the gas and swerve around traffic with Reaper and Brass following me.

Every black vehicle grabs my attention, and I'm about to lose my shit when I spot the van. I press the accelerator to the floor. I speed up alongside it and look over at the driver, who makes eye contact with me. His nose looks like it's broken, and he has a river of red running down his face. I pray he's the one whose blood was in the parking lot and not my pixie's. His eyebrows shoot to top of his forehead, and he starts shouting over his shoulder. Maybe he's shouting at Josephine, or maybe he's shouting at Jacob.

Whatever is said makes him step on the accelerator. I keep pace with him and roll down my window. The guy panics and shouts over his shoulder again. Another person comes into view and leans over the console of the van, staring at me.

Fucking loafer-dick himself.

Anger floods my veins. "Pull the fuck over!" I shout loud enough my voice shakes the remaining closed windows of my SUV.

Jacob gives me the finger and starts barking orders at the driver, who looks like he's about to have a panic attack. He yanks the wheel to the left and rams his van against my vehicle. I quickly correct my steering to keep myself from flipping the SUV. With a roar of frustration, I remind myself I can't ram them back because Josephine is in their vehicle.

Reaper and Brass pull up behind the van. Reaper darts up the right side and speeds around the van till he's in front. It's a dangerous move, but it makes the driver slow down. Since there's no way around, the van is forced to keep slowing down or do something drastic. The driver is not as much of a risk-taker as Jacob is, and he continues to lose speed as Reaper slows down more ahead of him. Jacob is screaming his head off.

Up ahead I see Punk and Gauge with the rest of the crew, waiting in the median. They pull out as they see us approach and create an impossible link to cross unless the driver plows them over. Highway patrol is coming into view ahead and has the entire highway barricaded, and more interstate officers close in behind us. There's nowhere for these fuckers to go.

The van comes to a screeching halt, and Brass has to swing right and into the ditch to avoid hitting the van. Thankfully he's able to keep his bike up and not crash.

I slam on my breaks and jump out of the SUV with my weapon drawn. "Get the fuck out of the van with your hands up," I shout, positioning myself behind the hood of my vehicle. I don't know if they're packing, which stops me from rushing the van. I have no tactical gear on for protection and getting myself shot or killed is not on my to-do list.

The driver jumps out and makes a run for it up the hill to the right. Brass is on his ass fast. The guy goes flying when Brass takes him out low like the defensive linebacker he was before becoming a SEAL.

My attention homes in on the van as Jacob emerges with an unconscious Josephine over his shoulder. He has a heavy duty hunting knife pressed against her side. "Don't come any closer, or I'll end both our lives," he shouts.

I'd shoot the fucker right now, but something about his demeanor tells me he wouldn't think twice about plunging the knife into Josephine.

I hold up my weapon. "Alright, Jacob, I'm backing off."

"You just had to come after her, didn't you? You saw how fucking pure and good she was and you had to fucking taint her," Jacob continues to yell, pointing the shaking knife against her side.

I swallow hard and take in how desperate he has become. My heart beats faster as I assess how dangerous this situation is. I need to appease him right now and hope he lowers his weapon.

"I had no right." The words chafe against my throat.

"You're damn right you had no right. She's mine! I was her first and I'll be her last. She ran away because she couldn't handle me wearing the pants in the relationship, but she needs a man to control and guide her. She would have seen it eventually and come back to me. I was close to having her come on her own free will, letting her believe she had a say in the matter to appease her stubborn side," he rambles with the knife still snug against her.

My teeth grind together. "I get it," I lie.

Jacob nods his head like he thinks I'm seeing his warped logic. "She's better off with me. She would never make it in your world. She's too good for you." His hold on the knife relaxes some.

I nod my head and take in Josephine's dead weight on Jacob's shoulder. "Is she okay?"

Jacob's eyes flicker with emotion. "She tried to fight me. I only wanted to love her, love her the way she deserves. But she resisted. I had no choice," he says with a slight edge to his tone. He points the knife at me. "She fought me because you poisoned her mind against me. But she will come to her senses, and I will be the one who rebuilds her."

My chest heaves with fear. "What did you do to her?"

Jacob's face contorts from anger to something resembling regret. "She wouldn't let me in. I—I strangled her. I had no choice."

My worry for her takes over, and I come around the vehicle with my hands up and approach him.

Jacob panics. "What the fuck are you doing? Don't come any closer."

"Jacob, put her down. She needs medical attention," I say firmly.

Jacob's expression twists with anger and tears run down his face. "I take care of her."

"Yes," I say. I make eye contact with Flay before looking back at Jacob. "You care for her by bringing her to a medic. You make sure she gets the proper care she needs, to ensure you can have a long and happy life together."

Jacob's eyes light up, and he nods. "Yeah, I make sure she has all she needs."

I nod my head. "You've got it all figured out. You know exactly what is best for her when she doesn't. And right now she's unable to decide, meaning you have to. You know, we've got a navy medic right here. If you want her to get the treatment she needs right away, this would be a good option, seeing as we're miles from the closest hospital," I offer.

Flay comes up with the medical kit he always carries on his bike.

Jacob looks leery but nods for Flay to approach.

"Why don't you lower her to the ground? I can take a look at her better there. You can stay next to her and be there when she comes to. She'll feel better knowing you're here," Flay suggests, appeasing to Jacob's self-righteous ego.

Jacob nods in agreement and pulls her from his shoulders, lowering her to the ground. He removes the tape from her wrists and holds her hand while Flay quickly gets to work removing the duct tape from her face. I creep closer to my pixie. She looks like an angel in her wedding dress—a beaten and bruised angel.

Flay regards Jacob with a serious face. "She's got a pulse, but she isn't breathing and is unresponsive. We need to activate an emergency response system. I need you to run to the ambulance over there and grab the AED while I start administering rescue breathing. We need the AED if her pulse stops and CPR doesn't bring her back."

Jacob practically wails, grabbing at his head. "Oh my God! What have I done?"

Flay grabs him by the arm and shakes him. "Jacob she needs you. Go now!"

Jacob jumps to his feet and starts racing at full tilt to the patrol cars and ambulance up ahead with the knife still in his hand, waving his arms above his head in panic.

The police order him again and again to drop his knife, but he doesn't hear their warning, caught up in his terror over possibly losing Josephine. I see what's unfolding, and I should stop the disaster happening in front of me, but I won't. The fucker deserves what's coming.

But Josephine needs medical attention!

I start to scream for the paramedics, but Flay lays a heavy hand on me, holding me in place. He stares at me with a firm gaze. I know he's trying to communicate something with me, but I'm so fucking worried about my pixie, I'm not registering anything. My head whips back to the scene in front of me as the police open fire on Jacob, peppering him with bullets. Jacob falls to ground and remains there, unmoving.

"Safe travels to hell, motherfucker," Flay says under his breath. "No one fucks with *our* first lady."

"But Josephine—" I start.

"Is fine," Flay reassures me. "Breathing and has a pulse. She's only passed out."

I rush to her side and hold her in my arms, thanking God that she's okay. Flay rips open an ammonia pack and holds it under her nose. Josephine's eyes fly open, and her mouth takes gulps of air.

Filled with relief, I cradle her to my chest and let the tears fall. The rest of the crew surround us, eager to see my woman. Josephine looks up at me and starts sobbing.

"I've got you, pixie. I've got you," I say as I take all of her in. Her lips are swollen, and the skin around them is red from where the tape was applied to her delicate face. A giant welt covers her right cheek where he must have hit her. Bruises cover her arms and her legs. My heart drops to my stomach when she winces in my arms and grabs at her side.

"Flay!" I yell.

Flay drops to her side. "What hurts, Jo?"

"M-M-My ribs. He kicked me," she pants between hoarse sobs.

Flay goes to lift up her dress, to assess the damage, and stops. "That fucker better be dead," he growls. "About face!" he shouts to our crew.

My men turn around, surrounding us with a sea of their backs.

I look down and see her panties have been removed, and her hips and thighs are bruised where fingers and hands dug into her soft flesh. Farther up her body, a giant bruise covers the entire left side of her rib cage. "Did he—" I choke out in pain, gazing into the face of the only woman I've ever loved.

Josephine sobs. "I—I don't know. He was trying to, and I was fighting him. He hit me. He choked me, and then I don't remember!" She wails and covers her face with her hands.

Desperate, I look at Flay.

Flay shakes his head. "I can't tell. She needs a pelvic exam at the hospital and to have a rape kit done," he seethes.

My control snaps. "Bring me the driver!"

Brass brings him forward. The guy looks distressed, but I feel no mercy at all standing to tower over him. I point at my beautiful woman. "Did he violate her?"

The guy squirms in Brass's grip, but my brother holds him tight.

"Did he rape her?" I scream in his face. All my men hiss in anger.

The guy pisses himself. "He was trying, man. I told him not to hurt her. He promised he wouldn't, but he was forcing himself on her. I don't know if he got that far because you and the rest of your guys got to us right after."

Relief washes over me, but I will encourage Josephine to have the rape kit done as a precaution. For her own health, she needs to know, and if the fucker isn't dead, it will be used to build a fucking huge case against him.

"Tell the cops I'm rushing her to the hospital. They can question her after we get her checked out," I tell Gauge. I pick my beautiful woman off the road.

She buries her face in my chest and I cradle her. I will get her the medical care Flay says she needs, and after I will hold her in my arms until she feels whole and safe again. Hell, who am I kidding? I'll never let go of her again.

I buckle her into my SUV and spin the vehicle around across the highway, heading north back into Fort Collins. All of my men follow on their bikes behind us. They care as much about their first lady as I do.

CHAPTER EIGHTEEN
JOSEPHINE

The rape exam takes a couple of hours, and the medical team charts, photographs, records, and examines every inch of me. I feel like a very sore pincushion every time the medical staff touch me —every surface of my body aches, and I want nothing more than to crawl into a ball against Maceo and cry myself to sleep.

I can't believe this happened to me.

Images of Jacob flood my mind before I can stop them. Jacob's cold eyes staring straight through me. His lips roaming over my body. His rough hand forcing my legs apart as the other was squeezing my throat.

I cringe hard, and sobs rake my body. *What if I was raped?*

Maceo, devoted and protective as always, sits next to me in the sterile room the whole time. He reassures me the exam is precautionary. We already feel confident I wasn't raped, molested yes, but not raped. His eyes demand my attention, and he stresses he's here to support me through whatever care I need. He holds my hand, and kisses my knuckles and my face after he's given the okay by the medical team.

He's so fucking sweet. How did I get this lucky? Don't know and don't care—he's mine and I love him.

I know this isn't easy for Maceo to witness. It's probably equally as horrible for him as it is for me. The cords in his neck strain when he sees me stripped bare, my black and blue body on full display. Maceo's face contorts in pain when he assesses me, like looking at me is hurting him—no, killing him. And I have to admit, the amount of bruising I have is chilling.

"It's worse than what I first saw on the highway," Maceo tells the doctor performing my exam.

The doctor nods in understanding. "Jo is pretty beat up. Don't be surprised if more bruises pop up over the next day or two. It's pretty typical after being attacked this viciously."

Well, that thought is really unpleasant. I don't know how this could look any worse. My back is scratched and a horrid shade of purple. My throat—which hurts like a motherfucker every time I speak or swallow—looks like Jacob squeezed my neck to the point it could have snapped. My fingernails are broken off or bent back from where I clawed and fought. The bottoms of my feet are bruised from where I kicked for my life.

Maceo is trying hard to control his anger, but I can hear him growling. "I wish I could kill Jacob all over again. The fucker got off easy."

My heart aches a little, hearing Jacob is indeed gone. As horrible of a thing Jacob did to me, I never wanted him dead. Honestly, I wanted him to get help and move on with his life. I feel slightly guilty, knowing I'll sleep sounder with him gone, but not enough to feel sorry about it.

Radiology confirms I have two cracked ribs from where Jacob kicked me, and my larynx is bruised from the strangulation. Upon pelvic examination, the doctor believes I wasn't raped, but laboratory tests will show if there are traces of semen or residue from a condom. The thought of Jacob having been inside me while I was unconscious makes me whimper with dread.

Tears run down my face. "What if he raped me, Maceo?"

Maceo jaw clenches. "He didn't."

"But what if he did?" I sob and it hurts my throat. "Will you think differently of me? Will you still want me, or will you want to end our relationship?"

Maceo shakes his head, his face red with anger and pain. He grabs the side of my face as gently as he can. "It makes no difference to me. I still want you no matter what. My feelings for you will only grow stronger with time. I'm not going anywhere, ever."

I hiccup and scratch at my skin. "But what if he gave me a disease? Do you think I'm dirty? God, I feel so dirty!"

Maceo's face scrunches up as he fights back his own tears. He cradles my sore face and kisses my forehead. "Baby, you're not dirty, and you'll never be dirty. Jacob never made it that far. Even the doctor thinks so."

Snot runs down my face along with my tears. I'm sure I look awful, but nothing can compare to how disgusting I feel on the inside. Maceo wipes my face clean with his fingers.

I chock. "But what if?"

Maceo's black eyes soften. "Then we'll deal with it, together. There's no STI that will run me off from you." He holds me tenderly until my tears stop.

The doctor performing my exam takes one of my hands in hers. "I've performed a lot of these exams over the years, and I'm confident you were one of the lucky ones. I don't see anything that would suggest you were raped, but let's wait for the lab to confirm my belief. In the mean time, heal and try to stay positive. I'm rushing the lab results and I hope to have an answer for you within two weeks."

Maceo looks over at the doctor. "We had sex this morning. Do I need to give a sample of my DNA to rule my semen out from any other semen that may be present?"

The doctor pulls out a couple sterile swabs, and swipes them along the inside of Maceo's mouth to gather some cheek cells for testing.

When my nerves finally settle, I ask Maceo another question I have been dreading. "Tony?"

I half expect Maceo to get jealous, since that's normally how he would react about any male I show a harmless interest in, but he surprises me. His eyes soften and he smiles, his thumb running up and down my unmarred cheek. "He's got a nasty concussion, cracked ribs, and a really bruised back, but thankfully, his skull isn't fractured. He's being monitored here at the hospital, and is in the best hands. He's going to be okay."

"I want to see him," I murmur, my throat throbbing.

Maceo nods, not a jealous bone in sight. "We definitely will, Pixie, but not today. Let him rest for a couple days, and then I'll bring you back to visit. I know you're concerned about him. I am too. But right now, you're my number one priority. I want to get you home to start your own recovery."

I nod and my voice cracks. "I'm holding you to it."

Maceo's dark eyes crinkle in the corners when he smiles. "I expect nothing less from you, *mi amor*."

After handing over my fake wedding dress as evidence, I put on the sweats Punk raced home to bring back for me. As we walk out of the exam room, the hallway is lined with all the Mercy Ravens MC men, eagerly waiting.

Happy tears spill down my cheeks and I make my way down the line, gently hugging and thanking each one of them. Out of the corner of my eye, I see them look to Maceo and he gives them a thumbs-up. They all visibly relax, knowing Jacob didn't manage to rape me.

When I get to the end of the line where Gauge, Chase, and Punk wait, I run gingerly to them and they cocoon me in their massive arms. I feel so loved. Punk cries like a fool, holding me close and kissing the top of my head. I take a quick peek at Maceo, praying he won't haul off on Punk for showing me affection.

Maceo only smiles at me and his brother. "The two of you are close. I know Punk loves you like a sister. He's as much your brother now as he is mine. They all are."

My heart melts hearing Maceo say that. I do love all his brothers.

I'm happy Maceo is fine with me being close with them, without fearing he's going to punch one of them out.

Detective Quire questions both Maceo and I rather quickly, and then he releases us. He knows enough of what happened to close the case regarding Jacob. He says he will reach out if he needs more information about Jesse, the driver. Honestly, I think he could see how much pain I'm in, and wanted to wrap things up for my sake.

Back at the rental, Maceo helps me into the shower. He climbs in after me to help clean me up, removing the rest of Jacob from my skin. He holds me after 'till the water runs cold.

Opal and Ebony push their way into the bathroom afterward, and they help fix my torn nails and apply ointments to my cuts and scrapes. Thankfully, they pay no mind to Maceo's toweled naked body while he watches them fuss over me. Red and Candy run in with a pharmacy bag containing my filled scripts, gauze, icepacks, and a heating pad.

Maceo is pushed out of the bathroom, pissing him off. "I don't want to leave her."

"You're in the way!" Candy hisses, before slamming the door in his face.

My face crumbles. I want Maceo with me right now. I start to cry and fall to my knees, clutching at my broken ribs. Red drops and wraps her slender arms around me.

Opal flies to the door and swings it open. "Flay, we need you."

My eyes flicker to the hallway and connect with Maceo's for a moment, before Flay comes running into view, blocking him out. The worry I catch in Maceo's dark eyes brings on fresh tears.

It sounds like there's a scuffle in the hallway, and I wipe away my tears to see Maceo pushing his way back into the bathroom. "What's wrong with her? For fuck's sake, let me in, dammit!"

Flay blocks him from entering. "It's her ribs. I'm going to wrap her and make her more comfortable. I need room to work."

Maceo snarls at Flay. "She's not fucking dressed." Well, I guess

Maceo's jealousy is still there. There's only so much he's willing to tolerate.

Flay shoots Maceo an annoyed look. "I'm a fucking medical professional. The last thing I'm going to do is check out your woman while I'm *treating* her."

"Come on, Atlas," Gauge says, pulling him out of the bathroom and closing the door.

I hear Maceo's muffled voice on the other side. "He's seen enough of her naked body for one day. She's been through hell. I just want to hold her and make her feel safe."

And then I hear Maceo breaking down in sobs—hard, gut-wrenching sobs.

My hands release my ribs and fly over my mouth, covering my own cries. The man I love is falling apart seeing me in pain. I can't let him hear me cry tonight, because I can't bear to hear or see him in emotional turmoil.

"And you will, brother. Flay's only helping her. She's in good hands. Let's get you dressed and wait out in the living room for her, okay?" Gauge says calmly, and the hallway goes quiet.

Flay squats down and helps me to my feet. "He's going to be okay, Jo. Just focus on you right now. I'm going to wrap your torso to help support your broken ribs. Is it okay if I remove your towel?"

I appreciate Flay asking permission to disrobe me after what I've been through, and I nod mutely. Red helps me out of my towel, and I stand in front of all the bunnies and Flay, completely naked. Under normal circumstances, I would be embarrassed to be nude in front of a crowd, but I'm too caught up in my head to care.

The bunnies take stock of my battered body before looking away with tears in their eyes. I know they feel bad for me, but this hits too close to home for them—judging by their faces, I'm willing to bet they've had similar experiences. Now I know why they're in here supporting me.

Opal assists Flay as he gently wraps my torso. True to his word, he didn't once try to check out my naked body. There's a knock at the bathroom door. Opal throws the towel around me, and I'm grateful. I don't want Maceo going wild if someone else sees me naked. Ebony answers the door, Triple and Stage are standing there with a Target bag.

"We thought Jo would want some soft, non-restrictive clothes while she heals," Stage says.

"We got extra-smalls. Hope that's right," Triple adds, looking into the bathroom at me.

"Thank you," I whisper, hoarsely. My throat is really hurting me now.

Flay tears into my scripts and pulls out my pain meds. "Here, Jo. You need to take this," he says, and places the pill in my hand. Triple darts off and comes back with a bottle of water. I take the pill with the water, but I have a hard time swallowing. I just can't get it down.

Seeing me struggle, Flay turns back to the guys. "Go grab a yogurt and a spoon." Stage goes to the kitchen this time. Flay makes me spit the pill out. He crushes it on the counter with the spoon and adds it to the yogurt. "Take small bites, but you will need to eat all of it to get all your medication."

I do as he says, and I manage to get it all down, but my throat bitches at me each time I swallow.

"When you're ready, Jo, come out to the living room. Reaper and Brass set up a bed for you and Atlas. They thought you might want to watch television while you recover. Butch and Ziggy even programmed Netflix with all the movies and shows they thought you may like," Stage says.

Triple smiles. "Yeah, Eagle even ordered your favorite Chinese takeout for the whole house. Everyone is trying to do something to help. Chase and Punk fed and took Hades for his walk—he was pacing the hallway carpet thin with worry over you."

I wipe away my tears and mouth "thank you" to them, unable to tolerate the pain of using my voice anymore. They close the door and more tears roll down my face.

Opal grabs a tissue and blots my face. Flay helps me get into a new silky-smooth pajama set.

When I finally emerge from the bathroom, Flay helps me walk, all the bunnies trailing behind us. The living room is jam-packed, but there's only one face I want to see.

Maceo sits on our new bed, Gauge sits next to him. It appears that Gauge is trying to keep Maceo calm by whispering words of support. I start to make my way to him, and Maceo's dark torturous eyes lock with mine. Gauge gets up and goes to Opal, making room for me on the bed. Maceo stands, holding out his arms for me to join him. Once I'm safe in his embrace, he relaxes, and he helps me into the bed, sliding in next to me, holding me close.

Everyone settles into the living room as dinner is passed around and some chick-flick plays on the television. The food looks good, but my throat hurts too damn much, and I'm feeling queasy on top of it.

Maceo coaxes me to take a couple bites. "I don't want the pain medication to upset your stomach. Throwing up with broken ribs would not be good for you, baby."

Ugh! That would be par for the course. The fear of vomiting and hurting myself more is the only way I manage a couple more bites before my throat screams 'enough.'

Mostly, everyone eats in silence or low whispers while we watch the movie. I don't say a word or laugh at any of the scenes playing on the screen. My body feels like it's shutting down. Hades whines at the foot of the bed. He knows something horrible happened, and my poor boy is worried, but I can't find the strength to comfort him at the moment.

I think I'm in shock.

Everything is catching up to me and I feel like my mind and body aren't connected. I desperately want to stop the awful memories from playing on repeat in my head, but my body is incapable of shutting it down. To say I feel violated or victimized doesn't cover the surface of my emotions. There are no words to describe what I'm feeling.

Anger, fear, sadness—so much and at the same time nothing at all. Maybe my pain meds are messing with me, or maybe I'm emotionally broken now.

Exhausted, I sag against Maceo and feel myself starting to drift off. My eyelids flutter closed, and my breathing evens out. I'm not completely asleep, but I'm close.

I hear the television turn off and everyone is quiet. They could go back to their normal activities or head off to bed, but no one seems to want to leave.

"Is it okay if we stay out here with you and Jo, prez?" Stage bravely asks on behalf of everyone.

"Yeah, it's okay," Maceo says, settling into the bed with me snuggled against him.

Everyone works to get comfortable for the evening. It's silent for several minutes before Punk speaks. "That was too close today."

Maceo groans. "No shit."

"The fucker is lucky the cops took him out and not us," Gauge growls.

"Well, Jo certainly didn't make it easy on either of them," Flay says, delighted.

Maceo chuckles. "She broke one fucker's nose."

"And fought like the hellcat she is to keep Jacob from going any further," Flay adds.

Red sniffles. "I'm just glad you were all there to stop him. Not every woman is that lucky."

The tension is thick in the air as Red's words sink in. She's right, not every woman has someone to help save them from danger, let alone an entire motorcycle club.

After a long silence, Reaper cuts the tension in the air by chuckling. "I'm just glad I'm not the one who got pissed on by the other weasel."

Brass groans. "Fuck off! It's bad enough I had to wait until late tonight to wash it off, without being reminded of it."

They all snigger, and I pass out from exhaustion.

CHAPTER NINETEEN
MACEO

J osephine rests through the rest of the week and into the weekend. She's starting to worry me. She hardly eats, barely speaks, has panic attacks, and when she sleeps she has night terrors. Getting stabbed in the heart would hurt less than watching her go through this.

By Monday, I'm frantic. I reach out to the VA and get the name of several recommended counselors who specialize in treating post-traumatic stress disorder. Having been around several men who have had it—I have a touch of it myself—I can pretty much diagnose her with it. I make her an appointment with one of the counselors.

My girl is broken, and she doesn't fight me when I tell her where I'm taking her. If this was my Josephine before Jacob's attack, she would be fighting me the whole way there. But this isn't—this Josephine is fragile and it's gutting me.

The counselor lets me to sit with Josephine through the session because my pixie has no objection to my presence. It doesn't take long before Josephine is breaking down in sobs retelling the events of that day. Hearing what she was feeling at the time and what she's feeling now rips a hole through me worse than any shrapnel could. I'm crying as hard as she is by the end of the session.

We're given good news at the end of the visit. Her counselor feels she's responsive to therapy, and that continued sessions will help Josephine deal with the stress and anxiety of the attack. We schedule for her to come weekly, and to taper off as she improves. The clinic psychiatrist gives her a prescription to help regulate when she's feeling emotionally overwhelmed. It seems hopeful, because she doesn't foresee Josephine needing it long term.

I don't know which of us feels better after we head home. The thick aura around Josephine seems to have dissipated and we both breathe a little easier. She actually reaches out for my hand for the first time in days, and I weep with relief.

We have a long way to go, but I know we will be stronger because of it.

Tuesday morning, I wake up to Josephine poking me. I grumble but say nothing. I get dressed to drive her to the hospital for a visit with Tiny Tony. When she enters his room, she bursts into tears and runs to his bedside. A concussion and cracked ribs don't stop him from pulling her into his arms while she cries. He may be a mafioso, but he's a decent enough guy. I let the two of them hug it out until her tears run dry.

By Wednesday, she's back at the build site with Hades by her side. Her crew nearly crush her, rushing to embrace her with Jared first in line. I would have let Jared see her sooner, but in light of how catatonic she was, I decided against it. Jared wasn't happy, but he understood. He filled in their team on what happened last Wednesday. Having her back at work has brought them more relief than anything.

Sore and in pain, she hobbles around the construction zone overseeing every detail like she always does. The normalcy of being back on the job should help with some of her anxiety, which is probably the only reason I agreed to let her come back this soon. By the end of the week, it's like she's the same old person at work as before.

The media has been hounding us relentlessly. My crew and I have been able to keep them at bay and shelter Josephine as much as possible, but I was still forced to give a press conference. I stressed the need for privacy as Josephine heals physically and emotionally. It got the media off our front lawn, but news outlets still blow up our phones with requests. Too bad for them they won't be getting any more information from us.

Hades is not happy going on his morning runs without Josephine. After the first day of me dragging him along, he refused to go, howling and barking up a storm. He hates being separated from her—just like me. All the guys tried to coax him out, but the dog is too damn stubborn.

Eventually Jo comes up with the idea to buy a bike and ride along next to me in order for Hades to get his exercise. I know it hurts her, her body jostles along, but she'd do anything for her dog.

It's finally Friday evening, and Josephine and I are ready to head home when her cell rings. It's the hospital, asking us to come in for the diagnostic laboratory results of the rape kit. We meet with the doctor who examined Josephine, hands clasped together in support. We're informed they found no semen or lubricant from a condom in their testing, only traces of my DNA inside of her.

We leave the hospital and breathe a huge fucking sigh of relief. Even though we knew the chance it happened was small, being able to put it behind us is what we're more grateful about than anything.

Always eager to make eye contact with my pixie, I look over at her in the passenger seat and see her eyelids flutter. She has been pushing herself too hard with work and not resting enough. Not wanting to hurt her, I've been driving her to work in her Subaru while my SUV is in the shop. Her eyes are closed, but she's wide awake.

She sighs. "I want to put the condo on the market."

"Whatever you want. What do you need from me to get it done?"

She sighs again. "I need help packing up my belongings and getting them into storage. We can store my stuff in one of the MC garages 'till we move into the headquarters. I know a realtor who will sell my place quickly."

"I'll get the boxes from the U-Haul store tomorrow. And I'll get the bunnies and the guys not out on assignment to help."

I gnaw on my bottom lip, bracing myself to ask the next question.

"Have you thought about the wedding at all?" I ask cautiously, afraid it may upset her.

She pulls out a white binder from her backpack, flips it open, and starts reading off a checklist she has inside.

"We're getting married the first Saturday of October. My dress needs a few small alterations and I've already booked the appointment. I've asked Opal and Ebony to be bridesmaids and I've picked out the dresses, but I need one more person. I'm letting you know right now I'm considering asking Jared to stand in as my man of honor since I don't have a maid of honor. My suggestion is that you guys should go with tailored suits, unless you want your Navy uniforms. I've booked the food and liquor vendors, cake bakery, DJ, florist, officiant, outdoor tent company, photographer, and I found the invitations I want to order. How many we order depends entirely on your guest list, which you will have to get to me by the end of next week. I only plan on inviting Jared and my crew."

My eyes bulge with shock. *When the hell did she do all this?*

"Oh, and we should decide where we're going to honeymoon, if we're going somewhere. I was hoping someplace warm, like an island."

"O-okay," I stammer.

She gives me a wry smile. "I'm good at multitasking. I was already planning the real one when we were doing the fake wedding."

No shit. Here I was, thinking we were going to have to postpone, or hire a wedding coordinator to get this ball rolling, but she's got the whole thing wrapped up with a bow.

My heart is jackhammering. October is less than two months away. The MC clubhouse will be complete, and we'll all be moved in by then. It won't take much to make our place ready to host the wedding. Everything is happening all at once.

Nervousness would be the rational emotion, but I'm feeling giddy as fuck. *Josephine will be my wife in less than two months!* Mrs. Maceo 'Atlas' Tabares sounds fucking hot when I apply it to Josephine. My dick starts to swell with excitement.

"Oh, and I've scheduled the removal of my implant for two weeks before the wedding," Josephine says with a seductive smile.

Holy hell! I yank the car to the side of the road down an old logger trail and throw it in park. I reach over and unbuckle Josephine, hauling her into my lap. My cock fights to break free of my clothes as I undo my pants. Chest heaving to drag in more oxygen, my lips crash against hers, and growl my desire.

Who would have guessed I'd get turned on by talk of weddings and babies?

"I fucking need you, Pixie," I say between rough kisses. My thick dick pops out from my boxers.

Josephine moans against my mouth, fumbling with her own pants. We haven't made love since before the attack, and to say I've missed being inside of her is an understatement—I'm fucking starving. I wasn't going to rush her after what happened, but I'm happy as fuck that she's yearning for this connection too.

My God, I need inside of her—now!

When her boots and pants are removed, she's quick to grab hold of my steel cock. It's already dripping with precome, and she lines it up to her warm, wet center. She sinks slowly, inch by agonizing inch, until I can enter her no further. She pulls back up, and sinks down again until I'm in her to the hilt.

My fingers gently take hold of her hips and I lean back in my seat, allowing her more room to move. Slowly, she grinds her hips, making my fingers dig a little more into her soft skin. As much as I want her to start working me, I won't push her. She needs to be in control right now and set the rhythm.

Her hooded eyes never leave mine, and she begins to move up and down at a torturous snail's pace. It's like heaven and hell all at once. I can feel every ridge and bump inside of her sweet pussy, enhancing the lust building inside of me. She's purring as she rides me, and I don't hold back my groans of pleasure.

"I've missed this sweet little pussy," I grit through my teeth. "I've been dreaming of my long cock getting milked by it for days."

"Yes," she moans. Her mouth parts in euphoria, encouraging me to continue.

"You like it when I talk filthy to you," I state, nipping at her nipple through her shirt.

"Yes. More," she begs and bites her bottom lip.

I pinch her nipple gently, making her buck. "You like when I manhandle you. You like it when I twist these perfect tits, and mark you all over with my love bites."

She mewls and starts to bounce faster on my hard shaft. Her teardrop-tits jiggle in my hands with the pounding of our hips. I have to remind myself not to blow my load too soon.

"You like riding my thick, hard cock, don't you baby? You like grinding your sweet little pearl against my pelvis," I growl, fisting her hair in my hands and pulling her lips to me.

She whimpers as I piston my hips up into her, meeting her thrust for thrust.

I claim her in a domineering kiss, forcing my tongue into her mouth. God, I love the taste of her minty mouth. I grind my tongue against hers, fucking her mouth the way I fuck her tight cunt.

It's not long before the wet sounds of our lovemaking are deafening in the car. *Smack, smack, smack.*

"I like how slick you get for me when we fuck. I love how your juices run down my shaft and coat my balls with your spunk," I snarl between kisses.

"Oh God," she pants. Her hips pick up the pace, and I feel her pussy tremble with need.

"I want you to milk me dry. I want to shoot my load straight to your womb. I want to overload your implant to the point we bust it. I want our come to mix together and weep out of you for days," I groan out, feeling my balls tighten up, aching for release.

She's practically screaming, riding me harder than she has before. The car is lurching forward and back in its parked position with how roughly we're fucking. Her round peach of an ass bounces against the car horn, setting it off again and again in rapid succession. Thank fuck we're on a deserted dirt road amongst the pine trees at dusk.

"I—I'm going to—" she doesn't get the words out before she explodes around me, soaking me with her cream. Her pussy pumps around my throbbing dick, making me see stars. I nearly black out when I come with her, ejaculating like a geyser. My hips don't stop jamming into her until the last wave of our orgasms subsides.

The air in the car is saturated with the musky scent of our sex—the fucking best smell ever. Josephine's forehead leans against mine, and we both struggle to regain our composure with my dick still snuggled in her tight little hole.

No words need to be shared except for three. "I love you," we say in perfect unison.

We get back to the rental, giggling like two teenagers, and Gauge is waiting outside with his arms folded across his chest. His composure is rigid and instantly, I'm on high alert.

"What is it?" I ask.

"Josephine got a delivery today," he says with a nod to follow him. Chase sits at the bench with Punk next to him. A flower arrangement of orchids sits between them. I recognize them as the *Flor de Mayo*, or the national flower of Colombia. Chase hands me the note that came with them.

Que te mejores, mami.

My heart turns to ice and I crumple the letter in my fist.

"What's it say?" Josephine asks.

"Feel better, little lady," I mutter, pulling her close to me. She doesn't ask who it's from. We both know.

Josephine gulps in lung-fulls of air, her body trembles, and her beautiful blue eyes bulge with fear. I hold her tighter to calm her down when her body seizes in a panic attack, cooing words of reassurance in her ear to help Josephine regain her composure.

Esteban Moreno is still a threat. I will need to finish our feud and soon.

EPILOGUE

MACEO

"When will you be home?" Josephine asks longingly over the phone.

I smile, loving how my fiancée misses me something fierce. Every time we stop for food or gas, I call or text just to feel closer to her. "We just got to Los Angeles, Pixie. This shouldn't take me too long. Just meeting with some people. We should be on the road home within a couple hours, and I'll have you back in my arms by tomorrow evening."

"You promise?"

"I promise, Pixie."

Josephine busted my balls all weekend about getting my guest list done. Considering she needs it to figure out how many invitations to order, I knew I couldn't put off this trip any longer. I didn't want to leave after Esteban sent her those flowers, but our sources say he's not in the states.

"Tell me, baby, how's everything going at headquarters?"

She giggles and it makes me smile more. "I'm still not used to you calling it anything other than a clubhouse."

I laugh, understanding. "We sound like a legit business if we refer to our home as a headquarters."

"Punk and Reaper are escorting me everywhere. Most of your crew is working the mission over in Florida," Josephine says.

"Good. I'm glad they're following my orders. How is Hades?"

I hear a bark in the background and Josephine laughs. "You're on speaker, and he heard you asking about him."

I chuckle, knowing Hades is waiting for me to address him. "How's my big boy?"

Hades barks and pants.

"You better be taking good care of your *mamá* and make sure to cuddle with her at night till I'm back home. Can you do that for me, big boy?"

He woofs three times, saying 'yes, I can.'

Josephine sighs.

I hear her anxiety through the phone. "Talk to me, Pixie."

"Lorenzo had another flower arrangement delivered today. I had Opal give them to the senior center this time. I'm running out of places to donate them. I wanted to call and ask him to stop since it wasn't Tony's fault, but Chase said to avoid any communication with Lorenzo because it may encourage him," she says with a tremor. "But he keeps sending things. That's something for every day since—since the incident."

Josephine still has a hard time talking about Jacob outside of therapy, and she refers to the attack as 'the incident.' Lorenzo has been showering Josephine with flowers and gifts every day, claiming it's his way of saying he's sorry for what happened to her while she was under the care of one of his men.

What Lorenzo doesn't realize is that his presents are reminders of what Jacob did to her. They disrupt her progress. Josephine has grown uncomfortable with his attention, and she came up with the idea to donate all his gifts to places in need. I'm pleased she feels no need to keep the things he gives her—it definitely keeps me from flying off the rails.

Lorenzo has been bugging the shit out of me about continuing supervision of my pixie, but he's getting too attached for my liking.

317

I'm no longer willing to have him anywhere near Josephine, which is all the more reason I want to get this over with, and head back home to my future bride where I can watch her myself.

"I'll have a talk with him when I get back." *Yeah, I'll talk to him, with my fists.*

She's silent for a few moments. "Do you think he's forming an unhealthy attachment, like...like..."

Like Jacob. She doesn't need to finish the sentence. I know it's too painful for her to even mention his name, unless she's with me or her counselor.

"I'll handle him, baby. I'm not going to let him or anyone else make you feel uncomfortable."

She sniffles and starts to cry, making my heart raw with emotion.

"Baby, baby, shh. It's okay. I'll be home soon, and take care of it."

"I just miss you," she sobs.

God, this woman slays me. "I miss you too, Pixie, more than you can imagine. I've got to go. I'll call and text when I can. Love you, Josephine."

"I love you, Maceo." And then she hangs up.

I pocket my cell and look over at Gauge waiting patiently for me. He just hung up with Opal a few minutes earlier.

"You ready to do this, brother?" Gauge asks from the seat of his bike.

I nod. "Yeah. I want to get this over with and go back home to my woman." We start our hogs and pull out of the gas station, heading deeper into the city.

To keep Josephine from growing suspicious, I asked Gauge to accompany me for the sixteen-hour drive to Los Angeles. I told her I had to meet with some people in the city, and that Gauge was coming with me. Josephine assumed it was business-related and didn't question any further. Had she pressed for details, I would have been obligated to tell her what I was up to. Gauge jokes Josephine's going to have my balls for this, but it's a legit fear of mine that she will lose her shit once she finds out what I'm doing.

We cruise to our destination, a more run-down area of the city. I wouldn't call it dangerous per se, but I wouldn't want my loved ones living here. We roll to a stop in front of a well-maintained bungalow with a nicely manicured yard. The residents on this block definitely take pride in their homes in comparison to the surrounding areas.

I walk the short path to the front steps, and I can easily see Josephine as a young girl growing up here. It was just over a year ago, my pixie stormed out of her parents' home because she felt she had no emotional support from her family. I love Josephine more than anyone in the world, and I'm here to confront her parents—I won't allow anyone to ever hurt her again. But I need to feel these people out for myself—make sure they're not malicious or bad people—before introducing them back into her life.

I really hope this family feud is more of a misunderstanding than a toxic relationship. If it is the latter, I'll have no problem telling them to stay the hell away from Josephine. My woman doesn't need anyone negative manipulating her life. But if it is the former, I'll do everything I can to help mend bridges between Josephine and her parents. She deserves to be surrounded by love and support, and I'm hoping her parents want that for her too.

I look over my shoulder at Gauge. He hangs back by our bikes and gives me a thumbs-up, letting me know I got this.

With a deep sigh, I take stock of my appearance. I decided it was best to wear something that didn't scream *biker*, since it seemed to turn her folks off. I settled on some new black jeans and a flannel button-down with the sleeves rolled up. I went as far as picking up new boots, anything to spruce myself up. Lloyd cleaned my face and hair real good before I rolled out. To an outsider, I didn't look like a biker at all.

I removed my leather vest for the occasion and wore my gladiator leather wristband with our club logo instead. The leather band let's me represent our crew and my position without it being in anyone's face. Plus, Josephine says it's hot, which is more of the reason why I've been wearing it.

I run a hand through my hair to put it in place, and I knock on the wood door.

A pretty woman around fifty answers. This must be Josephine's mom, Stella. She shares some of the same physical characteristics of her daughter. She's tiny, though maybe not quite as short as Josephine. But her hair is darker, and her facial features are completely different.

I clear the lump from my throat. "Mrs. Holland," I greet with a polite nod. "My name is Maceo Tabares. I'm the man who's engaged to Josephine."

Stella's gray eyes go wide before looking over her shoulder. "Jim!" she calls in a panicked voice.

I heave a sigh. It makes sense. She's worried since Jacob painted me as a 'big bad biker,' but I can't help that it saddens me. Will they even believe that I'm more of a businessman than a biker?

A man of medium stature comes to his wife's side. I know the second I look at him he's Josephine's dad. Same eyes, same nose, same lips, same sandy ashen hair. Josephine is a little cocktail of both her parents.

"Mr. Holland," I greet with a nod.

Jim doesn't need introductions to know who I am. He glances at his wife before looking back at me and opens the door wide for me to step inside. I feel like Goliath in this house. This home was built during a time when people were a hell of a lot shorter. My massive stature probably doesn't make her parents comfortable in my presence. I smile kindly to try and set their nerves at ease.

Jim takes a seat in a nearby lounger and motions for me to take a seat on the couch. I lower myself gently into the cushions, afraid of busting their tiny-ass furniture. Thankfully, it holds my weight.

"Would you like something to drink?" Stella asks me politely.

"I'm good, thank you. Please, have a seat. I'd like to talk to you both." I don't know what kind of man Jim is, if he likes to be the captain in charge, or if he runs his ship hand in hand with his wife, but I will let them both know why I'm here. Stella takes a seat in the armchair next to her husband.

I clear my throat again. "I'm sure by now you've heard what happened with Jacob Klein," I say, fighting to keep the malice out of my voice. There's no way they couldn't know. The story has been all over the national news.

Both her parents nod. "We tried to call her, but she must have blocked our numbers. We can't get through," Stella says, reaching for a tissue on a nearby end table to blot her eyes. "We would have come, but we didn't know if she would want to see us after the last conversation Jim had with her."

I nod. "I'm not surprised. Josephine is...stubborn. It's one of the reasons I fell in love with her. She's not a pushover and won't take crap."

Her parents look at me like I'm weird for loving that trait of hers. I shrug my shoulders. I can't help that I find her feistiness endearing. As long as I get to dominate her in our bed when I want, I'm all for her asserting herself outside of our bedroom. If Josephine and I have a daughter someday, I would hope she inherits the same trait from her mother.

Jim's face hardens. "How is she?"

Sighing deeply, I rub a hand down my face. "She's strong, so fucking strong. I apologize for my language. She went through a lot. Jacob had been stalking her since they broke up. He harassed her horribly, and he went over the edge when she decided to move on with her life. I'm not sure if I should mention any of this to you."

"Please," her father begs, and takes his wife's hand in support. "Please tell us what happened."

I look at both of them, and then down at my clasped hands. It's hard enough to talk about it during Josephine's counseling sessions. Talking about this with her estranged parents is far from comfortable.

"She got hurt real bad. Broken ribs from where he kicked her. Ripped and shredded skin from being dragged and handled roughly. Bruises, God the bruises—all over her legs, arms, back, and torso. He nearly crushed her windpipe from strangling her. He tried—he tried to rape her," I choke, dropping my face into my hands.

"Oh God," Stella cries.

I lift my face. "But she fought. She fought back until help came."

"Are you the one who put a bullet in him?" Jim asks.

"No, but I sure as hell wish I had been the trigger man. I was taking care of Josephine when the cops opened fire on him," I say honestly.

Jim presses more. "But you're the one who stopped him?"

"Yes, sir. Me and my crew all had a hand in stopping him from running away with her."

Her father nods. "I'm glad you were there. I'm glad you protected my little girl."

"I plan on doing it for the rest of my life," I say fervently. "I never did this properly. I come from a traditional family that believes in customs. I sometimes forget my roots, and I have to go back and make up for it. I would like to ask for your permission and blessing to marry your daughter. I know I'm not the type of man you envisioned Josephine being involved with, but whatever beliefs you have about bikers, I'm here to say my crew and I are not your typical stock.

"I run a security company that's doing rather well. We're expanding all the time. Your daughter recently built our new head-quarters. It's how we met, actually. My crew and I don't deal in illegal activity of any kind. We're active members in our community. We volunteer our services when families are in need of retrieving a missing loved one.

"Yes, we ride loud bikes, party a little too hard, swear a little too much, are tatted up, and may give off a tough guy vibe, but we're men of honor and integrity who do everything we can for our family. And we're all decorated retired Navy SEALs. We're the *good guys*," I say evenly, repeating Josephine's words.

"I love Josephine with all my heart. She's the only one for me. I want to build a life with her. Support her and her growing business. Take care of her at all times," I admit with a wide smile.

"Mr. and Mrs. Holland, please, give me a chance, and I'll prove to you I'm worthy of your daughter's hand."

Jim gets up from his chair and stretches out his hand for me to take. "You already have, son."

I stand and take his hand. "Thank you, sir."

Stella comes over and opens her arms to me. I bend down and give her a tight hug.

"Will she forgive us?" Stella asks with a sob.

I blow out a lungful of air. "I'm gonna be honest, I hope she forgives *me* after she finds out I came to visit you two. The one thing I know about my pixie is she's very forgiving. The hard part is getting her to listen to you. I've screwed up a lot myself, and as long as I can get her to hear my apology, she's always been gracious in giving forgiveness."

Jim and Stella look doubtfully at one another. Stella clears her throat. "We admit we liked Jacob, but we had no idea how manipulative he was. Even after Josephine told us what he did to her at the firm, we had a hard time accepting it. He called us constantly, filling our heads with these lies, and it was easy to believe him, especially after Josephine quit her job and came back home. She wasn't acting like herself, and she would hardly talk. When we started questioning her why she would just quit without notice, without another job, and asking how she was going to start a company with nothing..."

Stella shakes her head before continuing. "She got so angry and accused us of not supporting her when we were only concerned. And then she was gone the next day, moved out to Fort Collins. She refused to answer our phone calls or texts. For the longest time, we didn't even know where she lived. We talked to Jacob because she didn't talk to us, and we believed him over her. How is she ever going to look past our mistake?" Stella turns to Jim and cries into his shoulder.

"I'm not saying it's going to be easy and I'm not saying there aren't going to be hurt feelings. If you want a relationship with your daughter, you'll find a way to get through to her. I will do what I can on my end to see she at least gives you a chance. You have to under-stand your daughter truly believes you had no faith in her ability to start her own company, or to find a decent man. She's under the assumption you believe she's inept, or doesn't deserve a fighting chance. You have to be prepared for backlash," I confess.

Her parents both nod, and I hope they follow through. Josephine deserves to have her family's love.

"I would like you both to come to our wedding, Simone as well. We're getting married the first Saturday of October. If you could come maybe a week beforehand, I think that will give you enough time to get comfortable with each other before the big day. I'm hoping that by then, we will have gotten Josephine to hear you out. But please, let me talk to her first before you guys show up—she has been through enough, and if she's really adamant against this, I'm not going to force her to go through a family reunion."

Stella's eyes go wide. "Married this October? Why so soon?"

Eager for the big day, I smile down at Josephine's mother. "I know it seems like it's happening fast, but we've been waiting for each other forever. We're ready to start our lives together, give you some grandkids," I say, winking.

Stella's hands fly to her face and she turns to beam up at her husband. "Grandbabies!" She coos enthusiastically.

"I've got plenty of land up in Colorado. I can have Josephine build you guys a cottage on the property. You can visit as often as you want," I offer with a smile.

Stella is bouncing like Josephine does when she gets excited. Jim shakes his head and smiles at his wife adoringly.

Looking at both of them, I know I've done the right thing. Josephine is going to see my actions as treacherous and make me beg for mercy. But this is her family. As much as they may have screwed up, I don't believe they meant her ill.

"I should go," I say. "My VP and I need to head back before my future bride has my head."

"You and your friend should stay for dinner. I've been working on a brisket all day and it will be done soon," Jim offers. "Stella makes a great cornbread, too."

I smile at them because I can see a bright future ahead of us. I head to the door and whistle to Gauge.

"My in-laws invited us for dinner. Come meet the family," I say with a cocky-ass grin.

PLAYLIST FOR LIPS ON MY HEART

Maceo

1. Frank Turner—Photosynthesis
2. Lenny Kravitz—Again
3. Harry Styles—Adore You
4. Bruce Springsteen—I'm On Fire
5. Bon Iver—Skinny Love
6. Ben L'Once Soul—I've Got You Under My Skin (Frank Sinatra Cover)
7. Depeche Mode—Enjoy The Silence
8. David Gray—Please Forgive Me
9. Teddy Swims—Let Me Love You (Mario Cover)
10. Local Natives—When Am I Gonna Lose You
11. Wild Cub—Thunder Clatter
12. Ian Smith—The Man Who Can't Be Moved (The Script Cover)
13. Cold Play—Fix You
14. Kings of Leon—Wait For Me
15. Mumford and Sons—Woman
16. Kaleo—I Want More
17 Vance Joy—I'm With You

Josephine

1. Billie Eilish ft. Khalid—Lovely
2. Young the Giant—Superposition
3. The Gaslight Anthem—The Queen of Lower Chelsea
4. James Bay—Let It Go
5. LP—Tightrope
6. Vance Joy—Fire and Flood
7. The Noisettes—Cheap Kicks
8. Of Monsters and Men—Slow and Steady
9. Sara Bareilles—Gravity
10. The Chainsmokers—Inside Out
11 The Rolling Stones—Wild Horses
12. Peter Katz—Halo (Beyonce Cover)
13. Brandon Flowers—Crossfire (Acoustic)
14. Florence + the Machine—All This and Heaven Too
15. The Killers—Some Kind of Love

Enjoy on YouTube.com or purchase on iTunes.

COMING SOON

LIPS ON MY SOUL—A MERCY RAVENS MC
NOVEL 2

Their love story continues...

Maceo and Josephine have overcome so much in their new romance, but their challenges are far from over—if anything, their troubles are only starting.

The headstrong and independent Josephine Holland is a former shell of herself after surviving her stalker, plagued by night terrors and uneasiness of something—*someone*—lurking in the shadows. Josephine can't help but feel she is losing her grip on sanity, fearing the worst is yet to come.

The love of her life, Maceo Tabares, refuses to sit back and watch her shrink inside the recesses of her mind—he takes command and helps her rebuild herself into someone stronger than she could have ever imagined.

However, Maceo has not made it this long in his life without listening to his instincts. Taking a page out of Josephine book, Maceo follows the illogical route, taking Josephine's fears seriously, and digs to discover the root of her worries is far more serious than her imagination.

With Josephine's estrange family back in the picture, wedding preparations, unplanned build projects, Mercy Ravens missions, spies creeping, leaked personal files, and a hacker causing all kinds of headaches—life throws Maceo and Josephine lots of hilarious curve balls and heart-shattering moments. And of course there's always Esteban Moreno to worry about.

But a threat closer to home may be their biggest obstacle—Mafioso Don, Lorenzo Bianchi. Lorenzo's unhealthy attachment to Josephine is only growing by the day, and he has no intention on backing off, no matter how many threats Maceo makes.

Will Josephine be able to overcome her own personal fears and be able to use the safety techniques that Maceo has taught her to protect herself from all those who wish to harm her? Will Maceo be able to help Josephine to heal emotionally so she can move forward? Are they doomed to fall apart at the hands of their enemies, or will love, once again, triumph?

ACKNOWLEDGMENTS

I'd like to take a moment to personally thank some very special people who helped me in my writing journey.

First, my husband, Matthew. Thank you for your never ending love, support, and encouragement. You were the real driving force for me taking the leap into self-publishing. You are my #1.

Second, my three boys. Thanks for always being excited about your mom becoming a published author and keeping the volume down when I needed to work.

Third, my parents, Paul and Darrell. Even though you may be *slightly* embarrassed by your daughter's choice of writing, thank you for encouraging me to not give up.

Fourth, my sister, Sam. Thanks for being the first to read my story. Your enthusiasm was my drug of choice. You will always be my go-to person when I have new material.

Fifth, my grandma, Dorothy. Thanks for always sharing your personal stories with me. You made me want to be a writer.

Sixth, my girlfriends. Sarah, Laura, and Serena. Whether you supported me by reading and correcting my book, or offering words of motivation—you have inspired me.

And seventh, my editor, Christa Desir. I know it needed a lot of work when I sent you my manuscript, but you didn't back down. Your suggestions and corrections were over and above what I could have hoped for in an editor.

ABOUT THE AUTHOR

M.J Marino—lover of great stories and putting pen to paper. She lives in Waukesha, Wisconsin with her husband, Matthew, and their three boys. Walking away from her career as a chemist, she has plunged herself into writing, pursuing a lifelong dream, and has no regrets. She writes what she wants and makes no excuses for it. Aside from writing, M.J. loves to read, garden, listen to music while singing along, organize her home, coffee, and bourbon—lots of bourbon.

Need to get in touch? Email me: mjmarinobooks@gmail.com

Follow me on my website and learn more about me on my blog: http://mjmarinobooks.wixsite.com/website

STAY CONNECTED

Want to stay connected and see what's new with M.J. Marino? Then follow her on one or all of her social media accounts.

Facebook: http://www.facebook.com/mjmarinobooks2love

Instagram: http://www.instagram.com/mjmarinoauthor

Email: mjmarinobooks@gmail.com

Website: http://mjmarinobooks.wixsite.com/website

Made in the USA
Columbia, SC
04 November 2022

70421806R00207